Prosperity, PA

R. Lee Procter

ISBN: 978-1-68513-508-9
PUBLISHED BY BLACK ROSE WRITING
www.blackrosewriting.com

Printed in the United States of America
Suggested Retail Price (SRP) $24.95

Prosperity, PA is printed in Book Antiqua

*As a planet-friendly publisher, Black Rose Writing does its best to eliminate unnecessary waste to reduce paper usage and energy costs, while never compromising the reading experience. As a result, the final word count vs. page count may not meet common expectations.

PRAISE FOR
R. LEE PROCTER

Sanity Clause:
Many author folks who promise "humorous" or "hilarious" content fail to deliver, but R. Lee Procter dishes up grins and giggles galore in this soon-to-be classic holiday romp. The saga of Mike and Cookie, Magnus and Sugar Plum, Dudley is solidly holiday-delightful in every way. **–Gil Reavill**

Claude Monet Designs Yankee Stadium:
What an amazing, moving, and surprising book. R. Lee Proctor's novel transported me to another time and place in just the same way. It's beautifully written and full of wonderful and surprising twists and turns. **–Max Sand**

This improbable, but thoroughly worked out, zany plot makes for a delightful journey through the "what if" tale of a French impressionist artist with an unusual penchant for American baseball, and the fledgling artist who solves the mystery of how it came to be. Come along on the adventure? Highly recommend! **–Judith Stoffer**

Sugarball
I loved this fast-paced book for so many reasons. Procter conjures vivid characters (many of whom are historical) who stand up to the horrors of US racism and savage politicians. The writing is top-notch and Procter revels in world-painting and world-building: cliff-hanging games, musical numbers (Cab Calloway!), inter-team rivalries, kidnaping and daring escapes. No baseball knowledge necessary. A fascinating, provocative and thrilling read. **–Laura Morland**

AUTHOR'S NOTE

Some readers may consider this story to be a utopian flight of fancy. It's not. It's the result of research. Everything here really happened somewhere. I wrote this book to be useful to people, in the same way that Kim Stanley Robinson's book "The Ministry for the Future" was for me. Robinson created an engaging, fully immersive adventure into a future where we successfully defeat global warming. This book is about how we can come together to find a new way to create what Martin Luther King called "the beloved community."

At the end of this book, you'll find "The Underbook." These are the real events that support my story. As you read, know that this isn't the author wishing for an impossible world. It's the author conjuring a possible world, based on what people like us have done when they've coupled imagination with courage.

Prosperity, Pennsylvania

"We all, adults and children, have an obligation to daydream. We have an obligation to imagine. It is easy to pretend that nobody can change anything, that we are in a world in which society is huge and the individual is less than nothing: an atom in a wall, a grain of rice in a rice field. But the truth is, individuals change their world over and over; individuals make the future, and they do it by imagining things can be different."

–Neil Gaiman

CHAPTER ONE

MIKE DAVENPORT

People believe in all sorts of things: God, heaven, political candidates, vitamins, capitalism, socialism, and bingeing on cabbage soup to lose weight. I fought in Afghanistan because I believed what I was told: that we were there to help its freedom-loving citizens turn it into a secular democracy. I survived, but my idealism didn't.

So, what do I believe in now? Coffee. Coffee defies the laws of physics, blasting the body with endless energy even though it has no food value. No calories, fats, carbohydrates or protein, violating the laws of thermodynamics. It is the first mover of mankind. It is also addicting, thank goodness.

I own HuggaMug Coffee in Pittsburgh, Pa. Coffee will play a prominent part in this narrative. At every fork of the road, my friends and I took the path of foolish daring. We'd never have gotten into so much "good trouble" without it.

Saturday, March 13

That first morning, I was perking up my gang of regulars here in my coffeehouse in the East End of Pittsburgh. I opened in Lawrenceville for two reasons. One, this was the heart of Steeltown, a place just like Pulver Forge where I grew up. Two, I got a sweetheart deal on a derelict barrel house that had started life in 1922 as a speakeasy called "The Blind Pig." I guessed right about the arc (and velocity) of the neighborhood: just about all the shabby splendor I loved when I opened is gone, replaced by a Thai restaurant, an independent bookstore with poetry slams, and a brewpub. Can a Starbucks be far behind? Hope not, but probably. Bring it on.

My bookkeeper and business partner, Sergeant Darla Beachem, was working the "Beast" (our industrial-strength espresso machine). Her training for pulling perfect espresso shots was her service in Afghanistan as part of a Cultural Support Team: a team of female soldiers who supported Army Rangers by building relationships with Afghan mothers, wives, and daughters of the insurgency leaders who were trying to kill us. She runs our website and social media. She chats up the young gearheads who hang with us so she can stay current with all things cyberspacey. Me? I'm still grappling with the concept of email.

Steve Dorsey entered the shop and I asked Darla to take over the register. Steve is a bright-eyed, square-jawed, bemused-looking dead ringer for Young George Clooney. He owns my just-down-the-street neighbor, the Zymurgy Brewing Company, makers of a superior chuggable he calls his "Smokestack Artisan Ale." At 13 percent ABV, two of these beauties had me on the roof howling at the moon. Steve's day job is investment banking. He was here to talk me into franchising my business.

Darla handed us our drinks—Breve Cappuccino for me, Café Mocha for Steve—and we sat at a table in the back corner. He took a sip and winced. "You just can't make a mocha, can you?"

I summoned Darla. "Sergeant, how'd you make this drink?"

"As always, Captain. Layer of cocoa, double espresso shot, then steamed milk like in a latte."

I looked at Steve as I said to Darla, "And the cocoa…unsweetened, right?"

Darla was taken aback. "'Course. How the hell else would you make a mocha?'

"That's all, Sergeant." I smiled at Steve. "You've GOT to stop with the Starbucks shit…unless you prefer a hot, juiced-up chocolate Slurpee."

Steve smiled as he surveyed the shop. 10:30 a.m., every table full and five people in line. "Whatever it is you're doing, it's working. So, what's your secret?"

"That's easy." I took a sip. Perfection. "I buy my own beans, and roast 'em in small batches. I buy our pastries from Flour Power Bakery, run by a renegade priest who turns ex-gang members into solid citizens. Every espresso shot is fresh, pulled by a veteran of our Armed Forces from a real machine, not a push-button device designed by geniuses to be used by idiots. Oh, and no Wi-Fi, so people actually talk to each other, and every table isn't hogged by a high school kid trying to fake his way through a book report."

Steve watched as Darla handed a French Roast and a blueberry muffin to a hunched over duffer in a soiled track suit. "Plus, you give away your product. That's guaranteed to keep the place hoppin'."

"That guy?" I pointed to Track Suit as he eased his way into a just-vacated table. "That's Sarge. April 30, 1967, he was ordered to secure Hill 881 South. A hundred of his fellow Marines went up. Twenty-five dead, fifty-one wounded. He dragged three of his buddies off that hill, saved their lives. Still has shrapnel in his face. He has seven toes and sleeps in his van. So, yeah, a free cup of coffee is not out of the question."

He smiled. "Look, if I'm going to make you a millionaire, you're going to have to cooperate."

"How?" I knew what was coming.

"What you're doing is fine for a hobby project, but it doesn't scale. We're going to buy our baked goods from the lowest qualified bidder and pay your people just what the state says to pay them, as in minimum wage. And there *will* be Wi-Fi."

"And that's why we're never going to make a deal, Steve." I smiled. "I'm never going to do those things."

"Then you and Miss Tess Hudson are never going to retire to Kauai and spend your days drinking tropical rum drinks with tiny umbrellas." Ah, my fiancé, Sergeant First Class Theresa "Tess" Hudson. Beautiful, bright Silver Star recipient and owner of her own PR company, "FreeBooter Media". She has Ayn Rand's quote above her desk: "The question isn't who is going to let me, it's who is going to stop me." Answer? Nobody.

"Guess not," I said. "I guess I'll just...." Darla had stopped wiping down tables. She was standing stock still, her face pale. She was looking just past me at...nothing. She had her phone in her right hand, but she wasn't listening to it. "What?"

She turned her eyes to me, startled. She didn't answer for a long moment, and then said, "It's, ummm...Dave."

"Dave?" I searched my memory. "Dave...Bratton?" She gave me the smallest nod as she continued to stare at me. Dave and I grew up together, enlisted together, fought together. "What about him?"

"He's, ummm...he died." A long moment, then she answered the question I didn't have to ask. "Oxy overdose."

Dave Bratton was dead. Dave the hell-raiser. Dave the warrior. Dave, the best of them all. The one who saved me. Shit.

CHAPTER TWO

March 15

MIKE DAVENPORT

Pulver Forge, Pennsylvania was less than an hour from HuggaMug. So why had it been thirteen years since I'd been back? As I looked out my window, I knew. The place was a cadaver waiting to be buried.

A phrase kept running through my mind as I drove down streets I knew, past places where I'd hung out as a kid. *"It's not here anymore."* J.J. Winkler's Department Store? Gone. Wentzel's Original Coney Island, best hot dog in Pennsy? A vacant lot. Molly's Quik Lunch, 'A Meal in a Minute'? Boarded-up. The steel plant? Closed for good in 1986. I left for college in 1996. When did the Zombie Apocalypse devour this place?

In the distance, the Pulver Steel Works, the derelict mill, loomed over the city like a malign medieval fortress defeated by the Black Death. Pulver Boulevard, the heart of the business district, was a tumbledown wreck except for a tattoo parlor, a sell-your-blood storefront where Crandall's Meat Market used to be, a pawnshop…and the Five O'Clock Whistle, where I'd had my first (legal) beer, ordered up by my grandfather Chet.

Dave's wake was at the Holy Redeemer Community Church, corner of Foundry Avenue and Cloverdale. Dave himself never set foot in a church, because, as he'd yell at the television every Steelers game, "Sunday's for football!" The Church itself was a curiosity: a carriage house nestled amidst a street of decaying cottages in Cabbagetown, built by the Pulver Forge Steel Company to house workers in the 1920s. At some point a dome roof capped by a steeple had been cemented on top. Like a bad toupee on a bald man, this just called attention to how un-churchlike the house was.

Seventeen people had gathered for this affair. Five were from Dave's rehab group at "Second Chances." They were huddled around the battered urn of weak, lukewarm coffee-like matter. Another five were co-workers from MaxxMart, the mondo-humungo retail supercenter five miles outside of town. Dave's last job had been re-stocking shelves for minimum wage. Dave's ex-wife Cheryl was there, along with his mother Debra and her latest husband, sad-sack Darrel. Finally, there was Kate Walther. Dave, Kate and I were best friends in high school. Dave and I had both asked her to the Senior Prom. She chose me. Dave never let me forget that, and I never let him forget that she dumped me shortly thereafter for loser rock guitarist who broke her heart.

"Hey, Kate." Kate had been a beauty in high school, and brighter than both of us put together. She'd played Amanda Wingfield in our senior production of "A Glass Menagerie" and had broken every heart. Now she was an Emergency Room Doctor.

"Mike! Omigod! I'm surprised you…well, happily surprised," she said. "I wasn't sure that you'd…"

"I had to. He was my best pal."

The Reverend Cyril Wexler, a wizened wraith in wrinkled vestments, said "Good evening, friends. We're here to celebrate the brief but blessed life of our late friend Dave Bratton. Please come up here and share a memory of Dave, if you wish."

Debra took the stage first, using husband Darrel as a brace. She thanked us for coming, and then told us that her one solace was that her David was in heaven, out of pain, in the welcoming arms of Jesus Christ, who died for our sins.

After that, a couple of his rehab compatriots told us how hard he'd fought to stay sober, what a great, funny guy he was, and how they'd all work that much harder on themselves knowing Dave was in heaven rooting for them.

Then a feisty, late 20-something female stood up, eyes red from crying. She had heavily tatted arms and the square build of a hockey goalie. "I'm Betty Chapel. I knew Dave. The man could make me laugh. I gave him a job on my food truck and nobody worked harder when I could get him to show up. Such a sweetie, and so great with customers. I really thought he was going to make it…" She reached for more, but that was it.

When she stepped down, no one else moved. Reverend Wexler looked around nervously. This thing was supposed to last for two hours, and we'd only burned about twenty minutes. I wasn't planning to speak, but…I mean, this was Dave's wake, and he'd barely made an appearance. I shuffled up there.

"Hi, everybody, I'm Mike Davenport. Dave and I grew up together here in Pulver Forge. We enlisted together, trained together, shipped out to Afghanistan together." Everyone stirred, looked at each other. "Yeah, it was nasty over there, but having my best friend with me, that helped." I paused. Should I go there? Hell, this was my last chance to go there. "Something happened…well, it's important that you know what happened so you can know what kind of guy Mike was. I mean, really know."

I took a moment, gathered myself. "Our job was to shut down the Taliban. Their job—we heard 'em say this over the radio—they wanted to blow up our gun trucks, trap us in a kill zone, and grab us so they could behead us one by one and post the videos on YouTube."

Pin drop quiet. I had their attention.

"I was the CO and Dave was my XO. We were ordered into this village to meet the council of elders to see about building a school for their kids, a place where girls as well as boys could learn to read and write. Only guess what? There were no village elders when we got there, it was a set-up. There were fifty

Taliban on the high ground unloading on us with, oh my god, rocket-propelled grenades, mortars and AK-47s. I mean, I'd put us into the perfect kill zone. Our only hope was to run like hell for the gun trucks and start firing back, but I didn't make it. I got hit in the shoulder, and it was bad. I was dead. I mean, who was going to run across open ground in a kill zone, unable to fire his weapon because both arms were engaged dragging my sorry ass back to safety?"

Everyone was staring at me, including Kate. Debra's mouth was open. Good.

"You know the answer, don't you? Not only did Dave risk his damn life to get my sorry ass outta there, but he got hit twice as he did. One round blew his helmet off and creased his scalp, the other hit him in the chest. His bulletproof vest stopped it, but it cracked three of his ribs. Typical Dave: as he cleaned out my wound and shot me up with morphine, he kept telling me how lucky I was to get a ticket back to the world. Then he started yelling commands—he was in charge now, because I was out of it—and we held them off long enough for another platoon to arrive and save our ass. The last thing I remember before I passed out was this trickle of pink stuff coming out of Dave's ears. What the hell was that? Couldn't be good. Well, that bullet that creased his skull? His brain was bleeding, friends. I'm pretty sure this is where it all started: the headaches, the ringing in his ears, the dizziness. He went to the VA, they told him to take some Tylenol and call them when they gave a shit, which turned out to be never. The brain bleed, the swelling: this is what he was trying to medicate with that goddamn Oxy. And he got that wound saving my life, friends. My life. It's my…" I could feel myself losing it. "It's my fault, goddammit. Dave, I'm sorry. I love you, man, and miss you, so much. I'm so, so sorry. It should have been me."

Get your shit together, Captain.

"I, umm, just want to say one more thing that isn't going to make anybody happy, but that's okay because I'm never coming back here again." I could see Reverend Wexler's face fall. Darrel put his arm around Debra. "It's about this town. My God, Pulver Forge! We made the steel that built the battleships that kicked Hitler's ass! You ever see that New York skyline? That's *our steel*, people! For a hundred years people came here to make the steel that built this damn country. So, what happened? When did this town give up on itself? There's work to do, and nobody's doing it. If I had my way, we'd remember who we are and get to work saving this godforsaken town, give everybody a job who wanted one. I mean, where to begin? But...well, I'm done with lost causes. Thanks."

Debra was about to burst into tears. Kate was smiling, shaking her head. *"Same old Mike."* Of course, I couldn't let bad enough alone. I gazed at that crowd. "Final thought, and this is the truest thing I'll say today. Nobody's coming, folks. *Nobody.* It's up to you. Take care of business, you live. You don't, well, look around."

CHAPTER THREE

March 17

MIKE DAVENPORT

Two days later, I was working the Beast at HuggaMug, crafting mochas and lattes when two first timers strolled in. I recognized the woman from Dave's wake. "Betty Chapel, right?" She wore a battered bohemian camo jacket, faded khaki with the word "LOVE" embroidered on the back over some neon-scarlet wildflowers.

"Right. And this is my associate, the right Reverend Luke Bramlett."

"Hello, Michael." He was six inches taller than Betty: a trim, forthright Black man with a crown of grey curly hair. He was dressed in Christian-casual mufti: a Johnny Cash black sport coat and shirt with clerical collar, black pants and a Steelers ballcap. He had a baritone rumble of a voice that made me wonder if he needed a microphone when he preached. "Ms. Chapel and I would love to speak to you, if you can spare us ten minutes. We've got a kind of a proposition for you."

"An offer," said Betty.

"An...opportunity," said the Rev, smiling.

Hmmm. Sounded like trouble. I nodded at Darla. "Sergeant Beachem?" A moment later my two new "friends" and I were seated in the back corner, with three steaming cups in front of us.

"So," said Betty, "I loved your little speech at the wake the other night."

"Speech?" Hmmm. Did I give a speech?

"Your enlightened harangue," said the Rev.

"What did you mean when you said…" Betty paused, then pulled a three by five card from the inside pocket of her camo jacket. "If I had my way, we'd get to work saving this godforsaken town, give everybody a job who wanted one."

I took a sip of coffee as I pondered my words. What *did* I mean? "When I was growing up," I said, "Pulver Forge was a gritty town full of straight-ahead badass working stiffs like my grandpa Chet. Chet and his pals at the mill had this kind of, I guess you'd call it 'defiant optimism.' You got up every day, you went to the mill, and you kicked its ass, because you were tougher that it was, and it was damn tough. Now…"

"We've given up," said the Rev. "People step over the trash in the streets and complain how dirty the place is."

"Right. So, look around you, right her, now," I said. Betty and the Rev gazed around them. "What do you see?"

"The place is humming," said Betty.

"And notice the smiles, the energy. Know why? Because my people are happy. They're doing work that's worth doing. They're not just making coffee. They're making friends."

Betty continued to look about as she spoke. "Love this," she said. "How would you bring that kind of, oh, what did you call it…"

"Defiant optimism," I said.

"Defiant optimism to Pulver Forge?"

"I have no clue," I said, "or interest. I've got my hands full running this place."

"And that," said the Rev, "is precisely why we're here. We've got an offer for you."

"Offer?" I vaguely remembered something…

Betty said, "We want you to run for Mayor. Of, you know, Pulver Forge."

The blood drained from my face, and my heart started to thump in my chest. *"What?"* They both stared at me with tiny smiles. "Me? Hey, look, I'm not a politician…"

"Oh, God," said the Rev, laughing. "The last thing we want is a politician. We've already got one of those. Frantic Fred Bagley, our current Mayor."

Betty grimaced. "You know Fred's big plan to save Pulver Forge?'

"No," I said, "What?"

The Rev said "Our Mayor Bagley is going to make a sweetheart deal with Moses Creavey to build a casino where the old mill meets the river. Ever hear of Creavey?"

"He's…wait. He's like a big Vegas fat cat, right?"

"Right," said Betty. "Vegas, Atlantic City, Singapore. World renown felon and reprobate, Mister 'Too Big to Jail.' He says the casino will bring two hundred jobs to the town."

"Not including drug dealers, pimps, muggers and prostitutes," said Luke.

"And every job will be non-union minimum wage, and none are guaranteed," said Betty.

"Still," I said, "Two hundred…"

Betty cut me off. "There are currently two thousand, seven hundred and eighty-three people on unemployment in Pulver Forge."

"Which doesn't include everyone who has given up looking for work," said Luke.

Betty leaned in. "We need a native son, a warrior, who cares enough to try something new."

I was in shock. "I, ummm…. I'm flattered you'd ask me. And I appreciate the fix you're in. It's a tough spot. But…" I flashed back on my very first firefight in Afghanistan, the terrifying hell, and all I could think of was, *'I never signed up for this.'*

"What?" said Reverend Luke.

"I almost got killed fighting for one lost cause. This feels like another. Look, I like my life! So, I'm sorry, but…"

"STOP!" said Betty. "Don't say 'no,' at least not yet. Just…think about it. And…well, there's one thing you should know, Mike."

"What's that?" I was wary.

Betty looked at the Rev, who cleared his throat and said, "I, ummm, that is we already filed your name at City Hall," said the Rev.

"What?!?" My mouth dropped open. This was too much.

"There was a deadline," said Betty. So, your name will be on the ballot."

"You can still back out," said the Rev. "When you're elected, just resign and somebody else will step up."

I could feel my face start to burn. "How the hell could you…"

"We HAD to," said Betty. "You've got what we need!"

"Defiant optimism, Mike!" said the Rev. "The old spirit of Pulver Forge, the spirit that built this place here."

"You showed us something," said Betty.

"Something I'm not sure you see in yourself," said the Rev. "There's a candidate's forum in ten days in the old Pulver Library Auditorium. Frantic Fred will be there. So far, no one else has stepped up to challenge him."

"If you show up, we'll know you're in," said Betty.

The Reverend Luke added, "If you don't, well…" Those words hung in the air for several seconds. Then Betty and the Rev stood and stuck out their hands.

"You told us nobody's coming, Mike. It's up to us, right?" said Betty.

"Yeah," I said.

"Well, you're one of us. What you've done here is great, you're making a difference. But now you can make a bigger difference—maybe even a life-or-death difference—in the lives of thousands of people."

I opened my mouth to say something when the Rev stopped me cold. "What would Grandpa Chet tell you to do?" And with that they left me standing there. I knew what Chet would say. Shit.

CHAPTER FOUR

BETTY CHAPEL – THE QUIXOTE INSTITUTE
Betty Chapel was pretty sure Mike Davenport would agree to run for Mayor of Pulver Forge. She and the Rev had waited to find just the right person for the job. Mike checked every box on the list she'd worked up in her mind:

- Someone who didn't want the job. Pulver Forge didn't need another hollow man like Frantic Fred Bagley pushing an empty suit through the air.
- Someone who had lived in the town in better times: someone with a soul who was devastated by the wreckage of a once-thriving town.
- Someone who had been traumatized by a life-altering experience and was looking for redemption.

Betty knew what needed to be done. She'd gone through her own trauma. After she came out the other side, she'd tattooed her new mission on the inside of her right forearm: "I feed people."

She found her purpose through Reverend Luke: he's the one who spotted her in line at the Sunday Community Kitchen Free Lunch he hosted at his spiritual home, the "First Church of Jesus Christ, Troublemaker."

Betty was a de facto orphan at fourteen. Her feckless father had overdosed on opioids (she'd found the body), and her mother had vanished, lost in a haze of crystal meth. Betty was emaciated and jittery from washing down Vicodin and Adderall with slugs of whatever bargain vodka her friends could lift from the local Sav-Mor. She'd been stealing her mother's pills since she was 12. At 14, she was strung-out, homeless and hopeless, living from one high to the next.

As Reverend Luke sat down beside her at one of his battered red picnic tables, she knew he knew. He set his bowl of clean-out-the-fridge minestrone next to hers. "What do you think of the soup?" Before she could answer, he said, "I made it myself. It's terrible." This made her laugh, and when was the last time she'd laughed? Still, she wasn't interested in anyone wearing a clerical collar. She didn't want to be saved. She wanted enough Oxy for one, final ecstatic blast of joy, just like that first one she'd had in the bathroom of her double-wide, with her mom passed out in the next room.

But the Rev surprised her. He didn't quote scripture. He said "I read palms. Can I read yours?" Betty reluctantly opened her right hand to him. The Rev stared at it, then turned to her, eyes wide. "My oh my, young woman. Look at this lifeline. So long and straight." He looked back at the hand. "And this. This is your 'fate line.' Some call it your 'money line.' You are destined to have a rich and full life."

Betty laughed in his face, but he didn't flinch. Could this be true?

The Rev said, "Would you do me a big favor? Could you help us out here?"

"How?" No one had ever talked to her like this. He really seemed to be interested in her.

"Betty, we feed a thousand people every Sunday. One of my helpers just told me she's moving to California. I need a hard worker ready to open herself to the grace of God almighty by sharing Her love in the form of soup and bread. In return, we'll feed you, love you, and give you a place to sleep."

Love. No one loved her. "I don't think so." She didn't meet his eyes.

"You sure? I bet you'd be good at it." She opened her mouth, but his look brought her up short. That look, filled with love. Something flashed in her mind. She was at a crossroads. She was all set to kill herself when she got enough pills, but this other path seemed to be opening for her. She remembered Miss Burgess, her first-grade librarian, sharing a book about the life of Clara Barton, founder of the American Red Cross. The thought of helping people made her so happy back then! She felt a twinge of that now. What if…was it even possible…to change her life? To live? To let someone love her? She began to cry, and the Rev gathered her up in his arms, held her and rocked her.

Betty didn't know it then, but she was about to be initiated into The Quixote Institute. The Institute was an informal gathering of what the Rev called "wounded healers, reluctant heroes and unreasonable idealists": people filled with the crazy spirit of Don Quixote, who were determined to engage in the radical act of imagining a better, more loving world even though every shred of evidence screamed that it wasn't possible. The Quixote Institute had a manifesto that made this philosophy explicit. The Q.I. met on an irregular basis in living rooms and coffee shops in and around Pulver Forge. The members had nothing in common except a gleefully defiant bias toward hope and optimism. Most had been addicts. Many had tried and failed to kill themselves. Every single one was now committed to imagining a better world.

The first Quixote Institute member Betty encountered was Dr. Kate Walther. The Rev handed her off to Dr. Kate, who took her to a women's health clinic and watched over her for the ten days it took for the toxins to wash out of her system. Then the Rev moved Chef Betty to the church annex, into a spartan bedchamber reserved for visiting clergy, next to the food pantry and kitchen.

Now Betty was initiated into the challenge of feeding one thousand people a week. She rode shotgun as the Rev drove the church's rattletrap, rust-brown 1957 Chevy stake bed truck to the loading dock of every supermarket in Pittsburgh. They rescued whatever wilted produce, dented canned goods and expired bakery items were being discarded. Then they'd swing by community farms and gardens that had graciously agreed to share their fresh stuff. The last stop was always the farm of the Jarhead Sodbusters, a hearty group of war vets who worked their gardens as therapy to heal their physical and psychic wounds.

For the next three years Betty taught herself to cook. She watched cooking shows and YouTube videos and pored over cookbooks from the Pulver Forge Public Library. Her online search for recipes led her to websites decrying the horrors of factory farming, and soon she'd become a vegan. This worked out, because 99% of the food donations were veggies, rice and beans.

She amazed herself with her obsessive devotion to the work. The farther down the rabbit hole she went, the more she enjoyed herself. The same manic energy she'd devoted to getting high was now spent obsessing about the sixteen variations on beet ketchup she'd lined up in the kitchen window, so she could capture just the right crimson pigmentation.

The church's generic minestrone soup became "Betty's Butternut Minestrone with Sage, Chickpeas and Chard." The church's generic staple, "trashcan chili" became "Betty's Smokey Squash Chili with Quinoa, Pinto and Black Beans." Betty discovered the pleasures of helping others: she and the Rev would chat up their Sunday "customers," get them sober and put them to work in the kitchen. Soon the Rev was pointing out local "foodies" who would dress down and sneak in line just to savor Betty's offerings.

Betty knew the Rev was inviting local restaurant owners to the Sunday homeless feast to sample her wares. One such owner was Quixote Institute member Mashama Twitty, the 31-year-old owner of the Black vegan soul food joint, the "Meatless Mess Hall." Twitty made Betty her line chef. It was hot, harried work for demanding, impoverished regulars, and Betty knew she was home. Within a year Mashama was letting Betty prep the Mess Hall's signature "Black-Eyed Peas with Smoky Collards and 'Cheesy' Grits." And when Mashama and her sponsors branched out into the food truck business, Betty was made Mobile Chef Supreme.

With this move, Betty was invited to her first gathering of the Quixote Institute, in the Rev's living room. She laughed when she saw so many people that had helped her along the way. Now it all made sense. Now she had the chance to pay back what she'd been given. Her vegan soul food truck, "Bite Me," had a staff of five (including her) and each one was plucked from the ranks of the homeless by the Rev, then vetted and trained by Mashama. Each was like Betty: feisty, dedicated, devoted to feeding people, and happy to have a job. When one would backslide, the others would rescue her, rally around her and stay with her till she was good to go.

Betty and the Rev had been looking for Mike, and here he was. And it was time for the Quixote Institute to put all that theorizing to the test. Maybe...just maybe...all that idealism wasn't so unreasonable after all.

QUIXOTE INSTITUTE MANIFESTO

We Hold These Truths to Be Self-Evident:

- That we human beings have the inherent compassion, wisdom and fortitude to imagine and then create a circumstance where we can thrive.
- That we human beings have been given the gift of consciousness so that we can freely choose love over hate, cooperation over competition, and harmony over conflict.
- That we human beings can summon the power of intention to be kind, generous, loving and constructive in any circumstance. This intention will inevitably lead to the formation of deeply connected, mutually beneficial beloved communities.
- That we human beings can gleefully ignore circumstances and "the common wisdom" and act boldly to conjure the "beloved community" that Dr. King dared us to create.

We are peaceful warriors. We are not bound by circumstance, but rather by our commitment to go with joy in this world of sorrow. Like Sisyphus, we recognize this task may be never-ending, and yet we approach it with a smile. We are not doing this to save the world. We are doing this to save ourselves.

CHAPTER FIVE

THE CURSE OF PULVER FORGE
An Historical Essay by Calvin Mason McCoy, Editor/Publisher of the Pulver Forge Gazette from 1969 until it ceased daily, physical publication in 2004 and went to a once-a-week digital format.

Enoch Cornelius Pulver is still regarded as the patriarch of the town he named after himself. Those who hold him in high regard call him an "industrialist." He built the steel mill that gave jobs to five generations of our residents. He gave our town a magnificent library and recreation complex that has served us for more than fifty years. He built hotels, an Opera House, established our parks and built housing for his workers. And he's the one who put the curse on Pulver Forge.

In 1893, the men of the Pulver Iron Works called a general strike to protest a wage cut. These men were working twelve hours a day, six days a week, for ten dollars a week, half in company scrip. Pulver had cut them from twelve dollars a week two years ago. Now — in a year where the company cleared eight million dollars in profit — he wanted to cut them from ten to nine. He knew that whatever money they made went to their landlord, a man named Enoch Pulver. This Pulver also owned the Pulver Company Store, where they were required to use that scrip he issued: the store that charged them double what independent stores charged. Each year they worked for Pulver, they found themselves deeper in debt. They weren't looking for a raise, they just wanted to survive. They were desperate. They tried to negotiate, but Pulver pretended the union didn't exist. And so, as a last resort, they went on strike.

As the strike neared, Pulver left his estate to stay at his Park Avenue mansion in New York. On July 4, 1893, he enjoyed a fourteen-course dinner with Philander C. Knox at Delmonico's Restaurant, Fifth Avenue and Twenty-Sixth Street. Pulver's second-in-command was Grover Freeman Hendricks, a grim, hatchet-faced enforcer so chosen because he was a stone-cold killer, willing to do what his boss wanted without the boss getting his hands dirty. At the very moment that Pulver was savoring his Lobster Newburg, Hendricks signaled a group of strikebreaking hooligans he'd recruited from the Pinkerton Detective Agency to fire directly into the rowdy crowd of strikers. Eleven died. Nine of the victims were married. Seven had young children. The Pulver Forge police force, in the private employ of Enoch Cornelius Pulver, refused to arrest the shooters, who were hustled out of town. When the strike struggled on for another week, Pulver had his friend the Governor call in the National Guard of Pennsylvania to put them down. This was the same National Guard that had "restored order" by beating up strikers in the Railroad Strike of 1877.

Pulver had won. He ordered Hendricks to fire the strikers and hire a whole new group of workers at eight dollars a day. The mill didn't get a union until the mid-1930s under Franklin D. Roosevelt, and even then it took a mini-bloodbath.

My grandfather, Hiram C. McCoy, was killed that day in 1893. My father, Clancy McCoy, was three years old at the time. My grandmother, Bessie Walters McCoy, had to move in with her sister and their three kids in a one-bedroom shack over in Vinegar Bend. The town was broken. My father was broken. He went to work at the mill when he was seventeen, and he knew he'd never get out alive. He died in 1937 when I was six years old. I was at his bedside when he died. He couldn't breathe, too much metal dust in his lungs. He was gasping for air, literally choking to death when he asked me to do one thing for him: never to set foot in the steel mill. He told me it would kill me the way it killed him. That's why I became a newspaperman and amateur town historian.

I'm a storyteller. History is a story. It's not a moral lesson: it's most often a tragedy. The story that Pulver Forge tells itself is that if we, the people of the town rise up and decide to seize our destiny, we'll be crushed like our great-grandfathers were. But stories aren't set in stone: they can change. We're just waiting for our "what happens next" moment.

CHAPTER SIX

March 19

MIKE DAVENPORT

"Hey!" Kate Walther was surprised to see me reading a two-year-old copy of People Magazine in the lobby of her emergency room. She gave me a hug. "This is a nice surprise. What are you doing here?"

"Remember those heart-to-hearts we used to have when we were kids, walking by the river?"

"Of course."

"I need one now. Not the walk, the heart-to-heart. Over a drink, if possible."

The Big Smokey Steakhouse was one of those "Great Everywhere" lightly themed chain eateries that huddled in power centers across this great nation of ours. It was a massive sorta-kinda National Park lodge built of faux timber, with the wait-staff in lumberjack garb. But it had a good enough bar that served Glenlivet rocks (me) and Chardonnay (her). She'd changed out of her blue medical scrubs into a black and white floral print dress that made me smile. Her golden blonde hair was cut in a short bob now, but that mischievous angel face was the one I fell in love with back in 1994.

As the local football hero, I was one of five judges for the 1994 Miss Pulver Forge Beauty Pageant: the one that would choose the competitor for Miss Pennsylvania who then might become Miss America. Kate was a break-your-heart beauty in a high cut American flag one piece bathing suit and candy apple red high heels. The other, less stellar contestants oozed sincerity to win over the judges, but Kate was there to make mischief as she stepped up to the microphone for the talent competition. Mayor Randall Murkey asked her what her goal in life was. She said with mock solemnity, "To never have an argument with someone less privileged than myself." I'd never heard a more perfect spoof of pageant-speak. Then her pianist, Kevin Brooks, the gayest member of the Pulver High School Drama Club, sat down at the piano and Kate sang the most excruciating, just slightly flat, just slightly out of tempo version of "You'll Never Walk Alone" ever performed. This wasn't caterwauling: only someone with perfect pitch could commit an art-crime this heinous. The other judges were flummoxed, but I was thrilled. I couldn't stop laughing. I gave her a one-judge standing ovation, yelling, "Bravo! Encore!" She smiled, bowed gracefully and strutted into the wings. I hustled backstage, told her I loved her, and offered to buy her dinner. That night at Primanti Brothers (home of the "Pitts-Burger"), she told me what the deal was: her pushy stage mother had been grooming her to win the Miss America pageant since Kate was six. (Kate was never consulted about this.) Tanking this competition was the final stake in the heart of mom's dream: she was finally and completely done with pageant life. (Amazingly, she still finished third. That's what a knockout she was.)

"So," I said, "How's life?"

"Life is, you know, fine." She stared down at the table. "Good. It's all good."

Her body language told a different story. "Go on," I said.

She looked up at me. "Well, let's see. My oldest, Todd, is a junior at Penn State, so the nest is half empty. Amber is a high school senior. Spends her time with her friends and her phone. She's not pregnant and nobody's using drugs that I know about, so what more can you ask?"

"How's the marriage?"

She sighed and gave me a half-smile. "Scott just made partner at the law firm, which made him…happy is wrong word. Relieved. We're…I guess the word is 'steady.'

"Steady," I said. "Uh huh. And you?"

A rueful laugh. "Well, I finally got what I wanted. You know how I started as an EMT, and then became a nurse? Well, I worked my butt off to become an emergency doc, just so I could…" She stopped and gazed into the distance. "I was going to say, 'help people.' Do you know what it's like to tell a patient with pancreatic cancer that he was shit out of luck because his insurance won't pay for the proper treatment?" She put her face in her hands.

"And now?" I said.

She turned back to me, with a new fierceness. "Now I'm a goddamn prisoner of this sick system that puts profits before patients. Nobody ever says, 'Take your time, love your patients, listen to them, care for them, heal them.' All I hear is, 'Work faster, see more people, only do work you can charge for, and bill as much as possible.' And the hospital has been bought up by a corporate velociraptor that's slashed our sick leave, trimmed our benefits, and eviscerated our retirement program. Their answer to everything is, 'Don't like it, go somewhere else.'"

"Sorry."

"Me too," she said. "And it's not helping the marriage. I mean, we're not in trouble, but…"

"What?"

She stared at her half-empty wine glass. "The thing that you and I both shared — our bond — was getting out of that shit-hole town and doing something with our lives. And now we have, both of us. And it's just… "

"Not enough?"

She shrugged. "Not what I expected. Scott works fourteen hours a day to stay one step ahead of the Indiana Jones rolling boulder of death. Me? I work fourteen hours a day so our beloved CEO can pull down sixteen million dollars a year without ever seeing a patient or making anyone better." Then she forced a smile. "So, have I bored you to death yet? We came here to talk about you. So how are you? You still engaged to what's-her-name?"

"Tess. And yes, I am." Kate was allergic to Tess. "You should like her, she's a lot like you."

Kate blanched. "If you mean that as a compliment…"

"Smart, beautiful and world-class at what you do."

"Except what she does is bullshit."

"Lucrative bullshit," I said.

"Has she made her two million dollars yet?

"A little less than halfway," I said. "Me too, actually. With any luck, we should be in Kauai in two years." I saw that skeptical half-smile as she looked at her cocktail napkin. "What?"

She looked up and locked eyes with me. "I'd just be sure you're marrying her for the right reason."

"Like?"

"Like don't be stupid in that way that only men can be. I'm sure the sex is over the moon, but do you laugh at the same things? Does she 'get' you?"

That froze me. I'd never used that as a metric of romance. "Uhhh…"

She looked at her drink, near empty. "Everybody has an unspeakable secret, a terrible regret, an impossible dream and an unforgettable love. Does she know *any* of those about you?" I just stared at her for a moment. She was my unforgettable love, the first and greatest. She looked back at me. "Look, I hope it makes you happy. But that's not why you wanted to talk, I'm sure."

"No. No it's not." I wanted to ask her if I was *her* unforgettable love…but I chickened out. "I wanted to talk because…. well, two of Pulver Forge's finest came into my coffee house this morning."

"Let me guess. Chef Betty and Reverend Luke. Am I right?"

This surprised me. "R-right."

"And they want you to, what, run for City Council?"

"Mayor."

"Mayor, wow, right." She smiled. "So, big step. Are you going to do it?"

I looked down at my drink, took a small handful of over-salted pretzel bites from a dish on the bar. "No."

"Why not?"

"Look, I've got a life. I fought for that life. Now I got a guy, investment banker, who wants to put up seven-figure money to build out twelve HuggaMugs around Pittsburgh and Philly, maybe Collegeville and Pleasant Hills. This is my shot, and I earned it. Sooooo…."

She held up her empty wine glass. "You want my blessing to turn them down?"

I was surprised how she put that. "I just want your opinion. I really want to know what you think."

"I think you should do it." *What??* "In fact, I think you've *got* to do it."

I felt like she'd slapped me. My heart started to thud in my chest. "I…what? I think I just got whiplash there. We both agree it's hopeless, right?"

"Yeah, probably."

"So why…"

She turned her head and looked straight at me. This look: I remembered it from our fling-a-ding high school days, walking hand-in-hand at sunset in Waterfront Park. I was about to get it right between the eyes, no bullshit. "Because of what you said at Dave's wake."

"I said a bunch of stuff, including I was never going back there."

"You also said you loved him. Well, so did I. To see him laid out in that godawful plywood casket in that dumpy funeral home...." She closed her eyes. "I remember the three of us in high school. My gawd, we were carefree, immortal, and bulletproof."

"Yeah, before..."

"Before we found out that everything we took for granted was so...so fragile."

"Uh huh," I said, turning this over in my mind.

Now she turned to me, dead serious. "Pulver Forge killed him, Mike."

"I know, but what can I do?"

"What you said in your eulogy."

"But my business..."

"You can always make money."

"But..."

"You need to do this so Dave didn't die for nothing."

I let this sink in. "If I decide to do this, and it's a big 'if'..."

"Yes?"

"Will you help me?"

"You bet your ass." I was surprised how surprised I was. "I'm sick of what I'm doing now. Truth be told, I think I need this as much as you."

It all came back to me in that moment: the first moment I ever laid eyes on that beautiful, soulful face. I felt my eyes misting. "Kate, I...I..."

She put her hand on mine. "I know. Me too. Let's hold hands and jump off this cliff together."

CHAPTER SEVEN

March 25

MAKAYLA NICHOLS

"I think there's been a mistake." Makayla Nichols, Emmy-Award winning news reporter, was staring down at the thinning combover of WPTT-TV news director Geoff Walsh. She'd walked in without knocking. She was blocking his view of his beloved 85" big screen, which showed feeds of every cable news network and Pittsburgh TV station, all with the sound muted. She was pissed.

"Mistake?" said Geoff, all wide-eyed innocence. This is the same gosh-golly look Geoff used when he talked about "diversity," "inclusivity," "commitment to excellence" and "the big WPTT family where everyone has a seat at the table." Makayla always wondered why "diversity" never seemed to apply to white, middle-aged news directors who were gatekeepers of this "big family."

"Did you tweet out that you're going with Megan Baker-Hall to anchor the five o'clock?"

"Well…"

"The five o'clock you promised—PROMISED—to me?" Geoff's eyes finally met hers.

"Have a seat, Makayla." Should she? Or should she leap across his desk and throttle this smug douchewaffle? She pondered her options. After a long moment, she sat. "Megan…"

"Did you or did you not promise me that gig?"

He leaned back and tented his fingers. "I'm pretty sure I said something like, 'if things work out.'"

"'If things work out'? Dammit, Geoff, I've won you five local Emmys, a National Headliner Award, an AP Broadcaster Award..."

"You're good, Makayla! We love you! You are the best reporter this station has."

"Why do I feel like you're going to show me your great big 'but'?" Everything about this guy gave her the creeps: the Hermes tie, the Tom Ford dress shirt with the French cuffs, the spare, uncluttered chrome and glass office (for a news director??) with the fresh lemony scent. *He wasn't a news guy.* He'd come up through the station sales department, where everything was about numbers and ad buys. He was in news to check that box on his way to General Manager.

"But" he said, failing to disappoint, "we've all got to understand what business we're in."

This took her aback. "Aren't we in the news business?"

Geoff gave her that smug grin she hated. "We're in the business of renting eyeballs to advertisers, Makayla. Our job is to manufacture shiny objects that attract those eyeballs. Our shiny objects have to be shinier than the shiny objects made by our competition. The more eyeballs, the better our bottom line. That's it, end of report." He had a manila folder squared to the blotter on his desk. He opened it and handed her the single sheet of paper inside.

"What's this?" said Makayla.

"Market research, rating our on-air news staff and anchor personalities. Sixty-three percent of viewers in the greater Pittsburgh metro know who Megan Baker-Hall is. Fifty-nine percent like her, and would happily spend one hour each day with her, from five to six p.m. Those are big numbers. Your numbers...well, just look at the bottom of the page. Mid to upper forty percent name recognition. Not bad, but when it comes to likability..."

Makayla flicked the paper back at Geoff. It sailed over his head, settling on the alabaster wool carpeting. "When you hired me, you told me you wanted to turn this into a place that was…let me see, I think your words were, 'famous for news.'" She stood up and leaned over him. "You used that same phrase when you graciously accepted the Emmy for the enterprise series I researched, wrote, shot and edited on my own time, on the brain damage football was causing high schoolers…"

"STOP!" Geoff said. "That was a great set of pieces, Makayla. You are one of my stars. I want to keep you on the team, keep you happy, continue to give you a platform to bring home all those awards."

"Here comes the 'but'," she said.

"But…you weren't a first runner-up in the Miss Vermont contest like Megan. You don't have a boyfriend who's a big-name stud in the world of mixed-martial arts. You don't have half a million social media followers…

"…or a Newsroom Barbie body, a closet full of micro-mini skirts, a Pepsodent smile…"

"Look…" said Geoff, but Makayla's voice went up a notch.

"…or a peachy-cream alabaster complexion."

Geoff was about to parry this, but it was too much. He sighed, massaged his brow, and then looked at her.

"You saw the numbers, Makayla. You really want to make this about race?"

"Not unless it is, Geoff. Is it?" His face hardened. He squared the manila folder that didn't need squaring, leaned back and stared at her. She blinked, then turned away. "Look, maybe I went too far just now. It's just that…" She turned back to him. *Don't beg, just make your case.* "I'm twenty-nine years old. I've been here for five years working hundred-hour weeks doing every damn thing you asked of me. Everything. Ten stories a week, live shots, enterprise pieces, tweeting, Facebooking, Instagramming, TikToking, talking to civic groups, hosting career days for high school kids, all because of your promise. Shit, Geoff, our YouTube channel is *half my stuff!* Megan wouldn't know a scoop if a UFO landed in her back yard and Elvis got out. What do I have to do? Are you *ever* going to give me an anchor slot? Ever? Even on weekends?"

Makayla knew she was dead just from the pause. Finally, Geoff smiled. "You've done it all, Makayla. You're great, your reporting is smart and assertive. We'd be delighted if you continued to be a part of our WPTT-TV family."

"Uh huh," said Makayla. "Family." She couldn't muster the rage a second time. She just felt tired of trying to stay afloat in this sea of bullshit. "Okay," she said. "Got it. Thanks."

"Hey," said Geoff. "That thing you did last week on that Make-A-Wish kid going to Kennywood Park, with that plush kangaroo giving her a hug? Good work. More of that." She turned and walked away, whispering "what...a...weasel ..."

CHAPTER EIGHT

March 26

MIKE DAVENPORT

My plan was to make this short and sweet: stand on the doorstep and give Betty and the Rev a polite turn down. I'd done my best to come up with a plan to turn Pulver Forge around. Kate was the only one who thought it was worth doing. My conclusion? It was a great way to ruin my business, trash my relationship with Tess and wreck my life.

The Rev's simple white 1926 clapboard house was directly adjacent to "The First Church of Jesus Christ, Troublemaker," on the corner of Highland Avenue and Dewberry Street in the heart of Homewood, the African American district of Pulver Forge. This was a 1920s "hall" church, a cavernous whitewashed wooden rectangle with a peaked roof and long sides slit with tall, narrow stain glass windows. The illuminated glass panels lit up the room with glimmering shafts of crimson, gold and cerulean blue light.

The church property sat on an acre of land with a large Fellowship Hall in the back, with a community kitchen and residency annex. A generous patch of earth fronted the compound. What used to be lawn was now a thriving vegetable garden, with an early Spring crop of spinach, Swiss chard, and Red Russian kale just coming in. A wiry, dark-skinned man, about my age, clad in mud-spattered overalls and a straw sun hat, was using a water wand to hydrate his crops. He looked up at me and smiled. "Hey."

"Nice!" I nodded and continued to the front door, pressing the doorbell. When the Rev answered, I said, "Look, I just dropped by to let you know…"

Betty stepped forward, wrapped me in a bearhug and bumrushed me into the living room. "Come in, Mike. I just made some cookies. They go great with some fresh coffee!" She delivered me to the Rev as she disappeared into the kitchen.

Before I could reply, the Reverend Luke was nudging me into one of the oak Shaker chairs. "You're here to tell us you're not going to run, right?"

"Well, I…" Before I could finish, Betty handed me the cookie and a steaming mug of java.

"This," said the Rev, "is the best cookie you'll ever eat. Chunks of dark chocolate, almond flour, a pinch of sea salt on top."

"Friend of mine makes these," said Betty. "100% vegan, gluten-free. You should sell them in your shop."

I took a bite. Wow! The way that sea salt stood up to the sugar? She was right, our customers would love these. I looked around. Wall-to-wall, floor-to-ceiling bookcases, oak filing cabinets, and three computer workstations. "Is this your office?"

"Sort of. The Quixote Institute works out of here."

"The what?"

"I'll tell you later," said the Rev. "First, let's fight."

"No use. I've made up my mind, I'm not running."

"Uh huh," said Betty, glancing at the Rev, who was still smiling. "Can you tell us why not?"

"I've looked at it right side up, upside down and sideways. I don't see a way to save Pulver Forge. The town is dead and buried. Why dig up the corpse? It's a waste of time."

"What if…," said Betty. She leaned toward me, lowered her voice. "What if we could find a way to make your biggest, most outrageous idea come true?"

"Which was?"

"Putting everyone back to work. If everyone suddenly had a job, and the jobs were re-building the town, would that make a difference?"

It took me a second to get my mind around that. "Yeah, sure, of course, but I don't see how…"

"It can be done, Mike," said the Rev.

"I don't think so."

"It can. Because it has," he said.

"It has?" I was bumfuzzled. "Are you saying…that an entire town…"

"An entire country," said Betty.

"What? Where?"

"I could tell you," said Betty, "but why not hear it from a guy who lived it?"

That gardener I'd chatted up in the front yard was shaking my hand. "Yandy. Yandy Lopez."

"Corporal Yandy Lopez, Scout sniper, Second Battalion, 1st Marines. Silver Star earned during Operation Vigilant Resolve, first battle of Fallujah," said the Rev. He knew this would impress me. It did.

"Wow," I said, shaking his hand with more vigor. "Sniper."

"Twenty-nine confirmed kills," said the Rev.

I looked at Yandy. "Confirmed. That means that there were others…" He gave me his stone-cold sniper deadpan, and we both knew the answer. "That's…beyond impressive," I said. "I'm a little in awe."

"Don't be," said Yandy. "I know about your coffee place, what you're doing for vets. All I did was kill people. You're giving them jobs."

"So," said Betty, "Tell Mike what you told us about Cuba, when you were a kid."

Yandy pointed at my coffee mug as he plopped himself down in one of the wingchairs. Betty delivered coffee and a cookie, and he turned toward me. "Born in Havana, 1983. My dad was what they called a 'barefoot doctor.' They have a deal over there where they'd put you through medical school for free and then assign you to a neighborhood where you'd look after people, keep 'em from getting sick. It's a good system. So now it's 1991. I'm eight years old and…do you remember what happened back then?"

1991. I said, "Hmmm, Cuba…let's see, the Soviet Union fell apart, right?"

"That's right," said Yandy. "Literally stopped existing. Cuba went from getting seven million Russian dollars a day, including all the oil we could burn, to getting nothing. No warning, just 'Sorry, comrades, you're on your own. Good luck.' No gas. Forget about going for a Sunday drive, there was no gas to run shit like tractors, harvesters, city busses, generators for hospitals."

"Wow," I said.

"Yeah, it was a big shock. We were in a daze."

"So, what happened?"

Yandy smiled. "What do you think happened?"

"Well," I said, "I imagine the government…"

Yandy howled with laughter. "The government, ah, yes. The government treated us like we were mushrooms, as in 'keep us in the dark and feed us bullshit.' Lots of six-hour speeches from Maximum Comandante Castro blaming the Evil Americano Imperialistas, but nothing on the shelves of the grocery stores, or even, God help us, on the black market. My dad and his friends figured out pretty quick that the big shots had no clue about how to handle this, and that was scary. I was terrified."

"Okay, so get to the good stuff," said Betty as she handed out more cookies. I ate mine in three bites.

Yandy, dark eyes twinkling, leaned in, making me wait for the secret. "What happened…was that people—just average people, like me and my dad—started meeting in cafés. We knew no one was coming. We were on our own. If we were going to survive, we needed to get our shit together and fast. Do something, anything. So, we came up with an action plan, and then we got to work."

"Work," said the Rev, "As in grow enough food so you wouldn't starve."

Yandy said, "That's right, first things first. The shock troops were the garden teams. We went door to door, scrounged every garden tool we could find, and then we dug up every public park, vacant lot, soccer field and town square we could find and planted vegetables. We planted everywhere, including rooftops, we had veggie beds up there too. I was on Garden Team 31, Cervantes Park. There was even a team raising rainbow trout in the swimming pool at the Hotel Nacional. Must have protein, after all."

"When you say 'we'," said Betty. "Who was 'we'?

"Excellent question. 'We' was everybody who wanted to avoid starvation, which was just about the entire city of Havana. You didn't have to work, nobody put a gun to your head, but everybody on a work team got a share of what we grew. I was out there planting cassava and I'd have doctors like my dad working beside me, and lawyers and soldiers and teachers and car mechanics were out there working together, digging and weeding and watering and planting. Even the Mayor was out there. He was in charge of cleaning the filter of the pool-turned-trout farm."

"And you were eight years old. No school?" I said.

Yandy laughed again. "My teacher was out there weeding the zucchini beds! Besides, I was in the best kind of school, the one where you learn by doing. I was learning how to grow food, how to work together on a team. My math assignment was taking 'cañas' at the farmer's market..."

"Whoa, whoa. What's a 'caña'?" said Betty.

"You work an hour, you get a 'caña.' A 'time peso.' Like if a couple had young kids, they both got a caña for every hour they worked, which they could use to pay off the abuela who was watching their kids. And granny could use the time peso to buy what the couple was growing."

"So…it was like a barter economy," I said.

"Yeah. I mean, what could you buy with regular pesos? The markets were empty! It was our own system of money that let us actually buy stuff. And to get around town, we had these things we called 'camels.' It was this big truck with a special humpbacked rig on the back that carried, like, a hundred and eighty people. It would just drive around town all day, totally free. Hop on, hop off."

"If you didn't have any gas, how'd you run it?" I said.

"Veggie oil," said Yandy, "like what we used for cooking. Mostly corn oil, some peanut. Came from what we grew. Smelled like French fries when it drove by."

"Wow. And here you are," I said. "I guess you made it."

"Yeah," he said. "We made it."

Betty said, "Amazing what you can do when you have to."

"And people showed up to help us," said Yandy. "All these tree-hugging dirt worshippers from around the world showed up from organic farms and permaculture clubs. Australia, Denmark, France…they were a big, big help, because they could see all the mistakes we were making. We grew more stuff faster because of them."

"You've haven't told 'em the best part of the story," said Betty. "Tell them what happened after, like, a year of this."

"Yeah, what's the best part?" I said.

"What happened," said Yandy, smiling at the thought, "was that my dad practically went out of business. Like, everybody got *healthier*."

"Healthier?" I said, surprised.

"No shit! I mean, think about! Suddenly we're all outside, working together in the sunshine. All the shit that's bad for you—sugar candy, ice cream, donuts, fatty meats like beef and pork, plus cigarettes and liquor—nobody could afford that shit. We were eating tons of fresh lettuce and spinach and taro and yucca that was in the ground, like, two hours before. But that's not the *very* best part of the story."

"So, what's the *very* best part?" said Betty.

He leaned forward, excited. "The very best part—the part I think of when I think of life back then—was the part where we all got to *know* each other. We were all in this thing together. I mean, everybody! Our lives were on the line, and we were getting it done, together! We'd party like crazy on Friday nights, music, dancing, food, the works. So much fun! Another day, and we were still alive, and we were in charge of our own destiny! We were saving ourselves. It was a kind of heaven made in hell."

"So, what happened? I mean, this isn't still going on, is it?" I said.

"Naw," said Yandy. "Lasted four, five years. Then Castro loosened up his restrictions on tourism, so we started to get some Yankee dollars coming in, and Hugo Chavez made a deal with Castro to send him oil. The people that owned all that land gradually clawed it back, including the government. Tourism picked up. Things kind of returned to semi-normal. That's when my dad brought me to the U.S. But the funny thing is…"

"What?" I said.

"I'm still in touch with my garden friends, and…it's strange. Everybody misses those times. We worked our asses off, but on Friday night we'd feast on all this great, fresh food that we grew! It made us feel…I guess *powerful* is the best word for it."

"And" said Betty, "Cuba still has a bunch of farmers' markets selling organic produce from some of those original gardens."

"That's right," said Yandy, "some of those folks who took up gardening kept at it. And people like me took what we'd learned and started our businesses in the states. The Rev lets me cultivate his front lawn, and I sell the stuff at the Farmer's Market on Saturday."

"The Church gets twenty percent of the crop," said Reverend Luke.

"Wow," I said. I turned to Yandy. "You think something like that…I mean, is there any way this could work in a town like, oh, say, Pulver Forge?"

Before Yandy could answer, Betty said, "Pulver Forge needs jobs, Mike. And a purpose. And something like this, well…" My brain was on fire. *What if…*

"We're going to be at that candidate's forum, Mike," said the Rev. "We need somebody crazy enough to dare the people of Pulver Forge to bet on themselves. We hope you're that somebody."

CHAPTER NINE

March 27

MAKAYLA NICHOLS

"Well girl," she thought to herself, *"this is it. This is what the end looks like."* Makayla Nichols was standing in the back of the Pulver Forge Community Library Auditorium setting up her HD camcorder. She'd begun her TV career covering city council meetings in the suburbs of Pittsburgh, grinding hours of footage just to capture 30 seconds of anything resembling drama. Now she was back at the start, inside this moldy ruin of a building getting ready for a one-candidate "Pulver Forge Candidates Forum." A better story would be this building, she thought. It had been erected by "Sultan of Steel" Enoch Pulver himself as a magnificent, multi-faceted gift to his workers and their families: a two-story edifice built with Pennsylvania pressed brick, with floors of native marble and wood. When it opened, it offered a magnificent library, a pool, a gym, basketball courts and this civic auditorium. Now, like the rest of the town, it was crumbling through neglect, a rotting symbol of the disintegration of rust belt towns all over the American Midwest.

She was thinking about her next life as a field producer for nitwit reality TV shows when she heard a voice. "Ms. Nichols?" She turned. A sturdy young Millennial with heavily tatted arms and close-cropped brown hair smiled at her. "Betty Chapel. Thanks for showing up. So, what's your plan?"

"Well, since there's only one candidate and I've got a live shot in Market Square later tonight, I thought I'd do a quick back-and-forth with the mayor and then grab ten minutes of b-roll: the casino pitch, maybe some voter Q and A."

Betty smiled. "I don't work for Bagley. I wanted to give you a heads up about a bigger story, with a good angle for your viewers."

"Uh huh," she said. "Is there a new wrinkle in the casino deal? Is Creavey backing out?"

"No, it's bigger than that," said Betty.

"What then? Can you give me a hint?"

"Well, if everything goes right..." She paused, looked around. Mayor Bagley was on stage, glad-handing the civic-minded geezers who were setting up the two battered podiums that flanked a card table with a folding chair. A faded and stained red, white and blue banner dating from the Hoover administration hung over the stage: "Pulver Forge Candidates Forum." "...we're expecting a kind of surprise. Another candidate. A dark horse, you might say, to take on Bagley."

"Uh huh," said Makayla. "Who?"

"His name is Mike Davenport. Pulver Forge native son, runs a coffee house in Pittsburgh. Afghan war vet. He's got some fresh ideas about jump-starting the town."

"Is he against the casino?"

"Dead-set, and he'll say so on-camera. He's a fighter. Stick around, see for yourself."

Should she? The first voters had wandered in. Makayla noted that, as always, they were codgers, here for the fruit punch and cookies as much as the candidate bafflegab. Several had "Mayor Fred" buttons.

"This Davenport. He a Democrat?" said Makayla.

Betty pondered this. "Funny," he said. "I'm not sure what he is. You can ask him when he shows. If he shows."

"He might not show?" said Makayla.

"He'll show," said Betty, but Makayla could see she was a little jittery.

"Okay," said Makayla. "Ten minutes. I can wait ten minutes."

CHAPTER TEN

March 27

MIKE DAVENPORT

I walked in two minutes before the forum was set to begin. Kate had bumrushed me into Steve Dorsey's Porsche Taycan GTS electric, and now they were third row center, in front of Reverend Luke. On the aisle to their left, Betty was chatting up a young Black woman who was checking a video rig. Betty nudged her and pointed at me, and she looked up and nodded. I'd seen her before. Megan? Marla? Makena? She did live shots on the evening news. Did this sad little shindig rate a Pittsburgh TV station?

As I walked up the splintered wooden stairs to the stage, I was hit by the stench of…damp sweat socks. I looked around: five moss-green blotches of fungal nastiness decorated the ceiling. The place had devolved into an incubator for mold and mildew.

Betsey DeMarco was our moderator, town librarian. She'd been here since I was a freshman. She'd barely changed: ramrod posture, demure flower-print frock, and black-cat eyeglasses with rhinestones. Her auburn Dutch bob was now mostly pewter. "Hello, Michael," she said. "Are you joining us tonight? What a nice surprise."

"Nice to see you, Mrs. DeMarco. I swear to God I'll get that copy of 'The Great Gatsby' back to you by the end of the week."

She laughed. "No hurry." Then she turned and said, "Mayor Fred."

A beefy, balding pol in his early sixties presented himself, thrusting his hand at me. We shook. "A little bird told me you got talked into this. You can still walk away, no hard feelings. This job is a ginormous pain in the backside."

He said this sotto voce. All the voters saw was an affable Chamber of Commerce-type welcoming a neophyte to the stage. I knew he was right, but something in the way he said it set my teeth on edge. "Thanks. I'll know after tonight, Mister Mayor." I released his hand. He winked at me, and we stepped behind our respective podiums.

Nobody had told me the format of this thing: I didn't know until Betsey explained it. "I will ask the candidates a series of questions. Both will have ten minutes to answer. After I'm finished, you will be able to ask questions. My first question is for Mayor Fred Bagley." She turned to Fred. "Pulver Forge has been trapped in a cycle of unemployment and poverty since our steel mill closed in 1986. You've now been Mayor for eight years, and we've seen scant improvement. Do you have a solid, workable plan to improve the economic status of our town?"

His smile didn't reach his eyes as he wheeled toward the voters. "For eight years," he boomed, "I've been laying the groundwork for a major economic resurgence here in the great town of Pulver Forge…" And so we were off. I'm allergic to the kind of cranked-up, market-tested argle-bargle just about every politician uses today, and Mayor Fred was putting on a clinic. "Empowering our citizens…robust solutions… unleashing the power of civic enterprise…" Finally, he got to the punchline: the new SteelTown Casino. "Let's start with the best news possible: two hundred jobs. Two hundred! And that's just a start. This new gaming complex is going to revitalize our town, attracting other job-generating businesses. Stores, restaurants, hotels, and then who knows? Why not a performing arts center and a convention center? That's what happens when a town like ours becomes a leisure destination. This is the future, folks, and I'm proud to be the leader who is going to make it happen."

A smattering of applause, more polite than excited. Seemed to be a lot of skepticism out there, even amongst his fans. Betsey said, "Mister Davenport? What is your plan to improve the economic status of our town?" I froze. I had some vague notions, but nothing prepared. Steve grinned at me, and Kate did too, and suddenly I knew what to do. *You have nothing to lose, so let 'er rip.*

"Hi. My name, as you heard, is Mike Davenport. Am I running for Mayor? I'm not sure yet. My hat was snatched off my head and thrown in the ring for me. But here I am, for what that's worth. I, ummm, left Pulver Forge around 2003 and went into the Army with my best friend, Dave Bratton, who..." I choked for a second. *Stop. Deep breath. You can do this.* "...died of a drug overdose a couple of days ago. I run a coffeehouse in Pittsburgh, called HuggaMug. It's run by vets like me, folks who served in Iraq and Afghanistan. They know what I know: that bullshit can get you killed."

A small gasp from the startled crowd. Well, I had their attention. The TV reporter had been fiddling with her camera, but now she had the camera off the tripod, on her shoulder and she was striding toward the stage. "The Army told us were up against a bunch of ignorant goat farmers. Bullshit. They told us their people were eager for the United States to help them build a secular democracy. More bullshit. If I had kept on believing any of their bullshit after my first firefight, I'd be looking up at six feet of dirt in Section 60 of Arlington National Cemetery. Which leads me to what Mayor Fred just told you. That, my friends, is...can you say it with me? Capitol B BULL SHIT."

Fred's mouth was hanging open. I looked right at him. "A *casino* is going to save us? Really?" I turned back to the voters. "He's offering you two hundred minimum wage, non-union jobs. Every dollar of profit? Shipped overnight via FedEx to Las

Vegas, Nevada to Moses Creavey, an avatar of scumbaggery worth thirty-one billion dollars. Two hundred? When we've got over three thousand people out of work? That doesn't pass the laugh test."

The TV reporter was now on the stage standing behind Betsey, her camera pointed at me. Betsey said, "So what is *your* plan for Pulver Forge, Mr. Davenport?"

"My plan begins with remembering who we are." I paused, looked at the audience. I had 'em. "We're the people who made the steel for the guns and cannons and tanks that won a two-front world war. And then we made the steel that built the New York skyline. Now we're going to rebuild Pulver Forge, and we sure as hell don't need the help of a plutocratic scumbag like Moses Creavey."

Fred sputtered, "Two hundred jobs is two hundred jobs, Mr. Davenport."

I abandoned the podium and walked to the front of the stage. "Two hundred jobs...and you know what comes with those jobs? Ask the people of Atlantic City, Fred. Crime. Robbery. Murder. Prostitution." I looked back at Bagley. His face was red as a stop sign. Shock was morphing into outrage. "Tell me, Mayor Fred, how do we pay for our friends and neighbors who become degenerate gamblers out of economic desperation, plunge into debt and then kill themselves with prescription painkillers?" Back to the voters. "Because the company that's building that casino is just going to take our money and laugh at us." I turned to Fred. "Unless I misunderstood the deal. Do those jobs come with health care? Pension benefits?"

"A job is a job is a job, and we need jobs!" said Fred, just to say something but it was clear that he was losing the voters.

CHAPTER ELEVEN

March 27

MAKAYLA NICHOLS

Makayla smiled to herself. *"You just never know when you're going to trip over the next big thing."* She was living the dream: *shooting news.* This guy was on fire! And he had a seasoned politico gasping for breath.

"Who the hell are you to trash the work I've done, young man?" said Mayor Fred. "I'm laser focused on jobs. Have you ever created a job in your life?"

"As a matter of fact, I have, Mayor Fred," said Mike. "I own a coffeehouse. I built it from the ground up. I've created dozens of jobs, and I pay my people two times the minimum wage. And everybody has health insurance. And together we make a difference in the lives of our customers. We give them a clean, well-lit, friendly place to meet their friends and drink the best coffee in Pittsburgh." Mike turned back to the audience. "And unlike a casino, our place has never had a customer who has spent his entire paycheck on coffee in one night, nor will it ever."

"So let me bring you back to the question, candidate Davenport," said an amused Betsey DeMarco. "Do you have a plan to improve the economic status of our town?"

Makayla moved toward Mike, framing him in a waist-up medium shot. He looked at the floor, and then back at the audience. "Everyone here lives in Pulver Forge, am I right?" Nods all around. "Anyone here who doesn't think this place has gone to hell?" More nods, and some chuckles as Mayor Fred was the lone person to raise a hand. "My God, our neighbors, people we know, and their children are killing themselves with drugs. On that death certificate? Where it says, 'Cause of Death'? It shouldn't say 'Fentanyl.' It should say, 'despair.' What's killing us is the voice in our heads saying, 'We can't, it's hopeless, why bother.'"

Mike took a swig of water from the plastic bottle on the podium. Makayla pulled back into a long shot. She was focused on Mike, but she knew he had the audience. No coughs, no candy wrappers, nobody staring at a smartphone screen. They were his.

"So, here's my plan." Mike turned to Betsey. "We're going to get this place believing in itself, the way we used to believe. Optimism. Enterprise. Community. All three of these lead to the big word. Get ready for it." Mike held his hands out as if framing the word for them on a billboard. "Prosperity."

Mayor Fred snorted. "Who's not for that?"

"You aren't," said Mike. Mayor Fred glared at him. "No, really. Two hundred minimum wage jobs? Working on the plantation of a Vegas huckster? That's not prosperity, that's desperation."

Mike was at the front of the stage. Makayla hustled down the stairs, so she was looking up at him. Lucky her, Mike's head was framed by a halo of lights from a chandelier. *Oh, man, this is great stuff.*

"My first act as Mayor will be to outlaw pessimism, despair and cynicism." Mike just stood there and let that sink in.

Mayor Fred squinched his face. "What?!?"

Betsey, baffled, said, "Outlaw? You mean, you'd pass a law, have people arrested…"

"I mean, Mrs. DeMarco, that we will change the name of this dirty ol' town from Pulver Forge to PROSPERITY, Pennsylvania." Back to the voters. "We will own that word. Anyone who says a bad word about our fair city will be, umm, 'encouraged' to VOLUNTARILY toss a dollar bill into a five-gallon industrial bucket—let's call it a 'beef bucket'—that will sit just inside the door of City Hall. And we'll use that money to throw ourselves a hell of a party every July 4th."

"Bravo, Mr. Davenport," said Mayor Fred, voice dripping with sarcasm. Makayla swung over to him. "Only…it's funny, I still haven't heard anything about jobs. Two hundred jobs? Two jobs? One job? Oh, I guess you said you're opening a coffeehouse here, so that's, what, six jobs? Five? Tell us how many, please."

Back on Mike. He was calm, ready for this. "Starting on day one of my administration, any citizen of Prosperity, PA who wants a job will have one."

"Whoa, whoa, whoa," said Mayor Fred, stunned. "Anyone? How the hell…"

Mike glared at him. "When's the last time you got out of your Cadillac Escalade and walked around your own town, Fred? I mean, my gawd!" Back to the front of the stage, back into the halo of light. "Here's my plan. First—very important—every citizen of Pulver Forge will be entitled to one free cup of my French Roast coffee every single morning. Then, properly caffeinated, we will walk this town block by block and pick up every piece of trash. We will fix up everything worth fixing and bulldoze the rest, because we're gonna need farmland."

"Farmland?" Now Mayor Fred was just baffled. This thing had totally gotten away from him.

"Farmland. Didn't I mention that? We're going to grow food on every square inch of vacant land we can find. We're going to grow in vacant lots, in Memorial Park, and on front lawns. Maybe even on rooftops."

"That," said Mayor Fred, "is the craziest goddam thing I've ever heard. It'll never work. NEVER."

"Earth to Fred," said Mike. "It already *has* worked. World War II, Fred. Victory gardens. My grandparents grew their own lettuce, squash, tomatoes and rutabagas and what they couldn't eat they gave away to their neighbors." He turned back to the voters. "Maybe we'll fix up the ol' Bailey Brothers food mart, turn it into a Farmer's Market. Bring what you grow, take what you need. Nobody goes hungry, because everybody's part of the program. One people. One town. One generous, thriving tribe."

"STOP!" Makayla's camera battery had died. She was planning a half hour shoot. "Give me a moment, please." Everyone watched as she raced back to her gear bag and swapped out camera batteries. "Sorry." She trained her camera back on Mike. "Okay, go!"

Mike looked befuddled. She cursed herself for stopping his freight train of an oration. She cued him. "One people, one city, one tribe?"

"Right," he said. Well, that's basically…" Makayla saw him stare at someone in the audience. She swung her camera around: it was a blonde woman in the third row smiling back at him. His wife? She swung back to Mike who said, "No, no… There's one more thing we're going to do." He paused, took a deep breath, and said, in a voice choked with emotion, "We are…we are going find every lost soul snorting and shooting drugs behind every garbage dumpster. We're going to take them in our arms and tell them that they're not alone. We're going to stay with them until they get better, because the opposite of addiction is connection, and that's what this whole thing is about. Hell, we know what's best for us, we just forgot we had the power to do something about it."

Fred Bagley had had enough. Makayla swiveled toward the mayor as he huffed up to the front of the stage, "I have never, NEVER, in all my years, heard such a pile of airy-fairy, pie-in-the-sky horse hockey." Now he took two steps toward Mike, and with a knowing grin, said, "Three thousand jobs, Mike? On the payroll of this city? What magic lamp are you going to rub to make that pipe dream come true?"

Mike squared himself to the audience, and then said, softly, "There's no magic lamp, Fred. There's just us, in this auditorium.

There's just me, up here. I shouldn't even be here. I should be dead. One man, a guy named Dave Bratton saved my sorry ass because he loved me, and he thought he could. That's what happens when the power of the human imagination is inspired by love." He paused, collecting himself. "Let's imagine a brand-new town called 'Prosperity, Pennsylvania' where everyone has a job, everyone has enough to eat, everyone can see a Doctor when they need one, and everyone has a decent place to live. It wasn't so long ago that Pulver Forge *was that town*. It's not impossible. Our grandparents lived that dream. They went to work every single day to make it come true. So, let's stop complaining and get to work. Let's imagine a new dream—a better dream—*and work together to make it come true*."

Wow. A moment of silence, and then Makayla did a whip pan to the audience. A geezer in the front row stood up and started to clap. Then another, and then Mike was getting a standing ovation, complete with hoots, hollers and whoops. Makayla captured it all. She felt goosebumps, it was a dream shoot. After a minute of this, Betsey DeMarco said, "Now, if anyone out there has a question..."

Before any of them could speak up, Makayla shouted up at Mike, "What makes you think you can do this?"

Now Mike gave out with a full-body laugh. "Great question. But it's the wrong one. Can I do this? No. Can WE do this? I think that if we stay together, trust each other, love each other, and don't give up, we can do *anything*."

A bolt of adrenaline shot through Makayla's body as she moved in on Mike's face. *This is the guy everybody's been waiting for.' Holy freakin' shit...*

He turned to Mayor Fred, who looked like he'd swallowed a poison dart frog. "I grew up here, Fred. We built this country. And now it's time we built something for *ourselves*. Something we can be proud of."

CHAPTER TWELVE

March 27
MIKE DAVENPORT
What just happened? I wasn't sure, but I was being mobbed (if you call thirty people a mob) by the citizens who'd watched the debate. After I'd shaken every hand and bumped every fist, Betsey DeMarco said, "You acquitted yourself nicely, Mister Davenport. Well-reasoned arguments in short, declarative sentences with active verbs. You've exceeded my expectations."

"Not the same knucklehead you used to kick out of the library."

"Oh, I could always see your potential. Best of luck." She stuck out her hand. I grabbed it, and she pulled me just close enough to whisper in my ear, "Run. We need you" She smiled as she turned to leave. Mayor Fred was long gone. That left Kate, Betty and the Rev…and the news woman.

She held her camera in her left hand as she stuck out her right. "Makayla Nichols, Channel 7 news. That was impressive."

I shook it. "Thanks."

"Can I get a quick interview to frame up what I shot here?"

"Umm, sure, I guess."

She hoisted the camera on her shoulder. "Okay, don't look at the camera, look at my left shoulder, and answer in complete sentences, because my questions won't be in the piece. So…tell me why you want to be Mayor of Pulver Forge."

"I don't. Or at least I'm not sure."

She sighed as she pulled the camera down. "Okay, let's try again. Remember, complete sentences, 'I want to be Mayor because…'" She pulled the camera up. "Why are you running for Mayor?"

"Because…I mean, I'm running because…for Mayor, because two people I barely know put my name on the ballot without asking me."

She grimaced, then pulled the camera off her shoulder. "Forget it, I don't need it for tonight."

"Sorry. I've never done this before."

She studied me. "You've got something, Mike Davenport. I shoot politicians for a living. You've actually got something to say." And with that, she was gone. Which left my fan club.

The Reverend Luke Bramlett was grinning. "Good job, Mike. Mayor Fred never knew what hit him." He gave me a hug.

Kate was next. Another hug. "Great job, Mike. Proud of you."

Then, finally, Betty. "One thing before you go. Up there tonight? You're everything we hoped you'd be."

"But" said the Rev, "none of that makes a bit of difference if you're not going to run."

Betty said, "We can carry you across the finish line. We're ready to knock on doors, phone bank, whatever it takes. But we've got to know if you're in or out."

"Oh boy," I said. "Look, can you give me a night? Let me call you tomorrow morning?"

"No," said Betty, her mouth curving into a wry smile. "Because if we do that, you'll talk yourself out of it. If you're going to say no, tell us, in person, right now."

I scanned their faces. Smiles all around, including Kate. "Okay," I said. "I'll give you a 'yes, if.'"

"Yes if what?" said the Rev.

"Yes if I keep my business. Team HuggaMug has worked our butts off to get where we are. I'm about to make a deal that's going to put me on Easy Street, and I'm not ditching it now."

"You said you might open a coffeehouse in Pulver…sorry, Prosperity," said Betty.

"Yeah, I'd do that," I said. "If we're going to turn this sorry town around, we'll need plenty of high-octane brain juice."

"Agreed," said Betty. "What else?"

"I'm not ready to move here. Not yet. I live fourteen miles away, I can commute." Betty looked at Luke Bramlett.

"Your plan is ambitious," said the Rev. "It's going to be a full-time job."

I looked at him, dead serious. "Our biggest job is turning despair into hope into action. If we can do that, you won't need me around. If we can't, well…me being around won't make any difference." No one said anything. I could tell they weren't sold. "Look, I'm all in. Succeed or die trying. Those are my terms. If things change, we'll renegotiate."

"So, you're giving us a blinking green light," said Betty. I nodded. She stuck out her hand, and I shook it. A sick shiver went through my body, and I flashed back on the moment I signed my enlistment papers. *What the hell have I gotten myself into?*

CHAPTER THIRTEEN

March 28-30
MAKAYLA NICHOLS
Makayla's first story—the candidate's debate—ran as a 'kicker' on the ten o'clock newscast. That's the end of the last quarter hour, usually a human-interest story or "cutie" (new baby panda at the zoo) that aired just before sign-off. As Makayla expected (but Geoff didn't), her piece went semi-viral, generating the most social media posts, emails, and phone calls of any story that month. That meant Geoff had to give her the green light for a couple of five-minute follow up pieces.

March 28
First, Mayor Fred. He had the sweaty affect of a used car dealer who'd been arrested for rolling back odometers. He mouthed the usual fusty bromides about job growth, then shared his kludgy PowerPoint presentation about the new casino. He ended by warning voters not to entrust city government to "inept neophytes."

Then, Mike. As per her instructions, Mike was roasting coffee beans when she showed up to shoot B-roll. He came across as a brawny man of action, a hands-on job-creating entrepreneur. Thanks to her coaching, voters heard razor-sharp, provocative answers that dared them to take a chance on creating the future of their dreams. She ended with B-roll shots of Mike serving free coffee to grateful war vets.

Mayor Fred: smug hack. Mike Davenport: muscular young innovator. This kind of manipulation went against her journalistic principles, but those were out the window now: she had a new idea about where she was going and how she'd get there. Screw Geoff, screw the station, screw local TV news. She was in business for herself, and business was about to boom.

March 30

Two days later, Makayla shot a 'meet the voters' piece in Pulver Forge, using the downtown lunch crowd at Betty's "Bite Me" food truck. Betty and the Rev supplied her with just the right "Davenport for Mayor" faces: enthusiastic, young, diverse and well-informed, parroting bullet points from the campaign's direct mail piece. Lots of words like "positive" "inspiring" and "bold." And of course "jobs." Then she went to Snooky's Diner on Lincoln Avenue to capture Mayor Fred's supporters: crotchety denizens of the sixty-to-death AM talk radio demographic, mostly retired mill workers who knew Mike second-hand as a pot-smoking socialist rabble-rouser. Makayla used the shoutiest cranks with pastry crumbs in their beard stubble. The pro-Mike forces couldn't have cut a more effective campaign ad if they'd had a television budget.

At 5:30 p.m. on election day Tuesday, Makayla was sipping her vanilla latte opposite Mike and Betty at a corner table at HuggaMug. "So, here's the plan," she said. "If you win, you'll give your acceptance speech—hopefully no more than three, four minutes—and then you and I will do a live shot at 10:45 surrounded by a mob of joyous supporters."

"And if I lose?" said Mike.

Makayla laughed. "Then we'll do a live shot of you demanding a recount." She took a sip. "Have you scoped the yard signs in town? 'I Like Mike—Vote for Prosperity,' about two hundred. 'F-R-E-D Spells Jobs,' about fifteen. Nice job, Betty."

"Thanks," said Betty. "You could have told us this over the phone. Why the meeting? Not that we don't love you."

"So, here's the thing," said Makayla. "Right after the anchors sign off, I'm calling the station to give my notice."

Mike was startled. He glanced at Betty, then back at Makayla. "You're quitting your news gig? Why?"

"Because I'm going to become your Communications Director and 'Minister of Ballyhoo'."

Mike just stared at her, amazed. Then, after a moment, he turned to Betty. "Are we going to have the budget…"

Makayla cut him off. "You don't have to pay me, at least for a while. I've got some money saved up; I'll be fine."

Betty was intrigued. "Why?"

'Three reasons," said Makayla. "First, I got into this crazy business to make a difference." She snorted. "Silly me. On a good day I'm killing boredom, getting viewers to stick around for the mattress store ads. On a bad day…well, there are too many bad days, when I do stories that aren't worth doing. What you said at that forum…hell, if you can pull off ten percent of what you pitched, it'll make a huge difference in thousands of lives. Maybe I can help you do that."

"Second?" said Mike.

"Second, you clearly have no idea what the hell you're getting yourself into. Betty here, and Kate and the Rev…you need all the help you can get. This thing works, you're going to be in deep shit. You'll be a target."

Mike was taken aback. "Target? What do you…"

"Mike, why do you think Pulver Forge looks the way it does?"

"Well, because everybody's given up on it. Nobody cares, so…"

"There are people, a lot of them, who are perfectly happy with the way things are," said Makayla. "You think that casino guy is going to take this lying down? That he won't fight back? What about the people who've kept that Mayor in place for eight years?"

Mike looked at her skeptically. "I don't…"

"How 'bout the drugs that killed your friend Dave? You talked about getting people clean. You think the people who push that stuff want you wrecking their business? These people have power, Mike. And guns, lots of them."

Betty said, "So what's reason number three?"

Makayla took a deep breath. "A selfish reason. I had a personal reckoning not too long ago. I don't have the look, the connections, or the stomach to make it to the top of the news business. I need a new business."

Mike said, "So how will you…"

She reached out and put her hand on his. "If…and it's a colossal if…you can pull this off…if you can really turn this place around, make these people believe in themselves…." Mike was wide-eyed, hanging on every word. "…you're going to be a big deal, a celebrity." She squeezed his hand. "And I'll be right beside you. And when it's over, I'm going to write a book on how we did it. I'll get a two million dollar advance and a Netflix mini-series deal." She took a final sip and said, "After that, I'm going to choose amongst a number of lucrative offers and assume my rightful place as a primetime anchor on BlueNation."

Mike smiled and said, "When would you start?"

Makayla leaned forward. "I started a week ago at the candidate's forum. And also last night, when I wrote up these notes." She pulled a quarter-folded piece of paper out of her jacket pocket and handed it to Mike. "You need a simple, powerful message. Doctor King didn't say, 'I have a plan,' he said 'I have a dream.' Look it over. If you like it, use it."

CHAPTER FOURTEEN

April 6
TRANSCRIPT – WPTT-TV NEWS AT TEN 10:46 p.m.
BILL SLOCUM: Breaking news out at Pulver Forge where they're ready to declare a winner in that town's race for Mayor.

PEG DIVINE: And our own Makayla Nichols is there live. Makayla, sounds like there's a lot of happy people. What's going on?

(SOUND): CHEERS, HOOTS, HOLLERS, CHANTS OF "WE LIKE MIKE!"

MAKAYLA: I'm here at the headquarters of candidate Mike Davenport, the new Mayor here in Pulver Forge, beating incumbent Fred Bagley 1,653 votes to 971. I think…wait a minute…yes, Mayor Mike is about to speak.

(SOUND: CHEERING, CHANTS OF 'WE LIKE MIKE')

MIKE DAVENPORT: Thank you, thank you. Wow. First of all, I want to thank Betty Chapel and Reverend Luke Bramlett, they talked me into this. Next, I want to thank the people of Pulver Forge, and that means everyone, whether you voted for me or not.

(SOUND) CHEERS, MORE CHANTS OF "WE LIKE MIKE!"

MIKE DAVEPORT: We're through waiting for someone to save us. We're the people we've been waiting for. From this day forward, everyone in this town who wants a job will have one. Everyone who needs a meal will get one. Everyone who is ashamed of living here will feel nothing but pride. How are we going to do it? We're going to take the city we've been dreaming of, pull that dream out of the heavens and live that dream right here, right now. We're going to imagine the town we want to build and build it. So, here's to our new hometown: PROSPERITY, PENNSYLVANIA!

(SOUND) CHEERS, SHOUTS

MAKAYLA: Mike! Mike! Over here! Mike, you've laid out a very ambitious renewal plan for Pulver Forge…

MIKE DAVENPORT: Prosperity.

MAKAYLA: (laugh) Prosperity, right. Do you really think you can pull this off?

MIKE DAVENPORT: No, I don't.

MAKAYLA: You don't?

MIKE DAVENPORT: *I* can't pull this off. *WE*, the people of this town, can pull this off, absolutely. Isn't that right folks?

(SOUND) CROWD SHOUTS "YEAH!!"

MIKE DAVENPORT: Damn right! And one year from today? I want YOU, Makayla Nichols, to promise me that you'll come back here to do another live shot at our 'We Did It' celebration, okay?"

MAKAYLA: You got a deal, Mayor Mike. (turns to camera) Mike Davenport, the new Mayor of…

MIKE DAVENPORT: (off-camera) PROSPERITY!

MAKAYLA: …of Prosperity, Pennsylvania. Bill, Peg? Back to you in the studio.

BILL SLOCUM: (laughing) Quite a story there, Peg.

PEG DIVINE: Sure is, Bill. Here's hoping they can turn all that wishful thinking into some real achievements…

CHAPTER FIFTEEN

April 7
MIKE DAVENPORT
2:30 a.m. Love, happiness and beer. The very first meeting of Mike's Super Friends, in the Rev's Community Center behind the church. The Rev was helping Steven Dorsey tap the small keg the brewmaster had wheeled in. Makayla was…well, this is the first time I'd seen her in something other than her news duds. She was wearing straight-leg jeans, a man's Brooks Brothers blue pin stripe shirt, and a cute Penguins cap. I was gawking. She caught me and smiled, and I blushed. When was the last time I blushed? High school? I'd been up for twenty-two hours, and I was ready to rollerblade up Pike's Peak.

With a loud "SQUORSH!" Steve got the beer flowing as the Rev held out the red plastic cups to capture every drop. Steve saw me. "Ladies and gentlemen! We have gathered here to honor Pennsylvania's newest political shooting star…"

"And media studmuffin," said Kate.

"And so I offer you Zymurgy's latest small-batch brew, our 'Mayor Mike Davenport DropForge Coffee Porter, with even MORE coffee than our Smokestack Ale. Plus, a cocoa and blueberry infusion. It's a liquid speedball, a buzz within a buzz."

"A TOAST!" said Betty, "to Hizzoner, our new Mayor!" We raised our cups and quaffed his artisanal brew. Sublime.

"Well," I said, "The dog caught the bus. Now what does he do with it?"

"Demand a recount?" said the Rev.

"Too late for that," said Makayla.

"Announce your run for Governor!" said Steve.

"Or President!" said Kate.

Another gulp of beer, then silence. Finally, Betty said, "Can I share a thought?"

"Please," I said.

"The people of Pulver…that is, Prosperity…we're cynical. We know whoever becomes Mayor is going to disappoint us, and that nothing will change."

"That's because our mayor has almost no power," said the Rev. "We've got this crazy borough council. The six council members choose our borough manager who takes care of day-to-day municipal affairs. All you do, Mister Mayor, is break ties and oversee the police."

"Right," said Betty. "So, we expect you to vanish except for council meetings, funerals and ribbon cuttings."

"Soooo…" I said, "That means we need to flip the script. We need to come out with something BIG that wakes people up, tells 'em big changes are coming."

"Exactly," said Betty. "We've got a week before you take office. We should hold a community Charrette to get everyone involved."

"What's a Charrette?" I said.

"A Charrette," said the Rev, "is a creative meeting that ends in a workable plan that all the stakeholders sign. Takes place over two days. If we do this here, we'll spend day one asking what the people of the town want, and how to turn those wishes into workable plans. Day two, we'll divvy up the work. Who does what, by when."

"Do it all!" said Kate.

"In a year!" said the Rev.

I said, "Sounds good! With enough coffee…and beer like this…we can do anything!" More whoops and cheers, and then everybody stopped talking at once. We looked at each other, still smiling as the size of the task loomed before us. Could we really run enough go-go juice through the cadaver of Pulver Forge to bring it back to life?

"So," said the Rev, "I'm going to tell you a secret." Everyone leaned in. "A couple of years ago a very smart political scientist made it her business to analyze how ordinary people overthrew oppressive governments. What percent of the people do you think you need to do that?"

"Fifty-one percent," ventured Kate.

"Thirty," I said. All the other guesses were between those two numbers.

"The answer," he said, "is 3.5 percent."

"Really?" I was shocked.

"That's it. If we can get 3.5 percent of the people working for us right at the start, we win. The Civil Rights movement began with 3.5 percent of folks like Rosa Parks who were ready to give it up for the cause. We've got about nine thousand people, that means we need…"

Betty pulled out her smartphone, pulled up the calculator and punched in some numbers. "Three hundred and fifteen people," she said.

"Three hundred and fifteen on Day One," said the Rev. "These are the shock troops, let's call them our 'Hard Corps.' They're the tip of the spear in our campaign to give everyone jobs, food and health care. Our job is to give them the support they need to win."

"Where do we find these 315 people?" said Betty.

"We ask everyone we know, and then get those people to ask everyone they know. These are the people who come to the Charrette."

"You think we can get that many right off the bat?" I asked.

"How many voted for you?" said Kate.

"Sixteen hundred and fifty-three," said Betty.

"We need about a quarter of that," said the Rev. "The people in this town are desperate, fed up and ready for change. They'll join us. And when they do, we'll take very good care of them. Pretty soon, we'll be at twenty-five percent: two thousand, two hundred and fifty. That's our Critical Mass. That's when we know we've won."

Kate said, "Great! On to the Charrette." We lifted our beer cups. As I chugged the last of that dark, roasty craft brew I felt the kind of weightless exhilaration I'd felt once before: the day before I shipped out for Afghanistan. I was in, skydiving into a mystery land where I was sure to find myself neck deep in the best and worst life could offer. Bring it on, brother!

CHAPTER SIXTEEN

April 7
MIKE DAVENPORT
5 a.m. I was humming "Alive" by Pearl Jam as I jogged up the stairs to my fourth-floor corner studio loft. I lived in what used to be the "Bean Building" of the H.J. Heinz Company, when that mighty enterprise ruled the world from the north shore of the Allegheny River. The loft was basically a hallway of rooms: living room, kitchen, and bedroom joined by a skinny passage on the right side. I thought I'd stagger in, drag the futon mattress off my IKEA convertible sofa and sleep for a couple of hours until my 9 a.m. shift at HuggaMug. What I didn't expect was my fiancé, Tess Harper.

Sergeant First Class Theresa "Tess" Harper had served in Afghanistan as part of the Pennsylvania Army National Guard. Her military police squad was shadowing a supply convoy when some Taliban fighters ambushed the convoy with AK-47s, RPK machine guns and rocket propelled grenades. Tess muscled her fire team through the kill zone into a flanking position. She and her squad leader used hand grenades and M203 grenade launcher rounds to kill half the insurgents and disperse the rest. After accepting her Silver Star, she returned with a fierce desire to become wealthy enough to turn her back on the horrors of the fallen world that haunted her. She apprenticed with a genius marketing guru, then opened her own thriving p.r./advertising shop, "Freebooter Media." I met her at a networking party and was dazzled from the first moment. Here was a woman who knew who she was, where she was going and how she was going to get there. I never realized how wishy-washy most people were until I met the original human bulldozer. Just being around her woke me up to my own goals.

Tess was plopped in my gray IKEA wing chair. She'd angled it so she'd be the very first thing I'd see. I literally leapt back half a foot, my heart jumping in my chest. She was wearing a khaki racerback vest that showed off her sports bra underneath, skin tight shorts and gloves. She just stared at me. "Ummm, hi Tess. I didn't…ummm…how did you…"

"Your lock is a joke. It took me less than a minute."

"Uh huh. So, ummm, are you on your way to Crossfit…"

"I saw you on the news." She hadn't moved a muscle since I came in. "Quite a celebration." Her stare froze me in place. "I'm a little worried, Mike."

"Worried?"

She leaned forward. "I'm worried you're losing your focus. I waited a long time to choose a partner. I was looking for someone serious. Who understood what it meant to make promises and keep them. A no-bullshit, stone cold achiever. We're about a year away from living our dream, right? Kauai?"

"That's, ummm, right."

"So now you're suddenly, what, Mayor? Of this rinky-dink joke of a shithole town? Are you going to tell me that your duties there won't distract you from closing the deal to franchise HuggaMug?"

For the very first time since we met, the smallest squib of resentment sparked in my brain. Is this what the marriage was going to be like, with her barking orders as Generalissimo? My next thought calmed me down. She was right. I'd made a promise. We were two people with a single goal, and it was a worthy goal. "Look, Tess, when I agreed to run, I made a deal. I'm not moving to Pulver Forge. I'll be handing off the day-to-day stuff to my colleagues as soon as I can. And trust me, I'm birddogging the deal with Steve with all the ferocity you'd expect."

"Okay, then," she said. "Just know that I'm an interested party."

"I will."

"So, what's your plan?"

"For what?"

"For right this very second." She slowly rose and glided toward me. I could smell her signature scent: "Smoke Show," with a hint of roses wafting up from a base of sweet smoke and leather. She put her arms around my neck and gave me a long, deep, dreamy kiss. I suddenly lost all interest in sleep. I could feel her high-voltage vitality spark up my nervous system as I took her in my arms. She scissored her legs around my midsection, and I jounced us back to the bedroom. We didn't bother to drag out the bed, just plopped the sofa cushions onto the floor.

I remember thinking, "Okay, there is something better than coffee." It was the highest praise I could conjure.

CHAPTER SEVENTEEN

April 7

Moses Creavey

The saddest day of Moss Creavey's life was the day he got a certified check for three million dollars, delivered by bonded courier. A gaming resorts corporation made him a ridiculous offer on his first casino/hotel, the "Pair O' Dice" in Winnemucca, Nevada. Creavey had smartly picked up eight acres of adjoining property, so he could build the casino as part of a planned resort.

Why sad? His most cherished fantasy was that becoming a millionaire would transform him from a cynical, feisty outsider into a financial Master of the Universe: confident, serene and utterly self-assured. He'd become a 'made guy' who could enjoy his wealth and laugh at the world. When he looked at that check, he realized that nothing had changed except for one thing: he could no longer sustain the fantasy that money would turn this frog into a prince. Getting rich was nothing: he would always be a sweaty, insecure wannabe pounding on the door of a club that would never have him. Oh well. His despair lasted about ten minutes. There was work to do! It was no longer the money; it was the thrill of the chase: the insatiable need for MORE.

In the subsequent thirty years, he'd managed to turn those three million dollars into seven hundred million through perseverance, audacity, savvy timing, bare-knuckle negotiating skills and luck. It was almost too easy. He'd discovered the perfect market: struggling rust-belt towns in the post-industrial northeast and Midwest. The demographic was stellar: underemployed 50+ males ready to trade hope for distraction.

Free drinks, cheap lunch and dinner buffets and "Premiere Player Rewards" programs. He'd cut the ribbon, and they'd pour in, those lovely people. They had to know the odds were against them. They knew it was a pick pocket palace, and *still* they became regulars. They knew the odds: they just liked having a place where they could bury their dreams in the presence of beeping, clattering, strobing money-siphoning robotic bandits. They could be "amongst people" without having to get close to anyone in particular. They were happy to give Moses Creavey their money, and he was happy to take it, even if adding it to his humungous mountain of gold no longer made much of a difference to him. *Why wasn't everyone in this business?* he thought. It was a friction-free money transfer: capitalism, perfected.

So here he was, on the 45th floor of the Creavey-owned "Paradise Executive Towers," Paradise, Nevada, staring through the floor to ceiling smoked glass that walled his corner office. He gazed at the honey-amber light bathing the cacophonous jumble of faux global destinations (Paris, Venice, New York) that had become Las Vegas. Ahh, sunset. Not so long ago, sunset was the time he'd be teasing out his perfect evening: a ravishing pair of lusty escorts, martinis and steaks at the Palm, a front row table at whatever sold-out-for-months superstar showcase he wanted, then a pre-dawn afterglow party of rapturous carnal frivolity with champagne and fresh strawberries dipped in a fondue pot of white chocolate.

That was then. Now the man who was rich enough to do whatever he wanted couldn't do anything. Champagne? Alcohol triggered his atrial fibrillation. Same for caffeine: so long Irish Coffee! (sob) The list of foods that made his prostate swell could (and did) fill the entire menu of the Palm. Last time he'd had the Calamari Fritto Misto he'd gotten up nine times in the middle of the night to relieve himself. He'd even flushed the last of his Viagra down the toilet: it made his ticker race, and who needed to risk getting "Me Too'd" by some enterprising working girl?

All Creavey had left was his singular superpower: to want something and get it. And he wanted a Creavey casino in Pulver Forge, Pennsylvania. He'd had luck building gambling joints in three other Pennsylvania steel towns: Pulver Forge was perfect. The place had a downtrodden legion of resident suckers, and tons more in nearby Pittsburgh. He dry-rubbed his hands when he thought of it. Too bad Bumbling Bagley had figured out a way to screw up a sure thing. Hizzoner had let himself get beaten by a non-formidable non-politician of no known political party. What the hell? Creavey wanted that casino. It was rightfully his, a done deal, another money harvest for the Creavey Group. And he *always* got what he wanted.

He pulled a mini bag of "Skinny Pop" Kettle Korn out of his bottom desk drawer. So, it had come to this. No more butter-poached lobster rolls in spicy sauce, just his daily lo-fat vegan kale-and-quinoa "superfood" salad with braised tofu. This Kettle Korn, this was his "treat." He felt like weeping. Pull yourself together, man! You're Moses Creavey! "Look on my works, ye mighty, and despair!"

He squeezed open the bag and dumped the meager contents on his desk. He knew that this "treat" would just remind him of all the things he'd never enjoy again. He shoved handfuls of the stale confection into his mouth as he looked at the daily news summary his staff had put together. *Mike freakin' Davenport. A barista. A nobody nothing from nowhere.* Now it was Moses Creavey versus this Mike Davenport: an epic mismatch with all the suspense of a state-ordered electrocution. Creavey pulled out his smartphone. Time to go to work. He had something to win and someone to destroy. Life wasn't perfect, but, in this moment, it was sure as hell good enough.

CHAPTER EIGHTEEN

April 16-17
MIKE DAVENPORT
We held the Charrette in the Great Hall of the Pulver Community Library on April 16th and 17th. The doors opened at 7:45, HuggaMug Coffee and Flour Power bakery treats from 8 to 9. At 9 sharp, Betty Chapel stood in front of two easels holding 2 by 3-foot sticky-top white paper pads. Over the next two days she'd fill a hundred and thirty-one of these over-sized Post-It notes, covering the walls of the room.

One hundred and forty-nine citizens showed up to re-imagine their hometown. Forty-four attendees were members or "friends" of the Quixote Institute. Here's Betty's work product:

CHARRETTE REPORT

TO: Mayor Mike Davenport and the people of Prosperity, Pennsylvania
FROM: Betty Chapel, Charrette Facilitator

On April 16-17, the people of Prosperity, Pennsylvania met for a two-day Charrette to re-imagine their town.

• Day One was devoted to deciding WHAT KIND OF TOWN we want and creating our ONE YEAR GOALS FOR THE TOWN.

• Day Two was devoted to DECIDING WHO WILL HELP US MEET THESE GOALS.

CHARRETTE FACILITATOR: Betty Chapel

First, we came up with Mission, Objective and Theme statements to guide our progress and create indicators of success. All three of these statements were crowd sourced. Kate Walther projected possibilities on a screen. The group crafted them in real time, and then voted to approve the final version. Each represents a consensus of the community.

A MISSION STATEMENT is a motivational document crafted to inspire the people of the town by describing a singular vision that everyone can embrace. The new Mission Statement for Prosperity, Pennsylvania is:

Prosperity, Pennsylvania is our town: a hard-working community of people committed to taking care of each other. We have the vision, the commitment and the intention to make sure that everyone has enough: enough food, work, medical care, and friends. We once made the steel that built America. Now we're working for ourselves, to build the town we want to live in.

AN OBJECTIVE STATEMENT is a practical list of aspirational goals for the town. These must be measurable so we can know if we are successful. The Objective Statement for Prosperity, Pennsylvania is:

- *One year from today, everyone in Prosperity who wants a job will have one.*
- *Our homestead gardens will grow enough food to feed everyone at our community table.*
- *Everyone who wants health care will have it, including those suffering from drug addiction.*
- *We will measure our prosperity not in money but in happiness, community and the abundance of good food and good friends.*

A THEME STATEMENT is a "red thread" that offers the DNA of the project. This is the essence of the project: the glue that holds it together.

The following theme statements were proposed and considered:

- Happy, Prosperous and Healthy: Join Us!
- We are the Pennsylvania Miracle
- We Work So Our Town Works
- We Made America Great. Now We're Making Our Town Prosperous
- Prosperity, Pennsylvania: We Help Ourselves

The Theme Statement that was chosen by the group for Prosperity, Pennsylvania is:

Prosperity, Pennsylvania WORKS.

A breakdown of the theme:

Prosperity, Pennsylvania — that's us.

WORKS — We work hard. We work together. We work on what's most important. When everything works together, everything works for everyone.

The second half of Day 1 was about exploring our theme statement. Our people were eager to get to work. What did they want to build? We had breakout sessions, where small groups were encouraged to develop goals: the simplest goals that would have the biggest impact. They were asked to 'dream big,' knowing that the jobs they'd be working would come from these goals.

The final list of must-have "buildable dreams" is as follows:

- A JOB for everyone who wants one.
- A MEAL for everyone who needs one.
- A PLACE TO LIVE for everyone who needs one.
- MEDICAL CARE for everyone who needs it.
- CLEAN SAFE STREETS IN A BEAUTIFUL CITY

• OPPORTUNITIES TO COME TOGETHER to celebrate our new "Prosperity." (These opportunities include town parties, civic and political clubs, service organizations and block parties.)

(MAKAYLA NICHOLS COMMENT): Our volunteer town historian Calvin McCoy had one additional "buildable dream": a town museum/history center, where townspeople could learn about our heritage and visitors could celebrate the re-birth of the town. "For so many years," he said, "we've tried to forget our history. Now we can turn that tragedy into a prologue for our re-birth and triumph."

At the end of Day 1, the group walked four blocks north, up Ironside Way to Memorial Park to enjoy a potluck barbecue, with the ribs, brisket, hot links and chicken provided by Police Chief "Piledriver" Pooley. Chef Betty provided cole slaw, barbecue beans and potato salad.

DAY TWO
April 17

The group was given a list of "Ministerial Positions," part of the parallel administration for our "people-powered" all-volunteer advisory group separate from City Hall.

These new Ministers were:

• MINISTER OF FELLOWSHIP: Reverend Luke Bramlett (Over-all "Minister of Ministers" ensuring teamwork, collaboration and civic harmony.)

• MINISTER OF ABUNDANCE: Yandy Lopez (Community Gardens, etc.)

• MINISTER OF HOSPITALITY: Chef Betty Chapel (Running the Community Kitchen, Supervising and Serving Meals)

• MINISTER OF BEAUTIFICATION: Mike Davenport (Renovating Derelict Buildings, Fixing Up Property, Public Murals and Art for the town, Picking Up Trash)

- MINISTER OF WELL-BEING: Kate Walther (Medical Clinic, Community Medical Service)
- MINISTER OF BALLYHOO: Makayla Nichols (Creating Communications Infrastructure for the Town, Promoting the Town/Broadcast Media/Social Media)
- MINISTER OF FRIVOLITY: TBD (Mike, Kate, Betty and Reverend Luke agreed to do this until we can find someone permanent) (Town Parties, Civic Celebrations — This Has Got to Be FUN)
- MINISTER OF PUBLIC SAFETY: Police Chief Frederick "Piledriver" Pooley
- MINISTER OF FINANCE: TBD

COMMUNITY COUNCIL MEMBERS
The Community Council is a new advisory body empowered to work in partnership with the Prosperity Town Council. The Community Councils had certain powers in their districts and could advise the Town Council on larger matters.

COMMUNITY COUNCIL CHAIRS:
PRATTLEBORO: Hanna Jackson
VINEGAR BEND: Wilda Malone (Principal Pulver High, Quixote Institute)
LOWER SOUTH PULVER: Madison Hubbard
CABBAGETOWN: Chelsea Alverez (Quixote Institute)
HOMEWOOD: Dr. Nehrika Balakrishnan
FOX POINT (aka "The Heights"): Sheba Shane (Quixote Institute)
THE HOLLOWS/WHISKEYTOWN: Sylvie Grabowski

At 3 p.m. on Saturday, Charrette Facilitator Chapel thanked the participants for doing this great work. The group had created a clear path to a prosperous future with a workable plan and an engaged tribe of colleagues to carry out that plan.

One final bit of business: All the participants gathered around the giant sticky-note with the Prosperity, PA Theme Statement. Librarian Betsey DeMarco took a group photo to commemorate this event. This photo will be framed and hung in City Hall so everyone can see it. The group agreed to meet one year from today to revisit the Charrette goals and celebrate the completion of the Objective items.

Chef Betty laid out a lavish buffet of leftovers from the picnic the previous afternoon for those who wanted to linger. Everyone agreed her barbecue beans tasted even better the second day.

CHAPTER NINETEEN

April 19

MIKE DAVENPORT

7:18 a.m., Pittsburgh HuggaMug. I was pouring coffee, greeting my regulars, wiping down tables and re-filling sugar dispensers when Darla came up to me.

"Phone call for you."

"Take a message."

"She says she's your mother."

"What?" I didn't move.

"You want me to tell her you'll call back?"

"No. No, that's all right. I'll take it." I walked into my office and picked up the phone. "Mom?"

"Hi, Michael."

"Wow. Been a long time." Like, uhhh, twenty-five years…

"I know. How are you?"

"I'm fine. How'd you track me down?"

"I just used the Google. A very nice article in the Pittsburgh Business Times mentioned you. You have your own coffee shop!"

"Yeah, I do. Listen, umm, I'm kinda busy. Can I ask why you're calling?"

Short pause. "Well, I've got some good news, Michael. I'm engaged to be married!"

"Oh, that is good news." She'd moved to Florida more than a decade ago to find a husband, I guess she'd finally succeeded. "Who's the lucky fella?"

"His name is Frank Bendix. He's retired. He had a business running take-out pizza places in Michigan. We're here in The Villages, just playing golf every day and having fun. The good life at last."

"Uh huh." I decided to wait her out, find out the real reason she was calling.

"So, Michael...." Pause. "Frank served in the Marines in Vietnam. I told him about your service in Afghanistan and he perked right up." Pause. "He wants to know you." Pause. "He might call you someday."

"Uh huh."

"Like, you know, before we get married."

The light went on. When I was quarterbacking the Pulver High School Blue Devils to the state championship, I noticed a bunch of my football stuff—trophies, awards, game balls, stuff like that—started disappearing from my room. I was living with Grandpa Chet because ma had abandoned the family after she'd divorced my dad. I knew she was huffing crack cocaine when that was devouring the town. I set a trap for her and caught her trying to lift my high school letter jacket. I made her come clean. Turns out she'd been selling my stuff to a local dentist who was convinced I was going to be a big noise in pro football and thought the stuff might go up in value someday. We had a final screaming fight and I told her I never wanted to see her again. I heard from friends she'd finally cleaned up before heading south for her big husband hunt. Now this.

"So, if Frank Bendix calls me I'm supposed to say...what?"

"Oh, you know, Michael."

"No, tell me." I was going to make her work for it.

"Talk about the Army. Talk about your coffee business. Just don't talk about, you know...."

"What?"

A very long pause. I could hear her breathing. "I've worked hard to get past that whole terrible period of my life, Michael. I really want this chance. Frank isn't a saint, but, well, we have fun together."

"Uh huh."

"Michael," she said, her voice softening. "I understand I have no right to ask this of you. I treated you so badly. I failed as a mother. I think about what happened every day and I'm so, so sorry. I've never called you because what I did was so wrong, and I couldn't imagine you forgiving me. I don't expect you to forgive me now. I just…well…"

"Don't worry about a thing, ma. If Frank Bendix calls me, we'll have a perfectly nice chat about serving our country, my coffee business, and my pleasantly boring childhood with my dutiful mom. You're in the clear."

Another pause, and then I could hear her sniffling. "Thank you, Michael. Thank you." Twenty more seconds of sniffling, and a final "Thank you" and she hung up. I was half expecting an "I love you," but I waved that off. I'd made it this far on my own. I smiled when I realized I didn't need a single thing from her.

CHAPTER TWENTY

April 24, Saturday Night: The Town Party
MIKE DAVENPORT

So here we were in the "Fleetwood," aka The Lucretia Fleetwood Pulver Opera House, just down the street from the Pulver Library. Enoch Pulver built this arts barn for his opera-loving wife in 1910. It turned out she was the only person in Pulver Forge who liked opera, so it became—over the years—a vaudeville house, a theater for barnstorming thespians, a movie theater, a Baptist Church, an automobile showroom (Studebaker) and a lumber storage facility. Like most buildings in Prosperity, it was an impoverished dowager empress who'd been mugged, but still carried herself with pride and defiance. Still standing, and perfect for our purpose.

A gigantic (cheap, gaudy, homemade) banner hung from the ceiling:

A TOWN IS BORN:
PROSPERITY, PENNSLYVANIA!
EVERYONE WELCOME!

The first townsfolk were drifting in, clustering around our hospitality tables. HuggaMug had a Free Coffee station set up next to Zymurgy Brewing Company's "Pop-Up Brewpub." Reverend Luke and Chef Betty convinced some Pittsburgh supermarkets to donate a plenitude of day-old sandwiches, salads, snacks, wraps and pizzas. Flour Power had gifted us with sweet goodies at cost, and the homies were here, handing out paper plates with blueberry muffins, slices of cake, chocolate chip cookies and wedges of pecan pie.

The party was scheduled from seven to eleven p.m., with some brief remarks by yours truly at 9. We hoped for two hundred people, but we were pushing three hundred-plus by 7:45 when the band— "Dollar Bill Fortune and the Prosperity Blues Band"—kicked it off from the rickety stage. "Dollar Bill" was John Glickman, a 71-year-old bassoonist for the Pittsburgh Symphony Orchestra and a regular at HuggaMug. John and a gang of like-minded symphony chums shook off the pretensions of the classical canon by jamming on garage band oldies in his basement and performing under the name "False Morality and the Intangibles" (best name ever) at birthday parties, street fairs and on Tuesday nights at the coffeehouse. The band's repertoire featured 60s garage band hits ("Double Shot of My Baby's Love"), upbeat booty-shakin' soul hits ("Baby Workout," "Hold On, I'm Comin'") and even some country-western drollness ("You're the Reason Our Kids Are Ugly," "How Can I Miss You When You Won't Go Away?") They worked for "all the beer you can drink and a hearty handshake."

"Mike?" Betty Chapel had snuck up behind me. She was holding a red cup of Steve's finest, as was her guest, a beefy geezer with a buzz cut who looked like a retired pro wrestler. "Meet Nick Barlow."

"Ahhh, Mister Barlow, what a pleasure. I've heard a lot about you." We shook. Nick Barlow was bullet-headed mesomorph dressed in jeans, a Steelers hoodie and a CarQuest Auto Parts gimme cap. The silvery microscopic stubble on his face made his weathered skin look even darker. Nick was the owner of "Hell on Wheels," a beloved we'll-fix-anything automotive repair shop. I'd been told he was also a government-hating libertarian crank. He was noticeably absent from the Charrette. He looked ready to scrap. I liked him already.

"Leon Trotsky, I presume?" said Nick. "Here to save us from the horrors of the free enterprise system?" said Nick. "'A casino, oh the humanity.'"

"Hey, these fine folks had every chance to vote for that casino," I said. "But they didn't. Maybe they want to try something different."

"Mike was in Afghanistan," said Betty, eager to change the subject.

Nick's head jerked back in surprise. "Really?" He looked me up and down. "Well, I'll be." He stuck out his hand. "'Nam. 3rd Battalion, 187th Regiment, 101st Airborne Division."

I gulped. "The Rakkasans?" He nodded, surprised again. "Hamburger Hill?" Another nod, and a smile.

"Yeah." The snarkiness fell away.

"You made it," I said.

"Yeah, although to this day I don't know how." He cocked his head at me. "I heard a lot about your plan. No offense, but I think you're dreaming. That people-powered collectivist lefty-shit will never play here. Never."

"Well then you're just the man I want to see, Nick."

Reverend Luke arrived with cups of beer for everyone. "Gentlemen, I offer you liquid proof that God loves you and wants you to be happy."

God bless him. Nick and I both grabbed a cup and took sips. It was "Laughing Gravy," Steve's Belgian style farmhouse ale: lots of fruit, with a peppery/dry finish. Nice punchy mood-altering intoxicants. I turned back to Nick. "See, my whole program is about getting government out of the way."

"Which won't be hard," said Betty, "since Nick and I both know we don't have a functional government in Pulver Forge…"

"Prosperity," said Makayla.

"Prosperity, anyway."

I leaned in toward Nick. "True or false, Nick. Everything the state has tried here has failed. The more money they spend, the worse things get: more drugs, more squalor, more despair."

"You are singing from my hymn book, brother," said Nick, nodding.

"You want big government? That's Mayor Fred, shoveling your tax dollars at billionaires who take what they want and toss us table scraps. I say to hell with that. Let's get off our butts, try something, save ourselves. And I'd love it if you'd help us."

"I don't think so," he snorted. "I'm not a big joiner. I mean, what can I do?"

"Well, I'm planning to go visit the Governor." Makayla's head snapped toward me. This was news to her. "He's one of your people, right? A 'get-government-off-the-back-of-the-little-guy' guy?"

"Yeah," said Nick. "I like that about him."

"So, when I see him," I said, "I'd like you to come with us. We're going to ask him to put his money where his mouth is. Stop helping. Look the other way when we try some stuff, like turning our parks into gardens, ignoring zoning ordinances and bending some currency laws with our barter system. Interested?"

We turned our heads as the band kicked off a sloppy fun version of "Wild Thing" by the Troggs. Then Nick turned back to me. I could see he was intrigued. "Talk is cheap. How can I tell if you're serious?"

"Listen to what I say tonight, and then watch what I do."

"That's a deal," he said.

"Great," I said, raising my red cup. He raised his. Maybe I had a shot with this guy. And if I could get *him* into the tent…

CHAPTER TWENTY-ONE

April 24
MIKE DAVENPORT
9 p.m. Dollar Bill and the band had done their job, ending their set with their booty-shakin' cover of the Isley Brothers "Shout!" I was smart enough to grab some of that love. I rushed on stage, yelled "Give it up for the hardest working semi-professional garage band in show biz, Dollar Bill Fortune and the Prosperity Blues Band!!" The band members took their bows. I launched into my talk before the buzz died down.

We'd attracted over four hundred people: a real cross-section of the Pulver Forge citizenry. Half white, half-not. Half old, half not. Lots of weathered faces and hunched bodies of hard-working people who'd discovered the American Dream was a mirage.

Here goes…

"Thanks for joining the party." (A blast of feedback. I backed off the mike.) "I'm Mike Davenport, and I'm honored that you have chosen me to be the new Mayor of your new town. What was Pulver Forge is now PROSPERITY, PENNSYLVANIA."

The crowd, still buzzed up from the music (and the beer), gave me a hearty round of applause. So much for the easy part.

"When I was growing up here, we told ourselves a story. We were gritty underdogs with no quittin' sense who took iron and carbon, grabbed lightning from the sky and forged it into steel. That steel built the Arsenal of Democracy that won the Second World War, and then built the buildings and cars that made this country the envy of the world. It was a righteous brag because it was true."

The crowd had quieted down. I had them.

"But the people who ran the Pulver mill, they were telling themselves a different story. Their story was about quarterly profits and shareholder value and all that pension money that you earned that they could siphon into their own pockets. You thought you were partners with those people, but you weren't. You were disposable units of labor, and if they could find cheaper units in China or India or South Korea, well, the shareholders were happy, and the Wall Street Journal was delighted.

"And so, the mill closed down, and somehow—here's the crazy part—we told ourselves that it was our fault. That's wrong, and we're going to show the world how wrong it is. We're going to make this place the envy of the world a *second* time. Only this time, we're the workers AND the shareholders, and no one can take away what we're going to build for ourselves."

A guy in the back yelled "Yeah!" and everyone laughed, then clapped. This was fun!

"We're going to grow our food. Fix our homes, buildings, schools and streets. Make this a place we're proud of. And this will be our new story, the story of a town that rescued itself, and the hero of this story? YOU. YOU are the ones who will make the difference. In one year, you will be a vital part of a clean, hunger-free, drug-free, depression-free town. And you will know yourself as heroes who can do whatever you imagine."

CHAPTER TWENTY-TWO

April 24
MIKE DAVENPORT
"Not bad, Trotsky." Nick Barlow had a fresh cup of Zymurgy's finest in one hand and a floppy wedge of cheese pizza in the other.

"Thanks, Nick."

"'Course it's one thing to blow smoke up everybody's ass about what 'heroes' they are, and something else again to get 'em out there planting rutabagas."

I needed to shake this conversation up. "Nick, you could have died trying to take Hamburger Hill. Why'd you do it?"

He grimaced. Still a painful subject. "Orders."

"Yeah, sure. And something else, right?"

He stared at me. He knew where I was going. "My buddies. This was a suicide mission. They needed me, and I needed them. I lost..." He paused, gathering himself. Then, in a hoarse whisper, "I lost three of my best friends on that godforsaken piece of shit hill."

"I know all about it. You charged up that hill, what, nine times?

"Eleven."

"Eleven. My god. Finally took it."

"You are goddam right we took it."

Here's where I risked getting punched. "And two weeks later the Army walked away from it, just let 'em take it back. How'd you feel about that?"

Those laser eyes burned pinholes in my face. "How'd I *feel* about it? I'll tell you how I *felt* about it, Sparky. I felt like kicking down the door of whatever fat-cat Pentagon war room had tossed our guys into that meat grinder and lobbing in a big fat M61 fragmentation grenade, let those smug dickheads know what it's like to die for no good reason."

"So, the battle, you're sorry you fought it?"

"I'm sorry we HAD to fight it. I'm damn proud of what we did. We didn't quit. We stuck together. We kept going. And we finally got it done."

"What if I told you that what's going on right here can be some version of that same thing?"

He looked at me like I was crazy. "What the hell?"

Now I bore in on him. "A part of me hates, HATES what I went through in Afghanistan, Nick. But a part of me…." I took a long swig of that delicious beer, swishing it around in my mouth. "A part of me misses it. And what I miss is having buddies I could trust. We were all about looking out for each other, fighting for each other…" I paused, trying to choke out the next part.

"Dying for each other," he said softly. He knew.

"What if we could get that back? Here? In Pulver Forge?" We were eyeball to eyeball. "The world thinks what *you* think, that it can't be done. Well, the hell with the world. What if we could get the people of this town to believe in each other, fight for each other, to come together like we came together with our buddies? What if we decided to take this hill or die trying? Wouldn't that be a hell of a thing?"

He was doing a different kind of listening now. "Yeah, that would be. But, again, what can I do?"

"You fix cars. We got a couple of derelict busses behind the high school. We gotta figure out how we're going to move people around this town. You willing to take a look at those busses, see if you could fix 'em up so we could turn 'em into 'get-abouts'?"

"I don't have the people to do that."

"What if I got you the people? High school students you could train up, apprentices? You need hands, they've got hands. You've got skills, they need skills."

He was looking at me, the tiniest smile on his face. "Uh huh. Okay. Yeah, let me think about it."

"C'mon, join us," I said. "Just to keep me honest."

"Roger that. So, when are you gonna see him? You know, the Governor."

I smiled. "I got a call in already."

CHAPTER TWENTY-THREE

June 7
TRANSCRIPT OF CODY FORTUNE'S COMMENTARY,
"FIRSTNEWS"

CODY FORTUNE: Department of 'Really True or Too Good to Be True': Have ya heard about this guy Mike Davenport? Mike just got himself elected Mayor of Pulver Forge, Pennsylvania…only now thanks to Mike, the town is called 'Prosperity Pennsylvania.' Why? Because if we all say the word 'prosperity' and click our ruby slippers together three times, we'll be able to turn a hellhole that has been destroyed by fifty years of socialism into a paradise where everyone who wants a job can have one, everyone gets free health care, and everyone gets free food as they hug and pick daisies and dance under tangerine trees and marmalade skies.

That's a great big promise. Maybe I should back off the snark, because maybe…just maybe, Mayor Mike has the right idea. FirstNews has been listening to what he's been saying, and it seems to be more than another bunch of liberal big government b.s.

Mayor Mike is telling the people of Pulver Forge that no one is going to save them, including the federal government or the state of Pennsylvania! That's right! He's telling people the truth: that it's up to *them* to grow their own food, pick up trash, get their kids off drugs and do the hard work of building a real, working community.

So! Good for Mayor Mike! But we've heard this kind of happy talk before, haven't we? This is what lefty 'libidiots' and socialist demon-crats say right before they stick their hand into your pocket to finance their dreamy-schemey collectivist brainstorms. You know the kind: the ones that destroyed hard-working steel towns like Pulver Forge in the first place. It wasn't that long ago that Pulver Forge was a boomtown, making the steel that built that 1950s Motor City station wagon that drove the family to the bank every payday. That was before the labor unions ran wild and priced us out of the world steel market, turning towns like Pulver Forge into dystopian ghost towns.

So FirstNews is taking a wait and see attitude. If Mayor Mike can wave his magic wand and bring real prosperity to Pulver Forge, a certain yours truly will be the first one to sing his praises. If he's just another beansprout Bolshevik carnival barker selling socialist snake oil in libertarian bottles, we'll be the first to tell you that as well.

This is Cody Fortune, kicking ass for a living, and living to kick ass.

CHAPTER TWENTY-FOUR

GOVERNOR GOODWIN TUTTLE

Goodwin Tuttle, the Governor of the Commonwealth of Pennsylvania, thought about his career in two distinct ways. When he was wide-awake at two in the morning staring at the bedroom ceiling, Tuttle was terrified he'd be found out. He knew his career was an inexplicable series of lucky breaks, starting with the Boy Scout Jamboree back in 1983 when the Infinite, Unknowable Creator/Destroyer of All That Is chose him to shake hands with President Ronald Reagan, resulting in an above-the-fold photo in USA Today. His first real job was managing the Wendy's franchise in Punxsutawney, PA (by chance, the most conservative city in the state). He was talked into running for City Council, which led to his becoming the youngest Mayor in the Commonwealth. Each time he won by knocking on more doors than his feckless liberal opponents while papering the town with flyers showcasing the Reagan photo.

And then the luckiest break of all, the one that changed his life: meeting Burt McNally at the 2001 CPAC conference in Washington, D.C. Tuttle was on the "Tribute to Ronald Reagan" panel with Scott Walker and Paul Ryan when, trying to out-do those two, he testified how meeting the Gipper had literally saved him from the godless, dithering liberalism of his parents. Burt McNally, a ferociously bright political consultant, approached him and asked him to have dinner at the Olive Garden. Over chicken and shrimp carbonara, McNally told Tuttle everything that was wrong with him as a candidate: his look (dumpy), his communication style (garrulous), and his general affect (needy). Tuttle caught himself as he started to get offended. First, Burt was right. Second, he was doling out this tough love for a reason.

And the reason came over tiramisu and coffee: McNally thought Tuttle "had something." McNally was watching the audience when Tuttle was describing how Dutch's buoyant 'shining city on a hill' optimism had ignited the libertarian fire within him that caused him to stop reacting to the sordid, corrupt gamesmanship of this fallen world. Instead, he became a kind of Ronald Reagan Junior: upbeat, dynamic, contemptuous of lazy, liberal 'groupthink,' the very definition of an assertive 'maker,' not a dithering 'taker.' McNally said he'd seen that kind of captivating performance three times in his life. One was their mutual hero, Ronald Reagan.

Tuttle's insomniac ruminations then become a jumble of the campaigns that McNally had put together for him. The first was in 2002, the post 9-11 'Stomp Saddam' referendum that got him elected to the Pennsylvania State House. At McNally's instructions, he spent twenty percent of his time burnishing his brand on AM talk radio and eighty percent buckraking with pro-fracking energy lobbyists, conservative super PACS, and pro-business, anti-regulatory groups. He perfected what he called his 'rubber chicken talk' (rubber omelet talk for breakfast groups). Here, he was a righteous culture warrior, a man who did not shy away from controversy. No matter what anyone thought, Goodwin Tuttle was now and would always be PRO-GUN, PRO-LIFE, PRO-FLAG, PRO-CHOCOLATE, PRO-NASCAR, and PRO-STEELERS. He'd wash down his Pennsylvania State Fair corn dog with an Iron City Beer thank you very much, and his funnel cake with hot black coffee from the local diner, none of this effete, lefty-liberal "Starbucks" swill if you please.

All that fund-raising paid off in 2006 when he easily won re-election in a 'blue wave' year. His McNally-run campaign out-spent his Democratic opponent fifteen to one, turning the hapless owner of a chain of nail salons into a Wiccan-friendly, gay-marriage-loving socialist gun-grabber. In 2010—ahh, the Tea Party year, what fun that was! —McNally moved him up to the State Senate, with the clear intention of a run for Governor in 2014. This is when things changed big time. Now the PACs and lobbyists and big-money boys were calling *him* up, taking *him* out for martinis and prime rib, because *he* was the Next Big Thing. Now he was HOSTING the Ronaldus Maximus Panel at CPAC, and his 'Saved from Liberalism' speech had become a mini-doc on YouTube with eleven million views.

2014 was another glorious Republican tidal wave year, and Tuttle had been swept into office in a "McNally Special" campaign that cast the incumbent as a job-destroying prisoner of public service unions. This—and Tuttle's promise to cut red-tape, empower towns and cities and create 'enterprise zones'—swept him into office with 52% of the vote, not bad for a swing state. He'd barely survived another blue wave in 2018, thanks to divine intervention: his Democratic opponent had a seizure touring the Hershey chocolate plant thanks to an undiagnosed food allergy. Tuttle's years of pro-chocolate advocacy paid off, with McNally's minions passing out thousands of Hershey's kisses at every campaign rally.

So that was Goodwin "Cold Sweat" Tuttle at two o'clock in the morning, wide-awake and wondering when his luck would run out.

Then there was the *other* Goodwin Tuttle: the one currently perched at the head of the mahogany conference table in his office in the Pennsylvania State House. He was savoring the two words that Burt McNally had just whispered in his ear. "President Tuttle."

President Tuttle! *Why the hell not?*

He was as ready as anyone to be The Most Powerful Man on Earth, restoring the native 'can-do' attitude of the American people that put a man on the moon. President Tuttle, his Best Self emergent: compassionate without being squishy, bold without being reckless. He would return the spirit of Ronald Reagan to the Oval Office.

Those twin Goodwin Tuttles struggled in the single body that was sipping coffee, chatting with Burt McNally as they waited for the group of Pulver...no make that 'Prosperity' leaders due in ten minutes. "So, what's your blink on these folks?" said Tuttle.

"Working on it," said McNally. He helped himself to the hospitality sideboard, using a plastic spoon to fill a flowery paper bowl with vanilla yogurt, blueberries and granola. "This guy Davenport, the new Mayor, he's a neophyte, probably got elected 'cuz the folks in that godforsaken town just rage-voted the sad sack incumbent, what's-his-name, Bagley, out of office."

"Owns a, what, coffee shop?" said Goodwin. McNally nodded. "Seems pretty small time. So why should I meet with him?"

"Because Mayor Davenport ran on a platform I've never seen before. I mean, this is some crazy shit he won with, and he ought to be on our radar screen," said McNally.

"What kind of crazy shit?"

"Like promising everyone in that godforsaken dump a job, without raising taxes or begging funds from the state. Like planting victory gardens all over the place, then turning all that produce into a free lunch for whoever wants it. Like fixing up the town using volunteer labor. The crazy thing is..."

"What?" said Goodwin.

"I can't figure out if he's one of us or one of them...if he's some kind of loony-left moonbat, or a fire-breathing libertarian entrepreneur. Or neither? Or both? We need to get a fix on him."

"Think so?" said Goodwin.

"Yeah, I do." McNally gulped down the last mouthful of yogurt and picked up his coffee cup. "Because he's in your backyard and there's a one percent chance that he might be our ticket to the White House."

Goodwin was just about slurp up the dregs of his own coffee when he choked, spilling it on his white shirt. "I'm sorry. Did you say..."

"I said one percent chance. If somehow—I have no idea how—he can pull off twenty percent of the stuff he's talking about, he'll be somebody to watch."

"A rival?" said Goodwin.

"Maybe. Probably not," said McNally. "We'll have a better fix on the dude after we talk to him, see if he's the real deal."

CHAPTER TWENTY-FIVE

Wednesday, April 28
MIKE DAVENPORT

"So," said Governor Goodwin Tuttle, "Looks like you just made the worst mistake a politician can make." Quite an opening. He had my attention.

We—Betty, Makayla, Nick, Reverend Luke and yours truly—had arrived at nine thirty for our ten o'clock meeting. As we waited for the Guv, an intern served us each of cup of wretched coffee-like-matter: bitter, watery and stale, with a scalded-rubber after-kick. Makayla and I compared notes. How do you make a cup this bad? The project took on a kind of grandeur: buy the cheapest pre-ground beans from a supermarket, leave the lid off for a month, boil the grounds in dishwater for an hour and strain through a used surgical mask. Serve lukewarm.

At ten after ten we were ushered into a wood paneled conference room lined with gubernatorial portraits and a huge presentation screen on the far wall. The Governor's Chief of Staff, Burt McNally welcomed us, calling each of us by name. McNally had the square-jawed, handsome look of an aging soap opera star, complete with tailored suit and silver-streaked auburn hair. He was aggressively gracious in a practiced way belied by the hard, predatory look in his eyes. I flashed on Bernie Madoff. I patted my pocket. Yep, wallet still there.

The Governor himself bustled in ten minutes after the start of the meeting. Maybe it's the soldier in me, but my first read on Goodwin Tuttle was "soft." Soft hands, soft pink face, soft body that wasn't quite fat but would be in five years. He was the glad-handing high school student body president all grown up. I imagined him in my platoon in Afghanistan: life expectancy: thirty minutes. I pegged Tuttle as putty in McNally's hands. The eyes, though...Tuttle was shrewd. I had to be careful. "I apologize, Governor," I said, getting the joke. "This is my first week as a politician. So, what is the worst mistake a politician can make?"

"Easy," said Tuttle. "Writing a check you can't possibly cash. You promised the people of 'Prosperity'—awesome name, by the way—that anyone who wants a job can have one. I'm sure you're aware that every politician around the world would like to wave that magic wand, but none do. Why? Because it's not possible."

Good, I thought. *No niceties. Let's get into the Iron Cage and have it out.* "Governor, have you been to what used to be called 'Pulver Forge'?"

"I'm sure I have," he said, the reflexive non-answer of a practiced pol.

"Then you know our situation is desperate," I said. "Our people have given up."

"Mister Tuttle," said Betty, "You told us that under your leadership, Pennsylvania would thrive. Well, we ain't thrivin'. We're dyin'."

"We aren't dying," said the Rev. "We're dead."

This line hung in the air like a thundercloud. The Governor and I were looking each other right in the eye. Finally, McNally said, "And you think this is the Governor's fault?"

Before I could reply, Nick spoke up. "I voted for you guys twice, and I don't regret it. But I'm noticing that when you run, you make a lofty set of vague promises, with big words like "empowerment" and "entrepreneurship" and phrases like "thousands of new jobs." And then—at least in our town—not a goddamn thing changes. So, am I feeling empowered? No, I'm feeling pissed off. I'm sick of this shit. We all are, and we're doing something about it."

The Governor said, "We're looking at some proposals that will eliminate job-killing regulatory…"

"STOP!" I yelled. That look on his face: *no one talks to me like that.* "Sorry, Governor, it's just that…

"Your time is precious, Sir," said Nick, "so let's not waste it with bullshit."

"Fine," said Tuttle, looking at his watch. He was ready for this meeting to wrap up. "So, tell me why you're here."

"Governor," I said, "we're going to do you the honor of taking you seriously. We're going to stop waiting around for someone to, quote, "save" unquote, our little town. We are going to do every goddam thing we can think of to put our town back to work, to fix it up, to return it to glory. To do this, we are very likely to pursue some slightly unconventional ideas."

"Like what?" said the Governor.

"Like giving everyone a volunteer job who wants one," said the Rev. "There's plenty of work to do, and plenty of people who need to work. This includes high school kids who want to learn something they can use to make a living. We're very likely to create some kind of barter system, where people work for credits they can trade for food, baby-sitting, medical care, stuff like that."

"This won't replace what's there now," I said. "This will enhance it."

"Still," said McNally, "there's the matter of payroll tax, and worker's comp, and…"

"That's why we're here," I said. "That's a gray area, and we're going to live in that gray area for a while." I turned to Tuttle. "If you want to, you can probably shut us down for all kinds of reasons…like…we're going to adopt an attitude of benign neglect for certain zoning laws when we tear up the parks to create our Prosperity gardens."

"So, you're going to break the law," he said gruffly.

"We're just going to bend it a little," said the Rev.

"We're just asking that you look the other way, just for a while," said Betty. "Let us figure this out by ourselves."

"Uh huh," said Tuttle. "Let's say I agree to look the other way, for a while."

"That's all we want," said Nick.

"Great," huffed Tuttle. "What's in it for me?"

"I think I can answer that," said McNally. He fixed me with a knowing gaze. "You make a success of this; we get to brag about it. You're doing what we talk about every four years."

I nodded. "Jobs. Food. Health care."

"And if this all works out," Burt said, "the Governor gets to tell the nation that you were inspired by his leadership, because his policies work."

"Bingo," I said. "Our town stops being a tax burden on the state, as well as a source of shame. We'll invite you down to give a speech at our Fourth of July picnic where you take credit for the whole project. You can lead our little parade as you announce your run for President."

Tuttle couldn't help himself, breaking out in a grin at that last jab. "No decisions have been made about a possible presidential bid." Laughter all around the table. "But what if nobody gets on board for your little crusade? What if you fall on your ass?"

"Well then," I said, "we'll be right where we are now, won't we? So why not let us try?"

Tuttle snorted. "My base will say I'm encouraging an experiment in socialism. Lefties will demand the state take this over and pay minimum wage. The Unions will scream about slave labor. And the crazies will say I'm a puppet of the Red Chinese. I'll get pounded no matter what I do."

"So?" I said.

"So," said McNally, smiling, "We wish you the very best of luck."

"Thanks," I said. The best I was going to get, and all I really wanted. Handshakes all around, mumbled niceties, and promises to keep in touch.

As we left, Nick said, "What just happened?"

"The Governor just did the ol' 'winky-wink' that we have his approval to move ahead," said Makayla, "as long as everything goes perfectly. If something goes wrong, he'll be shocked, SHOCKED to discover perfidy in the Commonwealth! And he will order the state to move in and restore order." I was really getting to like her. She cut through the bullshit. Was she my Burt McNally?

"So, what do we do?" said Nick.

I turned to Reverend Luke. "Rev, what's our move?"

He stopped and addressed us as a preacher, his words bouncing off the marble walls. "What good is it, my brothers and sisters, if someone says he has faith but does not have works? Faith by itself, if it does not have works, is dead."

"Agreed," I said. "Let's get to work." Did I trust Tuttle and McNally? Absolutely not. Never trust anyone who can't make a decent cup of coffee.

CHAPTER TWENTY-SIX

April 28
MIKE DAVENPORT

THE THIRTEEN (Or Is It Fourteen?) PRESUMPTUOUS
PREMISES OF PROSPERITY.

NOTE: This document gives us a 'true north' to guide the
Prosperity Team as we work together to turn this town around.
These aren't rules or laws, and no one has to abide by them. They
are signposts, pointing to what we're trying to achieve.

1) Every Day is Day One

On Day One, we decide what needs to be done, then get busy.
On Day Two, we pretend it's Day One. Rest. Repeat. That's the
program.

2) Teamwork Makes the Dream Work

We're a tribe. Serving each other serves ourselves.

3) Unplug. Turn Off the World. Trust Each Other

If this thing is going to work, we're going to have to de-crazy
ourselves: shut off cable and quit social media so we can hear
each other without a bunch of cynical gasbags screaming in our
ears to keep us boiling with rage.

We're going to generate our own methadone for media junkies: create an ultra-low-budget micro-media empire. This includes an Internet radio station, an on-line newspaper/blog/Social media feed with email alerts, and some podcasts. The new rules are: ONLY connect, ONLY build bridges, ONLY celebrate what's working.

4) Lead, Follow, Or Get Out of The Way.

Everyone can lead, everyone can serve.

5) Nobody's Coming. That's Good News.

Pardon me while I rant. I've been told my whole life to work within the "system": an engaged citizenry and the free market will fix everything. So, here's what that's produced: shitty health care, gun violence, predatory pharma companies murdering people by the thousands to hype their stock, global warming, billionaires raping the middle class, and Black people being murdered by cops. Time to stop believing what everyone else believes and start getting folks like me to change the way we think about things. If we're not happy with the news, we'd better make some of our own. It's on us.

6) What Can We Do Right Now, For Nothing?

Well, let's see. We can make a friend, pick up trash, tell a joke, throw a party. We can share a cup of coffee, share a song, share a smile. We can find somebody who is living on the street who thinks she's alone and let her know she's not alone.

7) The Harder We Are on Ourselves, the Easier Our Lives Become

Got this one from a life coach named Steve Chandler. Once you get used to doing hard things, they're just habits, you don't even notice them.

8) Blame No One. Expect Nothing. Do Something.

Was watching football on TV, Bill Parcells had this on the wall of the New York Giants locker room. It's going up on the wall of our headquarters.

9) The Opposite of Addiction is Connection

Addiction isn't about getting high, it's about trying to numb out loneliness, alienation, and despair. It's not a substance problem, it's a social problem. We're going to feed, heal and connect people to their friends and neighbors as we work together to create a town that will fill them with pride.

10) Fail Better.

Our job? Keep trying shit until we kick this thing's ass, or the voters dump us in the river. We will be very good at not quitting.

11) It's Amazing What You Can Do When You Have To

Our town is destitute, defeated and hopeless. And that means we've got nothing to lose and everything to gain by trying some crazy, outlandish shit. Let's get busy.

12) All Life is Plan B

Mike Tyson said it best: "Everyone has a plan until they get hit in the mouth." The game begins when the plan breaks down. Whatever happens, say "Yes, and…"

13) When It Works Right, It All Works Together

Dr. Kate gets them clean. Betty and the Rev will feed them and house them. Yandy puts them to work in the gardens. Betty trains them up in the kitchen, Makayla puts them to work podcasting or cutting video. I work with them clearing lots, picking up trash, rehabbing buildings. Work hones skills, skills get jobs, and job-holders mentor the next wave. Everybody works, everybody learns, everybody teaches.

14) Laughter is the Sound of Freedom

Life's a joke, and we're the punchline. Nothing lasts, everyone fails, and we'll all die naked and alone, so let's take this thing we're trying to do seriously, but not ourselves. Never ourselves. Fun wants us to have it, so shut up and dance.

CHAPTER TWENTY-SEVEN

YANDY LOPEZ

When Mike asked Yandy if he'd be willing to become the Minister of Abundance and People's Garden Director, he had to keep himself from screaming "YES! YES! YES!" and kissing Mike on the forehead. For Yandy, putting a seed in the ground and watching it grow was more than a calling. It was a reason to keep going. Gardening had actually saved his life.

Yandy had been part of the original DIY "Special Period" city farming experiment in Cuba in the 1990s. He had joined the José Martí Young Pioneers at the urging of his father, to affirm the (non-existent) family commitment to Fidel's revolution: the one that was about to starve them to death through malign bureaucratic torpidity. Yandy worked the "Special Period" vegetable beds by day. At night, Yandy would practice his marksmanship. He'd discovered something he loved even more than growing lettuces: handling a Dragunov semi-automatic sniper rifle. His scoutmaster was a retired member of the Cuban Revolutionary Armed Forces. He was always looking for enthusiastic recruits with special talents.

There were two reasons that Yandy and his father fled Cuba in a ramshackle, open-air, wooden-hulled "chug," powered by the re-purposed engine of their 1953 Chevrolet 210 DeLuxe. The first was that the "Special Period" was no longer so special, and the government was asserting itself to ensure that Cuba's people remained impoverished and malnourished. The second was that Yandy had just turned 17. If he stayed in Cuba another year, he'd be press-ganged into the Revolutionary Armed Forces, which had been decimated as badly by the Soviet pull-out as the farmers had.

Yandy and his father almost capsized a dozen times as their chug took them from Cuba to the Yucatán Peninsula in Mexico. From there, they hitchhiked to El Paso where, thanks to the father's medical credentials, they were granted asylum. They settled in Houston where they both applied for citizenship. The country was still riding the adrenaline wave of the post-9-11 "Shock and Awe" Global War on Terror™. Yandy was thrilled with the idea of testing his skills in a real battle situation, and so enlisted in the Marine Corps. He was given his dream weapon: the M40A3, with a Unertl MST-100 fixed day scope. This was the weapon he used during Operation Vigilant Resolve, aka the First Battle of Fallujah: the one that got him all those confirmed kills and earned him a Silver Star.

It was during this battle that Yandy, working with a spotter, learned something about himself. He had a special set of talents. It wasn't just the killing; it was the whole skill set of becoming an elite sniper. Yandy discovered he was great at stalking. He could stalk his prey for miles and never be detected. He was great at waiting for the right moment. Only then could he express his greatest talent: executing the perfect kill shot. "One shot, one kill" was the Marine sniper motto. Unlike most soldiers, he got more relaxed the closer he got to pulling the trigger. He was in the zone. This was his moment. He could still picture it in his mind: lingering in the dark a thousand yards away, for hours if need be, waiting for his prey to step outside and light a cigarette. When he did, Yandy completed his mission.

And it wasn't just killing individuals. He used his M107 "Light Fifty," loaded with .50-caliber armor-piercing ammunition to light up supply convoys, radar stations and parked aircraft. That wasn't as much fun, because it wasn't "The Most Dangerous Game," going for the kill against big-brained hominids who were out to kill him first. But it was part of the job, and he did it impeccably.

Yandy did three combat tours in Iraq and could have stayed in longer, but the thrill was fading. He'd become a mechanic of death, and he wanted to come home and jump-start his life.

Back in El Paso, he struggled to find himself. From his life in the Marines as a very big "somebody"—a highly skilled, justly celebrated warrior—he suddenly became a nobody. In fact, worse than nobody: he was shunned when people got an inkling of where he'd been and what he'd done. Other men his age were moving up in the world. No one seemed to value the virtues he'd nurtured in the Marines: discipline, patience, courage, commitment. He spent half his days drinking coffee and punching out on-line applications for entry level jobs. The other half he spent smoking pot and visiting Internet chatrooms run by other disgruntled Iraqi and Afghan war vets. He started raiding his father's liquor cabinet, drinking brandy to take the edge off his pot buzz. He was in a downward spiral. He knew it, and he couldn't muster a reason to care.

It was a Wednesday, late afternoon when he found himself buzzed and fuddled, chugging slurps of blackberry brandy from the bottle. He was trying to numb himself after getting an auto-reject email turndown of his application to become a security guard at a shopping mall. The liquor wasn't calming him down, it was making his head ache. In fact, he could feel his aggravation boiling into rage as he listened to those goddam shrieking kids splashing around the apartment swimming pool. Shrieking! How many goddam times had he asked them to stop, asked their parents to get 'em under control? As if all this other shit wasn't enough! He flashed on the SIG Sauer P226 he had under his mattress, and how easy it would be to stop all that racket once and for all. I mean, nothing mattered anyway, so why not end the whole ridiculous charade? The noise, his life... And in that moment, a thought flashed in his mind:

"This shit has got to stop, right now."

Yandy sat bolt upright, still as a statue. That voice. He'd heard it in Iraq, and here it was again. He slowed his breathing. That voice had saved his ass more than once. That's the voice that warned him off whatever shit he got offered by the locals, and he got offered a lot of shit: pot, heroin, hash and pills like "Lebanani" and "Abu Hajib." Everybody around him was getting loaded on who knows what but he liked his job too much to take a risk that might make him careless.

Yandy stayed frozen, taking slow, measured breaths like the ones he'd take right before he pulled the trigger of his sniper rifle. He was cold sober and terrified. *Don't do anything.* Ten breaths followed by ten more, and then another ten. He understood that this was a big moment for him, maybe even life or death. Two paths, this one and that one. Which will it be? He flashed on all those poor guys he saw on television: *"I'd do anything to get that one moment, that one stupid moment back, but now it's too late…"* He heard the kids again, the ones in the pool. They were playing "Marco Polo." Just a bunch of rambunctious eight-year-olds doing what he'd done when he was that age. Hell, he'd done worse.

Slowly, deliberately, he killed the screen on his laptop. He screwed the top back on the brandy bottle and walked it to the liquor cabinet. Then he took the baggie of pot out of his bottom desk drawer and flushed it down the toilet. He booted up the laptop, went to Google Maps and searched for the Eastern seaboard town farthest from El Paso and still in the United States. Allagash, Maine was his first choice, but its population (239), climate (Arctic) and demographic make-up (97.5% white, median age 61 years) encouraged him to widen his search parameters. He shut the computer down and took a five-mile jog to sweat out the booze. Then he went at it again. After an hour he settled on Pittsburgh. One thousand, seven hundred and two miles was probably far enough for a fresh start.

He left at four a.m. the next morning, stopping only for gas, beef jerky and Mountain Dew. He slept in Wal-Mart parking lots on a futon in his 1983 Ford Econoline 3-door panel van. Before he'd sack out, he sat in the driver's seat staring at his laptop, searching for an Iraqi vet chatroom. That's where he stumbled on the "Jarhead Sodbusters," a group of ex-Marines who worked an eighty-acre homestead six miles outside Pittsburgh. The Sodbusters worked the land to heal themselves from combat trauma. What they couldn't eat themselves they gave away to food banks and sold at farmers' markets. Yandy emailed the group's point man, Sgt. Kelton Driscoll and they agreed to meet for Arroz Y Frijoles Negros at "Cuba Libre." From the first moment, Yandy felt almost giddy with gratitude. As Kelton told him about the sodbusters, Yandy understood what he'd missed over the last eleven months since he'd come back. *He'd missed being seen.* He'd become a phantasm, drifting through the world trying and failing to connect with his fellow humans. That last afternoon with those kids at the pool, that was a primal scream: I KILLED PEOPLE SO YOU COULD LIVE AND YOU DON'T GIVE A SHIT. NOW I CAN PROVE I EXIST BY KILLING YOU ALL. Now he realized he didn't need to murder anybody to get the world's attention. He just needed somebody to look him in the eye and ask him one simple question: "How can I help you?"

Yandy told Kelton his story over lunch, then Kelton told him all the ways their two stories rhymed. Kelton grew up on a small family farm in Willow Hill, PA. His father had been spooked by the Cuban Missile Crisis and moved the family into a bomb shelter where the six-person family (3 girls and Kelton) could survive two years underground. Kelton learned how to grow fruits and veggies, and how to hunt, fish, trap and forage. In 2003 he joined the Marines, rising to Gunnery Sergeant, 3rd Battalion, 1st Marines. He was part of the assault on Haditha in September 2005, fighting house to house, finding over a thousand caches of weapons like those that decimated Lima Company during Operation Quick Strike.

After the war, Kelton felt abandoned and superfluous, like Yandy. Kelton solved his crisis by doing what he knew best: 'dirt therapy" aka farming. He bought an eighty-acre farm from a 97 year old World War II vet, and put the word out: homesteaders wanted, Iraq and Afghan war vets only. He discovered that with just a little encouragement, vets quickly became great, dedicated farmers. They were outside in the sunshine, they were making new friends, and they were working hard — growing, harvesting and sharing food — for something the world needed. Pretty soon Sgt. Driscoll was offering classes on beekeeping, fermentation, canning and home brewing. Yandy became a 'Jarhead Sodbuster' for two years to learn Kelton's operation, but he didn't want to work for someone else. He wanted to be his own boss. And he didn't want to own a farm, he wanted to make money farming other people's land. That's when he worked up his nerve to go door to door asking people if he could "farm" their front yards. They'd get free yard care, and 20% of what Yandy grew.

Yandy knew he'd found his calling. He was practicing the same skills he used as a sniper: patience, focus, presence, commitment. When he worked his front yard farm plots, he remembered what he'd felt working the gardens in Cuba. With the right seed in the right soil, some sunshine and rain, paradise was right there waiting for him.

That first Spring he got carried away and almost cratered his experiment. Turns out friends and neighbors loved the idea of helping a vet, loved the thought of giving up yardwork on the lawn, and loved the idea of baskets full of fresh veggies every week. Yandy took on five plots, and it was too much. He found himself farming a hundred hours a week. He also planted too many kinds of veggies, many of which he threw away when they didn't sell at the Farmers Market. That first year he made twenty-two thousand dollars, but it was worth it. He graduated Summa Cum Laude from the University of What Not to Do.

The next year he dropped most of the land and most of his crops. He slashed the size of the farm to two plots right next to each other: fifteen thousand square feet, one third of an acre. He made friends everywhere. Joggers, dog-walkers, neighbors: they'd all stop and chat with him. He was still Yandy Lopez, Marine sniper and cold-blooded killing machine. But nobody who met him in his gardens saw him that way. He was this friendly guy growing lettuce. These people showed up at the Farmers' Market and happily bought his stuff. Better yet, they brought their friends and neighbors who also bought his stuff. And many became his friends.

In year two, Yandy tripled his income working an urban "farm" half the size. He did this by rating every crop he considered growing. He wanted things he could 1) grow quickly (fewest days to maturity), 2) give him the most product for the least space (high yield per linear foot), 3) pay him the most per pound, 4) give him the longest growing season, and 5) would sell at the Farmers' Market, and/or with restaurant owners. Spinach became a superstar crop for Yandy. It matured in 45 days, yielded one and half pounds per foot of growing space, paid him seven dollars per pound, and could grow for a full ten months of the year.

Year two—the year he figured it out, and every year since— Yandy worked thirty-five hours a week and cleared about sixty thousand dollars. That generated more than enough to finance a week-long bargain vacation in south Florida. But Yandy was always looking for a new challenge, and he had one in Prosperity, Pennsylvania. This was his shot, and he was going to take it.

CHAPTER TWENTY-EIGHT

May 5
MIKE DAVENPORT

"So," I said to Yandy, "tell me your plan." Yandy, Makayla and I were sitting in the cavernous back room of the Prosperity HuggaMug on Pulver Boulevard. When I was growing up it had been "Grumpy's Tap Room," an after-shift suds joint with six pool tables, tabletop shuffleboard, darts and foosball. It was just one of five beer joints on the Boulevard: The Five O'Clock Whistle was the last one standing. We'd divided the place in half: front half for the coffeehouse, back half for a de facto Mayor's office and meeting room.

"Okay," said Yandy. "First, the soil. I've already made some calls to my pals in the Jarhead Sodbusters. We've got a week with them to plow, water, and fertilize the soil, and train up our recruits. Then we plant, and six weeks later we harvest."

"That's great television," said Makayla, scribbling notes. "Pennsy Vets care, answering an SOS, neighbor helping neighbor. I can work with this."

"They have a place to stay?" I said.

"Betty has it figured out," said Yandy. "Half with the Rev at the church compound, the other half in homes around town. Hell, they're happy to camp out in the park if we feed them. They're Marines, they can sleep in a muddy foxhole in a monsoon."

"So, the plan," I said. "Continue."

"The first crop will be on three plots. We'll start with that big athletic field at the Pulver Rec Center, behind the library, used to be for baseball. That gives us an acre and a half. We'll divvy that up into three half-acre lots that'll be farmed by teams of eight per shift, two shifts a day. That plot will grow two big yield, fast-growing crops that everybody loves, lettuce and spinach. From field to table, six weeks and it'll keep producing through the entire season, probably enough for everybody in the program."

"Great!" said Makayla. "Our first home-grown feast by July 4, that's outstanding. The Sodbusters will be our guests of honor."

"Second plot is Pulver Memorial Park. Place is about four acres, we'll plow up two, leave the playground and picnic areas alone. They'll become four half-acre mini farms. Two of those will be lettuce and spinach. What we don't eat we can sell at the Squirrel Hill Farmers Market, the one on Sunday. The other half will go to stuff like arugula, Red Russian kale, carrots and squash. For the third plot, I've got my eye on the big garden up at the old Pulver family mansion, what was it called…"

"Rockhurst Castle," I said.

"Yeah, big open plot up there. We can grow specialty stuff, like cilantro, parsley, baby dill, micro-greens, stuff like that. Also a flower garden, just because. The idea there is to grow stuff we can sell to restaurants, to generate money we can use to buy the beans and rice we'll need for our community feasts."

"And you'll run this operation?" I said.

"I'll do more than run it," said Yandy. "I'll be out there getting my hands dirty. Each half-acre mini farm will need eight people working twenty hours a week, so that's four in the morning and four in the afternoon, fifty six people total with four on call when people don't show, that's sixty. Figure we'll have a lot of dropouts, so let's aim to sign a hundred. I'll be floating from farm to farm to make sure everybody's pointed in the same direction and having a good time."

Silence. "Yandy," I said, "you're a miracle worker. But…well…are you sure? About all this?"

"Sure he's sure!" said Makayla. She turned to Yandy. "Aren't you?"

Yandy smiled. "You gotta understand something, Mike. The people coming in—the sodbusters, my brothers—they've been waiting for a showcase project like this for years. They're connected to gardening clubs, organic food lovers, co-ops, and all the folks I know from selling at the Farmers' Market. You'll be amazed at how many tree-hugging dirt worshippers there are out there."

Makayla was beaming. "This story's got the whole DNA of what we're doing. People seizing their own destiny, going to work, making friends, feeding a town hungry for meaning." She cocked her head at us. "Think of the number of rust-belt towns out there that are food deserts, no fresh food for ten miles. Every single one of them has a public park and front lawns and sports fields and, I don't know, vacant lots just waiting to become gardens."

"And here's the thing," said Yandy. "It's hard work, but it's…ummm, fun is the wrong word. It's gratifying. It makes people feel useful. It's amazing to watch something you planted come out of the ground, go into a salad bowl and then into your mouth. People forget what fresh stuff tastes like. It's sweet, crunchy, full of flavor. Once people get hooked on what they grow themselves, you can't stop 'em. That's what keeps me going."

I felt a buzz of adrenaline shoot through me, and it wasn't just the coffee. *This thing could work.* "So seven, eight weeks from now we can schedule our first Prosperity Gardens Home Grown Community Feast?"

Yandy gave me a thumbs up. "Grown by us, served by us, enjoyed by us," said Makayla.

"We'll invite the Governor," I said. Nods all around. A thought flashed through my mind: "We're on our way." Followed by another, colder: "This is going too well. I'm missing something. What is it?" I shook that off and smiled. I'd know soon enough.

CHAPTER TWENTY-NINE

May 7
MIKE DAVENPORT

"You okay?" I spoke to Yandy Lopez without looking at him.

"Yeah," he said, and we both chuckled. Sunset, dark amber light blinking out just as the three (of eight) working streetlights flickered on. We were walking toward Pulver Memorial Park. I had a giant bag of plastic survey stakes slung over my shoulder. Yandy was carrying a canvas sack with rolls of braided twine. We were going to stake out the two acres we'd be using for our gardens…we hoped. I felt my nervous system crackle as I shifted to the hyper-alert status that kept me alive in Afghanistan.

"What's the closest you ever came to being killed?" I said as we walked.

Yandy's eyes stayed fixed on the park, now a half block away. "I was set up on a rooftop, locking in, doping the wind, waiting for the target to emerge from a kebab place. Dead of night, the world was asleep. I was ready to rock when I hear my spotter say, 'Oh shit!' I jerked around. This black shroud was rushing us with a wicked foot-long Ka-Bar, probably scrounged from the body of one of our guys. She shrieked like a banshee; says we killed her family. I froze, nothing in my hand when she leapt at me. I'm dead! Shit!"

"So, what happened?" I said.

"My buddy pulled his Glock and shot her in the head. Her blood spattered my face, soaked my chest. Did a body scan. Am I wounded? Dead? I was alive. I thought my heart was going to explode, and my hands wouldn't stop shaking, but I was alive. Not a scratch."

"You ever think back on that moment?"

"You mean, like, right now?" A laugh. "Yeah." And then, "There."

I saw them the same moment Yandy did. The hoodies. Five of them, faces shrouded by a drawstring sweatshirt hood. They were looming up out of the darkness, under a copse of bedraggled maple trees. Pulver Memorial Park had been the domain of drug dealers so long ago that no one but me could remember when kids used the swings, the monkey bars and teeter-totter.

"Hey," I said. Nothing. Then, louder, "We're here to mark out our new Prosperity Community gardens."

One hoodie seemed to be the alpha. Big man, wraith-thin, six foot four. "Ain't no days like that. This our place."

Yandy said, "Yeah, actually, it's something we're going to do. There's gonna be a lot of people using the park from now on, so you need to find somewhere else to…you know, whatever it is you do."

Now the four others moved up to flank the leader, two on each side. "The bookends are packing," I muttered, letting Yandy know I saw the Glock 20s barely hidden behind baggy denim pants of the two flanking hoodies.

"Got it," he murmured. Neither one of us had a weapon. We weren't wearing Kevlar vests either, which wouldn't stop a round from that weapon. We stared at them for about half a minute when I heard the crunch-crackle of tires on crumbling macadam, then two sets of car doors slam. We were now flanked by Police Chief Pooley and two of his deputies. The deputies had shotguns.

"Hey, Linc." No response. "Linc, we're not here to bust you, but you're gonna have to move along," said Pooley. "We got some business here." The five didn't move. Instead, six more hoodies emerged from the darkness, three on each side, eleven total. Four guns I could see.

"This is place is ours," said Linc, the alpha hoodie. "Been that way for a while, you know that."

"That was then," said Chief Pooley. "This is now."

The stocky fireplug hoodie next to the alpha, flashing anger, said, "Want it? Come and get it." Another stand-off. They didn't move, we didn't move. And then I heard the rumble of two big, beautiful Ford F-650 stake bed trucks pull in behind us. Thirty-one brawny Jarhead Sodbusters jumped off the trucks and double-timed next to us and behind us. The pungent scent of compost mulch perfumed the air. Yandy's friend and mentor Sergeant Kelton Driscoll stood front and center in khaki fatigues. Now it was thirty-six to eleven. The hoodies slouched. A few took a single step back.

Driscoll addressed his men. "You know the mission, gentlemen. It's our park. Let's take it." Sgt. Driscoll started to stride forward, followed by the deputies. He walked straight up to the alpha hoodie, followed closely by the two deputies with shotguns. Now they were nose to nose. A long moment…and the alpha took a half a step to the side. Driscoll brushed past him. We were in. The hoodies watched this, then faded back into the trees. Yandy led the way to the garden plots.

Yandy showed me where to pound the stakes, then connected them with twine. The Sodbusters, God bless 'em, didn't let the darkness stop them from soaking both acres, rototilling them and layering the plots with mulch. We weren't done till 3 a.m., and then one of the Sodbusters brought out a cooler with six six-packs of Iron City Beer. I don't love beer as much as I love coffee, but I loved every drop of that blessed brew.

We'd strategized it, planned it, and damn! We'd pulled it off! Yandy and I were grinning as we finished off that brew. Amazing what you can do when you have to.

CHAPTER THIRTY

May 15
NICK BARLOW

"Oh, shit." Nick Barlow knew he'd done it again. He was laid out flat on a creeper underneath the derelict 1979 Blue Bird All-American school bus: the one he'd towed off the vacant lot behind Pulver Forge High School to his repair shop, "Hell on Wheels." This was what Prosperity's Minister of Beautification, Mike Davenport, had asked him to fix up to become the free-for-everyone "Prosperity GetAbout."

What he'd done was prang his back AGAIN. He could feel the blaze of pain where he'd wrenched it: just where it always was, the third lumbar vertebrae, right where the medics had cut out the shrapnel from the VC rocket-propelled grenade on Hamburger Hill. Nick had stayed alive through the whole horrific assault—over three hundred American dead—and then, the final assault, BANG. He'd crawled to the top of the hill and then sunk into the mud. He still had a piece of metal the size of a bottle cap lodged in his back that predicted the weather better than any of those clowns on television. He used his grease-stained arms to roll the creeper out from underneath the bus. "JOHNNY!"

Johnny Austin was his geeky apprentice. Nick had given him the job as a favor to Chief Pooley. Austin was the nephew of a cop friend killed in the line of duty. Johnny's mother had overdosed with Fentanyl and his father had vanished, and the kid was fooling around with the stuff himself when Nick had given him a job and a place to bunk in the rear of the shop.

Johnny was 23 years old, a six-foot one inch, 135 pound high school dropout who showed up about half the time and had finally figured out how to do an oil change. "What is it, boss?"

"I-I can't…oh, man, can you pull me up? It's my damn back." Austin grabbed his arm and pulled him up into a hunched position. Nick felt like he was 110 years old, looking into an open grave. He launched himself upward, staggered over and collapsed into the filthy red vinyl bucket seat he'd rescued from a totaled '68 Pontiac Firebird. "Oh, God, now what?"

"I, ummm…" Johnny wanted to say something, but held back.

"What?" said Nick.

"I had something like that happen to me couple years ago, when I, uh, fell off my skateboard. A pal took me to this friend of his mother's, named, I think, Raven something. She fixed me right up. I could, you know…"

Nick cast a baleful glance at the kid, who took a half a step back. Then he grimaced and thought, "What the hell. Could it be any worse than this?"

The Craftsman cottage on Cloverdale Street had a well-trimmed lawn with a sign reading "I CRACK BACKS. Chiropractic Treatment $45." Parked at the curb was a dapper fire engine red 1953 Ford F-100 fat-fender pickup truck, with a single bumper sticker that said, "Kindness is Everything." Nick winced when he saw this. He didn't need woo-woo new-age bullshit; he needed a miracle. Or at least a fistful of painkillers.

Raven Washburn opened the door and Nick staggered in, his right arm slung over Johnny's shoulder. Raven was a sturdy, lean, straight-ahead Black woman: early 50s, blunt cut hair with bangs, dressed in a black sweatshirt with "Unapologetically Dope" in orange letters. She wore a small crystal heart around her neck. She didn't blanch when she saw him, and her calm, seen-it-all-before air put Nick at ease. As she plopped him on her treatment table, he looked around. The table was in the near corner of a sunny living room that also housed a barber chair, a stack of boxes filled with vegetables and a personal art studio. The walls were covered with Raven's vivid paintings of all things Pulver Forge. He saw one of the Pulver Library framed as a cathedral at daybreak, another of the Pulver family mansion bathed in the gold light of dusk, and a third of the Pulver Pennsy Train Station as it appeared on the day in 1922 when President Warren Harding delivered a speech from his presidential Pullman. The easel held a half-finished canvas of a backyard garden (hers?), with a rainbow-riot of daisies, zinnias, asters and Queen Anne's lace.

"Ready?" Nick nodded. He could tell Raven was examining Nick's scars. "You got wounded when?"

"'69."

"Mmm. Quite some time ago. Vietnam?"

"Yeah."

"Bad back since then?"

"You know, on and off. More on than off. This is nothing new, it usually takes me about six weeks to straighten up, only I don't have six weeks."

"Uh huh. Let's see..." She kneaded his back muscles, assessing his injury. With every tweak, Nick squealed. "Uh huh. Yeah. You're a mess, honey."

"Tell me something I don't know. Look, can you help me or not?"

Ten more seconds of probing. "Mmmmm, yeah. I think so." She pondered her approach. "I'm going to try something, it's a big move. It'll either fix you up, or..."

"Or what?"

"You won't be any worse than you are now. You up for it?"

"Is it going to hurt?"

She chuckled. "Yes, and then no."

Good answer, he thought. "Yeah, okay. What the hell, I'm ready. Do your worst."

Raven hooked her muscular arms under his arm pits, locking her fingers behind his head. "On three. One…two…" Before Nick could tense on the three count, Raven cranked his torso up and ninety degrees to the right, producing a firecracker-loud "POP."

"YEOW!" A red-hot shiv of pain burst up his spine, and then…nothing. Nick felt nothing. It was like…what? Like those morphine shots the Doctors gave him in 'Nam, the ones that parked him on Cloud 9. He gingerly straightened his back. A little soreness, but no shooting pains. He arched his back and heard a smaller 'pop.' He looked at Raven, smiling. She nodded, and he sat upright, slid off the table and straightened up. A little stiffness, but no pain.

"I…I can't believe it."

"Believe it," she said.

"You're…that's amazing."

"No, the human body is amazing. It wants to heal itself; we just have to help it out a little."

"Uh huh. What did you do?"

"Just got your back in alignment so the nerves that run up your spine to your brain work like they're supposed to. Want some coffee? Just made a fresh pot."

Nick sat at Raven's rustic-pine dining room table just off the living room, drinking her pretty-good coffee and nibbling on a raspberry tart. Turns out she knew who he was from friends who knew Mike Davenport. She asked about Mike's plan for the town, if he thought it had a chance of working. He said, "I was a skeptic. Still am, I guess. But the guy hasn't lied to me yet. He's got a healthy ten to one action-to-bullshit ratio. He even talked me into fixing up this old Pulver High school bus as a runabout so people can get around town."

"How's that going?" said Raven.

"It's a nightmare. Basically, I'm screwed."

"How so?"

"It's…it's a long story, you wouldn't be interested."

She grimaced. "You see that truck out front?"

"The '53 Ford?"

"I did that. Fully restored. By me."

Nick blinked. "Really?" *Who is this woman?* "You…

"I like being useful. You need a haircut?" She nodded at the barber chair. "I can do that too."

He took another sip of coffee as he sized her up a second time. That look in her eye, he knew it from his service. This woman had walked through the fire and survived. Just then a man and woman, weather-aged, late 60s, worn flannel and denim work clothes, came in the front door without knocking. They nodded at Raven and picked up the top cardboard box of vegetables from a stack of four. After they'd left, he looked a question at her. She sighed. "I grow more veggies than I can eat, so the neighbors…"

"Got it," he said. He squared himself to her and looked right into her dark brown eyes. "So, here's the deal. The Blue Bird, it's a '79 with a Cummins VT555 V8 Diesel engine that has a cracked block, which is why the town gave up on it. I tried to get parts, no luck. So, I thought about swapping in a Ford Super-Duty 534 V8 from a junkyard in Dooleyville, but it needs a new water pump which I could get off another junkyard in East Greenwich, but that's just north of Philly, which is, like a four and half hour drive and who knows if it'd work."

"Why not go electric?" she said. It took Nick a moment to figure out she was serious.

"Electric? Look, we're talking about a school bus. There's no way…"

She put her mug down. "This bus, it's just going to putter around the town, right?

"Right."

"Like 20, 25 miles an hour? Fifty, sixty miles a day tops.

"Yeah, right."

"So, you get a Torquey electric motor, bolt an adapter plate right onto the existing transmission. You've got all kinds of room for control electronics and charging systems."

"What about the batteries? Where are you going to get…"

Her eyes flashed with excitement. She'd been thinking about this. "So, all those Teslas out there? They're getting ready for their hundred-thousand-mile battery swaps, and those batteries still have 70 percent of their capacity left, which is, like 168 miles of range per charge, which is three days for your bus before you have to juice them up again. Tesla is trying to figure out what to do with those batteries. Recycling them into school busses? That's a win for Tesla and for you."

"Uh huh." Nick's head was spinning. "What makes you think…"

"Because I did it myself. Kind of a hobby project."

He stared at her as he put it together. "The pickup truck?"

She smiled. "Wanna go for a ride?"

Nick was having an out of body experience. *Who the hell is this woman??* Raven Washburn had electrified her 1953 Ford pickup truck, turning it into the zippiest ride on the planet. Raven drove them up Route 18 to Raccoon Creek State Park and back again. She got Nick to tell her his life story: his hardscrabble childhood as the son of an abusive, alcoholic Pulver Forge mill worker, his escape from that life by way of Vietnam, his return as a mechanic at the "Smokey Nolan Chevy" dealership on Bessemer Drive, and his struggle to keep his own shop alive after the dealership folded in '81 and the town went down the toilet. It took him quite a while to notice that he was doing all the talking, and this intriguing woman barely said a thing beyond quizzing him about his past. "So, what about you?" he said. "Back-cracker, barber, urban gardener, painter, shade-tree mechanic..."

"That bus. I could help you with that."

They were just turning back onto her street. He looked over at her. She looked at him. She wasn't kidding. "Help how?"

"You figure out how much it's going to cost. If it makes sense, you'll get the money, and we'll do it together."

"How..."

"The tech guides and manuals are in my garage," said Raven. "It's really pretty simple. I do have one condition."

"What's that?'

"You let me paint it."

"Paint it?"

"Paint it. The bus. You let me and my crew paint the bus, like we painted this truck."

Nick's mouth was open. "Uhh...yeah, okay. I'll make that deal. Thanks, Raven. Ummm..."

"What?"

Nick's first wife had left him by the time he came back from Vietnam. His second wife, the long-suffering Sarah who put up with him for 31 years, died of cervical cancer eight years ago. He had a daughter who dealt blackjack in Las Vegas and a son who waited tables in Nashville as he tried to kickstart his career as a singer-songwriter. He was done with romance, but this was something different. This was...what? He wasn't sure, but... "If I called you...that is, I know you drink coffee, would you be willing to, I don't know, meet me some morning? Not a date, just a..."

"Two friends having coffee. Sure, why not?" Nick felt something he hadn't felt in years, a pleasant surge of delight. He was happy! His face ached from smiling. What a goddamn day.

CHAPTER THIRTY-ONE

May 16
GUS FARNUM

Augustus "Gus" Farnum was beside himself. His eyesight wasn't what it used to be, but…no, there was no doubt: he was holding a crisp portrait of President James Madison that just happened to be on the first US five thousand dollar note he'd ever seen. It had come in a padded envelope postmarked Paradise, Nevada, with no return address. No letter inside: just a card that read, "Pulver Forge Patriots."

Gus didn't know a soul in Las Vegas. He hadn't been to Sin Town since 2009, when Wayne Newton stopped playing the Tropicana. He had no idea who sent him the money, but it couldn't have come at a better time, because the Pulver Forge patriots were getting ready to FIGHT.

Gus has gone to work at the Pulver Forge Mill in 1958, right out of high school. It took him fourteen years to work his way up to swing shift Foreman. He was fully vested in the pension fund after twenty-eight years of service when those greedy bastards shut down a perfectly good, hard-working mill. He can still remember the bile rising in the back of his throat as he and his cohorts listened to that smarmy "spokes-weasel" hired by BDM Holding, the company that had bought the mill from the Pulver family. How had he put it? "Unscrupulous foreign competitors and unforeseen domestic market forces have forced this closing, causing an unfortunate shortfall in available funding for the Pulver Workers' Pension Fund." In other words, the thieves who bought the mill from the Pulver family never gave a shit about the business. They were in it to loot the pension fund. And while they were yachting in Saint-Tropez, the people who made the steel that made them rich would be eating cat food and foraging in dumpsters.

Gus was in a white-hot rage. He vowed never to be suckered again. Lawyers, bureaucrats, the (useless) union, the media: it was all lies and bullshit, a bunch of rip-off-the-rubes make-believe designed to put him to sleep so they could pick his pocket. He put the thirty-five hundred dollars he'd saved up into a business, "Prep N' Save," a modest storefront on Wabash Street, next to the Dollar King. Gus sold everything from freeze-dried Fettucine Alfredo to bio stoves to the Scoped Ruger Takedown .22 LR Survival Rifle. The store was five blocks off Pulver Boulevard on the fringe of the business district, nestled between "2nd Chance Used Furniture" and "Village Cobbler Shoe Repair." He barely eked out a living, but he was able to cultivate a gang of regulars (including Nick Barlow) who saw things the way he did. Most of them were forcibly retired steelworkers. Many of them were like him: widowed, with kids scattered around the country. In 2010, this group joined the Tea Party as the "Pulver Forge Patriots."

Gus had watched as the rest of the country went down the toilet. The same fine folks who stole his pension money, shipped Pulver Forge jobs to South Korea and stole his tax money to feather the nests of illegals were all over television calling him a racist/sexist monster for speaking out about it. And when a few brave politicians finally did speak out, the media elites pounded them into the ground like tent pegs.

Gus and PF Patriots were outraged that elections were being stolen right out from under their noses. The proof was all over YouTube! And now the threat to their freedom was on their front doorstep. Now a group of radical lefties were here in Pulver Forge, running roughshod over the citizenry, hijacking the city government and taking over the town.

The plot was being exposed on the Facebook group "Pulver Forge Tattler": how a dodgy Pittsburgh carpetbagger named Mike Davenport, a bogus Afghan war "hero," had been recruited by a Wiccan cabal of Black radicals and lesbian feminists (the "Quixote Institute") to destroy a mayor who was trying to bring guaranteed jobs to the people of Pulver Forge. The thing that made Gus the craziest is the utter transparency of Davenport's agenda. He was hypnotizing Pulver Forge residents into doing slave labor…all work, no pay… in a scheme that the North Korean government would love. Could this really be happening? Right here in Pulver Forge? And that's the worst part! No more Pulver Forge! This great town, built and sustained by the Pulver family for eighty years, had lost the Pulver name! This bunch of radical crazies had renamed it, without a public vote, "Prosperity, Pennsylvania."

Farnum posted a request for donations on the Pulver Forge Patriots Facebook page. The group had gathered a scant hundred and forty-six dollars until the five-thousand-dollar bill had arrived. Now PF Pride could reach out to groups like the Keystone Free Men and the Righteous Ones to strategize about how to take back the town.

Gus had just turned eighty-one. He had arthritis, emphysema (unfiltered Camels, and all that goddam mill dust!), and macular degeneration. This would probably be his last chance to fight the scumbags who had taken everything from him almost forty years ago. He was surprised how often his anger toggled into a kind of glee. Nothing to lose! The PF Patriots were going to do this thing or die trying, and if he had to die, this was the way he wanted to go out: fighting for a free America, the one and only cause he believed in.

CHAPTER THIRTY-TWO

MAY 17
MIKE DAVENPORT
First Working Day for Prosperity, PA.
8:00 a.m. We were back in the Freeman Opera House cranking up the populace with coffee, along with a minivan's worth of baked goods (thank you Flour Power!) Four hundred folding chairs encircled a small round platform in the middle. The gym was a little over half full. Makayla, Kate and Yandy handed each citizen a packet that included our "Thirteen (Or Is It Fourteen?) Presumptuous Premises of Prosperity," an agenda, and an info sheet to sign up to volunteer.

We were getting a pretty good mix this morning. Lots of grizzled, fading Boomers, but also GenX, GenY and Millennials. I walked from the edge of the circle to the center, hopped up on the small platform and took the microphone. This is it. The first Day One of many, I hoped.

TEXT OF PROSPERITY, PENNSYLVANIA PUBLIC MEETING TRANSCRIBED FROM A VIDEO RECORDING

MIKE DAVENPORT: Welcome, friends! I'm Mike Davenport, Mayor of Prosperity, Pennsylvania. Prosperity! Today we begin doing what needs to be done. My list has five things.

First, food. Pulver Forge is a food desert. The nearest supermarket is the MaxxMart, that's seven miles away. We're going to change all that. To tell us how, I'd like to introduce our new Prosperity Minister of Abundance (laugh), Mister Yandy Lopez.

(applause)

YANDY LOPEZ: Friends, Prosperity, Pennsylvania has a ton of farmland! We've just been wasting it growing grass. So, we're going to use this land to grow food to nourish ourselves. We — that is, me and the people in this room — are going to plow up the fields at the Pulver Rec Center, half of Pulver Memorial Park and the gardens at the old Pulver Mansion and grow our own fruits and vegetables.

Twenty hours a week, that's all we're asking. If you can't give twenty, give ten, or five, or whatever you can offer. All we have to do is put seeds in the ground, then weed and water. God does the heavy lifting! And then everyone here will come together for our Prosperity Community Kitchen noon meal, hosted by our Minister of Hospitality, Chef Betty.

CHEF BETTY: You want a great job? I'll teach you how to prep and cook food that your friends will love. There's nothing more fun than feeding people, and once you're trained up you can take your skills into any restaurant here or in Pittsburgh and get a good-paying job.

MIKE DAVENPORT: Let's talk city beautification. Take a look at all that trash in the streets, friends. That trash is jobs. You won't be a trash collector, you'll be a 'city beautifier.' As you beautify the streets, you can tell us what houses need to be fixed up. If we can't fix it up, we'll tear it down and turn it into a garden, that's some great jobs as well.

We've got an abandoned hotel with a hundred and thirty rooms. How 'bout we give people living on our streets a place to stay? And a meal? And a chance to clean up their act? And then a job? That's what I mean by prosperity! Everybody counts, everybody works, everybody prospers.

Next is public health. Here's Prosperity's new Minister of Well-Being, Doctor Kate Walther.

KATE: We've got a health crisis in this town. It's addiction. The opposite of addiction is *connection*. We're going find people who need help. We're going to heal them, feed them, find jobs for them, and give them a reason to live. And helping me connect people? Your new Minister of Ballyhoo, Makayla Nichols.

MAKAYLA:I was part of the news media that sold you a fake story: that it was your fault the steel mill closed, and that nothing could be done. We're killing that old, fake story, and telling a new one. You want a job connecting with your friends and neighbors? See me. We're starting an Internet radio station. We need people to work our Prosperity website, stock it with blogs and podcasts. We're building a YouTube channel, shooting and editing and posting videos that will become a feature documentary called "How We Did It." It's our new story friends, and I can give it to you in two words: Prosperity works. And after work, fun. Reverend Luke?

REV. LUKE: Psalm 47, Verse 1 says, "Clap your hands, all you nations; shout to God with cries of joy." And that's just what we'll do every Friday night from seven to midnight. We're going to throw ourselves a great big party with live music, great food and joyous dancing, to celebrate the miracle of our new prosperity.

MIKE: That's it! Questions?

CHAPTER THIRTY-THREE

MIKE DAVENPORT
Q: What if I don't want to grow lettuce, or do any of this? Why should I?

MIKE: You shouldn't, so don't. If you've got a good-paying job here in Prosperity or in Pittsburgh or anywhere else, by all means keep living your life how you want. That said, we invite everybody to join us, buy into what we're doing, and do the work that's going to turn this place around.

Q: How is this going to affect stuff like our police and fire coverage?

CHIEF FRED POOLEY: Not at all. As you know, Prosperity has an agreement with the County to share these services. I'm thinking if we connect with each other, go to work, clean this place up and look out for one another, you won't need to call me so often. Then I can join you in those gardens.

Q: Yeah, I'm a Union guy. We worked our butts off for fifty years to get a contract we could live with. Some of us died for that. And now you're telling everybody we have to work for free? Why the hell should we do that?

MIKE: First of all, I want to acknowledge everyone here who was in the United Steelworkers. My father and grandfather were members. You are a bunch of stand-up folks who worked like hell to get a living wage. But that's been over for thirty years plus. What we're doing here is different. I'm not telling anybody to do anything. I'm just taking a good hard look at where we are in this town so we can figure out how to fix it by working together.

And you won't be working for free. You'll be earning TimeBucks that you can trade for goods and services in the community. And think of this: the quickest way to get companies with good Union jobs to come back to this town is to show them that Prosperity is full of enterprising, self-starting, hard-working people.

When you were in the Union, it was you versus the bosses. Now we're the bosses. We're working for ourselves. When we do our jobs, everybody benefits.

Q: What's the difference between what you're doing and socialism? Or Communism, for that matter?

MIKE: Great question. Both socialism and Communism are ways to organize a government that can impose its will on the people. In both those systems, the state is all powerful. They tell you what to do, and if you don't do it, you're sent to a Gulag.

This ain't that. It's the opposite. It's a kind of semi-self-organized anarchism. I'm your mayor, but none of what I'm doing comes from exercising my political authority. You want to join us? Great. That has advantages. If you opt out and this thing works, you'll reap some benefits. The town will be cleaner, livelier, safer and more fun. There'll soon be more real jobs, and your property values will go up. It's a win/win no matter how you look at it.

Q: I'm out of a job. How does working for no money help me?

MIKE: First of all, you'll get a delicious, healthy meal every day: and breakfast, if you count our free morning coffee. Second, if you need a place to live, we'll fix you up as we determine which buildings are habitable. Third, we'll give you a chance to learn a skill, like gardening, cooking, medical assistant, carpentry, stuff like that. And finally, it beats the hell out of sitting in your living room watching daytime TV. If this works right, businesses will move back here, and you'll be able to get a real, paid job with benefits. If you join us, you'll grow more than spinach. You'll grow a town you'll be proud of.

Q: What if this doesn't work? (Laughter, smattering of applause)

MIKE: Ahh! The best question of all! There is *no chance, none, zero,* that this isn't going to work. You know why? Because WE, THE PEOPLE of Prosperity are in charge of seeing that it works! Can you imagine those steelworkers showing up at the gate of the Pulver Forge mill wondering if they were going to succeed in making steel that day? Like it was a real question? Look around you, my friend! See all your friends and neighbors cranked up on that fine French Roast coffee, eager to get out there and get to work? We only have one real job, and that's not quitting! If we do that, it's going to work, big time! So...if there are no more questions...let's get to work!

(MALKAYLA) PROSPERITY REPORT CARD BY THE NUMBERS (1st Day of Work, Week #1)

466: # of HuggaMug Cups of Coffee Served
31: # Who Paid for Coffee (Surprised it was this many)
129: #Workers for Community Garden (GREAT!!)
81: #Workers for Food Prep/Service/Clean-Up at Prosperity Community Diner
47: #Workers for Town Clean-Up Duty (NEED MORE)
36: #Workers for Medical Clinic
293: Total # Workers who both signed up and showed up
358: #Lunches Served, Prosperity Community Diner (including workers)
1,314: #Total TimeBucks Issued

NOTES: In order to hit Betty's 3.5%, we needed 321 people to show up. We got 293 on the first day. Not bad. On the one hand, we'll probably have dropouts tomorrow. Still, Yandy can't stop talking about how people who see us gardening and cleaning up are going to want to join in. The bottom line: PEOPLE SHOWED UP. Sure, we had 65 freeloaders at lunch, but maybe they'll feel guilty enough to come out and help.

Our first mini miracle: Yandy was running the first crews working the gardens in Memorial Park. He'd recruited our most dedicated local gardeners to supervise the plots, and the crews were able to go right to work. After about an hour, people were getting to know each other, telling stories and jokes. The happy chatter attracted some on-lookers, and what do you know — three of them signed up for our gardening teams! Yandy dropped a well-deserved "told ya so." He said, "They did a survey a couple of years ago. You know the three professions happiest in their jobs? Lumberjacks, foresters and farmers. Why? Simple. They're outside, feeling the sun, smelling the soil, working with friends, and the work means something. This isn't pushing papers around the desk, this is growing food! What's not to like?"

Our second mini miracle: our "Prosperity" web portal is live. Members can track their TimeBucks, even cash them in using the handy barcode. The portal includes a tab for "ShareWhere," a community-commons "gift circle" that lets members list things they'll let others borrow (like a lawnmower that's used once a week) and lets them ask for things they need (like a sewing machine.)

CHAPTER THIRTY-FOUR

May 23
MIKE DAVENPORT
Tess and I agreed on our usual date-night time (7 pm). We'd agreed on the place to dine under the stars (Aspinwall Riverfront Park). We'd agreed on the Food Truck ('NamNamNosh', authentic Vietnamese street cuisine.) We'd even agreed to split a dish that was trending on social media: the Bun Cha, which was vermicelli noodles, grilled pork patties, a broth made of vinegar, fish sauce and sugar with pickled papaya and carrot, served with a basket of greens. My Steelers Picnic Time reclining camp chairs and tailgate table were all set up. I'd even poured two glasses of a completely adequate seven-dollar Trader Joe's Pinot Noir.

Tess had never been late for a date. Not only was she always on time, she was always eight minutes early: not seven, not nine, but eight. I knew something was wrong when my smartphone lit up at 7:22. Tess. "Hey, girlfriend."

"Hello," she said. Silence.

"I'm, uhhh, here."

"I had to work late."

"No, you didn't, or you'd have called. So, something's wrong. What's wrong?"

"I heard you're giving away coffee. Like, hundreds of two-dollar cups. For free."

Ahhh. Of course. "Not that many, and not for long, just long enough to…"

"I'm texting you a picture."

A second later the pic arrived. It was the two of us smiling in front of a Technicolor wall-sized color poster of Ke'e Beach on the NaPali Coast of Kauai. There we were in a booth at a 'Vacation Expo' to scope out a corner of paradise for our next life together. "Look, Tess, the coffee is nothing. It's all in the contingency budget. The deal is still on. I…"

"Have I ever stood you up, Mike?"

"No, never."

"I'm standing you up tonight so you'll know I'm not fucking around. We're this close to paradise, lover. We can have what's in that picture. We've worked for it, we've earned it, it's the life of our dreams. Stay focused. Stop the nonsense. Talk soon."

She clicked off. I shut down the phone and chugged half my glass of wine. Then I tilted my head back and stared up at the starry, starry night sky. What did I want? When I was a quarterback in high school, I wanted to be "Iron Mike" Davenport, 17 season franchise QB for the Steelers. When I got out of the Army, I wanted to make so much money I could wave adios to this fallen world and devote my life to the relentless pursuit of personal pleasure. In Tess, I'd found a soulmate/inspiration for that quest. We shared a glorious dream of giving the rat race a great big middle finger.

Another gulp of wine. That's what I still want, right? Isn't that why I've been working 18-hour days, six days a week for seven years to put together this sweet million-dollar deal for HuggaMug? Then what was I doing wasting my time in Prosperity, PA.? What kind of moron would turn down a life in Kauai with a smart, beautiful, loving woman and a vault full of hard-earned fuck-you money?

I lowered my head and checked out the line for the food truck. Saw an old, beefy guy in a black hoodie reading a paperback book. I flashed on one of my customers that morning. A geezer, late seventies, threadbare work pants and ragged flannel shirt: definitely a Pulver Mill lifer. Battered, sweat-stained fedora that didn't quite cover a jagged scar above his right eye. Before he'd take his cup, he insisted that I shake his gnarled hand. "Lou Fuller, Mike. Thanks." I saw him that afternoon spearing fast food wrappers with his trash picker and sticking them in a garbage bag he'd tied to his belt. He hobbled a bit, but he was smiling. He had a job. He'd have a meal. You know what? I had something to do with that.

A couple walked by, each holding a bag of 'NamNosh' take-out. Smelled good! I was hungry. Suddenly the idea of dining alone didn't seem so bad. In fact, it kinda made me happy.

CHAPTER THIRTY-FIVE

Monday
MIKE DAVENPORT
WEEK ONE DAILY SCHEDULE, WITH NOTES, PART ONE
4:30 AM – Alarm. Pitch black outside. Where am I? Right, the loft, Pittsburgh. Humans were not meant to rise at this hour. One thought: what is the shortest distance between my brain and a cup of coffee? Shower, shave, dress, out the door by 5.

5:15 AM – Arrive Pittsburgh HuggaMug. Darla and the new guy, Jarrett Strong (3rd Battalion, 1st Marines, Navy Cross) already there, God bless them, prepping for 6 am open. First cup of coffee. Coffee is my friend. Did I mention how much I love coffee? The morning's roast in good shape. Confab with Darla about financials, especially transfers to Prosperity City Fund for free coffee and the Prosperity Community Kitchen. God, if Tess saw my balance sheet, she'd strangle me with one of her Crossfit battle ropes. Onward!

6 AM – Open the store. The regulars. Lots of "where you been? We hardly see you anymore!" kidding-on-the-square. Interview a young warrior—Brad— six months back retired from active duty. Darla sits in. Brad is skinny, nervous, definitely on something—probably some psych meds—and makes the mistake of lying about it, like we can't tell. *We've been there, dude.* I was ready to let him walk but Darla told him to come back in a week. She walks him to his bike: she talks, he nods. She slips him a twenty. I hope he listens.

7 AM – Headed to Prosperity. "What's My Age Again?" by Blink 182 comes up on the oldies station. I remember the video (the three naked guys!), smile. Dudes must be in their 50s by now, probably playing state fairs and Indian casinos singing about how tough it is to be 23.

7:30 AM –Prosperity "Pay What You Can" HuggaMug. Line down the street, but it goes fast since we're just handing out cups, no espresso drinks. Makayla's there with me as I meet my constituents. Handshakes and selfies. A lot of inquiries about the Community Kitchen, as well as the Free Clinic. Most encouraging? The folks who have lived here their whole lives who smile, tell me how much they're loving "the big comeback." Me too! I thank them: they're the ones doing the work.

8:30 AM – Meet with Betty (and Makayla and the Rev) about what's worth saving in the town, and what needs to be torn down. The three blocks of decrepit row houses just across from the Pulver Forge mill, built around 1910, are a lost cause. They'll have to go. I was happy to hear that the Pulver Library/Recreation Center—the pride of the city when I lived there—can be fixed up, with a little money and a ton of work. The bones are solid: steel, marble and concrete, meant to stand for a hundred years. The Orpheum Theater, an old vaudeville house on Pulver Drive, is in pretty bad shape, but the less grand Majestic Theater on Highland Avenue can be re-opened pretty quickly. Great place for town meetings, concerts, community film events, maybe even comedy nights and a resident theater group.

J.J. Winkler's Department Store on Descanso Avenue can also be saved if we want to put in a lot of work: some water damage and a lot of vandalism. That said, it will probably be worth it.

We need the space for a Jobs Center, Day Care Center, Senior Center, etc.

The Keystone Hotel can be saved: this is the perfect place for families who just need housing. We can get them out of places that are falling down, into a place that's clean and safe. The Hotel Bessemer, an even older building, is in surprisingly good shape. Dr. Kate and her crew have already claimed the 130 rooms: this will become a halfway house, for detoxing the addicted and getting them straightened out. And that great big ballroom is perfect for our Community Kitchen noon meal.

And then finally the Downtown/Main Street area, anchored by Pulver Drive. The Rev tells me that these buildings need the most work, but they'll give us the greatest return on investment. The Arbogast Building can be our Arts Center, offering dirt-cheap rent to young artists/actors/graphic designers. Where there are young, energetic artsy types there are cafes, bookstores, galleries, clothing boutiques, etc. Then there are the ghost storefronts from the Pulver Forge that was: Elkins Hardware. Smokey Nolan's Chevrolet showroom. Bars like The Blind Pig, Chumley's, and the Royale Lounge. Quigley's Drugs and Sundries. Still standing after 97 years is Snooky's, a place that has served ham n' eggs through good times and bad. Right now, it's the breakfast hang-out for the Pulver Forge Patriots.

We'll bring this back, and it will be what it was: the heart of the town. I have a concern: what if we, the people of Prosperity, put in a million dollars of sweat equity, bring the city back, and outsiders buy this property to cash in on the comeback? Betty says we need to create a community foundation that can save this property for the people of the town. Let's do that! When? How??

10 A.M — Our clean-up crews are working miracles with the long-since abandoned Pulver Medical Building on Birchwood Avenue, new (temporary) home of the Dave Bratton Free

Community Care Clinic. More steel and concrete: the work is clearing out the rotted detritus of five decades of slipshod "renovations and improvements": the drop ceilings with asbestos soundproofing tiles, crumbling drywall from failed office sub-divisions, and miles of defunct fluorescent tube lighting.

Kate has recruited five retired nurses along with twenty-plus other volunteers to staff the clinic, and they are already treating patients on an ad hoc basis until all the permits and approvals come in. "We've got folks coming in who haven't seen a doctor in twenty years. We've got pregnant teens, battered wives, dope-sick twenty-somethings. We're going to have to add a dental clinic, and places for childcare and geriatric care. The thing that breaks my heart is that everyone is so damn grateful for the pitiful level of care we're giving them."

One of the volunteers is an FOK (Friend of Kate's) named Brad Beckham. Brad ran the business side of Kate's hospital until he was forcibly "retired" by the bean counting greedbags who bought the place. He's a whiz at getting the place set up to reap the goodness of every possible federal and state program. If you've got insurance (especially Medicare), you pay on a sliding scale. No insurance, you're covered. Checkups, pregnancy care, child care, substance abuse treatment, check ins, everybody gets seen, everybody gets helped. Kate and her staff are prescribing pharma drugs as a last resort instead of a fast way to get rid of patients. I haven't seen Kate this happy in quite a while. She actually thanked me! "For what?" I said. "Are you kidding? I'm back to helping people. It feels good." Her hugs are the only thing I like better than coffee.

11 AM — Meet with Wilda Malone, Principal at Pulver Forge High School. She's here to give us her list of students for our new summer intern program.

Wilda is someone who has touched everyone on our team. Kate Walther helped her survive and recover from breast cancer three years ago. Kate recruited Chef Betty to prepare special meals for her, as Wilda decided to build her cancer recovery on a rigorous vegan nutrition program. She chose Yandy to create and supervise the PF High School vegetable garden, a learn-by-doing project for 83 students. She's both a member of Reverend Luke's church and a soloist in the choir. Wilda convinced half of her student body to take summer jobs with us. These are real internships: "learn by doing" jobs that will train her kids how to grow, harvest, prepare and serve food, how to nurse people back to health at the med clinic, how to fix cars and how to create media to help us tell our story to ourselves, and the world.

11:30 AM—Met with Makayla about starting our Internet radio station. "I know a guy, did a story on him, he does one of these stations as a hobby, incredibly popular." Makayla's friend was Dan Dalrymple, formerly known as "Dapper Dan Diamond, dipping into the Diamond Mine of Your Mind" when he was the afternoon drive-time jock on KPPT, Pittsburgh's premiere Top 40 radio station. Now in his 70s, he has kept himself busy operating "DanTheManRadio" out of his garage. This was an Internet radio station that pumped out solid gold hits from the 50s and 60s along with jingles and period commercials. Makayla had told him what we were up to, and he agreed to come over and help us set up our station…as long as he got to do "The Diamond Mine," a weekly three-hour air shift playing his favorite oldies. That's a bargain I was happy to make.

CHAPTER THIRTY-SIX

June 7 Continued
MIKE DAVENPORT
WEEK ONE DAILY SCHEDULE, WITH NOTES, PART TWO
12:15 PM Lunch with Reverend Luke (and two hundred of his closest friends) at the Prosperity Community Kitchen. One of our most important goals was to show the town we could do big things quickly. The Rev and his sidekick Chef Betty shifted their weekly community kitchen efforts to the Hotel Bessemer ballroom. I was nervous about feeding all these people, but Yandy mobilized the Jarhead Sodbusters, and the Rev told me not to worry: "People will love a chance to be a part of something this crazy." He was right, as always.

A big decision—something we talked about for quite a while—was whether our Prosperity Community Kitchen should only serve the people who were working our program, or whether we should invite everyone who wanted (needed) a meal. Makayla, Nick, and I lined up on the side of just feeding our Prosperity partners who had joined our program. The Rev, Betty and Dr. Kate argued for letting everyone in. They wanted to serve the greater community and motivate the freeloaders to volunteer out of guilt. And so we fought, switched sides, and then compromised. Every one of our Prosperity partners could get a meal…and bring a guest. Those who didn't have a guest would be paired with someone in line outside the Kitchen. At the end of the meal, if there were still people in line and we still had food, they'd be allowed to come in and eat. So far, every single person who showed up had been fed.

This particular day—the third day of the program—we were doing pretty well. Just about all the seats were taken, and—the best part—just about everyone had been paired with a "neighbor" waiting outside. The meal started at noon, welcoming workers coming off their four-hour shift in the gardens (or wherever). The second shift also showed up for a meal, since they had to be ready to work at 1 pm. I tried a little of everything: Betty's "loaded vegan chili," mixed greens salad dressed with Balsamic vinaigrette, a slice of fresh sourdough bread, lentil casserole with mushrooms, and an apple crisp for dessert. "Well," I said to the Reverend as I handed him a coffee, "What do you think? You happy?"

"I'm happy that our friends here in Prosperity are getting fed," he said. "I'm happy they're out in the sunshine working rather than sitting at home marinating in the toxic stew of cable news and social media."

"So, you think this thing is going to work?"

He took a sip of coffee. "No," he said. "I don't."

I was shocked. It took me a moment to consider this. "You don't?"

"You asked my opinion. No, I don't think it'll work. I think we'll fail." He was smiling as he said this, gazing at the crowd of diners.

"Why?"

"Name one venture of this type, on this scale, that's ever succeeded. Besides Cuba."

"Okay. Then why are you here? Your whole life has been about…"

"My whole life has delivered me to this moment, Michael. I'm here so the cynic inside me can step aside and the holy spirit of our Lord Jesus Christ, creator, redeemer, sustainer and rescuer of sinners can flow through me into this fallen world and perform miracles like the one we both wish for."

"Fair enough," I said.

"How much do you know about me?" he said with a sly smile.

"Not much. I heard something about you being a big shot preacher a coupla years ago…"

"Let me tell you a story."

CHAPTER THIRTY-SEVEN

REVEREND LUKE BRAMLETT

There was a time not that long ago that Lucifer Divine Bramlett was the most influential African American evangelical Christian minister in America. He was invited to the Oval Office of the White House to discuss education policy. The sermons he shared with his six thousand parishioners were broadcast nationwide into eleven million homes. He was what today's young people would call 'a thing.'"

He had become a Christian minister because it was the family business. His father, Bartholomew Solomon Bramlett, built the first Black mega-church in East Texas, and when he retired, thirty-one-year-old Lucifer, by then known as Luke, was anointed to continue God's work. His job was to go out there every Sunday morning and sell the message of the prosperity gospel to his customers: that if they were righteous Christian soldiers who prayed hard enough and imagined themselves behind the wheel of that new Lexus (and tithed ten percent of their income to the ministry), then God would look on them with favor and reward them by making their dreams come true. Matthew 21:22: 'And all things, whatsoever ye shall ask in prayer, believing, ye shall receive.'"

It was a great story and Luke loved telling it. He knew it so well he didn't think of it as a story, it was the revealed truth of our beloved Lord/Savior/Holy ATM Machine. Luke certainly didn't question the two million dollars a year God bestowed on him, or the BMW M8 convertible he drove, or his three-acre estate at the end of a cul-de-sac in a gated, mostly white community.

The problem was this: if he was so blessed, why was he so miserable? No matter how much he had, he always felt this emptiness, like there was something more just beyond his reach. Why, that honky minister in Dallas drove a Bentley convertible and had a three-hole golf course on his estate! Luke was so much the better preacher than this pale pretender! Those things were rightfully his!

Luke had married his high school sweetheart right after they graduated from Abilene Christian College. She was the daughter of his father's lawyer, and it was a marriage that made the parents happy. Her job was to raise their three kids while he hobnobbed with political bigshots, guested on cable news shows and flew around the country attending evangelical conferences. He had a job and he aced it. He was a Black mascot for conservative politicians, living proof that there was no racial prejudice out there because 'look at Reverend Luke Bramlett, a righteous, wealthy bootstrapping Black man!'

He'd speak at crusades, twenty thousand people, and give his stump speech: *'Don't be pitiful! Be powerful!' You've got to have a breakdown so you can break through! That's when your wishbone turns into a backbone!'* Standing ovations everywhere he went…and that's when he really began to feel like a fraud. He felt like a hack Vegas lounge comic spoon-feeding the rubes market-tested applause lines, pandering to them, massaging their prejudices. Worse yet, he felt like a minstrel, doing the work of the white man to keep Black people from organizing, fighting for justice, and demanding their rights. He'd just turned forty and he was suddenly horrified that the rest of his life would be nothing but what he was doing now, barking out these motivational bromides on remote control. He'd made the easy, safe choice at every point in his life, and suddenly none of it meant anything. He was a hollow man play-acting in a drama written by someone else. It scared him.

And then…Maxine.

She was a white woman, one of his parishioners. She was a pistol: a former glamour-girl host of "Good Morning Houston!" Now she was one of those high-flying, super-achieving real estate dynamos. She was just bailing on an abusive marriage, and she gushed about Luke: the power of his words, how his sermons were the one thing saving her from despair. She showed up at a "Meet Your Preacher" coffee gathering after the 11:15 service and nailed him with those emerald green eyes. He invited her to lunch, and then…. Luke knew it was wrong, but he felt *alive* when he was with her. The whole thing was thrilling, including the notion that they might get caught. Soon they were meeting at the empty luxury homes she was showcasing for clients. They'd rendezvous, drink some wine, and then… cocaine.

Luke was shocked at how much he loved cocaine. Coke was the god he didn't know he was looking for. It was a revelation. It gave him the kind of rapture he'd expected from loving the almighty. He'd take a snort and the whole world would fall away and he'd ascend to a celestial realm of perfect, stupefied bliss. For that golden hour when he was buzzed, he was who he pretended to be the rest of the day, who the world told him he was: charismatic, wise, and immortal.

He started getting reckless. He was buying the stuff from a friend of a friend, a filthy-rich beer distributor in his congregation. He started "borrowing" from the church treasury to replenish his supply. And then one afternoon, the bill came due.

He and Maxie were enjoying a spirited afternoon in the bedroom of a hideous Zeppelin hanger of a McMansion she was trying to sell in Preston Hollow. They'd consumed a bottle of Chardonnay with foie gras and then gone for a nude swim. They got mellow in the hot tub and adjourned to the futon he'd set up in the sun room. They coked up and went at it like two feral cats. Luke was just about to climax when his vision blurred, and he couldn't catch his breath. And then an elephant plopped on his chest. Maxine was naked, screaming, trying to fish the cellphone of out of her purse so she could call 911.

And then Luke was hovering over himself, looking down on his twitching, prostrate body from the ceiling. He looked terrible! His skin was turning pale green! He yelled at himself to wake up. But nothing happened, it was like he wasn't there. Then the whole scene fell away, and he was plunged into darkness. And then *they* began to appear all around me, hissing and clawing at me.

Demons.

He'd never believed in God, REALLY believed, it was all just a business deal to him. The Bible was like Star Wars: a nice story that was fun to tell and made everyone feel good…and, of course, telling that fun story was making him rich. And in that moment, he knew he'd made a terrible mistake. He had sinned in the worst imaginable way: he had corrupted the sacred for his own secular purposes. He knew in a blink that he was going to spend eternity in hell…if his spirit wasn't snuffed out entirely. He opened my mouth to scream in agony…and no sound came out. He was a nothing nobody, nowhere. He was alone in his anguish.

And then…somewhere in the deepest recess of his mind, he heard a single, whispered word. 'Pray!' At first, he didn't believe it, but then the demons started to move in and he knew they were going to tear him apart. He shut eyes and began to pray the first thing that came into my mind, the twenty-third psalm. "Though I walk through the valley of the shadow of death, I will fear no evil: for thou art with me and I will dwell in the house of the Lord forever." He kept his eyes shut and said this over and over, whittling it down until all he was saying was, 'for thou art with me, for thou art with me, for thou art with me.' And then he saw the tiniest pinprick of white light, and the demons shrieked! Threw up their hands, started to back away. Luke prayed louder, and the light got brighter, and the demons backed away even further until they seemed to vaporize. And then he was swallowed by the white light and in a single instant he was in this celestial realm, kneeling before a kind of otherworldly radiance, a perfect illumination of the infinite spirit of a living God.

Luke was shocked beyond words, considering what a depraved life he'd led. He saw his entire life flash before his eyes. He expected an ESPN highlight reel. Instead, it was a cascade of moments where he either chose to love people or to use them: or worse, ignore them. He saw himself sleepwalking through his life, surrounded by people—his wife, friends, children, his flock—who were begging to be seen, to be loved. Luke was devastated as he watched himself blow off his daughter's cello recital for a rendezvous with Maxine, and then lie about it. The worst part was that he felt what his daughter was feeling. He felt her sadness, literally felt it in his chest and heart. He saw himself up in the pulpit mouthing a bunch of pseudo-religious argle-bargle to thousands of people who were desperate to be in the presence of God, to feel God's spirit inside them. They wanted to wake up to God's love, and he was putting them to sleep as he mused over what he was going to order for lunch at that French bistro Maxine loved. At every fork in the road, he saw himself taking the wrong path, feeding his own ego and mocking God.

When it was over he was weeping. He had no idea why he was where he was. It was clear that he was a hopeless sinner, unworthy of salvation. He begged God to hurl him back into that pit of hell and let him die. He had wasted this precious life he'd been given. And God told Luke that he was wrong. He asked God to name one good thing he'd done. And God told him that

Luke had redeemed himself, at the lowest moment of his life, by reaching out to God in prayer.

Of course, God didn't speak to him as a friend would. It was a psychic communication, spirit to spirit, soul to soul, and it was crystal clear. Because of an act of utter depravity resulting in a heart attack that produced scandal, disgrace and dishonor, Luke was finally ready to become the man he should have been all along! After a lifetime of sin, he was ready to lead his flock to the promised land. He was Paul rendered blind on the road to Damascus, returned with a message of good news so powerful it could make sinners righteous, crooked men straight and profane men holy. And all they had to do was see this new man for who he was and let the pure spirit of Jesus Christ flow through him into their immortal souls. Luke wept at the opportunity to share what had happened to him so that they could know the joy that was in his heart.

Just one problem: the hypocritical bastards who ran the church wouldn't let him *near* the pulpit. The scandal was too much, the lead item on the local news for a week. By the time Luke could leave the hospital, they had a new guy who was spewing the same rancid bullshit he'd been "preaching"! And then Luke understood that the church was a racket, designed as a firewall to protect the flock from the real, radical transformative love of Jesus. Nothing there for him. Luke couldn't stop laughing…and crying, of course.

His wife divorced him and took the kids, and he lost every single thing he didn't need. He had a new job now: to be with God's people, to feed them, shelter them, show them kindness, and give them the good news: that if they accepted God's love, they'll live forever with Him in heaven. This isn't something he "believed": it was something he knew. Every morning, he said to himself, "I am what God is doing on the earth. I will share this good news with my every breath until such time as, like my hero the Apostle Paul, I'm executed by the state and dumped in an unmarked grave. And my dying breath will be a prayer of thanks to God for my second life, a life of pure joy."

And that's how he ended up in Pulver Forge. He founded "The First Church of Jesus Christ, Troublemaker." He had a single picture over his bed: a Cubist dream of Saint Teresa of Avila, painted by Rachel, a fierce artistic spirit, nineteen years old, an overdose victim. Under the picture were the words:

'Christ has no body now but yours. No hands, no feet on earth, but yours. Yours are the eyes through which Christ looks compassion into the world. Yours are the feet with which Christ walks to do good. Yours are the hands with which Christ blesses the world.'

And so, his mission: be the hands, feet, eyes and body of Christ and bless the world every day. Do the work that's right in front of him. Believe in miracles, because one happened to him.

CHAPTER THIRTY-EIGHT

June 11
MOSES CREAVEY
"How much?" said Moses Creavey. His Cessna Citation XLS jet was over the Rocky Mountains, on the way back to Las Vegas. Creavey was nursing a Perrier with a squirt of cranberry juice and a wedge of lime, a pathetic counterfeit of his beloved Beefeater Gin double martini, three olives.

"Two million," said his only passenger, Gavin Cutler. Cutler was the latest go-to campaign wizard. Late 30's, tall and angular: designer jeans, Converse Chuck Taylors, and a hoody that said, "Rap is Something You Do, Hip-Hop is Something You Live." He wore nerd-genius black-frame glasses, like a video game mogul or an alt-rock music producer. He was a prize booking on conservative yak shows after he got Senator Kelby Dobbs re-elected despite Dobbs getting caught on smartphone video canoodling a foxy intern. He presented as smug, but Creavey needed him. Or did he? "That's two million all in, including the TV and Internet buys, 3 mailers, the FB and Instagram war room, working alliances with Pulver Forge Heritage and the R-Ones, five events for Mayor Fred and the GOTV operation, through election day."

"Two million is on the steep side."

"Is it? You told me you want to win."

"We're talking about a hick town of 10,000, that's got, what, thirty-five hundred voters? That's seventy thousand a vote. I think Mayor Fred spent twenty thou all-in the last time he won."

"Yeah, well, yard signs and Rotary luncheons aren't going to get it done this time, Moses. We're talking about rehabilitating a candidate who got slaughtered less than a year ago. Sixteen hundred to nine hundred? I've seen hangings less one-sided than that. And the climb is steeper this time. We've both seen the research. They like the new guy. The place is on fire, in a good way. This is a big lift, turning the town against him."

"So, what's your plan? Got something on Davenport?"

"Have we got a deal?"

"Tell me your plan. I'm not buying a pig in a poke."

"My plan is my product. You don't give away your product, I don't give away mine."

"Thanks for meeting with me, Mr. Cutler. I think we're done."

Cutler shook his head and let out a loud sigh. "Okay. So, I'll give you a taste. Your biggest problem? The new guy is world class at selling hope, and the people are buying. Good god, he's got 75-year-old ex-steel workers weeding spinach beds for four hours a day. He's feeding everyone on his own dime. They're getting health care. Kids are getting off drugs. There's a big town party every Friday night. And you know the best part that's the worst part?"

"Tell me, genius."

"The optics. He's not some windy, big spending liberal do-gooder. No government involved! I don't know why he bothered running for Mayor. He's the real deal, and people get that. That's why they're volunteering. He's getting community buy-in that…well, I've never seen anything like it. He's only got about ten percent working so far, but if this thing catches fire…"

"It's your job to stomp out that fire. So, what's your plan?"

"Your only hope is to strip the bark off this guy, make people believe he's a phony. What if this guy isn't who he says he is? What if there's some secret reason he's doing all this? What if this is something that's even scarier than 'big government'?"

"What's scarier than big government?"

Cutler smiled. "I call it 'the blob.' It's THEM. It's every shadowy group people rage at on the Internet. It's the evil cabal that's had its foot on the neck of these people for a hundred years."

"Oh," said Creavey. "You mean the Jews. Like me."

Cutler laughed. "Let's call them, 'the global elites.' And this is the final insult!" Cutler couldn't help himself. He loved his job so much he was going to show this skeptic his cards. "The Blob shut down the mill, shipped their job overseas, got them begging for shit minimum wage jobs at MaxxMart, shot new-fangled dope through a fire hose into the town square, and all just to fatten the bottom line and goose the stock price." Cutler leaned forward, his voice barely above a whisper. "And now—the killshot! The Blob wants them working *for free*. The whole town is its wholly owned plantation. Slave labor, the point from the beginning. We confirm their worst fears: that Davenport and his pals are cynical hucksters and everyone who works on their plantation is a dupe and a mark. The new casino is the only hope they've got. And that's all you get for free."

Creavey was impressed, despite himself. "Okay. I can see it. I'll give you a million."

Cutler leaned back and hooted. "You kill me, you know that?" He scrutinized him with a wry grin. "I'm betting that a million dollars is what your casinos make every, what, eighteen minutes? So, keep one of them open an extra eighteen minutes and give me what I need."

"For my two million," said Creavey, "do you guarantee a win?"

"I'm allergic to guarantees, because they don't mean a damn thing. So, what are you going to do if we lose, besides never hire me again?"

"Half up front, half at the election day victory celebration."

"Mister Creavey, there isn't a consultant in the world dumb enough to make that deal. Let's say we win. What's your motivation to pay me? And if we lose, well..." Cutler let that hang in the air. "Look, I've run Senate campaigns worth fifty million, where I cut myself a six-million-dollar slice. Two million all in? This is a frickin' hobby project."

Creavey stared at him for a very long moment, and then gave Cutler his smallest nod. Cutler gave back his smallest smile. "Okay. Just, you know, win."

"That's the plan. We go big on July 4."

Cutler settled back into his buttery-soft taupe leather lounger and summoned the flight attendant. He ordered a Beefeater gin double martini with three olives. And when she served it, Cutler gave it a loving glance, then savored it in a way that made Creavey loathe him. Slurping it? Smacking his lips? Really? "Two million," he thought to himself. "This is a hobby project for me too." If Cutler screwed him, Creavey would make sure he burned him to the ground with everyone on his political action list.

Creavey thought about ordering another Perrier and cranberry juice, and then thought the hell with it.

CHAPTER THIRTY-NINE

June 23

MIKE DAVENPORT

Another non-stop jubilee of toil and travail in Prosperity, PA. I was exhausted, but it was a good kind of tired: I'd spent the day grappling with the real problems of people who were struggling to make this thing work. Where could we get more mulch for the spinach beds? Who had the tractor with the newer rotary tiller? Who could pick up the truckload of day-old bread from the MaxxMart for the noon meal?

Now it was time to head home. I'd parked next to the HuggaMug pop-up on Main Street. I was almost there when a flash of light caught my eye: a block and a half down, blinking through an open doorway. The Med Clinic. That reminded me, I had some good news for Kate. One of Dave Bratton's junkie pals, Pete Vogler, had been cadging meals at the Prosperity Kitchen. The Rev befriended him, got him to 'fess up about his addiction, and walked him over to the Free Clinic. Kate got him set up on Suboxone and then got him a place to detox in the Hotel Bessmer, where Kate had a small group of reformed addicts to help people get clean. It took him a week, but he finally told Kate about the village drug store one town over in Struthers, where he was getting his stuff. She told the Chief, and the Chief rang up the FBI, who put the place under surveillance. Amazing how a humble pharmacy in a town of six hundred people could dispense more than two million pills a month. The pharmacists were trading drugs for sex, giving prescriptions to people they friended on Facebook, and making deals with local dentists to pull teeth to justify writing pain pill prescriptions. Now these scumbags were going down hard. A small victory, but sweet.

As I got near the clinic, I heard a voice that stopped me cold: the frantic rasp of someone having a psychotic break. I'd heard that kind of glottal howl before, in Afghanistan, and it was always followed by some eruption of ferocity, usually from an M4 Carbine. Then I heard Kate Walther's voice trying to calm the guy down. And I broke into a dead run.

I flew through the door, past the beat-up registration/intake desk and through the black vinyl curtain into the first examination room. Kate was cornered by a burly guy, shaved head, ragged clothes, wielding a Smith & Wesson "Extreme Ops" seven-inch knife with a wicked serrated clip point blade. Kate was having no success talking this guy down off whatever drug he was riding as her eyes flicked to me then back to him. "I haven't got them. If I had them, I'd give them to you."

"Bullshit, lady. I know you've got them; everybody knows. And I need them. NOW."

"I've got other stuff…" she said. Another eye flick so fast even I almost missed it. *Do something.*

"NO!" And with that he moved toward her, ready to stab her in the chest.

I launched myself at the guy's back, crashing him to the floor. The knife clattered toward Kate. As I moved to pull his arm behind his back, he shocked me by bucking me off him and flipping himself to his feet. He squared off against me, and I knew he had the advantage: his eyes were adrenalized pinwheels. He charged me. I ducked my head and used it to bash his solar plexus, crushing his diaphragm. His eyes widened as he realized he couldn't breathe. I grabbed his left hand with my right and clutched his throat with my left. Kate jabbed his arm with a needle: sedative, industrial strength.

Deputy Maggie Carson and Deputy Axel Doyle arrived from the Sheriff's Department. They got the cuffs on him and rolled him face-down on the floor. In the scuffle, his sleeveless sweatshirt had been ripped off. I stared at his back. Between his shoulder blades, there was a black tattoo of a skull-faced angel of death firing a Beretta M9 into the head of a dead ringer for Kate's attacker, with the crimson blood gush turning into red butterflies. And his torso? Five rows of etched names.

Kate looked at the names. "War dead. Everyone who was killed in Afghanistan when he was there."

"You know this guy?"

She continued to stare at him. Her blonde hair was an unruly mop, and her face was damp with sweat. "Max Stone. Maxton, to be exact. Homeless speed freak. He's not a criminal, he's just…you know, out of his mind. He's come around several times trying to get me write scrip for him. I'd give him Suboxone and beg him to let us help him: get him into the Bessemer, do our ten-day detox. He'd say he'd think about it and disappear."

We both looked at him, lying there unconscious. "What do you want to do with him?"

Kate turned to Maggie, who was taking pictures of the crime scene. "What happens if we call the paramedics?"

"That's up to you. Do you want us to file on him for assault, maybe attempted murder? If so, ummm…there was no bodily injury…twenty years."

I turned to Kate. "Guy's a vet. Afghan war, like me."

"Like Dave," said Kate. That hung in the air for a long moment.

Now I turned to the two Sheriffs. "You know what we're doing here, right?" They both nodded. "We're trying to look after our own, straighten people out without putting them away."

"What are you asking?" said Axel.

"We're both asking," said Kate. "What if we could get this guy over to the rehab center, get him into our program?"

"Lock him in a room with some of his fellow vets," I said. "Maybe they can talk him into going the distance, kicking his habit. If that doesn't work, we'll hand him over to you."

Axel looked at Maggie, who gave him a small nod. He said, "Yeah, if you're all right, I guess we could do that."

Maggie said to Kate, "You sure you're all right?"

Kate looked at me and smiled. "I said I'd help you. This is me helping."

CHAPTER FORTY

June 24
BETTY CHAPEL

Betty Chapel was happy she hadn't killed herself with a last blast of Oxy when she was fourteen. If she had, she'd have missed out on falling in love. Her beloved was a Black, elfin, bespectacled 22-year-old poet named Kimani Holloway-Truth, one of the first residents of the New Prosperity Arts Group in the back-from-the-dead Arbogast Building. She'd won Chef Betty's heart when she passed her this note after a meal at the Prosperity Kitchen:

"Love.

Grace.

Transcendence.

Your Vegan Jalapeño Popper Mac N' Cheese Casserole.

Mercy and Hope.

These are all I need to go with gladness in this world of grief.

(Oh, and your Honey Butter Cornbread.)

All Hail the Culinary Enchanter/

Conjuring Bliss with each lascivious taste of infinity.

May I write your name in the sky/

And conduct a symphony of birdsong to announce your sovereignty?

(And then have seconds?)

Betty tracked her down and asked her on a coffee date. Betty baked her best: carrot-quinoa breakfast cookies, made with pepitas and almond butter. Over two of these and cups of Huggamug's finest, Betty and Kimani swapped life stories.

Kimani was a throwaway kid like Betty: a runaway at 14, rescued by a Black lady librarian named Zosia Behati-Gzifa, who had a converted garage/guest room, no Internet and bookcases on every wall of every room of her cottage. As Betty saved herself with cooking, so Kimani saved herself with the words of Audre Lorde, Aja Monet, Toni Morrison and Lucille Clifton. She heard about Prosperity's pitch to youthful artistic freebooters, hitchhiked here and claimed a studio apartment in the Arbogast.

Kimani made Betty laugh with her ridiculous, exhilarating eruptions of jubilant prose. Betty understood where this came from. They both knew that hope was an act of self-will, that underneath the poetic rapture was a fierce commitment to affirm this new identity that obliterated what had been before: an unloved, unparented, hollow, hopeless, and doomed shuffle to oblivion.

Betty invited Kimani to Quixote Institute gatherings. The two of them noticed something about the great Prosperity experiment they shared with the group. Both of them grew up during the death rattle of the American Dream: the promise that life was fair, endless hard work was rewarded with material plenty, and that life would always get bigger, better, faster, newer, cheaper and happier.

Now, here in Prosperity, all of that had vanished. And what was left was a chance to relax in the mundane glory of "enough." Enough food, enough work, enough rest: enough time to enjoy the real pleasures of life, like love and friendship. Time to savor great food, create beauty, and make love in the afternoon whenever they felt like it. There was no need to chase happiness, it was right here!

Betty and Kimani were both on the same mission: to awaken their fellow townsfolk to the pleasures of this very moment. This taste, this sunrise, this flight of fancy: this instant that is all we have, all will ever be. So different from the history of Pulver Forge, and the history of western civilization, for that matter. No more hurling bodies into a charnel house of industry for the survival of the many and the enrichment of the few. No more self-flagellation for "failing" to prosper in a rigged global casino wrecking millions of lives and ravaging the planet by design.

Their lives were so simple. Kimani worked 12 hours a week growing spinach, and another 12 hours (at least) helping Betty clean and chop veggies, make sandwiches and prep casseroles. They had stepped outside the cultural hallucination that "*Today I will (blank) so that someday I will (blank) and then finally I will (blank), and only then will I be happy because everything will finally be perfect.*" Everything was already as perfect as it was going to get, filled with the blessings of 'enough.'

CHAPTER FORTY-ONE

June 25

MAKAYLA NICHOLS

Blade Kingston was almost done with his Keynote presentation to Mike and friends, and Makayla had to admit that it was slick. Kingston was a power Hollywood type, skinny nerd division: faux-vintage round-frame glasses, dark blue blazer over a black t-shirt, jeans, sneakers and a Pittsburgh Crawfords Negro League ballcap.

"So that's my pitch," he said. "As far as I can tell, there's absolutely no reason for you not to do this, and every possible reason for us to get in business together. This show is going to share what you're doing with the world. I don't have to make you into heroes, you already are. When this thing goes viral, Prosperity will become a tourist mecca. That means new restaurants, hotels, t-shirt shops…you'll have so much money rolling in you'll be able to bankroll every one of your best ideas." As someone who knew the television business, Makayla could spot an expert in fake sincerity, and this guy oozed it. "I'm sure you can tell how excited I am about this show. It's not just another project: it's something I'm passionate about. Something that's worth doing. Any questions? If not, I'll just…"

"I have one," said Makayla. "A couple, actually."

"That's great, uhhhhh…"

"Makayla."

"Makayla, right, but before I get to you, I'd like to get Mike's reaction." He turned to Mike. "Mister Mayor?" Makayla kept her face impassive as she thought *smug sexist dickhead.*

"You've certainly given us something to think about, Blade," said Mike. "God knows we could use the money this thing would bring in."

"Great," said Blade, grinning. "It's June 25 now, we can have a crew here grabbing your July 4th celebration, great way to kick this thing off."

"That said," said Mike, "Steve and Makayla are here to poke holes in your idea."

Before Makayla could speak up, Blade said, "Steve? Can you see the possibilities here?"

"I'm still trying to figure out the financials," Steve said. "We give you the cable rights to shoot this reality TV show here in Prosperity…"

"Actually, you give us 'all media' rights, but go ahead," said Blade.

"Wait a minute, you said this would be a cable show."

"That's what we think," said Blade, "But even as I was pitching it, I started to think we could push this onto a bigger narrative platform. Why not start with the networks? If they don't bite, we'll go to streaming services like Netflix, Prime, Apple, Disney Plus. After that, we'll take it to the cable nets. Wherever we sell it, my company, Zeitgeist Arts, will have the rights. Very small point, won't make a difference to the quality of the show, but I want to be clear on that."

"Okay," said Steve, "we sell you the rights, and we get, basically, a percentage…what was it?"

"Five percent," said Blade.

"Five percent of whatever you sell it for, which will be, what do you estimate?"

"Depends on who buys," said Blade. "Network? That's twenty-five grand an episode. Cable? More like ten grand. Streaming? Who knows? Ten, twenty, fifty…of course, it could be a half a million or even a million if the series runs for eight years. And you've got as many stories as there are people, so this thing could run eight years easy."

"Still, it doesn't seem like that much for what we're giving you…"

"Steve," said Blade with a patronizing smile, "I can tell you're a dealmaker. What I'd like you to do is research these kinds of deals." Makayla saw Blade turn on his ice-cold "closer" smile. She thought of her old news boss Geoff and grimaced. "You'll see that, most of the time, the subject of a reality TV show gets some kind of four-figure buy-out on the front end. What I'm offering you is on the generous side. The real payoff?" *Dramatic pause. Did he want us to beg him for it?* "Your town becomes known around the world. It becomes a brand. A buzzword. Can you imagine the impact on your town if people fall in love with this thing? If it goes viral? That's the business of reality TV: the money you make by being famous for something people want, and that thing is hope."

"So," said Makayla, knifing into the conversation, "Tell us about the show itself."

"The beauty of reality TV," said Blade in a well-rehearsed 'spontaneous' spiel, "is that people are interested in *people*, especially quirky, engaging people. Prosperity is full of people like this: gritty, real, hard-working, funny, courageous people. The heart of the heartland. We'll follow them around, get up close and personal with them. Watch them interact with their friends and neighbors as they work together to turn this place around. And their friends and neighbors will become America's friends and neighbors."

"When you say 'interact,' you mean what? Argue? Fight?" said Makayla.

This threw Blade just slightly off balance. "No. Not necessarily. I mean, no. Whatever happens happens, but…"

"If there's no fighting, there's no show," said Makayla. "The bigger the fight, the better the show. Conflict equals drama equals viewers. That's why somebody gets fired in every episode of 'The Apprentice,' right? You've always gotta throw somebody off the island."

"That's not our plan…"

"Your plan," said Makayla, "is to come into our town and do whatever you need to gin up some conflict. And that conflict has to happen fast, because you're on a tight budget and you've only got so many shooting days, right?" She turned to Mike. "Which means that Blade will make sure the low-life elements in town will know where he's shooting. They'll show up and do whatever it takes to get on television, and the quickest way to do that is blow something up, set something on fire or punch someone in the face."

Now Blade could see the threat. Makayla stood between him and the deal. "That's completely wrong. We're documentarians. What we put on film is the truth of what we find…"

"Oh, please," said Makayla. "You really gonna spend hours shooting people harvesting spinach, picking up trash and agreeing with each other? You're in the train wreck business, Blade, and if there's not a train being wrecked, you'll damn well dynamite the tracks yourself." She called up her best, sleazy cable commercial announcer voice. *"Tonight, on Prosperity, PA, a beer in the face becomes an epic brawl at the Friday polka party, and the town free clinic is under fire when social media lights up about rumors of a botched abortion."* She turned back to Blade. "And guess who is going to light up social media with those rumors, just to get a bunch of homicidal pro-lifers to show up for your cameras?"

He held her gaze. "That is bullshit."

"Your job in this meeting is to tell us whatever we want to hear so that we'll make the deal that you want, and then you'll burn what we're doing to the ground because that's what sells."

"Boy," said Blade, "I thought I was a cynic."

"I'm not a cynic, Blade," said Makayla. "I used to be a cynic because I was in a cynical business, and I hated it. I quit the so-called news so I could do something worthwhile. We're turning this town around. We're giving people hope. And that doesn't fit into any known cable series template, because what television likes is crisis, conflict, betrayal, rage, violence, fear and hatred: the big lizard brain emotions, out of control. You need the white trash to set themselves on fire, and you'll give them the blow torch. Sorry, Blade, you can't bullshit me. These are my friends; I just want them to know what they're getting into."

CHAPTER FORTY-TWO

MIKE DAVENPORT

"Wow," I said, "You just raised ass-kicking to an art form." Makayla laughed. We were sharing ginger scones and (what else) a cup of coffee. Blade had given up and hustled off to the airport. He was clearly stunned at his failure to close the deal.

"Thanks, I think." She took a bite of scone, washed it down with a sip of coffee. "I'm ashamed to admit how much I enjoyed that."

"Not as much as I did."

Another chuckle, then a pause. "If this thing is going to succeed, we've got to tell our own story. I'm getting terrific stuff: real people going back to work, making friends. We're starting to get thousands of hits on our YouTube channel."

I looked at Makayla. I had something I'd been meaning to say for a long time. I decided to chance it. "I'm starting to think that the best thing that's happened to us in this whole crazy adventure is when you signed up to be part of it."

She was startled. "Why do you say that?"

"Hell, I was ready to get on board with Blade just to get my hands on all those sweet Benjamins, but you stopped it, just shut the whole thing down by telling the truth. And that's because, well…"

"What?"

"You believe in this crazy dream more than I do."

She smiled, lowered her cup, and gave me a shy glance. "Can I tell you why I love what we're doing?" she said.

"Please," I said.

"Because there's something out there called 'What We All Know' and we're giving it a great big kick in the ass."

"Keep talking," I said.

She looked down into her cup. "I quit the news business because What We All Know is that Black people—especially Smart Black FEMALE people—will *never* be popular with white viewers. And I knew that that wasn't going to change, it would be the same ol' shit till I was 35, and then they'd bring in a younger, cheaper version of me to take my seat in the minstrel show. And then you come along with this ridiculous notion of turning around a beaten-down town by ignoring what everyone knows, and so maybe there's hope after all."

"Think so?"

"I do. That's why I had to take down that reality teevee creep. This story is so much bigger than the half hour of cultural mud wrestling. It's...it's what people like me have been waiting for our whole lives."

I looked in her eyes. "I guess I have to, Makayla."

"You and me...all of us...we're in this together," she said. And I thought of my platoon, what we meant to each other. *Yes,* I thought. *We are.*

(MAKAYLA) PROSPERITY BY THE NUMBERS (6 WEEKS IN)

Prosperity is getting cleaner, happier and more optimistic.

773: # of HuggaMug Cups of Coffee Served
293: # Who Paid for Coffee (BETTER!)
184: # Workers in Community Gardens (STILL GREAT!)
218: # Workers for Food Prep/Service/Clean-Up at Community Kitchen
325: #Workers for Town Clean-Up Duty (GETTING THERE)
318: #Workers for Med Clinic, including "Barefoot Doctors" (YES!)
156: #Workers at Radio Station/Newsletter/Podcasting
68: #Mobility Workers (including maintenance)
577: #Workers Miscellaneous Duty (babysitting, mentoring, teaching, caretaking)
1846: #Total Workers
41,766: #Total TimeBucks Issued Previous Week
1,957: #Transactions on "ShareWhere"
1,211: #People at Friday Nite "Hoe-Down"
$629: Money from "Prosperity Gripe Fund" Pretzel Jar

CHAPTER FORTY-THREE

June 26
MIKE DAVENPORT
I knew I was in trouble when I entered the HuggaMug backroom and saw their faces: Steve Dorsey and Darla, along with Makayla, Betty, Yandy and the Rev. The faces were grim and focused on me, like a jury about to drop a death penalty verdict. I'd just finished giving out coffee on the morning shift. "We've got to talk," said Darla.

"Uh oh," I said.

"That giant sucking sound you hear," said Steve, "is your finances." At my instruction, Darla had been pumping money into our little experiment until we "turned the corner," whatever that meant. I'd ignored all her previous "we've got to talk" entreaties.

"We're going broke, Boss." Darla always gave it to me straight. "The community giveaways are killing us: the coffee, the Community Kitchen…"

"That'll get better when we start eating what we grow, right?"

"Right, yes, that'll make a difference," said Darla. "But then there's everything else: the meds and the PPE for the clinic, the mulch and seeds for the gardens, the gear for the cleanup crews…"

"HuggaMug was making six grand a month four months ago," said Steve. "Now you're just breaking even, that's a twenty-four grand flop. Mike, we can't take these new numbers to the bankers. They'll laugh us out of the room."

"Uh huh." I looked at Makayla, who gave me a smile and a nod. So did Yandy. That helped. I said, "When we started all this, I wondered why other towns hadn't done it before. Now I know."

"We made a promise." Makayla's voice was quiet but confident. "We promised these people that if they believed in the dream, we'd be there for them with a meal, health care, and the tools they need to make the dream come true."

"And its working, dammit," said Betty. "They're excited. They can see the change."

"We're getting more volunteers every single day," said Yandy.

The Rev said, "Everything we're measuring—meals served, hours worked, medical clinic visits, buildings renovated, hours worked across the city in every category—every single one is trending in the right direction."

"Right, and good for you," said Darla. "You've gone a long way on a smile and a handshake, but stuff costs money. We have two choices." She paused and scanned the room. Everyone's eyes went to the floor except mine. I'd take it straight. "We can cut back big-time, or we can bankrupt Mike and the whole thing goes to hell anyway."

The Inuits have a word—Qarrtsiluni—which means "sitting together in the darkness, quietly, waiting for something creative or important to occur." That's what happened here. Everyone sat and thought, no one spoke.

Finally I said, "Sometimes you just gotta say 'What the hell.' Anybody here believe we'd get this far? You see those faces at the noon meal? The smiles, the laughter? The hope? Hell, people, I'm in. All the way. To my last dollar." I turned to Steve. "I'm sorry if I wasted your time."

"You didn't, and we're not dead yet," said Steve, but neither of us believed it. More silence. And then the silence was shattered by the braying honk of…what was that? A bus horn? Another honk, then another. Was that for me?

CHAPTER FORTY-FOUR

June 26
MIKE DAVENPORT

"Well," said a grinning Nick Barlow. "Whaddaya think?" My mouth was open. Speechless. Could this be the derelict school bus we'd towed over to Nick's shop? Now it was our new "Prosperity GetAbout." It was a dazzling, immaculate ice cream sundae of a bus, with graphic panels of chrome yellow and azure blue complemented by orange marmalade arrows pointing forward. "C'mon," said Nick, "let's go for a ride."

Nick plopped into the driver's seat and pushed a button on the dash. Second shock: no diesel rumble. The doors flexed shut and all we heard was a soft whrrring noise. We all looked at each other, and I suddenly felt a chill up my spine. "Ah, Nick, how did you pay…"

"I didn't. You need to meet somebody. A friend. That's where we're going."

The Oscar Wells Community Foundation was housed in the old Savoy Ballroom on Marcus Garvey Drive, five blocks from the First Church of Jesus Christ, Troublemaker. It was in the heart of Homewood, the dream of Pulver Forge's notorious (and beloved) numbers kingpin Floyd "Jelly Roll" Jenkins, great benefactor for the Black community in the 1930s and 40s. Jenkins got his start as a bootlegger, then moved into numbers after Prohibition died. He staged heavyweight prizefights in the Savoy and brought in every great Black big band (Ellington, Basie, Jimmie Lunceford, Cab Calloway) to play on Friday and Saturday nights. In the 1950s, the Savoy hosted R&B shows featuring Sam Cooke, Clyde McPhatter, the Platters and Little Richard. Jenkins finally went to prison in 1959 for tax evasion, and the Savoy fell into disrepair.

The Oscar Wells Foundation bought it in 2014, when it became a studio for "big art," especially murals. The place itself was a work of art: each wall was a gigantic fresco commemorating an era of African American history. A Black woman in denim coveralls was detailing the face of Medger Evers on the 1960s Civil Rights wall as we entered. Nick said, "Ahhh, Raven?" The woman turned, smiled and put down her paints. Nick turned to us. "This is Raven Washburn. She paid for the bus conversion, helped me rig it up, and then she and her crew painted it."

I looked at Raven. "Wow. That's awesome. Thank you."

"You're welcome," said Raven. "You're the coffee man, right?'

"That's right."

"I just made a pot. Would you folks like some? Let's have a cup and we'll talk."

We settled into the studio's confab corner: a big, poofy brown leather couch that felt like something from a Playboy Mansion yard sale. She poured seven mugs from a large French Press and handed around a platter of homemade lemon bars. The coffee was "amateur good": hot, clean, and strong. "This is a nice cup," I said.

She nodded her thanks. Then she moved to the center table and picked up a heart-shaped antique wooden box with an elaborate floral pattern carved in the lid. She handed each of us a small nugget of scrap steel. She said, "If you want to know what I'm up to, you have to know who Oscar Wells was."

"Please tell us," said the Rev.

"Oscar Wells was my grandfather. He was born in Georgia in 1898, arrived in Pulver Forge as part of the Great Migration in

1920. The mill folks started him at 33 cents an hour, six and half days a week. He and the other Black men got the worst mill jobs, like shoveling red hot coke-iron muck while they tried not to faint from the soot and fumes. The half-day on Sunday he got off, he played ball for our Negro League team, the Pulver Forge Iron Men. His nickname was Cannonball Wells, struck out 20 batters three different times."

"Holy shit," said Nick.

Raven continued. "He married my grandmother, Bertha Weems, in 1926. He was 28, she was 20. When the Depression hit, Pulver's son, Lambert Selden Pulver, who had inherited the Mill from his father, tried to do the right thing by the workers: rather than laying men off, he put everyone on a single nine to five shift. Unfortunately, men like Oscar couldn't survive on what Pulver paid them, so they took extra jobs. My grandfather worked eight hours in the mill, then another eight delivering coal, hauling ice, digging graves or shoveling snow. Bertha got a job as a housemaid in Rockhurst Castle, the old Pulver Mansion. That's where she met Lambert. Would anyone like more coffee?"

"I think we're good," said the Rev. "Please keep going."

"You all have your steel nugget?" she asked. We nodded. "In 1931, a sleep-deprived Oscar Wells tripped over a rigger's hose in the mill and fell into the foundry ladle full of molten steel. He was…liquified." She paused to let us take that in. I rubbed the nugget between my thumb and index finger. "This had happened before, and the mill had a policy: dump the tainted steel in a vacant lot. With no body to bury, friends of my grandfather took some of the polluted steel, formed it into nuggets and gave them to my grandmother in this box. What you are holding is the mortal remains of my grandfather, Oscar Wells." I squirmed. Raven said, "For years after Oscar's death, steelworkers swore they could hear his anguished cries in the mill, followed by demonic laughter. He haunted the place."

Another pause. Finally, I said, "So how did you…"

"I was born on May 28, 1964. My mother, Flora, was a single mom. She worked as an organizer for the NAACP right through the 60s and 70s. She was suffering from dementia before her death in 1997, and she kept repeating this tall tale: that we both had "Pulver blood." When she finally passed, just for kicks I got a DNA test, and—holy crap—she was right! When I went through her things, I discovered that I was conceived on the day that Dr. King gave his 'I Have a Dream' speech, and the sperm donor was a young white Civil Rights worker named Marshall Dodsworth."

"Marshall Dodsworth?" said Betty. "The politician? State Rep from, let's see, Connecticut, right?"

"Right," said Raven. "I rang up Representative Dodsworth and to his credit, he 'fessed up. He was relieved to hear that I just wanted one thing from him: to bankroll my lawsuit against the Pulver Foundation, which was very healthy thanks to Enoch's decision to have his millions of dollars professionally invested, with the heirs getting well-defined payouts at regular intervals as long as they didn't meddle."

"Oh my God!" said Makayla. "I heard about this. It was a big deal. You won, right?"

"Right," said Raven, smiling. "My mother was the illegitimate daughter of Bertha Weems and Lambert Selden Pulver. Born November 29, 1932."

"As you got…what…"

"Seven and a half million dollars."

Physicists say that at the dead center of an atomic bomb blast there's an infinite silence: that's what descended on the room. We froze: no sound, no movement.

Finally, the Rev said, "With all of that wonderful money, why do you still live here?"

"Because it's not my money," she said.

"It isn't?" he said. "Then whose is it?"

She took her time answering. "I did nothing to earn that money. It belongs to my grandfather, and all those men who worked beside him in that mill. They're gone, they can't do a thing. I can. That money is to make the world the kind of place where people don't have to risk death to make a living." She looked at me. "I've been watching you folks for months, hoping you were for real. Then fate delivered Nick to my door, and I had a chance to help. I enjoyed myself, and I want to keep helping. So, what can I do to make sure this thing succeeds?"

I turned to Makayla. She mirrored my grin. "About two hours ago," I said, "we—that is, these folks here—were talking about robbing a liquor store to keep our little experiment going. So the answer is, what you can do is whatever you want, which is…what?"

"First of all," she said, "I want to be your Minister of Public Art. My students and I want to paint everything in sight: murals on buildings, street lights, fire hydrants, city busses…"

"DONE!" I shouted, then looked around, abashed. "That is, as Mayor, I'll recommend it."

"Great," she said. She put her coffee mug down. "Look, you're getting the big stuff right. You're changing the way the town thinks of itself, that's huge. You're feeding people, helping them get well, I can feel the place changing just walking around town, it's exciting. You just need a plan to make it pay for itself."

"That's exactly…I mean, you've…I mean…" I was so excited I was babbling.

"Yes!" said Reverend Luke. "We do. And we're hoping you have some thoughts on helping us do that."

"First thing," she said, "you need a Community Bank, a kind of a civic credit union, where people—like me—can put our money so other people can borrow that money to start businesses that will pay fees to the city. That'll support the Prosperity Kitchen and the Med Clinic and fixing up all the buildings."

The Rev perked up. "And the businesses lease the buildings, and the town gets that money, along with the sales tax everyone pays for the goods and services of the business. And that pays for the gardens and the cleanup crews." He turned to me. "And that, my friend, is how Prosperity really works."

"One more thing," said Raven, "and it's a big thing."

"What's that?" said the Rev.

"If this thing works, or rather WHEN it works, people are going to move here, start businesses, fix up the derelict property. We need to form a 'Community Land Trust' to buy up that property now while it's practically free. When all our people are fed and healed and housed and start creating those businesses, we—the people of Prosperity—should own the land so we can make sure it's a local coffee shop that opens up, not Starbucks."

"What about a HuggaMug?" I said.

"You're giving away so much coffee, we'll grandfather you in," said Betty.

"That's where we'll start," said Raven, "because the more the community owns, the happier everyone's going to be five, ten, twenty years from now."

My mind was racing. Yes! This was it. What a find! I looked at the group: everyone was as jacked as I was.

The Rev said, "This town has been waiting for a miracle for 127 years. We've been waiting for you, Raven. This will redeem the memory of your grandfather. This will help lift the Curse of Pulver Forge."

Raven smiled and lifted her coffee mug. "You've been waiting for me? Well, I've been waiting for you." We lifted our mugs, and it was done.

As we walked out, the Rev smiled at me and said, "You know, Mike, I once told you I didn't think this thing would work. I'm starting to think I was wrong."

CHAPTER FORTY-FIVE

July 1
GOVERNOR GOODWIN TUTTLE
Governor Goodwin Tuttle was wrapping up his lunch remarks to the Macklin Grove Kiwanis Club, a must visit for every ambitious Pennsylvania Republican. Macklin Grove was 73.9% Republican, 96.1% white, with plenty of lawn signs in front of double-wide trailers in retirement parks that said, "Keep Your Government Hands Off My Medicare." Tuttle was humble-bragging about his many virtues: church elder, NRA member, Little League baseball coach (although his sons were 26 and 23), favored guest on conservative talk radio, and eater of cheesesteaks, Old Forge-style pizza and pierogis. They were smiling and nodding—this was a yearly visit to a friendly crowd—but Tuttle knew what they really wanted, and oh how he longed to give it to them. "Friends," he wanted to say, "If you do me the honor of making me your next President, I'll bulldoze every abortion clinic, make ownership of AR-15 assault rifles mandatory, revitalize derelict shopping malls by turning them into detention camps for effete liberal elitists, and make fealty to the Pittsburgh Steelers compulsory, with violators subject to televised waterboarding."

But he couldn't say any of those things. The best he could do was describe himself as a fierce warrior for the embattled American Dream and promise them that he'd continue to do what he'd always done: "wake up every morning, have my coffee, and then climb that rough-hewn ladder with my trusty Kentucky long rifle to the top of that wall of the Alamo so I can stand beside the great Davy Crockett and bash the homicidal intruders trying to invade our homes and strangle that American dream. That will never happen on my watch. God bless you, and God bless the United States of America." Hearty applause (three people standing) then some handshakes and fewer selfies than he was hoping for. Then back in his Jeep Wrangler with Burt McNally.

"So…what did you think?" Tuttle was hoping McNally would light him up with a gush of praise, but they'd been on the road for five minutes now, McNally at the wheel, with no conversation. He hated himself for feeling needy.

"You delivered a good meal at a reasonable price, and the customers were satisfied. That said…"

"Yeah?"

"We are still searching for the big new thing. The hobby horse we can ride to the White House. This year's 'RTR'."

RTR was rage juice: McNally shorthand for "rile the rubes." "What about Prosperity?"

"What about it?"

"It's got everything, Burt. This is bottom-up populism. They've put two thousand people back to work in, like, three months. They're growing their own food and cleaning the place up. Crime down, drug deaths down. This is our ticket. This is the people rising up and bringing innovation to the free market, to determine their own destiny, and it's happening on my watch! This is…"

"STOP!" Burt was frowning. What was going on?"

"What is it? We can *own* this thing. I'm the man who brought prosperity to Pennsylvania, can bring it back to America. I'm going to be speaking there on July 4th. That'd be the perfect time to…"

"No, you're not."

"I'm not what?"

Burt hadn't looked at him once, just stared through the windshield. "You're not speaking there on July 4th."

"What? Why not?"

Finally, Burt looked at him. "Because something's going on. All of a sudden, all our talk radio friends are gabbing about that place, and you know what they're calling it? Socialist hellhole, Communist gulag, that kind of stuff. Social media is going ape shit."

"When did all this…"

"Last two days."

Tuttle's brain took a moment to process this. "What could possibly…"

"I don't know, but something's up and we don't know what it is. Maybe somebody's got something on this Davenport guy. Maybe they're cooking their books. Maybe the whole thing is being bankrolled by a cabal of bong-huffing lesbians, or Venezuelan Marxists. We don't know what's going on, and until we figure it out, we're staying well clear of it, okay? We don't say a damn thing."

"But…well, yeah, okay, I guess." Tuttle couldn't fathom what had gone wrong, but McNally had pitch-perfect instincts about this kind of stuff. And nothing was more important than staying on the right side of the grand poohbahs that ruled the right-wing yak-o-sphere.

Goody and Burt drove the rest of the way in silence, with Goodwin staring out the window at the endless parade of fast-food outlets, dollar stores, tattoo parlors and used car lots. And it dawned on him that he envied the people he saw. They didn't live in fear that everything they'd worked for their entire lives could be taken from them in one news cycle.

CHAPTER FORTY-SIX

July 3
TRANSCRIPT OF CODY FORTUNE'S COMMENTARY,
"FIRSTNEWS"

CODY FORTUNE: Department of I Told Ya So: Remember a coupla weeks back when I told ya about this character Mike Davenport? Just got himself elected Mayor of Pulver Forge, Pennsylvania which he then renamed "Prosperity"? He was the media's latest magic man, but something about him didn't smell right to this reporter. The magic felt like pie-in-the-sky free-lunch malarkey, a sprinkling of positive thinking fairy dust on a problem that needed common sense and elbow grease. The reason I decided to do a 'wait and see' on this guy is because he wasn't some Boomer lib reaching for the sledgehammer of big government, big taxes, Big Brother to make this happen. He was a vet, my age, a guy who'd supposedly fought in Afghanistan. What he was proposing was people power: everybody rolling up their sleeves and going to work.

Well now this reporter has uncovered the truth. Tomorrow is July 4th and Prosperity is throwing itself a party. And what's going to happen at this party? I've got a very special guest to tell us. Meet Fred Bagley, the man that Davenport defeated in the mayor's race. Mayor Fred, thanks for coming on.

FRED BAGLEY: My pleasure Cody, love the show.

CODY FORTUNE: So what can you tell us about your hometown?

FRED BAGLEY: What I can tell you is that Mike Davenport is no savior. He's a Marxist-Leninist bent on enslaving the poor people of Pulver Forge who, I mean my God, haven't we suffered enough?

CODY FORTUNE: And you found this out how?

FRED BAGLEY: Good ol' shoe-leather investigating. Digging through records, looking under some rocks, talking to people who know things. The bitter truth is that Mister Davenport is a catspaw of one Raven Washburn…

CODY FORTUNE: Raven Washburn? You mean the Red Raven of Reparations? The one who finagled all that money she'd didn't earn just because her granny seduced the son of the Pulver of Pulver Forge?

FRED BAGLEY: That's right, Cody. At tomorrow's big 4th of July celebration, Mike Davenport is going to introduce her as Prosperity's new Shadow Mayor and Treasury Czar, meaning everyone in town is going to be working on her plantation, and I mean that literally! They'll be working her gardens, for free, so she can buy up the town and make millions when it comes back!

CODY FORTUNE: And there's even more to this story, isn't there?

FRED BAGLEY: There is, Cody. Here's the headline. Mike Davenport isn't the great hero of the Afghan War he pretends to be. He's a disgrace. And once the people of Pulver Forge find that out, there's a good chance they'll recall him, and we can restore some common sense to the government there.

CODY FORTUNE: Wow, that sounds huge, Mayor Bagley. Buzz us up when you find out more, okay?

FRED BAGLEY: My pleasure.

CODY FORTUNE:I had this Davenport character pegged as a Professor Harold Hill type from the git-go, and now? All the libs want is power, and they'll do anything—lie, cheat, steal, stuff ballot boxes—to get it. Be sure and tune in tomorrow night, 'cuz we'll be the only news outlet that will tell you truth about what just might be the scariest beachhead the Reds have ever established here in the good ol' USA. And on July 4th! I mean, what the hell? This is your friend Cody Fortune: when asses need kicking, I've got the boot to do it.

CHAPTER FORTY-SEVEN

July 4

MIKE DAVENPORT

Nick had warned me: something was up. Nick arrived as a skeptic and had become a friend and ally. He'd also become friends with Raven, which boggled everyone considering he was a libertarian curmudgeon, and she was a Black artistic free spirit. But that was the beauty of this experiment: it was about results, and they found common ground producing those results. "Teamwork makes the dream work." Nick and I had coffee on Sunday morning before the July 4th celebration. He told me what Cody Fortune had told his eight million true believers, especially the stuff about "Red Raven" and trashing my war record. We figured Moses Creavey might be cooking something up, probably a recall election. Maybe they'd be gathering names at our community party.

Nick was right. As Darla and I walked toward Pulver Memorial Park, we saw a hundred or so raucous geezers dressed in white short-sleeve shirts, blue vests and red ballcaps, with American flag bow ties. They were huddled under a giant banner that said "PULVER FORGE PATRIOTS: RECALL MOSCOW MIKE." Good ol' Gus Farnum was out in front. Gus stood in line every morning for his free coffee, and never failed to spray me with spittle as he berated me for changing the name of "his" town. (He did put a dollar in the Beef Bucket.) He was a squat octogenarian with a steel-gray flat top with shaved sides. He was yelling into his bullhorn, exhorting passers-by to sign his petition. "Take our town back! Stop the madness! Real jobs, not slave labor!" I decided to walk over and kill him with kindness.

"Hey Gus!"

Gus lowered his bullhorn and squinted at me. It took him a moment to bring me into focus. And then he smirked. "Moscow Mike himself. We're here to spoil your little revolution."

"Oh, come on, Gus, get your signatures then join us! We've got a beer with your name on it!" I turned to his feisty compatriots. "You're all invited!"

Gus took a step toward me. "You're wrecking this town, you Commie bastard, and we're going to put you in prison, where you belong!"

"Wrecking it how?" I said. "By putting people back to work?"

His face turned red. "Work? Slave labor! It's a goddam plantation!"

"Now that's what I don't get," I said, still smiling. "Who's forcing who to do anything, Gus? People are working because they want to."

"You're so full of shit," barked Gus. "You may have those sheeple hypnotized with your Marxist bullshit, but you're going down hard, because we're taking Pulver Forge back!"

"Whatever, Gus. If you're still here in an hour, I'll bring you a plate of barbecue beans." I grabbed a flyer as I walked toward the party.

Ahhh, the party. I was gazing at a thousand (or so) citizens of Prosperity, Pennsylvania celebrating the rebirth of their town in Pulver Memorial Park. They were feasting on the fresh-from-the-garden greenery— lettuce, spinach, chard, arugula—they themselves had grown. Makayla, Kimani and friends were serving up these greens in generous salads. Chef Betty and her crew (including the Rev) were dishing out barbecue beans at the Prosperity Mobile Party Kitchen, along with rice pilaf, steamed veggies, homemade sourdough bread and Dutch apple pie. I served up slugs of Huggamug coffee (of course), along with iced tea and lemonade.

The Sovereign Citizens of Prosperity were sitting with each other, talking to each other, and laughing with each other. Some of them were dancing to "Dollar Bill Fortune and His Beer Barrel Polecats," the polka-friendly mutation of John Glickman and his folksy cohorts in the Pittsburgh Symphony Orchestra. If the bounty of free food from the party kitchen wasn't enough, citizens could sample the wares of their friends and neighbors at homemade booths that ringed the picnic grounds: Kettle Korn, corn dogs, funnel cakes, cotton candy, bacon cheeseburgers, pierogis of every type, and deep-fried Oreos: all the best County Fair cuisine. And they could visit the Zymurgy Brewing Company pop-up for a frosty stein of "Uncle Sam's Red, White and Blue Prosperity Pale Ale."

Time for the speeches. "Four months ago," I said, "we renamed this town 'Prosperity, Pennsylvania.' We set up Beef Buckets where you were very politely asked…" (laugh from crowd) "…to donate one dollar every time you trashed this unlikely endeavor. Well, look around, my friends. We collected 813 dollars—on the honor system! — and it's made all the difference. Fred Bagley says…let me see if I can remember his words… 'I'm a Marxist-Leninist bent on enslaving the poor people of Pulver Forge.' Well, I don't see any slaves here. I see our townsfolk working together to help ourselves turn this town around. That's why we're throwing ourselves this great big, beautiful party, because we've earned it." I introduced our Minister of Abundance, Yandy Lopez, the man who deserved the accolades. This was his night.

Yandy was clad in blue jeans, a crisp white dress shirt, and his beat-up "Havana Sugar Kings" ballcap. "Sure hope you're enjoying all those veggies at the community table," said Yandy, beaming. "Because they were grown in this very garden here in Memorial Park by your mean green garden team. Can I have that team stand up and take a bow?"

A wildly diverse group of sixty-plus people stood up. There were kids in their late teens, men and women in their 70's, resurrected druggies in their 30s, and everything in between. "So, here's the thing. Everybody's having such a good time in the garden, we've now got a waiting list of folks wanting to get their hands dirty. So, we're going to be tearing up some more vacant lots and planting more veggies, only these veggies will be special. We're going to grow stuff we can sell to big-deal gourmet restaurants in Pittsburgh—I already have a list, they've been my customers for years—and you know what we're going to do with that money?"

The crowd shouted, "WHAT?"

"We are going to build ourselves some indoor hydroponic farms, so we can keep growing stuff all through the winter so we can *keep* feeding ourselves!"

Big applause from the crowd, along with chants of "YAN-DY, YAN-DY" as he handed me the microphone. "It is my very great pleasure to introduce the retired publisher of the Pulver Forge Gazette and our unofficial town historian, Calvin McCoy." I can only hope to be as spry as Calvin when I'm 91. He looked dapper in his blue seersucker sports jacket and red polka dot bow tie. He surveyed the crowd and smiled.

"July 4th: an historic day for this town. It was on this day— July 4, 1893—that Grover Freeman Hendricks ordered a mob of strike-breaking hooligans to open fire on a legally assembled crowd of persons in his own employ: working men who were on strike for a living wage, an eight-hour day and a five day work week. Those hooligans killed eleven men that day, including my grandfather, Hiram Gunther McCoy. And they killed more than men. They killed the spirit of this town…and today, because of what we're doing here, that spirit is being reborn!"

People stood up and cheered as McCoy took a long sip of water. "We will remember this day for another reason, my friends. This is the day that Raven Washburn joins us. She is the granddaughter of Enoch Pulver's son, Lambert —yes, she is, really— and she is going to use her well-earned part of the Pulver fortune—get this—to run a community foundation that is going to help us buy up all the derelict property in this town. When this boom reaches its full fruition, that property will benefit all of us, every citizen of Prosperity! Raven, stand up!" Raven stood, held up her plate of barbecue beans, and took a happy bow. Nick was next to her, smiling. Calvin turned back to the crowd. "Friends, let's remember that we've *always* had this power. The mightiest force for change is a community discovering what it cares about and creating its own destiny. Nothing can stop us! Thank you."

Another, longer ovation. McCoy embraced me as I moved back to the podium. "Thank you," he said. No way to top that speech. I nodded to Dollar Bill. The group had changed into 60s fringed cowhide vests and bell bottoms and announced themselves as "Dollar Bill Funkhauser and His Sweet Soul Men." What followed was a steamin' hunk of burning Stax/Volt funk: "Soul Man," "Midnight Hour," "Knock on Wood," "Respect," and "Walkin' the Dog." Makayla grabbed my hand and we joined the crowd in the 'picnic pavilion,' with the tables pushed away so we could get down with our bad selves on the polished cement.

As we danced, I thought about the last five months. I'd pretty much achieved everything I'd promised. The gardens were finally producing a bounty of greens. The cleanup crew was creating hundreds of places to live. The medical clinic was working twelve-hour days that often became sixteen or even twenty hours long as they helped people kick the drugs that helped kill Pulver Forge. Raven and the Community Foundation would float the town's finances long enough to turn the economic corner. Now I could get my coffee business in shape so I could make that million dollar deal I'd been planning for five years. And then I'd get married and spend my days windsurfing, snorkeling and drinking frozen rum drinks. What could possibly go wrong?

CHAPTER FORTY-EIGHT

MIKE DAVENPORT

Funny. The exact moment I had that thought, I saw them: a bunch of goons in ski masks filtering into the crowd. They were all the same age: mid-late twenties, with shaved heads and steroid-pumped bods, all dressed in black polo shirts, black chinos and steel-toe Doc Marten boots. It was the "Righteous Ones," the romper-stomper hate-everything group I'd seen marching in neo-Nazis rallies on television. There were eighteeen of them looking around, then glancing at me, smirking. My gut had kept me alive in Afghanistan. It told me these dudes weren't here to dance. I pulled Makayla off to the side.

"What?" she said. She followed my eyes to the R Ones and then to the flagpole that anchored the modest war memorial near the entrance to the dance floor. One of the R Ones had cut the rope so the American flag flopped into the arms of a colleague. That one showed it off for everyone as the rope-cutter doused it with lighter fluid, tossed it on the cement flagpole base and set it on fire with a Zippo lighter. My stomach lurched as two grinning R Ones grabbed footage of the burning flag with smartphones to the derisive hoots of the others. Then the pack waded into the crowd and started shoving people. Dancers crashed to the floor. The goons pushed others, taking swings and kicking people. Folks were stunned, so the tough guys got in a lot of free licks. Shouts, screams: the band stopped playing.

That ferocious beast from my Army days roared up inside me. Without thinking, I tackled one of these guys from behind. He was a monster, a broad-shouldered fullback who went down with a surprised "ooof!" then flipped over and kicked me in the stomach, knocking the wind out of me. Two of his pals grabbed me, yanked me to my feet and held me up so fullback could take his best shot. He was moving in when Nick came flying in, crashing the guy to the floor. His two pals moved to help him, so I bulldozed him off Nick. I felt a machete of pain in my bum shoulder. As I winced, the guy scuttled away. I dialed 911, looking up as I talked. Chaos. I remembered Makayla's words about making enemies of folks I didn't even know. I felt a chill down my spine.

The R Ones backed away as more and more people went on the offensive. Then I heard something strange. It took me a moment, but then I got it: the hornet-whine of a motorbike engine. No, not a motorbike: an ATV. More than one, a bunch of them. They roared by the dance pavilion: eight of them, manned by beefy yobbos in the same ski mask/polo shirt/chino garb.

Makayla, Yandy, Nick and I huddled. "What's going on?" I said.

"Where would you go if you wanted to wreak as much havoc as possible?" said Makayla.

"The gardens," I said. "I mean, ATVs…"

"Shit!" said Yandy.

"I'd hit the Med Clinic," said Nick.

I froze. "Anybody seen Kate?"

Nick looked at Yandy. "Mike and I will go there; you and Makayla go to the gardens. Meet back here in twenty."

As we rounded the last corner, we could see a "whumpf" of fire from the Molotov cocktail that lit up the entrance to the Clinic as an ATV roared away. "Holy shit!"

"Yeah," said Nick. "Let's pick it up."

"Roger that," I said. In an instant, I was back in battle mode, adrenalized by rage and ready to wreak a little havoc of my own. We ran past the flames and crashed through the charred barrier between reception and the exam rooms. Room Two: there was Kate huddled on the floor, holding an elderly woman who was gasping for breath. Kate was holding a damp washrag over her face with one hand, cradling a smartphone in the other.

"Fast!" yelled Nick.

"Back way!" I shouted. Nick scooped up the elderly woman and I grabbed a woozy Kate and we hustled them through the smoke toward the rear door of the clinic. The door was triple bolted, one bolt padlocked shut. The smoke was billowing toward us as I looked at Kate. "Key!"

"Back there," she said, "In my purse."

Shit. A wall of flame. I looked at Nick. He was wide-eyed, looking around for a crowbar. It dawned on me that we were in the kind of trouble that could kill us all. We were trapped. My mind raced. There had to be a next thing to do. "How much time we got?"

"Couple minutes," Nick said. And then a THWACK shook the door. What the hell? Another THWACK, and then another. The fourth THWACK splintered the door and we saw the red blade of a fireman's axe. Two more blows and the wooden door planks caved in, and in another minute and a half we were out of there, in the alley behind the clinic coughing our lungs out as we watched five County Fire folks hustle hoses into the building to douse the flames.

The woman was skinny, frail Minerva Clay, 82-years-old, who had stopped by to pick up her blood pressure medicine. Nick carried her around front to the ambulance as I checked in with Kate. "You called 911?" She nodded. "You saved us."

"Who did this?" she said. The fear was gone, but she was shivering from shock.

"Some young punks. Hired guns, I'm pretty sure."

"Who?" said Kate.

"I got an idea," I said.

"Me too," said Nick.

CHAPTER FORTY-NINE

July 5

MIKE DAVENPORT

2 a.m. Raven's house. Raven, Betty, Makayla, Calvin McCoy, Reverend Luke, Yandy, Dr. Kate, Chief Pooley, and Nick. My shoulder throbbed: I was still waiting for the Vicodin Kate gave me to kick in. "That fear you felt out there?" said Calvin. "That's what our grandparents felt everyday of their lives when they were trying to organize a union. Someone's out there who will do whatever it takes to stop us."

"So, what's the damage?" I said. "Yandy?"

"They wanted to tear up the gardens and they did a pretty fair job. They spun donuts in the soil till they wrecked everything. I'm hoping we can salvage some of the stuff in the neighborhood plots."

I frowned. "What does it mean in terms of feeding people?"

"It's bad," he said, frowning. "This'll put us back about, I don't know, three-four weeks. I'll call the Sodbusters; they'll help us out."

I turned to Dr. Kate. "How are you feeling?" I said, although I knew the answer before I asked.

"Angry. Sad. Full of rage, full of grief. I mean…dammit, what kind of sick, psychopathic bastards would fire bomb a free clinic? Minnie Clay hadn't seen a doctor in six years."

I turned to the Chief. "Any idea who did this?"

The Rev is the one who spoke. "Yes, we have a pretty good idea, although we'll never prove anything." Darla handed me one of the flyers she'd gotten from the "Pulver Forge Patriots."

My heart lurched. I saw my dream of semi-retirement sprout angel wings and flutter off into the sun, where it melted away. I was holding an 8" by 11" full color mailer on card stock. A grainy black and white photo of young soldier Mike Davenport was set against a full-color photo of a Special Forces grunt looking squarely at the camera:

"I KNOW MOSCOW MIKE DAVENPORT. HE'S A FRAUD. A FAKER. A PHONY. HE'S TAKING PULVER FORGE FOR A RIDE. IT'S TIME HE WAS STOPPED. JOIN THE RECALL."

"You know this guy?" Makayla looked at me.

"Nope." The flyer said he was "Army 1st Lieutenant Cal Crockett, Silver Star Winner."

"Read it," she said.

"I'm having a hard time getting my eyes to focus," I said. "Rev, you want to take this?"

He stared gravely at the copy. *"Mike Davenport says he's some kind of war hero. Baloney. It just so happens I was in Afghanistan when he was, quote, "injured" in that so-called firefight. His cowardice and incompetence put his platoon in harm's way. He panicked when the enemy attacked. He was saved by his best friend, the man who covered up his deadly ineptitude. That man was planning to come forward to expose his alleged friend when he died, under very suspicious circumstances. Mike Davenport used his death — a so-called "suicide" that looks to this soldier like murder — to promote the political fortunes of "Mayor" Davenport. I know that shadowy forces were behind his campaign: forces hell-bent on destroying an effort to bring hundreds of jobs to this town."*

The Rev looked up. Everyone was staring at him. He turned to me. I nodded. The whole thing, please.

"Now Moscow Mike Davenport has revealed himself for what he is: a radical left agent of Socialism, lining his own pockets as the people of this town work his plantation for free. He's reading from the Marxist-

Leninist playbook delivered straight from Castro's Cuba by his henchman Yandy Lopez, and by "Red Raven" Washburn, an organizer of the radical antifa left. Well, I've had enough. Enough lies. Enough Socialism. Enough slave labor. I'm heading the effort to recall "Mayor" Davenport so we can get Pulver Forge back on track. Sign our petitions. Vote for jobs, vote for truth, vote for the future of Pulver Forge. We can end this nightmare."

I felt like I was cornered in a dark room getting pummeled by hooded thugs. The tag at the bottom said, "Pulver Forge Citizens for Truth, Justice and Integrity in Government." And right below that, in one point type, the words "FreebooterMedia." Another fist to the gut, this one with brass knuckles. Tess? "'Scuse me," I mumbled. I turned to Betty. "Can I use your den?"

CHAPTER FIFTY

MIKE DAVENPORT

Three rings, then, "Hi, Michael." As if nothing had happened, as if ringing her up at two in the morning was perfectly normal.

"Hello, Tess." I was trying, and failing, to control my breathing. I could feel that beast, again: a raw, emotional demon surging up inside me. My face was beet red. I was trying not to crush my smartphone.

"This is about the flyer, right?

I almost laughed at her off-handed tone. "Uh huh, yeah, that's right. It seems that Army Lieutenant Cal Crockett, a man I've never met, thinks I'm a coward and a traitor. Do you know something about this?" A long pause. She was making up her mind whether to tell me the truth. I knew she would.

"Ummm, yeah, I guess I do."

"Uh huh." Silence. "So, tell me about it."

"It was a job, Mike. I did it, as per our agreement. Remember our agreement?"

My heart was pounding. I wanted to scream at her, but I choked it back. "Why don't you remind me?"

"You know, Mike. The agreement we made together. We agreed that work was work and love was love, and we'd never confuse the two. We agreed to make as much money as quickly as possible, and that neither of us would ask the other where the money came from. That agreement."

That was our deal. The corrosive, soul-killing weight of my nihilism hit me right in the gut. "Yeah, I remember."

"These people showed up with a dump truck full of money. They're my biggest client, by a factor of five. They pay big, they pay on time and they pay with certified checks. Without them, I'd be waitressing at Applebee's."

"And it doesn't bother you that these people are lying about me? Trying to destroy me?"

Her voice kicked up a notch. Okay, now we were into it. "No, that's not quite right, lover. The people paying me to do this, and it's really one guy, wants to destroy your stupid political career so you can go back to doing what you should be doing, which is getting your coffee house set up to sell for seven figures so we can live the dream, like we agreed to when we got engaged."

"So, you…so you're okay with this," I said. "You have no qualms about creating some lying trash that straight-up says I'm a gutless piece of shit who murdered my best friend so I could step on his body to become Mayor of this godforsaken town."

"If I hadn't done it, somebody else would have gotten the business. So, I got the business that pays four times my rate card. Do I believe any of the junk in that ad? Of course not. And that doesn't make a bit of difference."

"Did you ever think of giving me a heads up, incoming?"

"Not after they made me sign an iron-clad agreement not to, as I knew they would."

"Goddamnit, Tess…"

"MIKE!" Her shout startled me.

"What?"

"I'm surprised you're surprised. This is war. Tell me the rules, besides watch your back and kill the other guy first."

My face was burning. She wouldn't back down. I'd always admired that. Now the beast in me made me want to reach through the line and grab her by the throat. I took a very deep breath, and then another. "This is bad, Tess. This is…well, I'm not sure I can get past this."

"Mike…" Her voice was calm now, serious. "When we were serving, we both had the same sickening realization: that we were tiny little pawns in this great big game, and our lives were in the hands of folks who didn't give a shit if we lived or died. True?"

The beast backed down, and I started to go numb. I remembered all too well. "Yeah? So?"

"Guess what, lover. Same people. It's nothing personal, you're just in their way, and they're going to do whatever it takes to get rid of you. Whatever. It. Takes."

"When you say 'they'…"

"You know, Mike. Don't pretend you don't."

I opened my mouth to say something, but nothing came out. I hunched over, defeated. I knew.

"Mike? You still there?"

"Yeah."

"You didn't hear this from me, but there are two more direct mail pieces in the pipeline, plus an avalanche of social media, door to door canvassing and a phone bank come election day. You can just walk away now; we can forget all this. We can still make it, Mike. A year from now, in Kauai, this will be nothing." A long pause. "You said you loved me, Mike, and I loved you. I haven't changed."

I felt beaten up, defeated. "Did you at least…did you think twice about printing that thing?"

"Yes." More silence, then "Call me when you've had a chance to think about what I said." Click. Buzz. Nothing.

"Mike?" Makayla? How long had she been standing there? I turned.

"Yeah?"

"You okay?"

"How much of that did you hear?"

"Enough." She came in, sat down behind me, and put her arms around me. I let go and started to sob.

CHAPTER FIFTY-ONE

MIKE DAVENPORT

Some time passed. A minute? Ten? I finally got control of myself. "I guess I should get back out there…"

"No," said Makayla. "They can wait. Tell me what's going on."

I turned and looked into her beautiful dark eyes. "What if I were to walk away? Here, now?"

She leaned back. "Walk away?"

"You've seen the flyer; they've got a bead on me. On us. And they mean to take us down."

"So," said Makayla, "you think this is the end. That you're beaten."

"You don't?" I said.

"That firefight you were in, where Dave Bratton saved your life…did you run off and let your platoon fend for themselves?" Before I could answer, she said, "You fought like hell."

"Yeah."

"This is the *same fight*, Mike. When you decided to fight for this town, I knew I had to join up. Suddenly I had a reason to get up in the morning! They're coming after you because you're winning! *We're winning!*"

Something shifted for me in that moment. She was here, talking me off the ledge. She was the one who cared about me, who was with me. "What should I do?"

"There's a part of you that's been holding back, Mike. You never moved here, you're still trying to be the full-time boss of your business, planning your wedding, all that stuff from…

"My old life."

"Right. You've got to decide which life you want. What you believe in." She paused, and then, "What you'd die for."

"Uh huh." She was right. Shit.

"If you decide to fight, well…" She paused, then looked me in the eye. "I'm with you. We're with you."

"And if we get our ass kicked? What if I get recalled, and the thing falls apart and everything goes right back the way it was?"

She moved her face close to mine and whispered. "Would you regret *any* of this? Even one ridiculous moment? Because I wouldn't."

"But…" I said.

"Can I tell you something?" She looked at the floor, then back at me. "I have a job offer. It's the one I wanted. From BlueNation."

"That's…" I started to congratulate her. Then I remembered what this would mean to the town.

"Special projects and weekend anchor, with a track to anchoring weeknights."

"That's your dream, isn't it?"

"Yeah, it is," she said. "Or at least it was until…until I realized that it was just another news job. I'd be telling people what other people are doing, instead of…"

"What?"

"We're making news ourselves, Mike."

She had drifted close to me. I moved forward just an inch or two and then we kissed. Just a light kiss, just for a second. I felt a galvanic charge surge through my body, scalp to toes. Our faces hovered near each other for a long moment, and she whispered, "We should get back." She got up and moved to the door, then turned and smiled at me. And I knew that, once again, my life had changed.

And I knew just what to do. Starting with coffee, of course.

CHAPTER FIFTY-TWO

MIKE DAVENPORT

Making coffee from scratch—grinding the beans, heating the water, pouring it into a French Press, timing the soak and then pushing it through the filter into the beaker—was just what I needed. I had a skill! If everything went to hell, I could return to my core competency: creating chemical euphoria in strangers. This was a skill that couldn't be outsourced to China or rendered obsolete with a web app. I'd never be out of work. I was good to go.

Okay, so I was brewing the dreaded decaf, but hey: it was now 2:55 in the morning. Everyone got a mug. "Sorry, I was busy trashing my engagement because I discovered my fiancé is a high-functioning sociopath."

"And this was news to you?" said Kate. Laughs all around.

"Slow learner," I said. "And also, I made a decision."

"Which is?" said Yandy.

"To quit… (dramatic pause)…fooling around. To go all in." I could see their puzzled faces. "I'm moving to town. Live here, work here. I'm going to be out there twelve hours a day, working the gardens, the med clinic, picking up trash, dishing up chili. So…any revelations while I was gone?"

The Rev said, "It's Moses Creavey."

"Has to be," said Nick.

"Like all these entitled billionaires," said the Rev, "he's greatly aggrieved that the taxpayers decided not to give him his toy casino, so now he has to dynamite the rapscallions who got in his way."

"That would be us," I said.

"That vet slagging your service," said Betty. "I loved how he said he was 'there in Afghanistan' when you were injured in that 'so-called' firefight. Not in your platoon or company, not within a thousand miles of you, just the same country."

"Classic swiftboating," said Yandy. "The bastards..."

"We've got to fight this," said Reverend Luke.

"Yeah," said Yandy. "Great. How?"

There's a tiny bit of caffeine in decaf, and I could feel it spark me up: a micro-buzz. "I can answer that question. Or at least I can start, then you can pile on."

"Enlighten us," said Betty.

"First, most important, the Clinic will open this morning as usual. I don't care if it's a card table in the ashes or the middle of the park or…in fact, let's set up right next to the HuggaMug, so everyone who comes in for a free cup can see that we're open." I turned to Kate. "Can we do that?"

"You bet," said Dr. Kate. "I can make some calls, get people to come by with the basic stuff: thermometers, bandages, aspirin…"

"Good. Next, no weeping about the damage to the gardens, we get out there and start working the beds. Just a normal day." I turned to Chef Betty. "Same with the Prosperity Kitchen. You and the Rev call the supers and the food banks. Yandy and I will call the Sodbusters. Let's have the best spread ever. If we're short, I'll pay for whatever we need."

"Me too," said Raven. "Everybody's welcome, everybody eats."

"And" said Makayla, "everyone who gets a meal gets a flyer. Our flyer. Nothing fancy, just a statement that we're still in business, and the game is still on."

"Great!" said Kate. "When do you we put that together?

"How 'bout now?" I said.

Betty flipped open her laptop. "Okay, I'm ready."

"Okay, ummm…" I took a long sip. "Let's start with, umm, 'We must be doing something right…because somebody's trying stop us."

"Stop what we're doing," said Makayla.

"The good news," I continued, "is that they can't take what's ours unless we let them. Our jobs…"

"Our gardens," said Yandy.

"Our kitchen," said Betty.

"Our health clinic," said Dr. Kate.

"Our new friends," said Reverend Luke. "Our new…uhhhh…."

"Community," said Calvin. "Our new bounty of everything we need to be happy: food to share, neighbors to share it with, and work that means something."

Betty said, "Got it. Keep going."

We all looked at each other. What can follow that? I said, "For over a hundred years the people of Pulver Force worked for the bosses of the mill. Now we work for ourselves. We're building a new town."

"More than a new town," said the Rev. "A new *kind* of town."

"One without fear," said Calvin.

"That's good," said Makayla.

"Now it's the bosses who are scared," said the Reverend Luke. "What if this place, Prosperity, Pennsylvania, inspired people all over America…"

"And the world!" said Betty.

"…and the world," said the Rev, "to seize their destiny, help themselves, work for their own…ummm…I want to say 'salvation' here but that's too lofty…"

"Redemption?" said Raven.

"Same problem," said the Rev.

"Freedom, independence, liberation…" I said.

The Rev nodded. "Work for their own *freedom*: a freedom that they've earned through hard work and a commitment to community." He looked at us. Nods all around.

"It's our miracle," said Makyala. "Let's fight for it."

"Is that a first draft?" said Betty.

"Unless anyone can make it better, I'd say it's finished copy," said the Rev. "After Mike signs it."

"We all sign it," I said. "One team."

CHAPTER FIFTY-THREE

July 5
TRANSCRIPT OF CODY FORTUNE'S COMMENTARY, "FIRSTNEWS"

CODY FORTUNE: Department of 'Hey, this is a whole lot worse than I thought': You probably heard something about that riot they had down in Pulver Forge — oh, excuse me, I meant to say 'Prosperity', Pennsylvania last night. Didn't your ol' pal Cody tell you that Mayor Davenport was a three-dollar bill? Yeah, I did, and I also said he was a Commie who was trying to turn the town into a slave labor camp. Silly me, I thought he'd deny it! Well, here he is addressing the crowd at the big party they were throwing for themselves.

CUT TO: SMARTPHONE VIDEO OF MIKE

MIKE DAVENPORT: *I'm a Marxist-Leninist bent on enslaving the poor people of Pulver Forge.*

CODY FORTUNE: Wow! I mean…wow! That's not even the worst part. You can try and cut this guy all the slack in the world, but…

CUT TO: SMARTPHONE FOOTAGE OF BURNING AMERICAN FLAG IN CLOSE-UP

CODY FORTUNE: Mike and his pals burned the flag, friends. They burned the American flag…ON THE 4TH OF JULY! (SHAKES HEAD DRAMATICALLY) From what I've heard, they were having a dance and some young out of towners tried to join in the fun, but Mike and his minions were having none of it. They started shoving the visitors off the dance floor, and things got a little out of hand. So, what did Moscow Mike Davenport do when the fight started?

CUT TO: SMARTPHONE SHOT OF MIKE RUNNING AWAY FROM THE CAMERA

CODY FORTUNE: He took off! Look at him go! Those suckers he'd invited to celebrate his takeover of the town? They're back there fighting it out, but their so-called "leader" is in the wind!

WINDOW FOR FOOTAGE DISAPPEARS. CODY FORTUNE APPEARS FULL SCREEN CLOSE UP

CODY FORTUNE: This would be funny if there weren't real people in that town suffering because this jackass is strutting around giving orders. This thing turned into a riot. Word has it that one of Moscow Mike's minions, cranked up on who knows what, lobbed a Molotov cocktail that burned down the town's only medical clinic!

The people of Pulver Forge—the name has never been officially changed—have a chance to wake up from this tyrannical hallucination in a couple of weeks. Looks like the people have demanded a recall election to give Moscow Mike the boot, and if Mayor Fred Bagley wins, there's going to be a lot of new jobs in the town. We're on this story. This is your friend Cody Fortune. Kicking ass and taking names.

CHAPTER FIFTY-FOUR

JULY 6
MIKE DAVENPORT
Makayla and I watched Cody Fortune's commentary on "FirstNews" Monday night. I started to hyperventilate, but she smiled. "They had a shot list."

"What?" I said.

"A shot list," said Makayla. "Cody Fortune gave those yabbos a shot list, what he needed for his story. First, they videoed your speech, so they could up-cut that bite about you being a Marxist. Then those assclowns burned the flag and stepped away so the cameraman could get it clean and blame it on you. And finally, they got you running to save the clinic. Character assassination in three acts. Beautiful."

"What can we do?" I asked.

"Nothing," she said, still smiling.

"Really?"

"I called my TV news pals, and they'll have the story *we* want tomorrow night. And it's all about the miracle that's going to happen tomorrow morning."

July 7
VERBATIM TRANSCRIPT – WPTT-TV JULY 7 NEWS AT TEN 10:07

BILL SLOCUM: Sometimes the worst calamity can bring out the best in people. Looks like that's what happened today in Prosperity, Pennsylvania.

PEG DIVINE: Bill, two nights ago a Fourth of July celebration in the town of Prosperity was marred by violence.

CUT TO: CELLPHONE FOOTAGE OF THE BRAWL ON THE DANCE FLOOR, THE DAMAGE TO THE GARDENS AND THE FIRE AT THE MED CLINIC.

PEG DIVINE (VO): First a group of troublemakers started a fight at a community dance, injuring eleven people, including three that needed to be taken to a hospital. Then what locals described as hooligans on all-terrain vehicles tore up the community vegetable gardens. The worst damage was to the new Prosperity medical clinic: it appears that one of the assailants tossed a Molotov cocktail into the place, almost killing two people and causing catastrophic damage.

BILL SLOCUM: Would all this violence stop Prosperity in its quest to return this rust-belt relic of Pennsylvania's big-steel past to glory? Our own Velocity Blake has the story…

CUT TO: Young, blonde VELOCITY BLAKE in front of the charred remains of the Dave Bratton Community Health Clinic.

VELOCITY: Two days ago, this was a clinic that offered free medical care to thousands of residents here in Prosperity, and then…

B ROLL FOOTAGE: HEALTH CLINIC ON FIRE, COUNTY FIRE DEPARTMENT BATTLING TO PUT IT OUT.

VELOCITY (V.O.): …some arsonists set it ablaze. What would the people of Prosperity do for health care?

CUT TO: "WELLNESS ON WHEELS" 31 FOOT MOBILE MEDICAL CLINIC NEXT TO HUGGAMUG, WITH LINE OF PEOPLE WAITING FOR TREATMENT.

VELOCITY (V.O.): This is "Wellness on Wheels," a portable medical clinic that rolled up at 9 a.m. this morning and was seeing patients by 9:23.

B-ROLL SHOT OF DR. KATE WITH A CLIPBOARD TAKING INFORMATION ON PATIENTS WAITING TO ENTER WELLNESS ON WHEELS

VELOCITY (V.O.): Dr. Kate Walther is the Director of the Prosperity health clinic.

KATE: A day and a half ago I was standing in the ashes of our humble little clinic, despondent, thinking the world had ended. And then this great big, beautiful gift from heaven rolled up with a doctor and three nurses and we're back in business! We're helping people! It's a miracle!

CUT TO: TOWNSPEOPLE FILLING THEIR PLATES AT THE PROSPERITY COMMUNITY KITCHEN. A GIANT STAKE-BED TRUCK WITH A SIGN READING "JARHEAD SODBUSTERS" IS VISIBLE IN THE BACKGROUND.

VELOCITY (V.O): Those same bad news bikers tore up the veggie gardens: the ones that are feeding thousands of people here. The director of the community kitchen that's feeding this town wasn't sure how they'd re-open…

REV. LUKE SOUND BITE: We'd never missed a meal till now, but losing all that fresh produce, well, we thought we'd have to turn people away.

B-ROLL: "SODBUSTERS" UNLOADING CRATES OF PRODUCE OFF THEIR TRUCK

VELOCITY: That is, until the 'Jarhead Sodbusters' showed up with several day's worth of produce. They're a group of ex-Marines who've made a new life working a local farm. Here's their director, Kelton Driscoll:

KELTON DRISCOLL SOUND BITE: We were watching the news. Hot damn, no way we're going to let a bunch of knuckleheads force good people to go hungry…

B-ROLL: KELTON AND THE SODBUSTERS SITTING DOWN WITH THE REVEREND LUKE AND TOWNSPEOPLE ENJOYING A MEAL.

VELOCITY (V.O.): Plenty of great, fresh food for everybody. And about those gardens…

B-ROLL SHOT OF YANDY SURVEYING THE DAMAGED GARDENS.

VELOCITY (V.O.): Yandy Lopez is in charge of the garden project here in Prosperity.

NAT SOUND OF YANDY WALKING THROUGH THE WRECKED GARDENS: This was spinach, red leaf lettuce and chard ready to be harvested, just destroyed…

B-ROLL SHOT OF YANDY, RAVEN AND KELTON, FROM THE JARHEAD SODBUSTERS MAPPING OUT PLAN TO RESCUE THE GARDEN.

VELOCITY (V.O.): And then Kelton Driscoll and friends showed up with their gear to save this community treasure.

KELTON SOUND BITE: Truth be told, we live for this stuff. Yandy and his crew, these are our people, and we're going to help them because we're all in this together.

CUT TO: B-ROLL SHOT OF MAYOR MIKE WALKING DOWN MAIN STREET SERVING PAPER CUPS OF COFFEE FROM A HUGE TRAY, GREETING PEOPLE,

VELOCITY (V.O.): Maybe the happiest man in Prosperity was the saddest on July 4th: Mayor Mike Davenport, the new Mayor who promised to deliver Prosperity to what was Pulver Forge.

MIKE DAVENPORT SOUND BITE: Velocity, I am so happy…and proud…and grateful for what's happening here today. Can you believe this? I thought this was the end of our dream…but it was really the beginning. Bless the wonderful people of Pennsylvania, they're helping us keep the dream alive.

VELOCITY STAND UP, WALKING DOWN MAIN STREET: We take so much for granted every day—having enough to eat, feeling safe, having medical care—and yesterday, all that was threatened until caring people from all over Pennsylvania showed up to help a town in crisis. And now Prosperity is getting a second chance. Bill? Peg? Back to you…

CHAPTER FIFTY-FIVE

July 6
MIKE DAVENPORT
After a full day of helping, everyone who'd come from everywhere was our guest of honor for supper. Raven Washburn staked Chief Pooley with the funds to host his "dream barbecue": Texas-style brisket, Carolina-style pulled pork, Memphis-style ribs and Alabama-style chicken with "Pooley's Soon-To-Be Famous Magnificent Mop Sauce." This was all cooked over a roaring flame, and the Chief liked it that way. "I will not cook unless danger is involved." He made enough to feed over a thousand happy people, with Betty and her crew fixing the side dishes. The crowd parted so the Jarhead Sodbusters could be first in line.

Steve Dorsey arrived with something special: two chilled kegs of "Zombie Tears," a hair-raising, kick-ass lager based on a Bavarian doppelbock "extreme" beer brewed up at the Eggenberg Castle in Austria. (All Steve's beers had names that could double as names for 80s metal bands: Coffin Varnish, Zombie Tears, Killdozer, Yeastus Kee-rist, etc.) The brew was as subtle as a Mike Tyson leaping left hook, and it was so rich it was practically chewy. The hearty goodwill of the tribe rocketed into the stratosphere after Steve served cups of this joy juice.

I was on my second cup when Makayla and Betty plopped down on either side of me. Makayla had the brisket, Betty a plate of ranch beans and cole slaw. "This recall thing is going to be shitshow," I said. "Moses Creavey's budget is 'whatever it takes.' Think we can survive?"

Makayla washed a bite of brisket down with a gulp of Zombie Tears. "I think," she said, "that we should be glad you're not running for President, or Governor or even State Representative, where advertising might make a difference. The Creavey gang has to convince these happy campers right here…" She waved her fork at our Prosperity Kitchen customers. "…that you're a fake, a phony, a covert Commie. My advice?" She looked a question at me.

"Please."

"Don't waste your time fighting Creavey, it just keeps all his lies in play."

"Agree," said Betty. "Let's keep feeding people, putting 'em to work, helping 'em make new friends. These folks remember what this place was like before we got here. If they buy Creavey's bullshit, we're wasting our time."

Somebody yelled for a speech, and that turned into a chant: "Speech, speech, speech!" and people held up their beer cups and looked at me. The last thing I wanted to do was put the brakes on everybody's fun, so I stood up on my chair and said, "Everybody know James Baldwin? The writer? He once said, 'The world is held together by a small number of kind people.' I am honored and happy to find myself amidst those people tonight, and because of that I hope this lovely evening never ends." I held up my cup. They held up theirs. We drank. And I knew I was having a deathbed moment: a moment of perfect happiness. No matter what happened, every goddam bit of this crazy adventure was worth it.

CHAPTER FIFTY-SIX

Wednesday, July 14
KATE WALTHER

10 pm, Room 303, the renovated Hotel Bessemer. Kate Walther had arrived at the "Wellness on Wheels" mobile medical clinic at 6 am that morning, ate the lunch Mike delivered from the Prosperity Community Kitchen, and left at 6 pm. From there she walked to the soon-to-open Prosperity Community Wellness Center on Bessemer Drive. The Center was a re-purposed upgrade of the Pulver Forge Hospital that had opened in 1923, one of the last gifts of Enoch Pulver to the town. It was about a mile from the mill. It had handled thousands of amputations, burn cases, head wounds and lung disorders of mill workers. When it closed in 2003, the nearest full-service hospital was 14 miles away in Pittsburgh. This was Kate's work: she and Brad Beckham enlisted Raven to join Allegheny County health officials to re-open the 24-bed Hospital, using money from state agencies and the new Prosperity Community Foundation. The new/old hospital would have a small number of paid staff alongside the volunteers. It would offer more comprehensive medical, dental, and behavioral care; chronic-disease management; and wellness coaching. It would, of course, be open to all.

Now she was room-hopping in the Hotel Bessemer for a final check on her rehab cases. After she was done, she'd walk up the stairs to the top floor, where she had a pocket-sized one room flat. What started as a just-when-she-needed-it crash pad had turned into her primary residence as her duties expanded to overseeing the new wellness center. She and her husband Scott were taking a break from the marriage. Kate had tried to explain how happy she was in this new job. Scott pretended to understand, but she knew he didn't. Still, he told her to take all the time she needed. She'd never spent less time with him or felt more gratitude for the relationship. Even if they divorced, she thought they could salvage a friendship.

"How are you doing?" She sat next to an empty bed. Max Stone was on his feet, staring out the window. His wrinkled pajamas bagged around him: he'd lost twenty-two pounds.

He turned to her. "You're here to kick me out, right?" No anger, just a mournful near whisper.

"Kick you out?" Kate tried to hide her surprise.

"Three weeks today," he said. "Isn't that what everybody gets? Three weeks?"

"That's right. I mean, that's the rule, but…you think you're ready to leave?"

The mask of pure fury she'd encountered three weeks ago was gone, replaced by a furrowed map of pain, regret, and anxiety. "I can. I will if I have to. I've leveled out from the drugs. But I…"

"What?"

He walked over, sat on the bed, and looked in Kate's eyes as he held her hand. "I'm scared. It's the same world out there that got me in such deep shit. I got no job, no home. I…" He went silent and shrugged himself back on his bed.

As he stared at the ceiling, Kate noticed a tattoo on the inside of his forearm. It was a small heart-within-a-heart. Very softly, she said what was under the hearts. "Matt 5-19-17." He turned to her, then glanced at his forearm. The look of worry dissolved into anguish. "Your son," said Kate. It wasn't a question.

Kate did more listening in this new job than she did in her last. After a very long moment, Max said, "Yeah. Matthew. He was a great kid. Seven years old, full of beans, just coming into himself. I'd just gotten him his first baseball glove. Brain tumor. Ependymoma." He put his head down, winced, and began to shudder as he cried.

Kate moved from her chair to the bed and put her arms around him. "I'm so sorry."

"When he died," said Max, "that was the end of everything. My wife couldn't deal with it, I mean, how could she? She took off. I stopped showing up at work…"

She let him go. "What did you do?"

He snorted, wiped away the tears and looked straight ahead with a sardonic smile. "This will make you laugh. I was a home health aide. Early Alzheimer's patients, stuff like that. They needed a big guy to get people wrestled into wheelchairs then back onto beds."

"Were you good at it?"

"Yeah. I liked helping people. And the relatives were so grateful. But after Matt's…you know, after he died…I felt numb. I stopped caring about anything. Started stealing meds from my patients, especially the speedier stuff, you know, like Methylphenidate. Pretty soon I was doing bumps of coke. Got caught, got fired, couldn't pay rent, got bent on meth, and…"

Kate felt his shame. How could she help this guy? Kate shifted so she was facing him. "I have a thought. How'd you like a job?"

"Huh?"

"Look, who stayed with you when you were kicking?"

"Ozzie, the Black guy, and, oh, let's see, who's the little guy with the red hair, squeaky voice…"

"Cooper."

"Yeah, him."

"You know they're like you, right? Except Oxy instead of meth. They work here because helping people kick gives them a purpose, something worth doing."

"Takes an addict to know one," he said.

"Exactly. You've even got experience caring for people. We need people to do what they do. To start, you'd be paid in TimeBucks. Place to stay here in the Hotel, free lunch everyday with your friends. What do you say?"

For the first time, she saw a light in his eyes. "I say yes. I say hell yes."

"The thing is," she said, "You have to show up. You use, you lose, one strike and you're out."

"I get it," he said. And then he pulled her into an awkward hug. "I've been to hell. The idea of staying here, helping people like me, that would be…" He tried to find the words. "Thanks. I, ummm…

"What?"

"I know you could have had me arrested. Should have had me arrested. I'd be in prison now, doing twenty years. Feels like you're saving my life again."

She felt a rush of dopamine, the kind she'd given up feeling when she served the Beast of Mis-Managed Care. "You're welcome, Max." She got up and headed for the door. She turned back to him. "You know, I like to take walks along Riverfront Drive just after work. I could swing by sometime to see if you're free. You want to come with me?"

"Yeah. That would be nice."

As Kate entered her flat, she texted Mike. "Just saw Max Stone. I think we might have saved another soul."

He texted back, "Have I mentioned lately that you're my hero?"

CHAPTER FIFTY-SEVEN

July 21
MIKE DAVENPORT

8 p.m. Roasting beans at the Prosperity HuggaMug after a full day of work. After all the nonsense of the last few weeks, I loved working a discipline that had rules, involved judgment, required focus and produced a righteous result in a reasonable amount of time. I was well into the roast, just about to achieve the second crack when my smartphone rang. I looked at the screen. Mom? I put her on speaker. "Hi, Mom."

"Hi, Mikey. How's it going up there?"

"Fine! Great! How's the marriage?"

"Oh, it's fine, fine." Long pause.

"Uh huh. How's the golf?"

"I broke a hundred and ten last week! I shot a 106, with two pars. Frank took me out to dinner at the Lobster Barrel. We had vodka martinis; it was a lot of fun."

"Great." Long pause. So much for small talk. Get to it, ma.

"Are things really okay where you are?"

"Of course. Why?"

"Oh, no reason. It's just that Frank heard some things on the news about that place where you're living…

"Prosperity."

"Uh huh. Frank said it's called Pulver Forge."

"It used to be, but we changed it. Now it's called 'Prosperity.' What kind of things did he hear?"

"He has these radio shows he listens to. I don't know why. I tell him if they make him so mad, he should stop listening. And then he turns up the volume to drown me out."

"What did Frank tell you, mom?"

"Well…he said that your town has been taken over."

"Taken over?"

"By Communists. Not the Russian kind, the Cuban kind. They're grabbing people from their homes and forcing them at gunpoint to work on these slave labor farms."

"Wow, that sounds terrible. What else?"

"Well, he said there are people, old people like me, dying on these farms, and then they stack the bodies on funeral pyres where they're cremated in some kind of Satanic ritual. They use fires to burn American flags. He showed me some pictures."

"Does Frank know I'm the Mayor of this town?"

"Ummm…well, I've told him. A bunch of times, actually. So, I think he knows. It's the radio. The radio says…"

"What?"

"That you're a puppet. Of this Cuban fellow Randy Lopez…"

"Yandy Lopez, mom. He's a friend of mine. Highly decorated American war veteran."

"Well, that's not what the radio says. The radio says he was sent here by Fidel Castro as a sleeper agent to take over the country. Starting in Pennsylvania."

"Can you put Frank on the phone?"

"This is his poker night, down at the Club House. That's why I can call you."

"Frank doesn't let you call me?"

"Oh, he doesn't, you know, stop me. That is, he didn't tell me I can't. In so many words, that is. It's just that he…well, he thinks you're a, I think he said…"

Long pause. "What, ma? You can tell me."

"Brain-dead Commie snowflake libtard."

Mike guffawed. "Uh huh. He knows I fought in Afghanistan, right? Purple Heart? Silver Star?" A very long pause. "Mom?"

"He says that…well, he doesn't believe that."

"Really?" Pause.

"He thinks you made it up. It's the radio, Mike, that's where he gets these crazy ideas."

"What do you think, Mom?"

"Oh, I know you'd never lie about something like that. I love you, honey."

"Uh huh. But you're not sure about some kind of Communist funny business going on around here?"

"Well…I don't know. Frank shows me these sites on the computer, and they have pictures of people working on these farms at rifle point, and then burning bodies and people dressed in black hoods wearing pentagrams."

"Wow."

"And then there's the microchips…"

"Whoa, wait a minute. Microchips?"

"Yes, that's how they control people."

"They?"

"The Communists, dear. There's a medical clinic in town where they pretend to give people vaccines but they really plant these microchips so they can find people and control their minds and force them to work at gunpoint. Our Minister says these chips will keep people from entering the gates of Heaven."

That last one stopped me. What do you say to that? "Mom, have you ever considered that people are just making stuff up to scare people?"

"There are so many people saying these things, Mike. Frank says that where there's smoke…"

"Mom, I've got a great idea! What if you and Frank come to Prosperity? Have a look around for yourselves. Talk to some people…"

"Well…"

"This is very alarming! Doesn't Frank want to see for himself if his son-in-law is a devil-worshipping Bolshevik?"

"I'm not sure when we could do that, Dear. We've got our golf group and I've got my scrapbooking, and Frank has his real estate investing club, and we're set to take a cruise to Puerto Vallarta next month…"

"Thanks for calling mom. Good luck with the golf."

(MAKAYLA) PROSPERITY REPORT CARD BY THE NUMBERS AUGUST 2

815: # of HuggaMug Cups of Coffee Served each day, on average
541: # Who Paid for Coffee (including TimeBucks)
290: # Workers in Community Gardens
401: # Workers for Food Prep/Service/Clean-Up at Community Kitchen
431: #Workers for Town Clean-Up Duty (GETTING THERE)
227: #Workers for Med Clinic, including satellite "Unconditional Positive Engagement" units with fentanyl test strips, naloxone, and clean needles (YES!)
181: #Workers at Radio Station/Newsletter/Podcasting
112: #Mobility Workers (including maintenance)
228: #Workers Miscellaneous Duty (babysitting, mentoring, teaching, caretaking)
1,870: #Total Workers
52,801: #Total TimeBucks Issued Previous Week
2,683: #Transactions on "ShareWhere"
1,883: #People at Friday Nite "Hoe-Down"
28: Weekly Posts on Prosperity YouTube Channel (4 a day)
63: Podcast Episodes (21 shows, 3 episodes each)
11,899: Podcast Downloads
$242: Money from "Beef Buckets"

AUGUST 2 NOTES:

• We're now able to see the impact of this project on crime. Pulver Forge had 31 murders last year. This year, so far, we've had 4 (all drug deals gone wrong.) Pulver Forge had 284 robberies last year. So far, we've had 91 in Prosperity. Last year, 958 "crimes against property." This year, 399. When people know their neighbors and look out for them, good things happen.

• The PROSPERITY COMMUNITY WELLNESS CENTER is now open! 24 beds! Drug treatment and detox! Medical, dental, and behavioral care! Chronic-disease management and wellness coaching! Thank you, Kate Walther, (and Raven, of course, and the state of Pennsylvania for some generous grants.)

• WE'RE FEEDING OURSELVES! Big celebration at the Prosperity Community Kitchen: The "Earth Angels" from the "Dirt Candy Heaven" Garden delivered the first post-riot baskets of spinach and lettuce. Reverend Luke brought heaven down to earth with a prayer of praise for our gardening brigade. The meal was served by Mike, Yandy, Raven and me. Glorious.

• The SECOND HIT PIECE arrived in Prosperity, PA mailboxes today. The smears escalated, as we knew they would. This one had Mike engineering the overdose death of Dave Bratton to protect the drug profits he used to finance his "coffee empire." Oh, and people are dying in our gardens from overwork, and Mike is covering it up in league with Yandy and Raven who are minions of North Korea by way of Cuba. No, I'm not making this up. Oh, and Mike killed babies in Afghanistan.

• The PROSPERITY COMMUNITY FOUNDATION now has title to 511 abandoned homes and 384 vacant lots in town, and 27 derelict business locations on Pulver Boulevard and Lincoln Avenue. These include the Arbogast Building, the Majestic Theater, the "Dutch" Devlin Ford car dealership, and what used to be Elkins Hardware.

• The RAVEN WASHBURN CITY ART PROJECT has almost finished its first city mural, an awesome panoramic visual pageant of Pulver Forge history on the outside of the Majestic Theater. Six other murals are in the works, as is the plan to paint every fire hydrant, manhole cover, and derelict storefront (including the plywood covering the broken windows). Young freebooting artists from the around the state are arriving to take advantage of the art spaces in the re-purposed Arbogast Building, which is now the most colorful edifice in town. It is, in fact, a perpetual art project itself, much to the delight of our citizens. This includes an ongoing, ever growing Perpetual Chalk Art Festival on sidewalks up and down Pulver Boulevard.

CHAPTER FIFTY-EIGHT

August 10
MIKE DAVENPORT
Makayla and I were in the musty basement of my new/old house, 317 Grover Avenue, in the Prattleboro district of Prosperity (where the Poles and Slavs settled: my great-grandfather, the one who first moved here, was named Hanusz Drzewiecki). The house was derelict, a tear-down in most cities but not for me. This was the place I moved after my mom deserted us: I lived here with my grandpa for fifteen years. I bought the place from a perplexed realtor for $19,500 cash. It had no front door. The paint was faded and chipped. Lots of rotting wood, and most of the windows were gone, but it was still standing. It reminded me of my grandfather: squat, solid, stubborn, built to last a hundred years. It defied anyone to tear it down. It was waiting for me.

My grandpa built this place himself with the help of his steel mill pals back in 1947. That's how they did it in those days: buy a plot of land, tear down whatever shack Pulver Steel had built at the turn of the century, get some blueprints from the Pulver Public Library, and build the place on weekends with your buddies. Chet had worked on their houses, so now his buddies got to work on his. One guy knew about plumbing, others could wire up the electrics, still others knew about roofing, masonry, drywall, and cabinetry.

It was a Craftsman style house, with a second story master bedroom with four big windows under a gabled dormer. It had a covered porch fronted by river rock, boulder columns and pier supports. What grandpa called the "gathering room" had a large hearth. This room opened to the dining room. The kitchen had a breakfast nook where I had my first cup of coffee at age eleven courtesy of grandpa. He made terrible coffee, from giant supermarket tin cans of inferior, pre-ground beans. I thought it was wonderful: I was hooked from my first slurp. *"Where has THIS been all my life?"* Behind the gathering room was a kind of den, where grandpa would read the Pulver Forge Gazette and the Pittsburgh Sun-Telegraph. My home office will go there. Upstairs, there was a giant, airy master suite and a guest bedroom with its own bathroom.

The place had been abandoned for fifteen years. The ground floor was littered with crack pipes, malt liquor bottles, a filthy, stained mattress and fast-food trash. Whatever could be stripped and sold has been stripped and sold. Makayla recoiled when we walked in, but I...well, I was both horrified and delighted, because I was *home*. I *remembered*. That hearth? We put the Christmas stockings above the fire, and the tree right in the corner next to that. And the hardwood floor in front, that's where I sat while grandpa read me what the sports writers said about the Pirates and Steelers. And the dining room, that's where I'd open my birthday presents.

The basement had been locked up all those years. We pried off the lock, inhaled the musty smell, and looked around. What we saw was a frozen-in-time graveyard of Grandpa Chet's hobbies. Makayla was looking over Chet's tuba (he played in the steel mill polka band, "Looney Louie and the OomPaPahs") when she said, "How are the wedding plans going?"

That one surprised me. "Off," I said.

"Really?"

"I'm surprised you're surprised. Do you think I'd shrug off what she did to me with those flyers?"

"Hey, you were together a long time, right?" Makayla turned and looked at me. "And I'm sure she said it was nothing personal."

"Yeah, well, but…" I stopped. Something had changed. What was it? "Six months ago, I might have shrugged it off, but…"

"But what?" She straightened up, took a couple of steps toward me.

"But you," I said. "Every time I've blinked, you've been there for me. Without you, this thing might have folded two months ago. You're…I just…" She wrapped me a long, glorious hug, placing her warm, smooth cheek next to mine. I hugged her back, loving the feel of that lithe, beautiful body.

"Hey, what's that?" She was looking over my shoulder.

"What's what?" I said, breaking the clench. She was pointing at a musty brown box on the top shelf of an alcove against the back wall. The label had two words: "MIKE/KENNYWOOD." Makayla held the wobbly stepladder as I reached up and grabbed it with both hands.

The rotted cardboard tore when I opened it. Inside were a number of faded 9" by 12" manila envelopes, each with a year on the outside written in marker pen. And inside each was a record of that year's visit—the two of us, grandpa and me—to Kennywood Amusement Park.

Chet and I went to Kennywood every year from the time I was eight until I was nineteen. We'd go one summer day a year, for the whole glorious day. Twelve years, twelve visits, twelve envelopes. He'd get one of those single-use send-it-in-and-get-your-pictures-back disposable cameras as soon as we'd walk through the gate. 27 pictures. That's what was in the envelopes.

I could feel my hand trembling when I opened the picture packet from the 1987 visit. I was twelve years old. Till this moment, I didn't know there were any photos of the younger me outside of my high school yearbook. Here I was with Grandpa Chet in front of the Thunderbolt roller coaster, my first time on a real, adult scare-the-living-shit-out-of-you coaster. There we were on Raging Rapids, and on my very favorite coaster: The Racer, a clattery wooden relic from the Roaring 20s. It wasn't that fast, but it was noisy as hell, rattling and shaking. It seemed like it would come apart on every clackety-clack turn. Chet and I both screamed our heads off every time we rode.

I was in every picture. Half of them had Chet: he'd ask folks to "snap us" as we toured the park. There I was stuffing a chili dog into my mustard-covered face. And this one, wolfing a box of popcorn and — my favorite — slurping up a great big soft-serve vanilla ice cream cone that had been dipped in hot fudge, so the ice cream just under the shell was nothing but melty goodness. And the 27th shot — I knew it'd be the same in every envelope — was the two of us, bathed in the amber glow of a late summer sunset, standing under the "Kennywood" sign above the entrance portal. I felt a rush of emotion: how I remembered the bittersweet feeling of being so happy with that glorious day and so sad it was over for another year!

Makayla looked over my shoulder as I flicked through the photos. I stopped at one, just stared at it. There we were: the two of us in one of those tiny cars at the "Auto Race," a ride Kennywood had built in the 1930s. It was just like everything in the park: hand crafted by locals out of local lumber. It was a relic: clunky and charming. I thought of Chet. He loved me, and that love had saved me. Makayla put her arms around me and hugged me from behind as I stared at my grinning twelve-year-old self. My mom had vanished three years before, my father had taken up permanent residence on our living room sofa, so sick he couldn't work. And here I was, so happy.

In that moment, I knew what I had to do. I'd rebuild the house, just the way Chet would have wanted it. He taught me to be a man, to stand up and do what was right. Once I was pulling on a crescent wrench, battling a rusted lug nut on junkyard car. He said, "Secret of life? You gotta be tougher than it is." Best lesson I ever learned. He was the reason I'd come back to this town. When the house was ready, I'd throw a big party for all my Prosperity friends and the final touch would be hanging a painting over the hearth. I'd pay Raven to do it: the two of us in that car at the "Auto Race."

CHAPTER FIFTY-NINE

Tuesday
MOSES CREAVEY

Moses Creavey was sipping a Fresca on the forward deck of his super-yacht, "Dolce Vita." Sweet life: as if! Owning a super-yacht had one benefit, thought Creavey: it was the quickest and most efficient way ever devised for incinerating thousand-dollar bills. Why had he bought this damn thing in the first place? A woman, of course. It was that bouncy blonde flight attendant on his personal jet, what was her name? "J" something, a stripper kind of name…Jubilee, that was it. A George peach, ripe for the plucking. Everybody told him to wait at least a year after the divorce to start dating, and he tried to be good…but then this foxy firecracker made him feel like a teenager again. He still remembered reveling in the afterglow of a fiery coupling on the couch of the private jet, and Jubilee murmuring that they deserved a new toy — a super-yacht — because didn't Steve Wynn have one that had fourteen bedrooms and wouldn't she look great sunning herself in a string bikini on the deck, miles from anywhere, where no one could spy on them, hint hint?

And so, it began. Of course they couldn't just buy a super-yacht. It had to be a small-ish cruise ship that would be so darn easy to convert to a super-yacht, which (of course) ended up costing half again what it would have cost to buy a brand-new super-yacht. And (of course) Jubilee left him for De'Aron whats-his-name, that cocky power forward on the Toronto Raptors before the conversion was even finished, and so here he was: docked in Marina Puerto Escondido in the Sea of Cortez, spending thousands of dollars a minute to enjoy all the luxury he could enjoy just as easily back at his suite in Vegas. But did his condo have a heliport? A gym? A screening room? Two swimming pools? Yes, yes, yes, and yes.

His smartphone blurped. Gavin Cutler! About time. "So, genius, tell me it's a lock and we're good to go."

"Just shipped flyer number three, should arrive in Pulver Forge mailboxes tomorrow or the day after. I just texted it to you." Creavey liked the way Cutler used "Pulver Forge" instead of "Prosperity." It was the right kind of pandering.

Creavey flicked over to his text app and punched it up. There was a pic of a very young Yandy Lopez holding his sniper rifle. He'd been Photoshopped next to a menacing Fidel Castro. Juxtaposed to young Yandy was a sweaty, disheveled modern-day Yandy in a garden yelling at his workers. The image was manipulated so that Yandy was wearing a khaki Che Guevara shirt and a Cuban "Red Star" commando cap, and his skin had been darkened to a deep tobacco brown. The headline read, "COMMUNIST PUPPET MASTER DIRECTS TOWN TAKEOVER…BUT THERE'S STILL TIME TO FIGHT FOR FREEDOM!"

"Why the Cuban?" said Creavey.

"The stuff with Mike was working, but Che Guevara? Tested off the charts. The whole point is to get the sixty-to-death 'Pulver Forge Patriots' out of their Barcaloungers into the polling places. This will do the trick."

"It better." God, he wanted a martini. Just one: bone dry, frosty, with three olives. Was it worth the racing heart, the trip to the Emergency Room, getting zapped by those paddles, then taking that godawful Metoprolol for a year? It was a toss-up…

"You there?"

"Uh huh. So how about my November surprise?"

"Done."

"Really?" Creavey was startled. "Okay, give."

He heard Cutler chuckle at the other end of the line. "What's the fondest wish of every one of those slugs? What do they talk about after their third beer at the Five O'Clock Whistle?"

The light bulb went on for Creavey. He couldn't help but smile. Maybe this guy was worth the money after all. "The mill."

"Bingo."

"It's going to re-open, right?"

"No. Better. A brand-new mill is going up on the old site, and you're the man that's going to make it happen, you miracle worker you. You and your billions. We're planting a well-sourced, very convincing rumor with our friend Cody Fortune on FirstNews that Moses Creavey has formed an audacious alliance with a major South Korean steel mill that is going to install the latest, most efficient electric arc furnaces in order to revitalize the steelmaking business in Pulver Forge, and re-hire two thousand-plus workers."

Creavey whistled. He felt dizzy with joy. "And when is this going to drop?"

"Has to have enough lead time to sink in, but not so long they can debunk us. I'm thinking a week before the election, during the Pulver Patriots parade. That gives us the perfect amount of time to talk it up."

"Beauty," said Creavey. His brow furrowed. "And, uhh, what happens after we win and no steel mill?"

"Who the hell cares? You get your casino, and we blame it on, you know, liberal bureaucrats and woke tree-huggers who snarled the thing up in environmental red tape, blah blah blah. The usual." Pause. "Anything else?"

Creavey thought. "Do I have anything to worry about?"

Another pause. "Well, here's what the numbers tells us. The people who like what's going on really like it. The Prosperity folks have a little over a third of the town in their pocket. Another third's on our side. The key is that middle third that's on the bubble. They haven't figured out which way to jump.

We've got to nail them down, fast. And that's what we're doing. That Cuban piece is our hammer." And with that, he signed off. Creavey liked to be the one to end the call, but…he was happy. How to celebrate? He grimaced. Maybe he'd go wild and have an iced decaf Americano, with TWO decaf shots. And in that moment, the guy who used to suck down three vodka martinis and do an amyl nitrate popper during an amorous all-nighter seemed like a fictional figure from three lifetimes ago.

CHAPTER SIXTY

August 24
MIKE DAVENPORT
"About as subtle as a car alarm." Makayla said, looking over the latest flyer. We were sitting in Raven's living room: Makayla, Yandy, Nick and Raven, Kate and the Reverend Luke. The house, as usual, was filled with savory fragrances thanks to the feast that Chef Betty had prepared. Even Nick, Steak Lover Magazine's "Carnivore of the Year" couldn't resist her roasted cauliflower and lentil tacos with creamy chipotle sauce. "Not bad," he said. "Am I turning into a rabbit?"

"Why me?" said a smiling Yandy, enjoying a third helping of roasted Brussels sprouts with honey-sesame glaze.

"Because you're scarier than Mike," said Makayla, "and we're five weeks away from the election. Scary brown people are here to take your stuff. Time to blast those dog-whistles from the rooftops. It's a great example of Brandolini's Law."

"What's that?" asked Nick.

"It's the Bullshit Asymmetry Principle. It takes a lot more energy to refute bullshit than to produce it. Hence, the world is full of unrefuted bullshit."

"Here's a question nobody's asking," I said. "So, what if they recall me? So what if I'm not Mayor? The mayor's job is a joke. Why can't we just keep doing what we're doing?"

The Rev took this one. "Mike, if we lose, I guarantee that everything we've done goes away: the gardens, the clinic, the drug rehab program, the community meals, the parties, gone, gone gone, probably inside a month."

"Why do you think they're spending so much money on this?" said Betty. "They're spending millions on a recall election in a broken-down town of ten thousand. Good god! Flyers, radio ads, billboards, door to door voter sign-ups…"

"Their social media stuff is out of control," said Makayla. "Did you know that you were injected with CIA mind parasites in Afghanistan? So the Deep State could control you and direct this whole plan by remote control to enslave people?"

"Whoa, whoa," said Yandy. "I thought this was being run by the Communists."

"It's all the same thing!" said Makayla. "It's THEM! The BLACK HATS! Take the red pill! Do the research!"

"The point is," said Nick, "that angry white guys like me who look at Mike out there getting his hands dirty in the spinach beds need to have some reason to fear him. He doesn't look scary, but what if he's just a meat robot being manipulated by evil puppet masters?"

"And also," said Kate, "You'll be shocked to discover that I'm running an abortion mill out of the basement of the Wellness Center, which of course doesn't have a basement, and then auctioning the fetal tissue to fictional Chinese billionaires on the dark web."

"And I'm the illegitimate offspring of Hugo Chavez and Hillary Clinton," said Raven, which made everyone laugh, even though we knew it was a real FB post.

"So, we have five weeks," said the Rev. "We all want to fight." Nods all around. "How do we win?"

"More flyers?" said Makayla.

"We could ask some of our garden teams to go door to door for Mike," said Nick.

"What if we don't do a single thing that looks like regular campaigning?" I said. "People are smart. They like what's happening."

"The only people who are buying what Creavey and Bagley are selling are folks in the PF Patriots who are spending fourteen hours a day in doomsday chatrooms," said Makayla.

"Speaking of the PF Patriots…" I said.

"What?" said Betty.

"They want a parade permit for October 26, a week before the election," I said. This stopped the conversation. Everyone pondered this.

Finally, Makayla said, "I'm thinking Creavey's going to have a ton of media there—news crews, maybe Cody Fortune. So, what if we do a little energetic counterprograming?"

"Like a parade of our own?" said the Rev.

"Think bigger," I said. "Like a great big…let's see…Prosperity Harvest Festival/Open House. Invite the state of Pennsylvania to celebrate what we've done, with a big party and a garden-to-table community feast."

"And a chalk art competition," said Makayla. "Give the artists something to do, and the news crews something to shoot."

"The biggest damn dance party we've ever thrown," said Kate.

"And the biggest damn feast the town has ever seen," said Betty. "'A Taste of Prosperity.'"

"I like it!" said the Rev. "How many tastes?

"I'm thinking five," said Betty. "We can do American, Mexican, French, Polish and Cuban."

"Great!" said Makayla. She looked at me. "Let's just be ready for a surprise. Creavey's all in to win this thing. Last time he had some yobs throwing Molotov cocktails. We need to be ready for anything, including more violence."

CHAPTER SIXTY-ONE

August 27
MIKE DAVENPORT

"So, you really don't remember what day this is?" Sunset, a picnic at Memorial Park. I was gazing at the lovely visage of Kate Walther as we sat at a concrete picnic table between a kid's playground and a spinach garden. She's the only woman on earth who could look sensational in teal medical scrubs with six pocket cargo pants. She was thin bordering on skinny, and dark circles made her blue eyes even more vivid. I'd brought the food: a couple of "Pitts-Burgers" from the Primanti Brothers, with fries and cole slaw. I was gobbling mine, and she was picking at her slaw.

"No. Sorry," she said. She seemed distracted.

"Everything okay?" I said.

"Yeah, good." She turned, looked at me. "In fact, very good. Great." This surprised me. The last shards of burnt umber sunlight revealed a face that wasn't downcast, just reflective. "So tell me," she said. "What's today?"

"This was the day…back in 1994…" I wanted to drag this out as long as possible. "…we had our first date." I could see her cast back in her memory, and then the light went on.

"The 'Pitts-burger,' right. Of course. Omigod. Ridiculous then, ridiculous now."

"I was trying to impress you."

"You did, you did. You were trying too hard in just the right way." She finally took a bite of her burger. "Good thing Chef Betty isn't here. She'd beat you to death with a zucchini."

"I know, I know. We're eating poison. We're destroying the planet. We're killing ourselves with saturated fat. I won't tell if you won't."

"It was right after the godawful beauty pageant debacle, right?"

"Debacle? Are you kidding me? The way you tanked that thing was…well, it was a piece of transcendent performance art that lives in my imagination. I said to myself, 'this woman is a goddess.'"

"Thank you. That's why I agreed to go on that date, you know." I cocked my head. "The way you responded, the one-man standing ovation. You got what I did, at every level. You and Kevin."

"Whatever happened to him?"

"Or we're still in touch. He runs an art gallery in Chelsea. Married to Steve, a bass clarinetist in the New York Pops Orchestra. Happiest couple I know."

I dipped a French fry in a splat of ketchup. "Speaking of marriage, Tess and I have called it quits. Or rather, I did. We are an ex-thing."

"Good. I was worried."

"Boy, you really didn't like her, did you?"

"She was…what's the word…damaged. Something was missing. All that demonic energy, like she was trying to out-run something."

"Yeah."

"You were nothing to her, Mike. All she wanted to do was get rich and blow town, and you were the getaway driver." Wow. I'd never heard it put just that way. So true.

"So," I said. "What about you?" I was surprised by the very long pause, the look off into the distance, and the look down at the ground.

"I want to thank you, Mike."

That's not what I expected. "Why?"

She finally looked back up at me. "This whole thing you started, it's…changed me. It's let me find out who I am. What I want to do."

"Well, that's…"

"Scott and I are getting divorced."

This brought me up short. "Really?"

She nodded. "I tried; I really did. Two weeks ago, I went to a cocktail party for the law firm and I found myself holding a glass of white wine trying to think of something to say to people who didn't…we just had nothing in common. All I could think about was my friends at the clinic and the people we were helping. That morning I'd been giving a footbath to a homeless guy. You ever done that?"

"No."

"The thing with homeless people is that their feet are always sore. And you can tell by their feet what's wrong with the rest of them. So, you take a plastic tub and fill it halfway up with Bentadine, put their feet in, and you're there kneeling in front of them, and you say, "How are you, Mr. Jones?" This is the first kindness anyone's shown this person in ten years and you hear the most astonishing, heartbreaking things. Helping these people makes everything from my old life feel like nothing."

"I'm sorry," I said.

"I'm not. The kids are out of the house, Scott's got work he enjoys, and now, so do I. And I'd never have found this work if we hadn't decided to jump off that cliff together."

I felt such love for her as I looked in that radiant face. "You once said to me that everyone has an unspeakable secret, a terrible regret, an impossible dream and an unforgettable love. My terrible regret is that I ever let you go. And my unforgettable love…"

She dropped her burger, moved over and crushed me in a hug that went on and on. I could feel her body shake with sobs, and then I started to cry. Not with sadness, just with…I don't know what. Life? After what seemed like both several moments and an instant, we parted. "We're going to make this work, Mike."

"Maybe. I hope so."

"The funny thing is, we're not saving them. They're saving us."

CHAPTER SIXTY-TWO

Friday, September 10
YANDY LOPEZ
Yandy and the Rev were just finishing their spinach/arugula salads with quinoa and Cuban black beans. The Rev looked over the crowd, more than a thousand people, all sitting at community tables passing plates and bowls and chatting each other up. He smiled at Yandy and said, "How can anyone doubt this universe was designed to give us an abundance of everything we need to live happily? We're given the seed, all we do is work the earth, plant it and wait. Rain, sunshine, and time work their magic. We weed, we compost, we harvest, we share, we thrive."

Yandy nodded. He flashed back on his time as a sniper. He'd taken lives, that was his job. He was a mechanic of death, albeit for a righteous cause (or so he thought then). So, this was him balancing the cosmic scales. Now he was a mechanic of life: a channel for the fruitfulness of the infinite, mysterious universe.

Gardening had saved him: WAS saving him, even now. It pried him away from his smartphone and computer screen with their toxic cascade of neural uproar that spiked his anxiety and fed his nihilism. Gardening got him outside, engaged in physical, doable tasks: planting, watering weeding, irrigating, composting, harvesting. He wasn't so much "out" in nature as *in* it: an enabler of this unfathomable miracle of photosynthetic generosity, harnessing the alchemical power of the catalyzing enzyme ribulose 1.5-bisphosphate carboxylase oxygenase (took him a week to memorize that) that transforms a tiny tomato seed into 150 pounds of succulent fruit in a single summer.

When he was gardening, Yandy was around others who were also being healed. They were all immersed in what the poet called "the felt presence of immediate experience." What made Yandy happiest was watching people take the dare: "Can I do that? Looks kinda fun." More helpers, more people working the earth instead of staring at screens, more sunshine, more strangers becoming friends. Working the gardens meant slowing down and syncing their souls to the speed of nature.

Even composting had a strange kind of benign effect. After the harvest, the "waste" (*there is no waste)* got put in the compost bins. Decay, regeneration, rebirth: the cycle of life began anew. It all worked together. It took him a while to remember what he first learned in Cuba: what a garden really grows is friends. They start out to save themselves, and they save themselves by finding themselves in a community of like-minded souls.

"Agree," said Yandy. "You should start holding your services in the gardens. In the sunshine."

The Rev looked at him, wide-eyed, and then laughed. "Yes," he said. "Of course. Celebrate the miracle where it happens. Would you consider delivering the sermon?"

"The sermon," said Yandy, "should be a salad." Now they both laughed.

"Just so. Hey, I'm ruminating on the promise of that peach cobbler. Would you care for some?" Yandy nodded and turned back to the lunch crowd. He was a part of this. That made him happy.

CHAPTER SIXTY-THREE

September 14
MIKE DAVENPORT
If I'm not careful, my job can devolve into one continuous meeting. I had my twice-a-month Borough Council meetings, my meetings with Mike's Super Friends, and I was always meeting with citizens' groups and ad hoc committees on the gardens, the community kitchen and the town clean-up. And then, every other week, I'd look in on the Community Council meetings. This was the advisory council created in the Charrette. This council met in the (vast) Rehearsal Room in the back of the Lucretia Fleetwood Pulver Opera House. The Council reported out the results of the district councils. They could meet either weekly or bi-weekly and had the freedom to act as they wished within the intentions of Prosperity's Mission, Objectives and Theme.

The Community Council Chair tonight was my friend, the Principal of Pulver High, Wilda Malone, representing Prattleboro. I'd brought along Raven Washburn and Reverend Luke for moral support. The Council had just heard an impassioned demand by Nevaeh Nadiyah-Lundy and a group of young artists, poets and writers from the New Prosperity Arts Group who were living rent-free in the Arbogast Building. Their demand was to tear down the statue of Enoch Cornelius Pulver in front of the Pulver Community Library. The eighteen-foot bronze "great man" statue was sculpted by Antonin Mercié, the President of the Société des Artistes Français and creator of the Robert E. Lee equestrian bronze that used to bestride Monument

Avenue in Richmond, Virginia. The Pulver bronze was a gift to the town from Pulver himself. It was perched on a twenty-four-foot sculpted marble base. As far as I could tell, no one but incontinent pigeons had paid a bit of attention to it for seventy years. But now…

"This is a monument to patriarchy, oppression and racism that cannot be allowed to look down upon us. It must be removed *now*," said Nadiyah-Lundy. "It is a slap in the face of every working person, every person of color, and every person who believes in social justice. Pulver was a monster, no better than Vanderbilt, Rockefeller, Andrew Carnegie or Henry Ford. Tear it down. Not tomorrow, not next week, NOW." Wild applause from the young artists in the gallery.

I raised my hand. "Can I say something?"

Wilda nodded to me. "Mayor Davenport." Had to play this one carefully.

I walked from the gallery of folding chairs into the arena. I turned to the council members. "First, I'd like to acknowledge Nevaeh Nadiyah-Lundy and the members of the New Prosperity Arts Group for bringing this up."

"We're not 'bringing it up'," shouted a goth kid from the gallery. "We're demanding it." Shouts of support.

"Uh huh," I said. "Look, Enoch Pulver was no saint, just ask Calvin McCoy. He was your typical plutocrat/robber baron of the time. A lot of people died in that hellscape of a steelworks he ran. But he did start and sustain this town and provide gainful employment to hundreds of thousands of people. There are lifelong residents here working with us in those gardens who think fondly of Pulver. They should have a say in this decision."

"Why?" said Nadiyah-Lundy.

"Does everyone remember the Charrette, that created this Council?" Nods all around. I took the Charrette report from my back pocket and read it aloud. "Quote, 'we will measure our prosperity not in money but in happiness, community and the abundance of good food and good friends.' I looked toward the gallery, then continued. "Jobs, food, medical care, clean, safe streets and an opportunity to come together and celebrate." I looked up at the Council members. "That's what we're here to accomplish: things that bring people together. We need to stay focused on that."

Kimani-Holloway Truth, Chef Betty's partner, vaulted up in the gallery and strode toward me. "This is just more 'mansplaining' from a smug, patriarchal white male who doesn't know what it feels like to have to walk by that damn statue, to feel the weight of a hundred years of oppression staring down at you. You don't get it."

"I think maybe he does." Reverend Luke was standing up, smiling. Bless you, Rev. How I loved that deep, rich, Biblical rumble of a voice. "If we're going to make a success of this thing, we need to listen to each other."

"He's not listening to us!" shouted Kimani-Holloway Truth, pointing at me.

"I am," I said. "Patriarchy. Oppression. Racism. I heard every word you said. I didn't say we'll never tear it down. I'm saying we won't tear it down right now, because we need to finish building up this place first."

"HE MURDERED BLACK PEOPLE," shouted Nadiyah-Lundy. She walked up to me until we were nose to nose. "*You* will never know what that feels like. Never."

"But I do," said Raven. Every head swiveled toward her. She stood, walked up to the two of us, turning to Nadiyah-Lundy. "My grandfather, Oscar Wells, died in that steelworks. Was murdered, really. I think of him every day. My community foundation is named after him. But tearing down that statue won't bring him back, or any of them, and it will divide the town, turn us against each other. Black versus white, old versus young. What we're building here will dissolve into yelling and finger-pointing and we'll become just another clot of angry, polarized villagers lobbing stink bombs at each other as nothing gets done."

She turned to the gallery. "We're building a movement here that includes everyone. This isn't a movement about hairsplitting and gatekeeping and performative moral outrage."

This set Kimani-Holloway off. "You think…"

Raven cut her off. "Our job here is finding converts, not fingering heretics."

The Rev stepped between them. "Kimani, we're all part of something that's new, never tried before, and it's as fragile as a soap bubble. It's welcoming and merciful. It's about giving a hug instead of picking a fight. That's all. Nobody's ignoring you. You're a part of this, we all are."

A long moment of silence. Kimani-Holloway Truth, head down, walked back to the gallery. "Whatever."

Wilda Malone said, "The proposal to remove the statue of Enoch Cornelius Pulver is tabled to a future time."

After the meeting broke up, I gave Raven a grateful hug as I said, "Converts and heretics: genius." Then I walked up to the Rev. "Up to me," I said, "I'd tear down Mister Pulver and put you up on that pedestal."

He laughed. "No more pedestals, Mike. Let's melt down that statue and let those young artists run wild sculpting something wonderful out of the bronze."

CHAPTER SIXTY-FOUR

September 26
NICK BARLOW

Nick Barlow had seen a lot of life. He'd (barely) survived his stint in Vietnam. He'd been married and divorced and married again and widowed. He was 73 years old: old enough to know that he was never going to change the world into the one he wanted. That was the "free minds and free markets" place his father dreamed about. That dream turned to dust in his hands when the folks he voted for treated him like a 'useful idiot' and did whatever the big business types told them to do. Anger became bitterness that melted into a puddle of cynical resignation. He was good at fixing cars, so that's what he did. The rest of the world could go to hell (and it was).

So, what was he doing here, in Raven Washburn's living room, standing next to Raven in front of the Reverend Luke Bramlett, hearing himself saying the words, "I do"? As in "I do take you, Raven Washburn, to be my wife, to love from this day forward no matter what happens, until we are parted by death."

Nick and Raven were surrounded by their friends: Mike, Makayla, Kate, Wilda, Darla, and Yandy. Chef Betty was prepping the wedding feast. Everyone was smiling, and he had the biggest smile of all. Why?

When his Sarah had died of cervical cancer eight years ago, Nick was certain that was it for him. He'd adored Sarah. She brought up their two kids as he put in fourteen-hour days at his shop. She was the kindest, most caring person he'd ever met, and when she died, he felt as if he'd lost a limb. He knew he'd never fall in love again, so he put no effort in finding another mate. The worst part was that he'd never experience the kind of lighter-than-air 'crazy love' he'd dreamed about as a teenager: the kind Jerry Lee Lewis sang about in "Great Balls of Fire": "*You broke my will, but what a thrill!*" This might be his best-kept secret: he watched vintage romantic comedies on Turner Classic Movies just to feel, vicariously, what was like to fall truly, madly, deeply in love. A lot of movie and rock stars got tangled up in wild, messy, failed romances. He envied them for daring to risk everything on love. He'd played it safe. It was probably the right decision, but still...

And then Raven Washburn had cracked his back and taken him for a joy ride in her electrified 1953 Ford F-100 pickup truck. *Who was this woman?* They started having coffee together, then lunch, and then dinner. That led to nightly walks along the river, just talking about everything and nothing. Nick thought Raven was the most interesting person he'd ever met. She was outgoing and friendly. She seemed to know something about everything. All that money she'd been awarded meant nothing to her except as a way to help other people. She was fiercely opinionated but in a smart, funny way: debating her was a delight, and she would give it up when he boxed her into an ideological corner. And crucially, her progressivism and his libertarianism collided right here in the crucible of Prosperity, Pennsylvania. They both subscribed to Mother Earth News, the monthly Bible of self-sufficient living. "Live small, need less, do it yourself." Raven helped Nick install a solar water heater on his roof, with the hot water sent by small direct current pumps to his water tanks. He helped her switch to a custom-made, ultra-efficient, super-insulated refrigerator that used 80% less power.

And so, finally, he knew what "crazy love" felt like. There were still those (including his pals at Snooky's, and the Five O'Clock Whistle) who looked askance at this inter-racial romance, ESPECIALLY with a "rad-lib Commie" type,

ESPECIALLY at his age, and it just made him laugh! He could give a shit! Who cared what they thought? His daughter Kathy, a blackjack dealer at the Golden Nugget in Las Vegas, thought he was out of his mind, but his son Karl (for Karl Hess, legendary freethinker) was thrilled for him.

He remembered his proposal. Raven was sponsoring a special garage/workspace at Pulver-Bledsoe University. They were trying to figure out how to electrify the sweet 1962 white-with-red-trim Rambler American 400 convertible she'd just bought at auction for six hundred dollars. She'd gotten PBU to partner with her as a project for young people interested in doing something about climate change. They rebuilt the body, and now they were helping turn this car into a full electric. Raven got free labor for her project, and the kids got trained up so they could turn this into a business that could change the world. Talk about fun! Nobody could find a manual for the Rambler, so it was all seat-of-the-pants, take-it-apart-and-figure-it-out DIY stuff. They scoured junkyards and Internet message boards for parts, and when they hit a dead end, Raven got the students to use the university's 3D printers to make the parts.

Nick and Raven had just had a peak moment: firing up the car's full digital Bluetooth sound system. Raven punched up a playlist from her smartphone with "Love Train" by the O'Jays. All the kids were gone, so she grabbed him by the hand, and they started dancing, laughing, working off the stress of six hours of focused labor. That song segued right into "Let's Get It On" by Marvin Gaye. Nick pulled her close and they began slow dancing. It was just everything—the song, the moment, the warmth of her body, the ridiculous joy of hearing that song coming out of that phone being played through that sound system of that car—that made him start laughing.

"What?" she said as they danced.

"I don't know," he said. "Just…everything. This thing shouldn't work. We shouldn't be here. I shouldn't be having this much fun. We shouldn't even know each other…"

"We shouldn't?"

"What possible reason would a smart, rich…."

"Stop, stop," she laughed.

"Look at me! I'm just this cranky geriatric gearhead."

She pulled back in mock anger. "Are you saying we should stop hanging out together?"

"NO!" he said, so loudly that she laughed again. The song ended, and she gave him a huge hug before letting him go. Even as they parted, he couldn't stop looking at that radiant, smiling face. Without thinking, he blurted out, "What would it take…that is, is there a way where we could figure out…"

"Yes? Figure what out?"

He sighed. He just needed to say it, but he couldn't. Or could he? "You…you make me happy in a way I never…I can't remember being this happy. Would you laugh at me if I asked you to…to…

"What?" She was smiling.

He gulped. Then, almost a whisper: "M-marry me?"

All at once he felt sick to his stomach. Had he blown it? She didn't laugh, but she seemed surprised. She opened her mouth, then closed it, thinking. He wondered if he was about to be humiliated. But she said, "No. I wouldn't laugh."

"You wouldn't?"

"No."

Gulp. Pause. "Well then," he said, "Would you, you know…will you…ummm…marry me?"

Another pause. And then, "Yes, Nick. It's kind of ridiculous, but…I think…I think that would be something I'd like." They just looked at each other for a long moment, and then came together for a kiss, and then another long, luscious hug. She must have been scrolling through the song list on her smartphone, because "God Only Knows" by the Beach Boys started playing. The hug turned into another slow dance: or was it their first slow dance as an engaged couple? He could feel hot tears streaming down his face.

"You're a Beach Boys fan?" he said.

"Surprised?" she said.

He pulled away from her, wiping away the tears. "Raven," he said, "Absolutely nothing about you surprises me anymore…except, you know, everything."

CHAPTER SIXTY-FIVE

October 26
MIKE DAVENPORT
It finally landed with a resounding thud: the October Surprise.

Makayla, Yandy and Raven were angry.

Nick Barlow was shaking his head. "I know these people; I should have seen it coming."

Reverend Luke was sanguine. "We have delivered on the promise of prosperity, friends. We're feeding people, giving them hope, and offering them an opportunity to sing, dance and hug each other. The rest is in the hands of the almighty."

"You got that right," said Makayla. "We thought they might try something, but this…" She face-palmed, shook her head. "We let the story get away from us. We lost the day. And we might lose the damn election. Because they were more devious than we were."

"Hey, c'mon, people." I felt kind of giddy, like being shot at and missed. What had just happened was so cynical it was kind of awesome: a pure expression of brazen, amoral audacity. "We didn't know what it would be. Now we know. That's good for us." Everyone stared at me like I'd lost my mind. Maybe I had. I said, "People are smart. We've got a week. Let's get busy."

So, here's the story of the day.

Makayla did a magnificent job setting us up to look good in the media. She got left-wing media darling Maggie Atwater, primetime anchor of BlueNation's most popular show "Right Now" to come to Prosperity to do a feature on our Harvest

Festival/Open House. Atwater showed up because her competition, Cody Fortune of FirstNews, was here covering the Pulver Forge Patriots parade and political rally.

The Patriots' parade wasn't until 2, so Makayla programmed our Festival to start at 10 am, with our Sidewalk Chalk Art Contest. The artisans provided the BlueNation news crew with some great, energetic interviews and enchanting visuals. I was a judge, along with Calvin and Raven. The winning work was a spectacular 1930s WPA Diego Rivera-style mural that took up the sidewalk of an entire block. It divided the history of the town into two halves: the grim half (a soot-covered, black and white Pulver Forge) and the radiant half (a dazzling full-color-mostly-green Prosperity).

At 11:30, the BlueNation crew captured hordes of ravenous citizens savoring our "Taste of Prosperity Community Feast." Chef Betty and crew outdid themselves, with five food stations serving hot, fresh, vegan takes on American, Mexican, French, Polish, and Cuban cuisine. For dessert, five kinds of homemade pie: pecan, pumpkin, apple, cherry and key lime.

At 1 p.m. I took Maggie and her crew through our "Prosperity Preview Center" in the old fire station on Dinwiddie Street, where we'd cobbled together some artwork that showed our plan for the next year. New cafes! Trad and hipster restaurants! Art galleries! Clothing boutiques! A food co-op, featuring our homegrown produce! Yandy showed off plans for some innovative greenhouses we were going to build with profits from the gourmet greens we were selling to Pittsburgh's best restaurants. We'd now be able to grow spinach, chard and arugula when it's snowing outside. And Kate showed the news crew through her new Prosperity Community Wellness Center that was sending out neighborhood volunteers to give at-risk citizens monthly wellness checks.

The Pulver Forge Patriots had their raggedy-ass parade — guns, flags, pickup trucks, Harleys and Cody Fortune, holding an AR-15 rifle, sitting in a Barcalounger wedged into the cargo bed of a black 2003 Cadillac Escalade EXT — at 2 p.m. It ended at Memorial Park. Maggie's crew shot this, and interviewed Fred Bagley (Cody Fortune begged off). Our crew was loving the contrast. We were smiling, they were scowling. We were generosity, they were grievance. We were creating hope and beauty, they were a bunch of geezer commandos waving their guns. Cody Fortune spoke, giving the codgers a straight shot of snake venom, invoking the word "patriots" thirty-seven times in ten minutes.

Then Fred Bagley got up to speak. I expected the usual character assassination spiked with some hairy-scary "we're on the brink of extinction, take back America" boilerplate, and that's what I got…until the finale. That's when he dropped the bomb. *"Good people of Pulver Forge, when we take back this town, we're going to enjoy some REAL prosperity, yes sirree bobcat. That's because our benefactor, Mister Moses Creavey, in addition to all the jobs he'll give us with his beautiful new casino, will be bringing us 2000 — you heard me right, that's 2000 — new jobs. How? With a brand new, twenty-first century steel mill! Built right on the site of our heritage facility! You know he's a deal maker, right? Well, he's in business with a South Korean steel company, and they are going to build the latest, most innovative, most efficient electric arc furnaces that will return Pulver Forge to the forefront of steelmakers in America and the world! We'll forge a brand-new future for Pulver Forge! We are not gardeners, trash collectors or slaves. We're steelworkers! And we're going to make the steel that's going to rebuild this country, and that all starts in exactly seven days!"*

Makayla was watching this with her mouth open. Maggie laughed, it was such a bare-faced fraud, but it was news, and she was duty-bound to report it. She moved in to interview Bagley. He was well rehearsed: he rattled off a bunch of specifically vague not-quite-promises that always ended with "at least two thousand new jobs." The deal was huge, but he couldn't reveal the details. It was one of South Korea's biggest steel companies, but he couldn't reveal which one. Bagley was surrounded by joyous geriatric patrons of the "Five O'Clock Whistle" who had been dreaming of this day for thirty years.

As disgusted as I was, I admired the nerve of the play. This was a mega-whopper, a lie so humungous that surveillance satellites could see it from the exosphere. This was a lie that looked you in the eye as it picked your pocket. The idea was to pound this astonishing pipe dream into the frontal lobes of waffling voters and squeak through the election. Then they could shut us down, shrug their shoulders when the "new steel plant" turned out to be bullshit and get busy building Creavey's gambling joint. So how could we fight this? Should we? Would it sink under the weight of its own dishonesty? We had a week to figure it out. Personally, I was looking forward to it. We'd finally get this settled, once and for all.

CHAPTER SIXTY-SIX

October 30

TRANSCRIPTION: Remarks by Mayor Mike Davenport at Citizen's Forum Regarding the Matter of the Recall Election (8 p.m. Pulver Forge Community Library Auditorium)

MAYOR DAVENPORT: Thank you. That's quite a presentation from Mayor Bagley! If I were to meet myself on the street, I'd be terrified of such a reprehensible traitor, a man without virtues. Abandoning my platoon on the battlefield! Murdering my best friend, the man who saved my life in Afghanistan! A Communist turning God-fearing Americans into soulless robots!

And I'm masterminding this heinous cosmic conspiracy while running a humble coffeehouse in Pittsburgh and serving as Mayor of this very town. Where do I find the time for all this villainy? I mean, I'm spending forty hours a week renovating derelict buildings, another thirty attending town meetings and another ten hours serving eight hundred cups of coffee to you fine folks every morning.

I guess this is the part of my remarks where I'm supposed to defend myself, but I'm not going to, for two reasons. First, you're smart enough to see what's going on. You know there isn't going to be a new steel mill in this town, because any foreign steel company would open in a place with cheap labor and no unions, like Arkansas or Alabama. Plus they'd demand a "greenfield" to build on, not a "brownfield" like Pulver Forge where they'd have to pay half a billion dollars to pull a hundred years of toxic debris out of the ground before they could even start building. This is the worst kind of lie, because it preys on our hopes and dreams so that we'll abandon what we've built together, and when we find out they lied to us, we'll have nothing.

The second reason I'm not going to defend myself is because what's happening in this town isn't about me and my political ambitions, of which I have none. This is about you…or better yet, us: what we've done together in five months. We aren't hapless rust belt casualties. We're self-reliant citizens with a promising future that we're creating ourselves. We're creating our own opportunities.

The other day I shared a cup of coffee with Jake Dawkins. Some of you know Jake, he's that big friendly bear of a guy who serves you lunch at the Prosperity Kitchen and drives you around town in our 'Lectric Get-About. Jake told me he'd been in the emergency room three times from over-dosing on painkillers, and you know what got him clean? A job. A job serving people. You saved him, friends. The opposite of addiction is connection. Connection produces prosperity. Prosperity means having enough for ourselves, and some left over to share with our neighbors.

My message isn't, 'Please keep me in office.' My message is, 'Don't give up on what we've created together.' We've created over two thousand jobs in five months. We're feeding those two thousand people every single day with fresh produce we're growing ourselves! We're housing over a thousand people. A lot of them used to sleep under bridges and next to trash dumpsters. We're seeing over a hundred and fifty of our friends and neighbors in our wellness center every single day.

And every single day we're having four thousand, two hundred and seventy-one friendly conversations we didn't have before. We're producing over six thousand smiles a day. We're telling two thousand, seven hundred and nine jokes. We've formed three thousand, nine hundred and eighty-one friendships, and we've cut this town's cynicism and negativity by a mind-boggling ninety-one percent! And all I've done is served enough coffee so that you could do this yourselves!

So, when you step into the voting booth, ask yourself one question: are you better off now than you were five months ago? Don't vote for me, vote for yourself and your neighbors. Vote for the future. Vote for hope. Thank you, my friends.

CHAPTER SIXTY-SEVEN

October 31
CALVIN MCCOY

A Saturday night World Premiere movie screening! I was the only member of tonight's audience who had attended the last motion picture to premiere at the Majestic Theatre, corner of 7th Street and Maple Avenue in Pulver Forge, PA. The date was August 14, 1946. I'd just turned 16. The picture was "Men of Steel," a Republic picture starring Sonny Tufts, Victor Jory and Czech skating star (and notorious non-actress) Vera Hruba Ralston. In this brisk 63-minute B-picture, Tufts is a steelworker who tangles with his supervisor Jory over the affections of Ralston, comely secretary to mill boss Porter Hall. The film was premiered in Pulver Forge because the Republic team spent two days shooting background footage of the mill. (The steel-making plant in the movie is called "Thunder Forge," in the fictional town of Thunder Forge, Pennsylvania.) The only "star" who showed up for the premiere was Ralston. I still have her autograph on that evening's program. I kept it for twenty years hoping it would increase in value. Nope.

For seventy years, from 1927 to 1997, the Majestic Theater invited Pulver Forge movie patrons to enjoy a sturdy buffet of blue-collar crowd pleasers. The much grander Orpheum, an ex-vaudeville house, was the local palace of the cinema arts, hosting everything from "Gone With the Wind" to "Casablanca" to "Quo Vadis" while the Majestic played Abbott and Costello comedies, Gene Autry and Roy Rogers westerns and black and white crime melodramas like "I Wake Up Screaming." The

Orpheum closed in 1991 and fell into disrepair. The Majestic stayed open long enough to play "Titanic" in 1997. Although it shut down, the Majestic had a guardian angel: a movie lover named Morven Hoonigan. He was the last projectionist, and he spent his life savings to buy the place when it closed. For the next twenty-plus years, Hoonigan hosted the yearly Pulver-Bledsoe University student film festival, along with a week's worth of "It's A Wonderful Life" screenings the third week of every December.

Morven Hoonigan is now eighty-one years old. He still loves movies. He's the reason we were able to host Prosperity's first cinematic World Premiere in seventy-plus years. The movie was "Creating Prosperity," a documentary produced and directed by Makayla Nichols, shot by her precocious acolytes, and starring the people of Prosperity, PA.

Nick actually found a beat-up red carpet in the sub-basement of the theater, so the people of the town would feel like stars as they entered. The film was 79 minutes long. Mikayla had her kids use the video app on their smartphones to capture the lives of five Prosperity residents.

The first—and most obvious—was Mike Davenport. We meet Mike at that first candidate's forum. We feel his joy the night he was elected Mayor. We watch him serving coffee, working the gardens, picking up trash, and making friends at the noontime meal. He's a happy warrior who likes getting his hands dirty.

We meet Chef Betty in the Prosperity Community Kitchen, prepping lunch for 800 people. As she works, she tells us her story, from 14-year-old addict to apprentice chef to Vegan Gourmet Goddess, the "Woman Who Feeds People." Interview bites with Reverend Luke, Betty's beloved poet/partner Kimani, and her culinary mentor Mashama deepened the story. The takeaway here was how Betty's devotion to feeding people turned into a million smiles from grateful customers who donned homemade "FED BY BETTY" buttons.

Next was Raven Washburn. This story begins with the death of Oscar Wells, continues with the Lambert Selden Pulver's forbidden love affair with housemaid Bertha Weems, and peaks with Raven's discovery that she is an heir to the Pulver family fortune. Makayla makes an inspired link between Martin Luther King's "I Have a Dream" speech, delivered the day Raven was conceived, to Raven's own dream, to fill Prosperity with a riot of glorious art work as she re-vitalizes the town through a Community Bank that holds town property in a citizen's trust.

The Raven story flows neatly into the story of Nick Barlow. His journey from Vietnam vet to conservative/libertarian cynic to Prosperity Goodwill Ambassador is told with wry humor by Nick himself, with his narration complementing footage of him teaching his gang of apprentices how to fix and electrify every kind of vehicle on the road. We see Nick and Raven driving a sporty vintage convertible Rambler through town, stopping in front of one of Raven's glorious murals.

Makayla saved the best for last: the story of Max Stone, the homeless methamphetamine addict who almost killed Dr. Kate at the Bratton Free Clinic. This story brings in everyone. We see the damage he created at the clinic as Dr. Kate gives a harrowing description of his attack on her. We see Max going through withdrawal as two volunteers watch over him, supervised by Kate. Next, we see Max outside in the sunshine, the newest member of the "Earth Angels" as they garden their "Dirt Candy Heaven" spinach garden. The "Earth Angels," all ex-addict service veterans, heap praise on Max as they plant, water, weed and tend to the beds. Finally, we see Max back in his room at the Bessemer Hotel, helping a sixteen-year-old girl kick her Fentanyl addiction. "I'm so lucky to be alive," he says. "So lucky I can give something back."

The film ends with the whole gang at Nick and Raven's joyous wedding, followed by a Chef Betty feast and a dance-the-night-away party. We think the film is over...until Makayla shows a grainy video clip of Mike at Dave Bratton's memorial service. "Nobody's coming, folks," he says. "Nobody. That's the best possible news I can deliver. The truth shall set you free. It's up to you. Take care of business, you live. You don't, well, look around." Then a quick series of shots as we look around Prosperity today. Gardens. Murals. Happy people eating, dancing laughing. A final shot of Raven's rainbow-colored banner over Main Street, "Welcome to Prosperity." Fade out.

Makayla got a standing ovation as she stood up from the front row. She summoned her crew; everyone took a bow. Then Mike came in, and then Yandy, the Rev, Dr. Kate, Chef Betty, Raven and Nick and finally Max. The ovation lasted for ten minutes, which was nine minutes longer than the applause for Vera Hruba Ralston back in 1946. Makayla had really captured our story. Now we had something to show the world.

CHAPTER SIXTY-EIGHT

November 2 (ELECTION NIGHT)
MOSES CREAVEY

Moses Creavey was on a losing streak. This morning, he discovered that his female Bantamweight UFC hopeful, 'Terrible Terry' Savage had been banned from fighting for fourteen months after she tested positive for Dehydroepiandrosterone. So stupid! And then he discovered that he'd been pushed out of the top 50 on the Forbes list of the richest people on earth, dethroned by a software dork and a Wal-Mart heiress. 31 billion dollars didn't buy what it used to.

Now Creavey was neck deep in the scalding waters of his penthouse Jacuzzi, on the far end of the cantilevered pool that hovered past the edge of the 81st floor of the Creavey Alcazar Resort: best view in Vegas, and he had no one to share it with. His phone quivered. Gavin Cutler! About time. "Gavin, I've been waiting for your call. Good news only, please."

"Well, let's see. You tasked me to get the geezers to the polls, and we did, every single one. Last time our Mister Bagley got nine hundred seventy-one votes, and Davenport won with one thousand, six hundred and fifty-three. This time two thousand, three hundred and eighty-eight of the fine people of Pulver Forge cast their ballots for Frantic Fred Bagley."

Creavey's stomach clenched. He could see where this was going. After a short pause, he said, "You're about to make me unhappy, aren't you?"

"It is what it is, Moses. Mike Davenport got three thousand, one hundred fifty-three votes."

Creavey was suddenly aware that he was boiling to death. His face was red before this call. Now he felt his head might explode. He hauled himself onto the edge of the Jacuzzi and swung his feet over to the chilly water of the pool. The shock of going from hot to cold made him woozy. "We were supposed to win. I paid you eighty thousand dollars for every vote we needed. You guaranteed me that we'd win."

The barking howl of laughter was so sharp, Creavey had to pull his phone away from his ear. "You kill me, Moses. You fat cats think you can buy anything. I never promised you a damn thing, and you know it. I delivered the goods, and the goods were damn good. That October surprise? The best, and perfectly timed, a work of art. You got a beef? Move to Prosperity, Pennsylvania and have it out with the voters."

"What went wrong?"

"Jobs, jobs, jobs. And healthcare. And free lunch. Too many voters like what's going on. And the folks who believed what we said about the new steel mill were going to vote for us anyway."

"You ripped me off, Cutler. I'm going to ruin you. I know people, I'm going to tell them you're a bullshit artist."

Another laugh. "Take your best shot, Moses. Before you put too much time into that project, you should know that I'm booked for the next three election cycles." And with that, he hung up.

Creavey stared off into the Las Vegas night. What was his next move? He'd call Goodwin Tuttle in the morning and light him up. You want to be President? Then you have to do me a favor…

Or should he bother? He'd already spent more on this stupid recall fiasco than he'd realize in casino profits for the first ten years he'd be open in Pulver Forge. He flashed on the memoir he'd yet to write. A new title popped into his head: "What 31 Billion Dollars Can't Buy."

CHAPTER SIXTY-NINE

November 2 (ELECTION NIGHT)
MIKE DAVENPORT
11:53 p.m.: Makayla took the call from City Hall. "YEAH!" she shouted, ecstatic. "How much?" She turned to the group and said, "Recall Yes, 2,388. Recall No, 3,153!" Deafening cheer, followed by whoops and banshee cries. The best news besides the margin of victory was the number of voters: almost three times as many people voted this time as last.

We were packed into the backroom of the Prosperity HuggaMug, which had been our makeshift campaign HQ. With an ear-splitting "SQUORSH!" Steve Dorsey tapped a keg of his latest celebratory one-off micro-brew, "I Like Mike Imperial Victory Kick-Ass Stout." As he was filling red cups with the stuff, he said, "Just be warned, this isn't on the Little Leaguer menu. I was fooling around with the ABV, and I got it up to 15%, that's about twice what my normal stuff has." Everyone got a cup, and everyone looked at me for a speech. "To paraphrase the great Winston Churchill," I said, "This isn't the end. It's not even the beginning of the end. But I'm betting it's the end of the beginning. We're really on our way." Laughter, sip, laughter, sip, followed by huzzahs and "Wow, that's some powerful shit!"

I didn't feel the full force of the elixir. Didn't want to. I quit after half a cup. I was loving the moment, and I couldn't feel any better. So, what did I feel? A blessed relief, certainly, and something more. You work so hard for something, fail so often, and then, suddenly…you've done it. It's shocking. You're in it, the victory moment. So delicious the way time stops: no future, no past, just this one perfect moment. And then the certainty that the moment passes, the feeling fades and the next catastrophe shows up right on schedule. I guess that makes it even more special. "The most incredible thing about miracles is that they happen." They do, and I'm proof.

Wednesday, November 3
1:15 a.m.

Makayla and I were both too wired to sleep. We meandered through the town until we found ourselves on Bessemer Road where we could see the haunted remains of Pulver Forge Steel Mill #3. We could smell the swampy tang of the mighty Monongahela as we approached. A right on Pulver Drive, and we were standing at the gates where workers entered the mill. The gates themselves were long gone. Now there was just some tangled, rusty chain-link fencing that had been cut up by vandals. Anyone could wander into this hallowed hellscape. The only people who did were thrill-seeking teens, looters and druggies. "You know what we should do with this place?"

"What?"

I stared at it. I could hear echoes of what used to be: the thunder of the Bessemer converter, the deafening sizzle of the three-thousand-degree open hearth furnace, and the shriek of the factory whistle that let everyone know there'd been an accident. And ghosts: I saw the ghosts of those sweat-soaked, grim-faced men like my father and grandfather, forty going on sixty. "Use it to tell our story."

"Like what?" she said.

I held my arms out, as if I were gathering this whole filthy monstrosity in a bear hug. "This, right here, is where we should put our 'Prosperity, Pennsylvania History Museum and Cultural Heritage Center.' I mean, the history of Pulver Forge is the history of the American labor movement, the birth and death of the middle class. Why can't we use this place to tell our story?

Not like a regular museum, but the *real* story, warts and all. Take people into the darkness and filth. Scare them, and then inspire them."

"We could re-create the Pulver Forge Massacre," she said.

"Damn straight. Line 'em up, turn out the lights, let 'em hear gunshots, screams. How many folks show up to re-fight those Civil War battles? This will be the very first 'massacre reenactment.' Would Maggie Atwater show up for that?"

She laughed. "Interactive historical atrocity guest experience, with simulated gun violence? She'd love it."

"Great!" I said. We were kidding on the square. I mean, this was ridiculous, like, say, turning Alexander Hamilton's life into a Hip-Hop Broadway musical. "We'll invite people to see our history for what it really was."

"And exit through the gift shop," she smiled.

"Always!" I said. I held my hands up to frame a t-shirt. "'My Folks Got Gunned Down in the Pulver Forge Massacre, and All I Got Was This Lousy T-Shirt.' The whole July 4th celebration can begin and end here, followed by fireworks and a dance."

"I like it," she said. "So, what's in this museum? What do people actually see and do? Pitch it to me. No budget, dream as big as you want."

There was something inspiring about being in the belly of the beast on this particular night, immersed in this surreal moonscape: the steampunk engine room of a lost robot civilization buried in decades of sooty dust. "Okay," I said. "First of all, we keep as much of these ruins as we can, as grimy as possible. We blaze a path through the rubble so our visitors can get to our museum space, with the shows and exhibits. Then one of our personable hosts meets them with a genuine Prosperity, Pennsylvania hospitality welcome."

"Jobs, jobs, jobs," said Makayla.

"That's right. Hell, this place can give us more jobs than Creavey's casino."

"Good. So, what's the story we tell?"

"First, we meet Enoch Pulver, your classic 19th century robber baron: the paradox of capitalism in human form. Family man, philanthropist, friend of Presidents, candidate for governor. And, at the same time, a money-obsessed sociopath, a stone racist, and a man who didn't blink when he ordered the murder of his own workers so that he could create a slightly bigger pile of filthy lucre."

"The perfect person to anchor our story," said Makayla. "Dynamic, bold, greedy, charismatic, smart, ruthless, ambitious. Is he an evil man looking for redemption, or a good man corrupted by an obsession with becoming the richest man alive?"

"Or both?" I said.

"Yes. Visitors decide for themselves."

I had a brainstorm. "Oh my god," I said. "That goddam Pulver statue? We move it here, right in the middle of the exhibit."

"Perfect," she said. "Now what?"

"Now," I said as the story clarified in my mind, "We do the massacre like we said, big and dramatic, some kind of super-realistic holographic image of Pulver's goons shooting into the crowd of guests. Only this doesn't stop thousands of desperate immigrants from flooding into Pulver Forge. These are the folks who fought for a living wage, who risked their lives to build this country. We create one of those big over-the-top shows like they have at theme parks, with live actors and flying scenery and three-dimensional visual effects."

Makayla laughed. "Great! No budgets today!"

"We're dreaming!" I said. "Dreams are free!"

"Okay, yeah, I'm with you. But what's the story that goes to the heart of the audience?"

"Pulver Forge builds America. The heaven of America's golden years was forged in the hell of this place. This steel made America the Arsenal of Democracy. Think of the ending: V-J Day, the whole theater lights up, red, white and blue confetti drops from the ceiling."

"Love it," said Makayla.

"Yeah," I said. "And then we plunge them into more darkness: the 1970s. The betrayal. Fly-by-night greedbag owners ship our jobs overseas. The mill shuts down when there's nothing left to give away. Our friends and neighbors are thrown onto the trash heap without a second thought. Drugs, crime, misery. Pulver Forge left for dead. Then we turn a corner, and…"

"What?"

"A miracle!" I said. "Pulver Forge becomes Prosperity, and everyone goes back to work. Our visitors find themselves smack dab in the middle of our 4th of July picnic. White fluffy clouds in a blue sky, the smell of Kettle Korn, joyous dance music, and greenery everywhere. This is an interactive exhibit area where people can discover for themselves everything we're doing: the gardens, the wellness clinic, the town meetings, the whole bit."

"And then they…" We both said it together. "…exit through retail!"

"Damn straight!" I said. "T-shirts, jackets, hats, coffee mugs, commemorative posters, and autographed copies of the DVD of your movie and book about this place. Have I missed anything?"

"Yeah," she said. "The most important thing: a framed certificate of honorary Prosperity citizenship, signed by the mayor, just nineteen ninety-five."

"Perfect!" I said, laughing. All this had come out in a big rush of enthusiasm, and now I was spent. It seemed almost possible for a moment. I mean, why not? It was a great story with a happy ending.

"Can we really do this?" said Makayla.

"Hell, we just trounced Moses Creavey, how can building a fifty-million-dollar history museum be tougher than that?"

CHAPTER SEVENTY

November 3
MIKE DAVENPORT
"So, you won," said Tess.

"I won," I said. "Not exactly a landslide, but…"

"Good for you. That makes me happy." Tess lifted her stemless plastic wine goblet in a toast. We bumped and took sips. Our last date was like our first: Steelers folding chairs and tailgating table on a sidewalk off River Front Drive under the 40th Street Bridge in Millvale. Tonight, we were enjoying the cuisine of the "La Cocinera Loca," a Nicaraguan fusion truck that was trending on Social media. The wine, a pinot grigio, was (as always) the very best we could find at Trader Joe's for under six bucks. As we dined, I stole glances at her: that handsome moon face with those smart, flashing brown eyes. I remembered the first time I saw her, which was the moment I fell for her.

"You got my check for the wedding planner?" I said.

She nodded. "I think she was more upset than I was," said Tess.

"Are you sorry it's not going to happen?"

"Are you?"

"I asked you first."

She paused, took a sip of wine, and stared at the sky. "Let me answer that question three ways. First, yes." My smile broke into a laugh. She lowered her head and gazed at me. "Second, my worst nightmare would be to marry someone whose heart wasn't in it, because they felt obligated by a past promise. Third, I…" She stopped, looked away.

"What?" I said.

"I've been thinking about what's happened. About who you are now, what's happened to you. And about what I did to break us up."

"You didn't do anything," I said. "I'm the one who changed. I still feel…" I paused. What did I feel?

"What?" she said.

"I can still feel what I've always felt for you. Affection. Fascination. And respect. You're one of a kind, girl."

A wistful look. "Maybe…I don't know…I'm changing too."

"Really? How?"

"You know me, work is work. Tess the freebooter, this gun for hire, count the money and move on. No job ever bothered me…until this one. Most promotion has an element of hooey, but this…this was complete, malignant bullshit, the worst kind of lying." A sip of wine. "I stopped eating. Broke into tears for no reason, couldn't sleep. Turns out that maybe, I don't know, there's a such a thing as a soul. And maybe I've got one."

Now it was my turn to sip the wine. "I think maybe we've both got souls. Maybe we've always had them. And life has this funny way of pushing our noses in that fact."

Silence, then an owl started hooting. I counted the hoots: seven. A great horned owl, like the one that used to live outside our house when I was a kid.

"You know what I wish?" she said as her head lolled back, gazing at the night sky.

"What's that?"

"I wish we could stop time and live in this moment forever. Forget Kauai, just us, here, this sky, this food truck, this mediocre wine, this bittersweet feeling that, for one unlikely moment in a world of eight billion lonely people you and I found each other, loved each other, could see our futures together, a happy future that would go on and on. Why can't we live in this moment forever, with that beautiful future just ahead? Why do things have to end?"

"I don't know, but they do," I said. "Nothing lasts." I looked at her. My heart was breaking, and hers was too. "No matter how much you want it to go on."

She held out her wine glass. Clink. "And let's not forget Kauai," she said. We both sipped. "It's probably better as a dream, because the dream will always be perfect."

On the way home, my phone beeped twice. The first message was from the Rev. We'd hit the two thousand three hundred sign-up number in our work community. "That's the ballgame, Mike," he said. "That's 25%. Critical mass. The recall election moved the needle for us. We're going to make it. Congratulations. God loves you, and so do I."

The second phone call was from Makayla. "Burt McNally called. Governor Tuttle wants to see us. Wouldn't tell me why, but said it was urgent. I said yes. Call me."

CHAPTER SEVENTY-ONE

November 9
MIKE DAVENPORT
The Goodwin Tuttle for President campaign headquarters was on the first floor of the Gridley Sheldrake Building on Market Street in Harrisburg, three blocks from the Governor's Office. The building was a steel and white marble wonder that had dazzled the world in 1888. Team Davenport had been summoned by Burt McNally for a "vital discussion" with the Governor. To no one's surprise, Tuttle had announced his intention to run for president a month before so that he could share the benefits of his "Pennsylvania Miracle" with the rest of America.

Different building, same heinous coffee-like matter but this time I made sure the whole team was fortified with my own brand of brain juice before the meeting. The gang— Makayla, Nick, Yandy, the Rev, Betty and myself—bantered about the purpose of this summons. The Rev thought he might want to make us the hood ornament of the "Pennsy Miracle" strategy. After all, we *had* conjured thousands of jobs out of thin air in less than a year. Betty thought it might be a grip and grin photo op and an offer to get on board his juggernaut to the White House. Makayla was less sanguine. She reminded the gang that Tuttle had backed out of his speech at our Fourth of July picnic. Nick affirmed her gloomy view: the zeitgeist in the right-wing yak-o-sphere was that we'd become a Sister City of Havana, Cuba, although most of this chatter had faded away after the election. The crazy train may have moved on, thank goodness.

We were ushered into the Tuttle "War Room" by a perky pair of young female interns. Burt McNally strode in first, shaking hands and thanking everyone for coming. He saved the Bill Clinton handshake for me: a smile, eye contact, a firm grip with his right hand and forearm grab with the left, two resolute pumps. A headline flashed in my mind: "Governor's Aide Nabbed in Ponzi Scheme." Whatever magic powers of heartfelt persuasion Bernie Madoff had, this guy had those same powers. No, I wouldn't like to join his Amway team, and crypto currency just isn't for me.

McNally was pouring himself a Diet Coke as Governor Tuttle entered five minutes later. He'd shed about ten pounds and upgraded his wardrobe, but he still looked more like the General Sales Manager of a Doylestown Lexus dealership than President of the United States. Had this guy ever taken a punch, missed a meal, hitched a ride or bagged groceries to make ends meet? Had he ever served a meal to a homeless person? Or been homeless himself? We had a word for guys like him in the Army: "Fobbit": someone who never left the bunker of the Forward Operating Base except to freshen up his Cinnamon Dolce Latte.

McNally congratulated me for beating the recall. I wished Governor Tuttle good luck on his run for President. "Actually, Mike, that's why you're here. You, my friend, can play an important role in our winning the White House."

That surprised me. "Me? Really? How?"

Tuttle glanced at McNally. Burt said, "Your story has the power to inspire people. Change them."

"Wounded warrior comes home, refuses to wallow in self-pity," said Tuttle. "Instead, he builds a business from the ground up. Then he returns to his hometown to build something yet greater. He harnesses the spirit of enterprise to empower the community."

There's something about that word 'empower.' It's a perfectly fine word: it's just that I've never heard it used by anyone but prosperity preachers, self-help gurus with bleached teeth and smarmy corporate spin merchants: inductees in the Huckster Hall of Fame. I downgraded Tuttle from G.M. of a Lexus dealership to sales associate, major appliances, Best Buy. "What do you want from me, Governor?"

"As your president, I'll be adding a new position to my cabinet: Secretary of Prosperity. I'm going to campaign on it, and I want you by my side because you, my friend, will be the first to sit in that chair."

I felt dizzy. What the hell? "I, ummm, don't…that is, I've already got a job. In fact, I've got two jobs, Mayor and running my coffee business."

Tuttle waved his hand. "Well, you'll leave all that behind, Mike. Your president needs you. Together, we're going to make this the United States of Prosperity." He gave me his victory grin as he fingered the flag pin on his lapel.

Silence. "Well," I finally said. "I don't know what to say. I guess I'll have to think about it."

Makayla, God bless her, looked askance at Tuttle and spoke up. "What happens to the town if Mike takes this job?"

Tuttle broke eye contact and looked at McNally. "Well, see," said McNally, "that's the thing. When Mike joins us, uhhh, what you're doing…that is, there will be a transition period, where things will evolve to a new normal."

Weasel word alert. "Evolve?" I said. "How?"

"If you're going to climb aboard our victory bandwagon," said Tuttle, "we need somebody one hundred percent squeaky clean. And that operation you're running over there in Pulver Forge…"

"Prosperity," said Betty.

"Whatever," said Tuttle. "It's problematic. I mean, by our count you've violated over…" He looked at McNally, just as they'd planned. "How many was it, Burt?"

"A hundred and thirty-one," said McNally.

"A hundred and thirty-one laws and regulations," said Tuttle. "Zoning violations, licensing laws, using underage labor…"

McNally said, "Every single person you've got bartering their time for food is liable for criminal prosecution unless they report the fair market value of their work on their taxes," said Tuttle. "Are you figuring that into your plans?"

"I didn't think we had to," I said. "I mean, it's called 'volunteerism' because…"

"You can call it anything you like, but the IRS has got to be paid," said McNally.

"I seem to remember a meeting where we told you exactly what we were going to do," said Nick. "We asked you to look the other way, just for a couple of months, and you nodded your head. What happened?"

McNally looked at him, then at me with a scary aura of calm. This wasn't someone interested in negotiating. This was a saltwater crocodile taking a bead on a baby gazelle.

"We respect you, Mike. That's why we're going to honor you by telling you the truth. Give it to you straight."

"Okay," I said. We all looked at each other, except for Makayla. She looked at McNally, like she knew what was coming.

McNally took a last swallow of Diet Coke, swished it in his mouth and then fixed me with that laser glare. "You have any idea what's been happening around your little town while you've been doing your thing?"

"No, not really," I said.

"Well, let me fill you in. Sales at MaxxMart, in the power center off 337? Down twenty-six percent. Fast food restaurants in that same center? Down thirty-nine percent. Pharmacies in and around your town, their sales are off forty-one percent. Every business within twenty miles of your town is getting hammered."

"Okay," I said. "I'm sorry to hear that. But why is that my problem?"

"My job is to make the people of this state feel good about what's happening,' said Tuttle. "And none of those businesses feel good right now."

"I see where this is going," said Nick. "By depending on ourselves, we've managed to piss off just about every plutocrat who's floating your campaign."

McNally glared at Nick. "What if your little experiment causes other rust belt Mayors to do some version of the same thing?"

"Yeah, what if that happens?" said Nick, leaning in, real fire in his voice. "What a train wreck that would be! People in towns all over America taking back their power, growing and eating their own food, getting healthier, getting off the bullshit medication that numbs them out so they can't understand what's really making them sick. People working, making friends, solving their own problems. What a freakin' catastrophe! How can we head off this nightmare?"

Everyone sat there in stunned silence until Makayla and Yandy went over and gave Nick a fist bump. He'd changed a lot in five months, and he hadn't changed at all. He'd never believed in government, always believed in people saving themselves. "I have nothing to add to that," I said to Governor Tuttle. "We've got work to do. We don't need you making your problems our problems. Good luck running for President."

"If only it were that simple," said McNally, cobra-grin in place. "Governor Tuttle and I are offering you the opportunity to wrap up what you're doing, take a victory lap, then let things settle back into a new normal. That will happen, one way or another."

"What do we tell the voters?" I said. "The people who just told us how much they like what we're doing? Who are working their butts off to make things better for themselves?"

"Easy," he said. "Tell them they can do whatever they want as long as they stop breaking the law. And tell them they'll be getting that casino, and the jobs that come with it."

Ahh. Clarity. I said, "because Moses Creavey is writing you a fat check."

Both McNally and Tuttle grimaced. McNally said, "The benign forces of American enterprise have an entirely healthy sense of self-preservation. These forces are, in fact, the engine of our real prosperity, and you are not going to obstruct them with your socialist cosplay fantasy camp."

Ouch. Tuttle said, "Think it over, Mike. It's a good deal. More than that, it's the only deal on the table. A cabinet post in the White House, a national platform for your ideas, book deals, a cable news platform, an open doorway to higher office...or prison."

CHAPTER SEVENTY-TWO

November 9

MIKE DAVENPORT

"Thought I might find you here." Makayla, of course. She's the only one who would think of this place. The graveyard.

I motioned her over. "Want a beer?"

She nodded. I tossed her a lukewarm can of Iron City. "This your dad's favorite?" she asked.

"They were all his favorite." She cracked it open and took a swig. We were standing in front of my father's grave. An orange half-moon glimmered up just enough light to illuminate his name and the single word beneath it. The two of us stared at that word, "FIGHT."

"How'd your father feel about you joining the Army?"

"He was dead set against it," I said. "And then he did something that made it impossible for me to step away." I finished off my beer, put the empty back in the paper sack and thought about opening a second. I didn't need a DUI. But still…

"Want to tell me about it? Sounds like a story."

I gazed up at the sky, misty drizzle washing my face. "He was in the hospital, dying of brain cancer. He was one of those poor suckers they got to spray Agent Orange on the mangrove forests of Vietnam, and that shit killed him dead. One of our very last visits, right before he died, he became obsessed with having his death 'mean something'. He was pretty excited by the idea. He said, 'Hey, you know about that Buddhist monk back in '63? Doused himself with gas and then got a buddy to light the match?'" My dad said he wanted to go out like that: on

Pennsylvania Avenue, in front of the White House, surrounded by other Agent Orange victims. A human blowtorch, on national TV. I was going pour the gas on him, light the match, then film it for the nightly news. I hadn't seen him that animated in two years."

"Holy shit," said Makayla, and we both chuckled. "What did you say?"

"I said that the White House had a zillion surveillance cameras and snipers on the rooftop, and if they saw a guy in a wheelchair and another guy with a big gas can and a Zippo lighter stopping traffic, we'd both be dead before the wheelchair stopped rolling."

"Good advice."

"So, then he asked me about getting a suicide vest, like those terrorists have in the Middle East, and sneaking into some veterans' event with the Secretary of Defense, blowing his ass to hell. This scheme was even crazier than the first one and I told him so. He got really agitated. He started yelling that I was against him, that he was dying, and I didn't care, shit like that. People were looking at us. He said, 'We can't let the bastards win. Don't let the bastards win. This is my last chance, Mike. Help me, I'm begging you.' I finally got him calmed down and he came up with one last request. And I this time I said yes."

"What was it?"

"My dear old dad died on October 17, 2003, five days after my last visit. At his request, I had him cremated. On November 5, I walked into a conservative political conference at the Hyatt Regency Hotel in Fairfax, Virginia. I made a beeline for retired General Fletcher Hardcastle, one of those 'Smoking Gun, Mushroom Cloud' bastards who couldn't wait to send eighteen-year-olds to die in Afghanistan and Iraq. I said, "General?" He said, 'Yes? What can I do for you, son?' I opened up my dad's Steelers cigarette case and blew his ashes in the General's face."

"Wow." I could tell she was impressed. "How did it make you feel?"

"Pretty good, for about ten seconds. I'd fortified myself with a big belt of vodka and I knew I was going to catch hell, but I'd made my dad's last wish come true."

"So, what happened?"

"I got jumped by some security goons who beat the living shit out of me and turned me over to the Fairfax Police, who beat the shit out of me again. Hardcastle was an asshole, he wanted me prosecuted for assault with a deadly weapon."

"What the hell?"

"He said the ashes were toxic, and that I knew it. At the preliminary hearing the Judge told me I could either go on trial and risk a prison sentence of 25 years, or I could join the Army. What the hell, it was right after 9-11, I thought I was signing up to fight evil."

We drank our beers. The drizzle gave her face a nice luster that the moon turned into a soft ebony glow. She finally said, "What if it all came true?"

"What if what came true?"

She looked at me, black eyes shining. "What if what we're doing really did, you know, catch on? What if every sad sack, rust-belt town did what we're doing: started community gardens, opened free clinics, gave everybody a job who wanted one? That really would change things."

I started to say something glib, but it hit me: *that's what they're afraid of.* "Wow," I said. "I can see why they're freaking out. We've started a brush fire that could burn down the whole freakin' forest."

"And that means…" she paused. The full force of the thing hit home. "…they really will do whatever it takes to stop us. Whatever…it…takes."

Now we both stared at the scraggly grass around the grave. "Are you sorry you gave up a perfectly adequate job in TV news for this?"

She surprised me. She put her beer can on the ground, walked up to me, and kissed me: I mean, really KISSED me in a way that sent a delicious high voltage jolt of joy juice through my body. I love this woman! She held my head in her hands and looked me straight in the eye. "No," she said, and kissed me again and this time I put my arms around her and put my body into it. When we finished, I had that feeling I've had just a few times in my life: that feeling of being just slightly "love drunk" after a lusty clench. "I'm the one who believes in you more than you do. And if we quit now, I won't have the boffo climax for my bestselling book and TV docu-series."

"Uh huh," I said, still a little woozy. "Yeah, the book. The one that's going to pay my legal fees."

"Uh huh. And then the movie, with Bradley Cooper playing you and me playing myself."

I felt like I was seeing her for the first time. She was my love, and also my Burt McNally: the pile-driving, can-do realist yelling YES into a world of NO. "So," I said, "Dad says fight. So, let's fight. How?"

She turned away from me and started to pace. The beer fuzzies had vanished. She said, "They think they've got us in a box. Two options: give up or go to jail. If we accept their framing, we play their game. So, we've got to change the game, make them play our game. We need them back on their heels, reacting to us."

"Great!" I said. "How?"

"There's a simple answer that's hiding in plain sight. We're not in their box, because there is no box."

"No box," I said.

"That's right," she said. "It'll come to you, give it time."

We kissed for a final time, and then I observed every speed limit driving home. "There is no box," I said to myself. "When I wake up tomorrow morning, the box that isn't there will be gone. And I'll have the answer to the riddle." I thought of that first kiss tonight and I hoped that, maybe, this beautiful ride was just beginning.

CHAPTER SEVENTY-THREE

Thursday, November 25
MIKE DAVENPORT
Enoch Cornelius Pulver began building Rockhurst Castle in 1895 on a bluff overlooking the town. He finished it in 1902 and looked down on the town he built till his death in 1927. Pulver's last remaining heir, Winthrop Merriweather Pulver, tried to sell it two years after the family sold the steelworks in the 1970s, but the town was already coming apart so there were no takers. It was vacated in 1979 and abandoned in 2003, allowed to languish. Raven's Community Foundation secured the land, and I led the town reclamation team that cleaned it up.

The place we entered was a botanical jungle, mold incubator, wildlife habitat and bird sanctuary. We removed two and a half tons of flora and fauna, including a troop of shaggy mane mushrooms in the wine cellar and a bat colony in the attic. Luckily the mansion, like so much of Pulver Forge, had terrific bones: plenty of red sandstone and granite supported by a steel skeleton, with marble floors. It was a grand example of the English Manor style, designed to last 500 years, with a garden created by Frederick Law Olmstead. We stripped it down to those good bones. And so here we were: Makayla, Nick, Raven, Chef Betty, Calvin McCoy, Yandy, Steve Dorsey and myself, in the cathedral-inspired Grand Hall, sitting on folding chairs at portable tables enjoying an informal Chef Betty Thanksgiving feast as we figured out what to do with this place.

"This should be our Prosperity Celebration Center," said Calvin. "Starting with this Christmas day. That was the one day the Pulvers invited the town into their home. That tradition can live again."

"Okay," said Makayla. "Christmas, and…"

"Christmas can be a whole week," said Yandy.

"Or even the month of December," I said. "A Christmas marketplace, homemade crafts and gifts, with Dickens carolers and cookie pop-up stands."

"And then New Years," said Betty, "with a countdown and champagne toast at midnight. And Valentine's Day, that's another week-long event, maybe serve dinner for two by candlelight, and then show romantic movies."

"The day the town was re-born, that's another week," I said. "Prosperity Homecoming, Help Celebrate the Day Everything Changed."

"And what about July 4th?" said Yandy. "That's our day."

Makayla, getting into the spirit, said "And Memorial Day, Labor Day, Veterans Day, and Halloween, that's another week…"

"And don't forget Easter week," said Betty.

"I insist," said the Rev.

"That's a pretty healthy number of holidays," I said. "Any other ideas?"

"Let me put on my tourism hat," said Makayla. "What we've got here is a one-of-a-kind monument to robber-baron splendor. No one will ever build another castle like this."

"Or a garden like this," said Yandy. "Frederick Law Olmstead, a genius."

"This is a good, ol' fashioned tourist attraction," said Makayla, "like the Carnegie Museum in New York, or Hearst Castle or the Vanderbilt Mansion. We can host guided tours, exhibits about Pulver's life and times…"

"Wait a minute," I said. I looked around. "Oh my god, we're missing a bet. This place would be perfect."

"For what?" said Betty.

"If we're going to look back in time, we should look forward too." I looked at Makayla. "What Tuttle said, about what if every rust belt town did what we're doing…"

"Uh huh," she said. "Sooo…"

"So, let's make it our business to make that happen. You see? This becomes the new home for the 'American Center for Creative Prosperity.' We share what we're doing with the world. We give classes and seminars. We've done it, you can do it too, here's how. We hold a great big national convention every year where every Prosperity Club, the ones we're going to start, come here to learn, to teach, to share, and to celebrate."

Makayla started to laugh. "Friends, we're going to do everything. A celebration center for the town! A year-round tourist attraction! And a place where we teach the world how to create their own do-it-yourself civic revolution."

The group was quiet. We'd figured this out! "Shouldn't we be writing all this down?" said Chef Betty. "Better yet," said Makayla, taking out her smartphone and hitting the record app, "Give me that again. Everybody. Slowly."

CHAPTER SEVENTY-FOUR

November 26

MIKE DAVENPORT

Friday, the day after Thanksgiving: a special meeting of Mike's Super Friends in the backroom of the Prosperity HuggaMug. I was pouring coffee from the stash I kept in the locked bottom drawer of my battered desk. This was my Volcanica Hawaiian Kona Extra Fancy Beans, twenty-six dollars for ten glorious ounces. A flimsy, grease-stained magenta box of assorted pastries from Flour Power sat on an end table. I'd already wolfed down a hazelnut chocolate chip scone and was eyeballing the red velvet cinnamon roll when the meeting began, right on the button at 11 a.m. Now it was my Super Friends—Nick, Raven, Yandy, Makayla and the Rev—here to help me figure out how to get out of the box that wasn't there.

The Rev took two big sips of coffee, acknowledged me by raising his cup— "The Master!"—and then turned to the group. "Friends, we are uniquely qualified to crack this conundrum. Collectively, we are a genius."

"Agreed!" said Nick, with nods all around.

"Okay," I said. "So…. what do we think we think?" Silence.

"This isn't a solution and I'm not proposing we do this, but…" Raven turned to me. "Well, what if you just took one for the team? Let them arrest you. Make you a, you know…"

"Martyr?" I said.

"Yeah, that," she said. "You being a jailbird gives a lie to everything Tuttle says he stands for. He'll look like such a hypocrite that…"

"Raven," I said, "I think you're underestimating our tormentors."

"How so?"

"You think the Governor is going to sweep in, arrest me, and sit by as I become the Nelson Mandela of eastern Pennsylvania?"

"Right," said Raven.

"So here's what I think will really happen. I'll be nibbled to death by ducks, a million tiny zoning infractions and tax violations levied by an army of faceless bureaucrats. And the Guv will stay above it all, maybe even tsk-tsking about big government interference with the noble civic activism of this well-meaning citizen. But, of course, nothing he can do!"

"Okay," said Nick. "Sounds about right. So, what if we go in the other direction?"

"What's that?" I said.

He jabbed his finger at me. "You, my friend, do just what Tuttle wants, become his 'Secretary of Prosperity.'" He had everyone's attention.

"So, the town gets shut down...," said Makayla.

"Right," said Nick, "BUT...Mike is out promoting our ideas, talking about what we did here. It's a powerful story, we all know that." He turned to me. "You might bring some people over to our side, get them to try some things."

"Let's say I take the offer, campaign for Tuttle, and Tuttle wins," I said. "Then they give me a cubbyhole office in the dank sub-basement of the White House. I will have my own Chief of Staff, speechwriter, and media wrangler, all chosen by Burt McNally to ensure I do nothing but provide frequent and lavish tongue baths for my beloved President. And after a decent interval, say, a year and a half, I will be tossed into the dustbin of history to make way for an ambitious, Ayn Rand-loving son or daughter of Tuttle's biggest buckraking supporters."

"Well," said Nick, brow furrowing. "Where does that leave us, besides screwed?" Another deep, infinite silence.

"Okay," said Makayla, pulling out her smartphone. "Desperate times call for desperate measures. Here's something we used to do in the newsroom when we were stuck for stories." She punched up the clock function on her phone. "Five-minute round robin, everybody has an idea, no exceptions, no idea too stupid." She punched the stopwatch function. "I'll go first. We turn Tuttle down and run Mike for Governor. He's 'Mister Prosperity,' exactly the miracle worker that Tuttle says he is." She turned to me. "How does 'Governor Davenport sound?"

I laughed. "Why the hell not?"

Makayla turned. "Nick? You're next. Go."

"Ummmm.... okay." Eyes to the floor, then up at us. "We form the 'LPRC': the League of Pissed-Off Rustbelt Cities, like a National Rifle Association of Pennsylvania left-behinds. Mike's our leader. We fund-raise like hell, show up everywhere, arm the peasants with torches and pitchforks and make it our business to send Tuttle back to the Chamber of Commerce."

"Nice," said Makayla, clapping her hands together. "Yandy?"

"Hey, I'm Cuban. When they come for us, we vanish into the hills of the Sugarloaf Knob. Then we go village to village convincing the peasants to join us, and at just the right moment, we roll into Harrisburg and overthrow the Tuttle regime in a bloodless coup."

Laughter and cheers. Makayla said, "Rev?"

"We form a secret society, like the early Christians: 'The Universal Order of Prosperous Publicans.' We pledge ourselves to keep the dream alive. No matter what Tuttle does, Prosperity lives. If he shuts us down, we go to ground until he gets bored and leaves, at which time we come out and pick right up where we left off."

"That's great!" said Makayla. "See? There's a lot of stuff we can do. Raven, you're next. Go!"

Raven stood and opened her arms to us. "We have an 'I AM SPARTACUS!' moment. We create a viral website with our manifesto about what Mike caused us to believe in: community, volunteerism, self-sufficiency, prosperity. Then we get a hundred people to agree to each recruit another hundred people to sign the manifesto. That's ten thousand people. They can shut down Mike and even put him in jail, but they can't shut down ten thousand people in a town of nine thousand."

"Okay, beautiful!" Makayla turned to me. "Mike?"

My mind went blank. "Uhhhh…how can I top that?"

"Forty seconds left. Don't think, say anything. GO!"

"Uhhh…how about this. I give in to Tuttle, tell him I'm on board and become his most loyal foot soldier. Then we get to the convention, I use my nominating speech to put his shit in the street big time, reveal what a sniveling, hypocritical piece of garbage he is."

"Wow!" said Makayla, whooping with delight. "As a retired reporter, I'd say that's inspired. Campaign story of the year: from the penthouse to the outhouse in three minutes. Beauty."

"Caffeine plus panic equals creativity," I said.

"Those were some good ideas," said Nick, smiling.

"Yeah," said Yandy. "Just add courage."

Makayla was deep in thought, staring into the distance. "You know what's funny about all this? I mean what we're doing here, now."

"Besides everything?" I said.

"What's funny," she said, "is that we're all sitting here worrying about what Tuttle's going to do to us."

"So?" I said.

"Well, think about it. Why are we giving him all this power? Why do we care?" Makayla turned to me, dead serious. "The whole point of what we're doing is that we've stopped waiting for someone to bail us out. We're in charge of us! We control our own destiny."

"We're taking care of each other," said the Rev. "Neighbors loving neighbors."

"Why do we care what he thinks?" said Makaya. "Shouldn't Tuttle be, you know, scared of us?"

The words hung in the air, and everyone nodded. And then it happened, just as Makayla said it would. The clouds parted — suddenly I could see the sun! It was up there shining in that astonishing blue sky, and I could feel that delicious warmth on my face. The walls were gone! The box had vanished! In fact, it had never existed! "I'm having it," I said, excited.

"Having what?" said Yandy.

"My 'oh shit' moment. The box is gone! All because of what you said."

"So, tell me what I said," said Makayla, mystified.

"You said the box would disappear. You said…" I opened my mouth, eager to share…and then I stopped. "No."

"No?" said Nick.

I turned to him, big grin on my face. "No, I need to do some thinking first. Some research. This is a big idea, and by big, I mean 'it's sure to get us arrested' big. This is a 'fly to Vegas, take your life savings and bet it on a single roulette number' big."

"And after that you're not going to tell us?" pleaded the Rev.

"Look, Christmas is in a month," I said. "Let's have a Prosperity Christmas in the Pulver Mansion. Let's throw the mother of all parties. And after everyone is stuffed and happy, I'll get up and share my brainstorm…that might be a brain fart, but what the hell."

"Can you at least give us a hint?" said Nick.

"Sure. All I'm going to do is take everything we've done to its logical end point. Tuttle gave me two choices — join him or go to jail. This is a third choice, the one that will push Tuttle back on his heels."

"You're not even going to tell *me*?" said Makayla, half-kidding.

I thought a moment. "Yeah, I'll tell you, because I need you to make this work. The rest of you? I'm doing you a favor. You have a whole month to out-guess me, and when you hear what I've got, you will laugh out loud. This could actually get me hanged, but the road to the gallows is going to be paved with loud, braying guffaws. And as the wise man said, 'Laughter is the sound of freedom.'"

Thursday, December 2

MAKAYLA PROSPERITY REPORT CARD BY THE NUMBERS

997: # of HuggaMug Cups of Coffee Served

901: # Who Paid for Coffee (including TimeBucks)

326: # Workers in Community Gardens

410: # Workers for Food Prep/Service/Clean-Up at Community Kitchen

466: #Workers for Town Clean-Up Duty (GETTING THERE)

380: #Workers for Med Clinic (YES!)

311: #Workers at Radio Station/Newsletter/Movie Crew/Social Media/Podcasting

118: #Mobility Workers (including maintenance)

659: #Workers Miscellaneous Duty (babysitting, mentoring, teaching, caretaking)

2,670: #Total Workers

61,331: #Total TimeBucks Issued Previous Week

2,758: #Transactions on "ShareWhere"

24: Posts on Prosperity YouTube Channel (4 a day, 6 days a week)

27: Podcast Episodes (9 shows, 3 episodes each)

14,105: Podcast Downloads

$77: Money from "Prosperity Gripe Fund" Pretzel Jar

NOTES: Today the town dedicated its two new INDOOR FARMS:

Thanks to a generous grant from the Prosperity Community Foundation (i.e. Raven Washburn), Prosperity, PA dedicated "Vine & Dandy" and "Budliciousness," our first two indoor gardens. Yandy bought the two forty-foot-long shipping containers from a salvage outfit. Then he and a special crew (including Jarhead Sodbusters, still helping!) turned them into indoor farms, capable of growing 4,000 plants, herbs and leafy greens including lettuce, kale, chard and arugula.

Yandy gave the tour. The gardens are 50% solar powered. The crops are grown vertically in hydroponic towers. They're exposed to red and blue LED light strips. Water packed with nutrients flows down through the top of the towers, bathing the roots along the way. (NOTE: each container uses 10 gallons of water per day, 90% less than what we're using in our regular gardens.)

Yandy wowed the crowd by showing how he controlled the water, temp and light conditions inside the gardens with an app on his phone. If these work, we'll get six more: local restaurants will happily buy fresh, local produce during Winter.

CHAPTER SEVENTY-FIVE

December 25: Christmas Day
CALVIN McCOY

For fifty-three years—1901 to 1954—the Pulver family hosted a day-long Christmas party at the Pulver Mansion. This was the only day the estate opened its doors to the people of Pulver Forge, and some of the older folks still remember those celebrations. I know I do.

Christmas Day, 1940. I was nine years old, and this was my first Pulver Family Christmas. It was more than just a wondrous event: it was a chance to leave behind the soot-stained, paycheck-to-paycheck town of Pulver Forge and enter a fairy kingdom of impossible abundance. The mansion was a secular cathedral, a monument to a benevolent god unknown to us: a bountiful deity of grace and goodwill who granted every wish.

I held my mother's hand as we walked through those massive iron gates and saw a breathtaking dazzle of red and green lights that turned night into day. I walked in and gazed up at a huge, majestic, fully decorated 40-foot Norway spruce in the foyer. I still have that sweet holiday scent in my nostrils. After the coat check, there was a groaning board of welcome snacks like stuffed mushrooms and bacon-wrapped potato wedges. This table was flanked on both sides by servants serving flutes of champagne (Coca-Cola for kids). Every room was lit with incandescent Edison bulbs with the filaments twisted into a double helix. These bulbs washed the rooms in a honeyed amber glow, just like a dream.

I sat on Santa's lap, of course, and told him what I wanted for Christmas: a Gilbert Electric American Flyer "Tru Model" 3/16 O gauge 2-6-4 Northern Pacific Freight AC Train Set. Delivery of my treasure assured, I walked into the Great Hall. The walls were adorned with stuffy 18th century portrait art. I ate like a young prince at the help-yourself buffet banquet of everything that made Christmas dinner special. There were carving stations for turkey, roast beef and ham, and heaping tureens of stuffing, mashed potatoes, gravy and roasted vegetables like carrots, potatoes and parsnips. And the desserts! Oh my lord, a separate table for cakes and pies, including apple, raisin and pumpkin pie, soft molasses cookies, Christmas pudding and fruitcake. Plus strolling Dickens carolers singing "Oh Come All Ye Faithful" and a string quartet playing "Joy to the World."

I remember it all: not just the sights but the smells and sounds and textures. My most vivid memory is what I felt inside my chest. All year long I carried an ache of anxiety that was so much a part of me I forgot it was there. It was the banked terror that I was always this close to losing everything, that our family was dependent on my father surviving another day in the infernal hellscape of the Forge. Here, that ache vanished. What a relief! I exhaled a breath I'd been holding for as long as I could remember. I was finally in the place I knew only from Sunday school lessons, where God's children were rewarded for their good behavior by living in His Loving Kingdom as described in Second Corinthians: "And God is able to bless you abundantly, so that in all things at all times, having all that you need, you will abound in every good work."

As I left that wonderful celebration, Lambert Selden Pulver, Mr. Pulver's gaunt, sullen son, he must have been in his late 30s, handed every child a gift. Girls got a kewpie doll. Boys like me got a toy soldier forged from Pulver steel: a West Point cadet complete with ceremonial saber and plumed shako hat. A servant handed us Christmas cookies wrapped in red and green tissue. That toy soldier and a Buffalo-head nickel I got from my father on my fifth birthday are the only things I've kept from my childhood, and I take both from my desk and hold them at least once a month. It never occurred to me to resent the Pulvers for having everything while we had nothing. I was just so happy our monarch shared his palace that one beautiful day every year.

And here I was again, eighty-one years later. I never did get that model train set, but now I was getting something even better: one more splendid Christmas in the palace of the Pulvers, this time with my friends from the town. In fact, more than my friends. Just about everyone in Prosperity was here, even people who fought what we were doing. Even the rehab patients from the Hotel Bessemer. Especially them.

I was filled with the same serenity I enjoyed when I was nine, but for a different reason. What I felt as a child was a mirage: a feeling of tranquility that evaporated as soon I was on the other side of those iron gates. Here, now, with these people I felt a kind of peaceful reverie. What is it we all want? Enough friends, enough food, enough love. We had that here, not a frown to be seen. And there was a feeling that we'd earned this. We'd worked for eight solid months to grow this food, to clean up this place, to make these friends.

The party had started at 6 p.m. with a tradition begun by Enoch Pulver: the lighting of the tree. His was forty feet tall and illuminated by hundreds of hand-colored Edison bulbs. Ours was a twenty-foot Douglas fir that had fifty-plus strings of commercial red and green lights. It had been decorated at a party that afternoon by the kids of the town: popsicle stick Santa hats, strings of popcorn, pinecone-head reindeer ornaments, pipe cleaner candy canes and egg carton Christmas bells. Then a one-hour pre-feast "Jolly Hour" with Zymurgy beers, non-alcoholic egg nog (bring your own flask) and Irish coffee made with fresh HuggaMug brew, mixed and served by Mike Davenport. John Glickman and three of his symphonic cohorts played Baroque arrangements of Christmas carols. "Mrs. Claus" (Makayla) walked about handing out "North Pole snow crystals" to every child under ten.

We had a Santa Claus, too: Reverend Bramlett. I gave serious consideration to plopping myself on his lap and taking one last crack at getting that train set but thought better of it. The Rev gave every supplicant a candy cane and a smile, and the room was filled with a joyous glow even without those Edison bulbs.

The meal was a proper "fill your belly" Christmas feast courtesy Chef Betty: Wild Rice and Mushroom Casserole, Whole Roasted Cauliflower with Pistachio Pesto, Stuffed Portobello Mushrooms, baked root veggies, salad greens, mac n' cheese, baked beans, potato salad, and a table full of desserts, including homemade pumpkin pie. (NOTE: Chef Betty allowed Police Chief Pooley to smuggle in roasted turkey, for traditionalist carnivores like Nick.) The Rev said the prayer, another soaring paean of gratitude for the blessings of community and fellowship. The servers served, and then the servers were themselves served. The Great Hall was filled with happy chatter spiked with laughter, buoyed by Christmas music.

After everyone had gone back for seconds, thirds, desserts and cups of HuggaMug coffee served by Mike and Yandy, a videographer set up at the front of the hall. Makayla had her media squad positioned throughout the hall with smartphone cameras. Our mayor was going to bless us, every one…and maybe say something more.

CHAPTER SEVENTY-SIX

Saturday, December 25: Christmas Day
Transcription of Mayor Mike Davenport's Remarks, Great Hall of Pulver Mansion, 8:30 p.m.

MIKE: Thank you, friends. Are you stuffed? I am. What a celebration! The greatest gift that we celebrate this Christmas is the simple journey we've taken from strangers to friends. I've made so many new friends, and I treasure each one.

I had a talk with our Governor and maybe even next President recently. Much to my surprise, he was less than thrilled with what's been going on here in Prosperity. I thought I was doing just what he wanted. I thought the Pennsylvania Miracle was sovereign citizens standing on our own two feet and going to work! Creating the town we've always wanted by growing, harvesting, serving, cleaning, building, planning, dreaming and doing, helping each other to help ourselves!

Turns out that what we're doing is upsetting the people who are paying him to run for President. We're too busy working for ourselves to shop and eat fast food, and we're having too much fun to fool around with the drugs that Big Pharma is pushing on us. Is it possible the Governor was happier with Pulver Forge than he is with Prosperity? It really doesn't make any difference because none of us long for the bad ol' days when we were sick, hungry, lonely and afraid.

In this meeting, the Governor made me an offer. He told me I could either resign as Mayor, quit everything we're doing and become his ceremonial 'Secretary of Prosperity,' or I could go to prison for a few hundred wholly invented violations of zoning and payroll tax laws. What to do? I had a meeting with my most trusted associates. In that meeting my friend Makayla Nichols asked a simple question: 'Why are we afraid of what the Governor might do? What power does he have over us? What do we need him for?'

These questions led me back to the promise of America itself. This country was founded on a radical idea: that we didn't need a king to tell us what to do: that we, the people could rule ourselves.

It had been a while since I'd read the Declaration of Independence, so I printed out a copy. I'm pretty sure everyone knows the first part of what Mr. Jefferson wrote, but you may not know the second part. Here's the first part:

We hold these truths to be self-evident, that all men are created equal, that they are endowed by their Creator with certain unalienable rights, that among these are life, liberty, and the pursuit of happiness.

Okay, here's the second part:

That, to secure these rights, governments are instituted among men, deriving their just powers from the consent of the governed. That, whenever any form of government becomes destructive of these ends, it is the right of the people to alter or to abolish it, and to institute new government, laying its foundation on such principles, and organizing its powers in such form, as to them shall seem most likely to affect their safety and happiness.

Governor Tuttle has power over us as long as we give our consent, and that consent is based on whether we feel safe and happy with what he's doing. I don't know about you, but I felt neither safe nor happy after that meeting. He was telling me that our successful effort to seize our destiny and live the promise of self-government was—what's the right word—*inconvenient* for him, so he was shutting us down. His campaign donors had spoken. So far, his campaign has received eleven million dollars from Ellsworth Waverly, the CEO of MaxxMart, which is…wait for it…the largest dispenser of opioid drugs in the U.S. His campaign has received four million dollars from Moses Creavey, the man who dragged my reputation through five miles of broken glass and tried to have me recalled because he's going to ram his casino down our throats whether we like it or not.

So where does that leave us? Well, it's right there in our founding document, the DNA of our democracy:

"That, whenever any form of government becomes destructive of these ends, it is the right of the people to alter or to abolish it, and to institute new government, laying its foundation on such principles, and organizing its powers in such form, as to them shall seem most likely to affect their safety and happiness."

Our Founding Fathers are speaking to us across eleven generations and two hundred and forty years to give us an answer that's hiding in plain sight. They are telling us that it is our right to abolish—their word—this oppressive form of government, and institute a new government that will provide for our safety and happiness.

Friends, we have created this government already. We did it in those very first days when we came together and formed an intentional volunteer community that was committed to that safety and happiness. And so here we are, asking ourselves Makayla's transformative question, 'What do we need Tuttle for?' You know the answer, don't you? The answer is 'not a damn thing'. That's why I'm proposing that the town of Prosperity, Pennsylvania secede from the Union on March 1st of next year and become the sovereign republic of Prosperity."

Okay, I can tell by the gasps and the murmuring that you think this is a pretty bold move. And it is. But think about it. When we pay our state and federal income taxes, what do we get back? We pay Tuttle's salary so he can turn around and stop us from building the kind of community we want.

We pay the salaries of our senators and representatives so they can create trade agreements that give steel companies incentives to ship our jobs overseas. We pay for wars we don't win, for nuclear weapons that are specifically designed never to be used, and for trillion-dollar fighter planes that can't fly. They've forgotten we're here, because we can't put an eight-figure check in their campaign coffers. We're nothing to them. They won't miss us when we're gone, except for one thing: other communities like ours will look at what we're doing and say, 'Hey, we could do that.' We might be the first domino that falls, and once more dominoes start falling, then we'll have their attention. But that's not our problem.

Can we really do this, friends? Could those freedom-besotted radicals back in 1776 actually break away from England and start a new kind of country, where the inmates run the asylum? A wise man once told me, 'You can do anything you want in this crazy world as long as you're willing to take the consequences. But don't underestimate the consequences.' And I don't. It'll be challenging, but…wouldn't it break your heart to let go of everything we've achieved together, just because it was *inconvenient* for some politician's presidential election campaign? Were you happier one year ago than you are now? Were you healthier? Were you safer? Did you have as many friends? Aren't these the most important questions we can ask?

When I was talked into running for this crazy job, I had no idea we'd all end up here, on Christmas Day, talking about starting our own country. And at the same time, I have this sense that every single thing that's happened to me, beginning with being born here, October 29, 1975 has led to this moment. I'm through waiting for someone else to make things better. It's up to us. We are the people we've been waiting for.

As with every single thing we've achieved here in Prosperity, I'm not telling you what's going to happen. I'm putting it out there. Do we want this? Let's meet in our neighborhood councils and then come together to figure it out. It's a big dare, but then this whole shebang was a big dare from the time we changed the name of the town and decided to believe in ourselves. Thank you, and Merry Christmas.

CHAPTER SEVENTY-SEVEN

December 25: Christmas Day
MIKE DAVENPORT

After Makayla stopped laughing, she gave me the terrible news that was also the best news possible: this ridiculous idea was doomed to fail. AND it would instantly become catnip for the mainstream press who would lavish media coverage on us. We (and by 'we' I mean 'she') had to shape this coverage as best we could so I came off as a feisty underdog, not a buffoon. We got the gang involved. We broke this down into narratives that quickly proved irresistible to the media:

• Mike Davenport: earthy, reluctant rebel. Vet with a mission: put people back to work, redeem the honor of forgotten rust-belt town. (all true, with a bit of hyperbole about my earthiness and reluctance)

• Governor Goodwin Tuttle: grasping, hypocritical political hack who preaches community empowerment and practices top-down, money-driven corporate capitalism (gospel)

• Secession as controversial: esteemed legal experts on both sides have compelling claims (shaky ground here – this was just show biz, but the media needed a "both sides" argument to keep this in play)

• Citizens of Prosperity: grateful to be working, happy to be part of a thriving community, wondering what all the fuss is about. The experiment is working! (Mostly true, with the outliers again feeding the "both sides" media narrative.)

Makayla had another precious bit of sagacity that came from her years in the news biz: reporters are harried, smart and lazy.

The more story elements you can hand them (especially engaging eye candy), the more positive press coverage they'll give you. What reporters really want is for you to hand them the story so all they have to do is drop themselves into the piece with a couple of stand-ups. We happily did this. The result was a segment on "Need to Know," network TV's top feature news show, Sunday nights at seven. Here it is, as broadcast:

CHAPTER SEVENTY-EIGHT

TRANSCRIPT "NEED TO KNOW" NEWS MAGAZINE January 17

IN STUDIO ANCHOR TOSS by the silver-haired, avuncular show host Gavin Darling:

DARLING: Next, a small Pennsylvania town that's making a very big noise. The town is Pulver Forge, only these days it calls itself 'Prosperity, Pennsylvania' thanks to its controversial new Mayor, Mike Davenport. Mayor Davenport may soon be President Davenport, or maybe even King Davenport. Confused? Here's our own Cheyenne Danvers with the report:

CUT TO: B-ROLL SHOTS OF ABANDONED PULVER FORGE STEELWORKS

CHEYENNE (V.O): Welcome to Prosperity, PA, the battered buckle of the Pennsylvania rust belt. Here's what's left of the famous steelworks, a place that made the steel that built the battleships that won World War II, and then built the New York skyline. It's quiet now, rotting away since it closed in 1986. When Pulver Steel finally went out of business, half the citizens left town and the other half got trapped in a cycle of unemployment, despair, crime and drug abuse. That's until this man, Mike Davenport...

CUT TO: MIKE DAVENPORT, SERVING COFFEE AT THE HUGGAMUG IN PROSPERITY, GREETING PEOPLE, SMILING, SHAKING HANDS.

CHEYENNE (V.O.): …launched an improbable campaign for Mayor. He's an Army vet who fought in Afghanistan, and an entrepreneur who had never run for political office. He won, and that was only the beginning for Mike. This was Mike last week, at the town Christmas celebration that shocked the nation:

(SMARTPHONE B-ROLL SHOT PROVIDED BY MAKAYLA) Mike: "That's why I am proposing that the town of Prosperity, Pennsylvania secede from the Union on March 1st of next year and become the sovereign nation of Prosperity."

CUT TO: B-ROLL SHOTS OF THE TOWN

CHEYENNE (V.O.): That's right. Take a look, folks. If Mike has his way, this will soon become the…what? Nation of Prosperity? Kingdom of Prosperity?

CUT TO: MIKE'S FACE, SIT DOWN INTERVIEW

MIKE: Republic. The Republic of Prosperity.

CUT TO: B-ROLL SHOTS OF TOWN WALK-ABOUT WITH CHEYENNE AND MIKE

CHEYENNE: I decided to put Mike on the spot. The mayor of a town of nine thousand people becoming its own country? Was he serious?

MIKE: You bet I'm serious. I'm as serious as Jefferson, Adams and Washington were when they declared their independence from King George of England.

CHEYENNE: (sit-down, reverse shot): Why? Why would you do this?

MIKE: Instead of telling you, how about if I show you? Are you up for a look at what real democracy is all about?

CHEYENNE: Please, lead the way.

CUT TO: MIKE AND VELOCITY INSIDE A PROSPERITY INDOOR GARDEN FULL OF BUSY WORKERS

CHEYENNE: What Mike showed me was extraordinary: a town that has gone to work to bring back its economy. Every one of these people you see here? They were all out of work a year ago. Now they're growing…

CUT TO LIVE INTERVIEW BITE

CHEYENNE: (OFF CAMERA) WITH LARK FENNIMORE IN THE INDOOR GARDEN: What is this stuff?

LARK:This is arugula. That's Romaine, and over there…what is that, Rashid?

RASHID:The best Red Leaf lettuce on earth!

CHEYENNE (OFF CAMERA): And you're getting paid for this, right?

LARK: I'm earning TimeBucks! I can use 'em for lots of things: medical care, babysitting, coffee and lunch. Come on with me, I'll show ya.

CUT TO: PROSPERITY KITCHEN. LARK IS INTRODUCING CHEYENNE TO CHEF BETTY, AND THEN TO REVEREND BRAMLETT, WHO GETS IN THE SALAD BAR LINE WITH HER

CHEYENNE (V.O.): This is the Prosperity Community Kitchen, where all those gardeners meet their friends and neighbors as they spend their TimeBucks. It's run by Chef Betty and a group of young helpers she's mentoring. And it's all supervised by a disgraced evangelical minister who has become a resourceful street preacher, Reverend Luke Bramlett

CUT TO: B-ROLL SHOTS OF REVEREND BRAMLETT BUILDING HER A MAGNIFICENT SALAD

(NAT SOUND) CHEYENNE: And all of this produce was grown here, in Prosperity?

REV: That's right, every leaf. In the middle of winter, by these people right here!

CUT TO: B ROLL SHOT OF CHEYENNE SURROUNDED BY TOWNSPEOPLE, ALL EATING LUNCH.

CHEYENNE (V.O.): Who were these people? And how'd they get here?

SERIES OF SOUND BITES OF TOWNSPEOPLE AT LUNCH TABLES

ABNER: I'm Abner Doolittle. I'm 76 years old. I worked in the Forge for eighteen years, was there the day it closed. Now I'm in charge of the post-meal clean-up crew.

BRAYONNA: I'm Brayonna Watkins, I'm a bus driver. I was a cashier at the Bailey Brothers supermarket until it went out of business eighteen years ago. Now I drive people to the gardens, the health clinic, wherever they want to go. And I'm a Community Council member.

THALIA:My name is Thalia Garroway. I was hooked on Oxy and also Vicodin. I was declared legally dead twice. I've been sober for five months. I work at the medical clinic helping people get off drugs, and I work at the community radio station, the one on the Internet. We broadcast eighteen hours every day. Plus, I serve meals here five days a week.

CUT TO: MIKE DAVENPORT INTERVIEW

MIKE: When I became Mayor nine months ago, we had almost three thousand unemployed people, out of a population of nine thousand plus. And you know what? Nobody cared. We were collateral damage in the rush to globalize and out-source everything. We were left for dead. Today, we're back to work, working for ourselves this time. Every resident of Prosperity who wants a job can have one.

CUT TO: SERIES OF B ROLL SHOTS OF PROSPERITY – PEOPLE PICKING UP TRASH, GARDENING, REHABILITATING BUILDINGS, CLEARING VACANT LOTS, GETTING MEDICAL CARE AT THE CLINIC

CHEYENNE (V.O.): It looked to me like Mayor Mike was that rare politician who makes promises and keeps them. This town was buzzing. So why did he want to do a crazy thing like secede from the United States?

MIKE: That's the last thing I want. But Governor Tuttle looked at what we were doing here—everything you just saw—and told me to shut it all down.

CHEYENNE: Shut it down? You mean stop what you're doing? Put all these people out of work again?

MIKE: That's right.

CUT TO: INTERVIEW WITH BURT MCNALLY

CHEYENNE (V.O): Governor Tuttle's chief political advisor and strategist, Burt McNally begs to differ.

BURT: That's absurd. The Governor said no such thing, Cheyenne. Prosperity is a part of Governor Tuttle's Pennsylvania Miracle. God bless those fine people! Governor Tuttle just has a responsibility to make sure that state and federal laws aren't being trampled, that's all.

CUT TO: B-ROLL SHOT OF NICK BARLOW WITH MIKE AND FRIENDS IN FRONT OF A WHITE BOARD, MAPPING STRATEGY

CHEYENNE: Nick Barlow is a lifelong Libertarian gadfly and supporter of Mike Davenport. He says Mister McNally is mistaken.

NICK: Tuttle and McNally say that every volunteer who now has a job is an employee of the city, so we have to file paperwork and pay payroll tax. That would cost us millions of dollars we don't have. The last time I looked, there was no law against spending your free time any way you want, including volunteering. Volunteers may not get paid, but that's not because they're worthless. It's because they're priceless."

REVERSE SHOT OF CHEYENNE: But they are getting paid, aren't they? In TimeBucks?

NICK: It's a trade. They're trading their labor for a meal, or a doctor visit, or an hour of babysitting. It's barter. No contracts, no paperwork, nobody's forcing anyone to do anything.

CHEYENNE: Then why is Governor Tuttle trying to stop you?

NICK: Because the Tuttle presidential campaign is being financed by the kinds of fat cats who would be devastated if everyone did what our people are doing.

CHEYENNE: Which is?

NICK: Working together, cleaning up our town, feeding ourselves. Working, serving, living.

CUT TO: MIKE SIT DOWN INTERVIEW

MIKE: Cheyenne, all we've done is call Governor Tuttle's bluff. He talked about empowering people and creating ways for them to lift themselves up by their bootstraps. We believed him. We created the very system he asked for, and you know what? Our people love it! And all we're asking is that the state get out of the way, leave us alone. They didn't lift a finger when we were coughing up blood. Now they're trying to stop us from doing the hard work of saving ourselves.

CHEYENNE: Yes, but secession! Is that even legal? Didn't we settle this back in 1865, with the Civil War?

MIKE: You'd be surprised. We've been talking to some experts, and they tell us we have a very good case.

CHEYENNE DOING A B ROLL WALK AND TALK WITH DR. CLEMENT BLACKWOOD AT COLLINGSWOOD COLLEGE

CHEYENNE: One of these experts is Dr. Clement Blackwood, professor emeritus of American political history at Collingswood College and a fellow at the Institute for American Exceptionalism.

CUT TO SIT DOWN INTERVIEW WITH DR. BLACKWOOD

DR. BLACKWOOD: Cheyenne, this country was founded on secession. Our Declaration of Independence, the one we all learn in fourth grade, is the most famous secessionist document in world history. The founding fathers argued, rightfully, that governments derive their just powers from the consent of the governed, and whenever that consent is withdrawn, it is the right and duty of the people to "alter or abolish" that government and "to institute a new government."

CHEYENNE:But didn't the Civil War really end the argument on secession?

DR. BLACKWOOD: All the Civil War proved was that the Northern states had more men and a greater ability to produce armaments than the South. There was no debate about the legitimacy of secession. President Lincoln refused to engage the issue, and considered the Confederate states renegade governments that didn't represent the people. It's time we engaged in a robust debate. If we do, I believe Mike Davenport has a very good chance of winning.

CUT TO: CHEYENNE WALK AND TALK WITH DR. VERTASHA BATES, AFRICAN AMERICAN HISTORY PROFESSOR ON HER COLLEGE CAMPUS

CHEYENNE: A more mainstream opinion came from Dr. Vertasha Bates, Distinguished Professor of Race and American Culture at Dunhill University in South Putney, Vermont.

DR. BATES:The Civil War established that secession is treason, and those who choose to pursue this path risk imprisonment and death.

CHEYENNE: But Mike Davenport is saying that this country was born in act of secession, and the founding fathers…

DR. BATES: …were almost all slave owners. And the South seceded to perpetuate chattel slavery and thereby committed an act of treason. And a great, bloody war was fought to end it. Cheyenne, we are the UNITED States of America. There is nothing, I repeat nothing, in the Constitution that gives a state or a city or a town the right to secede. Indeed, the entire document is predicated on the assumption that there exists a union of states designed for perpetuity.

CHEYENNE: So what happens if the town of Prosperity moves ahead with secession?

DR. BATES: Once an entity — a state, or in this case a town — attempts to secede, it becomes a foreign nation and thus subject to all power that the federal government has over foreign nations. This would include the power to declare war on the seceding entity and thus force it back into the union. Now, Cheyenne, who is going to win that war, and how long will it last? Please give me your answer in hours, not days.

CUT TO: SIT DOWN INTERVIEW WITH MIKE DAVENPORT

Cheyenne has just played Vertasha Bates sound bite for Mike.

CHEYENNE: So what do you think, Mike? Are you prepared to repel an invasion by the Pennsylvania National Guard, or even the United States Army?

MIKE: I was in the Army, served in Afghanistan. I know what it's like trying to force a government on a people who don't want it. We had the best weapons, the best leaders and the best soldiers…and we never had a chance because we weren't giving them something they wanted. What they wanted was the ability to decide their own destiny. Victor Hugo said it best. He said, 'Nothing is more powerful than an idea whose time has come.' The time for people to decide for themselves what they want — our time — has come.

CHEYENNE: So what is your idea?

MIKE: I knew that if we — the people of our little rust belt town — could find our way back to each other, we could work together to create prosperity for everyone. And by prosperity, I mean enough: enough food, enough shelter, enough health, and enough love. You've seen it, Cheyenne. We've become necessary to each other, and that's all I ever wanted. And we're not going to let the Governor take that away from us because it's inconvenient for his presidential campaign. We can't. We mean too much to each other.

CUT BACK TO MIKE SERVING COFFEE TO TOWNSPEOPLE
– THEN A MONTAGE OF SMILING CUSTOMERS

CHEYENNE: The people of this town aren't wealthy by conventional standards, but from what I observed, they are the very definition of prosperity. They've got enough of what they need to live…and are rich in the things that make life worth living. Gavin?

CHAPTER SEVENTY-NINE

January 17
GOODWIN TUTTLE

Burt McNally clicked off the sixty-inch LED television monitor mounted above the fireplace in the Governor's office, flanked by portraits of Milton Friedman and Ronald Reagan. He chuckled.

"What's funny?" asked Governor Goodwin Tuttle, popping another peanut butter cup into his mouth. Thanks to the "Halloween Big Bag" he'd bought at Costco, he was good for six months. He'd already gained back ten of the twenty pounds he'd lost for his presidential run and could barely fit in his new power wardrobe. And he didn't care, because the PB cups were helping him manage his anxiety.

"You pay me to game out every possible scenario," said McNally. "I've been in this racket more than thirty years, and I thought we were ready for any goddam thing that would come our way. Except for secession. Secession! I mean…" He threw his hands up and laughed.

"What did you make of that story? I mean, they've got nothing, right?"

McNally turned and looked at Tuttle. There it was again, just for a flash: that hint of contempt, like 'do I really have to explain this to you? Are you really that dim?' Then it vanished and McNally was back pretending that the Tuttle visage would soon be chiseled onto Mount Rushmore. "They've got one thing, and one thing only. Legally, secession is a joke, but that's not the point. The one thing they've got…" He laughed again, shook his head and grimaced.

"What?" said Tuttle. One of his phones shivered in his pocket: not his official on-the-books Pennsylvania state smartphone, the other one. The Batphone. Uh oh. He fished it out and took the call. "Mo?"

"Did you see that?" Moses Creavey was shouting, as per usual. He had one volume setting: TOO LOUD.

"Moses, I'm here with Burt McNally, can I put you on speaker?"

"Whatever." Tuttle flicked screens and scrolled up to the speaker button. "Mo? You there?"

"Yeah, I'm here. Did you guys see that? Right now, on television? That goddamn 'Need to Know'?"

"We saw it, Mo," said Burt.

"Just like those media whores to give Mayor Mike a big wet kiss. They made him look like a combination Jimmy Stewart/Mother Theresa!"

"Mo...," said McNally.

"This is our last shot, and it's getting away from us. You know that don't you?"

"Nothing's getting away from us, it's under control," said Burt. Tuttle noticed he'd been cut out of the conversation, but he couldn't think of anything to say.

"You want another seven-figure lollipop from Uncle Sugar, you're going to get on that phone right goddamn now and order the goddamn National Guard to march in there and shut this down. I want see Davenport in jail by tomorrow night, can I be any clearer?"

"Mister Creavey, with all due respect..."

"I don't want respect, I want action!"

Burt paused, choosing his words carefully. "If you want to turn a new, fresh media celebrity into a martyr, then by all means let's arrest him. That turns a hand grenade of negative press into a hydrogen bomb. Can you imagine how social media would react to that?"

"Good!"

"No, bad," said McNally. "People *like* him. He's a Vet, he's a fighter, he's a businessman, he's put that town back to work…"

"He's a Marxist rabble-rouser, and you and I both know those jobs are bullshit."

"That's not what fourteen million people just saw."

"Okay, so what's your plan, genius? Tell the public that Tuttle is going to be President of the United States except for one rust-belt town in Pennsylvania, which is now its own country? You don't think other towns are going to get onboard with this Commie bullshit? And cities? And states?"

Tuttle opened his mouth, but Burt McNally was ahead of him. "Here's what we're going to do, Mr. Creavey. We're all going to take a very deep breath. I'm going to wash a Xanax down with three fingers of Pappy Van Winkle Kentucky Bourbon. And then we're going to call the crew from Pulver Forge and hash this thing out. How does that sound?"

"Sounds like chickenshit. Sounds like surrender. Sounds like you want to be the one who puts a crown on the head of King Michael the First."

"You're dead wrong," said McNally. "This is our best, maybe our only chance to survive this. This is chess, not whack-a-mole."

"I want to be in that meeting," said Creavey.

"No, you're going to let us handle this," said McNally. "It's one meeting, just to see where we are and what happens next."

"One meeting," said Creavey. "And at the end of that meeting you arrest the sonofabitch for treason, or you're dead to me." CLICK. Both men stared at the smartphone and then at each other.

"One thing," said Tuttle.

"Huh?"

"Before Creavey called. One thing. You said they have one thing. What is it?"

"It's the one thing you need to win an election. They have the public. As in voters."

"Think so?"

"You don't?"

"Convince me."

"Governor, what are people looking for, more than anything else? They want someone they can believe in, someone who makes big, optimistic promises and then keeps them. Mike Davenport promised to create jobs…and he did! Did you see how happy those people were in that town? He's a hero! And who was the villain? *You* were. Governor Goodwin Tuttle, that hypocritical arm waver who gives lip service to creating jobs but shuts down someone who actually does."

"But what he's doing, it's ridiculous…"

"That's a feature, not a bug. He's a crazy American dreamer and he's creating the real Pennsylvania Miracle, and it looks like you're trying to bury him."

"Is that what you think?

"No, dammit, that's what THEY think. You pay me to get inside their heads. They're rooting that guy on, and they're the people you need to win the White House. We have two choices: break up the parade or get in front of it. Either one comes with consequences, so what's it going to be?"

This was his chance to be decisive! Only…he didn't have a clue. "What do you think?" said Tuttle.

"I say we have our meeting and decide."

CHAPTER EIGHTY

January 21st
MIKE DAVENPORT

"Politics," said Bumptious Burt McNally "is the art of compromise." The five of us—McNally, Governor Tuttle, Makayla, Nick and myself—were gathered in a neutral location: a beige meeting room in the Hilton Harrisburg, a blander-than-bland business hotel within walking distance of the state capitol. "But before we begin the real negotiation, we need you to agree to back off this secession nonsense."

"So," said Nick, "your idea of compromise is that we throw away our biggest bargaining chip before we start."

"We all know it's a bluff," said Tuttle. He turned to me, bemused. "You ready to go on trial for treason? Stand up in front of a firing squad?"

"Yes." I wasn't smiling and I wasn't kidding. That brought him up short. "Thomas Jefferson was. Adams was. Washington was. I've already been shot at. You?" He frowned and looked at McNally.

"We assume you've seen the latest Straight-Up Politics polling," said Makayla. "Governor Tuttle is at 31 percent approval. Mike is at 58 percent."

"Governor Tuttle arrests Mike and puts an end to this silliness, those numbers flip," said McNally.

"Maybe," said Makayla. "And maybe Mike's number goes to 90, and your guy goes to 10. And your next campaign is for Mosquito Abatement Warden."

"You mentioned compromise," I said. "What do you have in mind?"

"You drop the secession thing," said McNally. "You come on board as President Tuttle's Secretary of Prosperity. You won't just be a hood ornament: you'll have some real power to try out your programs in towns across the country. Plus, you'll get a ton of publicity. This will be the best possible platform for your next move: Governor, Senator, whatever."

"Say I do this," I said. "What happens to our town?"

Tuttle laced his fingers and gave him his best 'we're all in this together' sales face. "I'll appoint a five-person Blue Ribbon commission to evaluate what you've done there. You and Nick will be two of the five, I'll appoint two, and the fifth will be appointed by a bipartisan panel of judges. In six months, a report will be issued, and we'll move forward on the findings."

"Which will be to appoint another Commission," said Nick.

"What happens for those six months?" I asked. "The ones where you're running for President?"

"We'll simply go back to what we know are lawful protocols until we get a definitive ruling on best practices," said McNally.

"Oh," said Nick. "Right. So…everything we've done just goes away. All those jobs gone. Gardens gone. Medical care gone. Everything just disappears, is that it?

"Relax," said McNally. "You'll get some wiggle room. The community garden can go on where zoning permits, without the barter element. That way there's no payroll tax problem. Nothing wrong with volunteering, and if they want to share what they grow with their neighbors, we're not going to stop them. But everything else gets put on hold. That's our best and final offer."

Makayla and Nick looked at me, and I could tell we agreed. "It sounds like you get everything, and we get screwed," I said. "And everybody in town will think I let you screw them because I want that bullshit show-pony job. I don't think I can sell that to my constituents," I said. "I didn't become Mayor to break their hearts."

"You have a counteroffer?" said McNally.

"Sure. We drop the secession thing," I said. "You do what you said you'd do in the beginning: ignore us. Hell, come down and take credit for what we're doing, people will love you for it. Just let us have the kind of town we want."

"Not going to happen," said Tuttle. "If you don't back down, I'll have you arrested and charged with treason."

"Uh huh," I said. "Are you going to put me to death? When I was shot up by the Taliban, I spent my time in that hospital bed thinking about what's worth dying for. That war? Not worth it. But my friends in Prosperity? Yeah, I'll die for them."

I paused. I had their attention. "Governor, let's get real. You and I both know you're a sock puppet for Moses Creavey. He and his pals are worried that their stock might tank if everyone does what we're doing. I've tried hard to care about that, but I can't. So, here's our compromise. We drop the secession idea. You get out of our way. That probably means that you won't be President and I'm sorry about that, but that's our deal, take it or leave it."

"And if I leave it?"

A long silence in the room as we stared at each other. I took a deep breath and reminded myself to talk softly and slowly. "If you leave it," I said, "then on March 1st, the whole world will see your fully armed National Guard troops, with tanks and Humvees, rolling into our little town to stop a bunch of people from growing red leaf lettuce and sharing it with their neighbors." I paused to let that sink in. "And Governor, I guarantee that will be the first line of your New York Times obituary. You will be the Orval Faubus of Pennsylvania." I framed my fingers to box a headline in the air. "'Tuttle Dies, Sent Federal Troops to Put Down Peaceful Social Experiment.'" I turned back to him. "That might make you a hero to some voters, but not the ones you want, believe me. Because you and I both know that what we're doing is the *real* Pennsylvania miracle. So, I guess we'll see you on March 1st."

And with that, we picked up our stuff and marched out. I felt good. Just talking to Tuttle and McNally had clarified my thinking. It's always good to know what you're willing to die for.

CHAPTER EIGHTY-ONE

MARCH 13

TRANSCRIBED REMARKS BY MIKE DAVENPORT, FIRST ANNIVERSARY PICNIC, OSCAR WELLS COMMUNITY PARK

MIKE: Thank you, friends. One year ago, when I took office for my two year term, I told you I was only going to do this for the single year, and then I was going back to my real life, making and selling the best coffee on earth. A funny thing happened during that year. I discovered what people can do when they turn optimism into action. And I discovered what it feels like to fall in love with a town: my hometown. Our hometown.

I'm not your leader, and you aren't my followers. I'm the patient, and you're my doctor. Or maybe I should say, we're all patients, and we're all the Doctor. We've awakened from a nightmare of victimhood and healed this town, and ourselves, and the healing continues.

In fact, we're just getting started. Pretty soon, our Community Councils are going to have to decide if we want all the things other thriving cities have. Thanks to what we did when we started this effort, we own all that great real estate on Main Street and beyond. We're hearing from people who want to be a part of Prosperity! So, ask yourselves: do we want art galleries? Clothing boutiques? Pricey bistros? A Starbucks next to my HuggaMug Coffee joint? Over my dead body, that's a deal breaker, because, let's face it, Starbucks isn't going to give their coffee away. Anyway, we've got some exciting choices to make, and we'll make those choices together.

There's one more announcement I want to make: something that will make you happy. I'm pretty sure you saw Governor Goodwin Tuttle at his press conference last week telling the world that all we had was a silly disagreement, and he's decided to bless what we're doing here in Prosperity. Now that he's decided he can't shut us down, he's taking credit for what we're doing. Friends, we ARE the "Pennsylvania Miracle"! And he did this even though his worst nightmare was looming on the horizon: the chartering of the one hundredth "Prosperity Club" in America, this one in Steubenville, Ohio.

So, my announcement is that sometime this Fall—my guess is early October, but we'll figure it out together—Prosperity, Pennsylvania is going to host the first National Prosperity Club Congress up at our new Conference Center in Rockhurst Castle. This is going to be a four-day celebration with people coming from all over America to take a gander at what we're up to. We're going to welcome them into our homes. We're going give tours of the town. We're going to share what we've done and how we've done it, and we'll listen to how other folks are improving on our methods. And every single night…well, we're going to have the biggest, most joyous series of picnic-and-dance parties we've ever hosted. This is our Open House for the world.

As I look over this past year, I just have one regret, and it's a tiny one. I'm not sure 'Prosperity' was the right name for this town. Sure, it gave us a North Star, and it pointed us in the right direction. But today I'd offer a different name. If I were giving that speech I gave a year ago, I'd have called this town 'Redemption, Pennsylvania.' That's the journey I've taken. I'm a different person than I was a year ago. I understand the word 'realism' in a whole different way. What's realistic? Being optimistic, being kind, being generous, trusting your neighbors, that's realistic behavior. And one more thing: it's completely realistic to plan for a miracle. It just depends on enlisting enough like-minded co-conspirators like you, and then getting to work.

There's still work to do. And if past is prologue, that work will just make us happier and prouder of this great town we've built together. Now let's eat, let's dance and let's laugh together. And then let's get back to work.

EPILOGUE – TWO YEARS LATER

MIKE DAVENPORT

Everything changes. The goal is to get things changing in the right direction. Take HuggaMug Coffee, for instance. After a year of offering free coffee as an elixir to the citizenry to fill them with optimism and resolve, we transitioned to a "TimeBucks and Cash" model (with free coffee to anyone who couldn't pay.) Then we leased what used to be the Scotty Barnes Oldsmobile dealership around the corner. That's where I began this particular day: roasting, grinding, brewing and serving the best coffee in the Commonwealth, God Bless It. Our Prosperity HuggaMug is five times bigger than the original. It now offers the complete complement of espresso drinks along with homemade savory treats (quiches, paninis) and Chef Betty Flour Power pastries. Our patrons can take a book (and leave one) at the satellite Book Exchange, and they can watch—or join—a public affairs show from the coffee house satellite of our Prosperity community radio station. Prices are posted on the giant chalkboard above the brewing stations and espresso machines, but everyone knows they'll get a great cup of coffee for whatever they can afford to pay. (Lattes and mochas are a different story…)

In case you're wondering: I never did make that deal to franchise the coffee house. We just have the two locations, Pittsburgh and Prosperity. Darla runs our Prosperity store. Steve Dorsey helped me work a deal where the employees own both businesses. Everyone has a voice in what we serve and how things are done. And we still don't offer wi-fi at either location, because our customers like it that way.

When I finished my shift, I walked next door to what used to be Bottomley's Finer Foods, which housed the All-Cuts Meat Market back in the day. It's now the Prosperity Food Hall, a jam-packed tourist magnet and town center of commerce. This is another of those "happy circles" of circumstance. Growing our own food created an opportunity for hundreds of people to prep, cook and serve. As the Prosperity Community Kitchen evolved, Chef Betty Chapel created an apprentice program of sous chefs that she trained up in different cuisines (to the delight of our daily customers). The more they worked with Chef Betty, the better they got. We turned this derelict market into a culinary bazaar, and Betty's students started a happy, thriving, ridiculously diverse bunch of mini eateries.

Did I say diverse? Here you can find pizza, cheesesteaks, Thai food, vegan dishes, soul food, Japanese, Chinese, burgers, fish dishes, baked goods, juice drinks, cookies, pastries, chocolates, and craft beer. Oh, and pierogis. And fresh Prosperity produce, craft items, and custom jewelry. Phillipa Langstaff will capture you in the whimsical image of your choice (caricature, super hero, anime, etc.) and Chelsea Alverez will write, record, and post a song about you on social media. The people of Prosperity own this building, and the vendors are part of a Co-op that polices itself. They just produced the "Chef Betty's Taste of Prosperity Cookbook," all profits going back to the Co-op.

Now I arrived at my next shift: four hours at the Clean Machine Vintage Motorcycle Shop. Raven and Nick started this project: taking vintage choppers and swapping out the gas engine for an electric. I pretended to help, but I was really there to hang out and admire the handiwork of the two owners and seven apprentices from Prosperity High School. Today's project was a Triumph Norton Villiers Triton: beautiful bike with a new lithium-ion battery slotted in a featherbed frame. A great café racer that was quicker and faster than the original.

After that I headed for home. It's Saturday morning, and I stopped to gaze with wonder at our thriving Farmers' Market. Today we got over two thousand people from the greater Pittsburgh metro area to buy what we had grown. This was above and beyond what we grew to feed ourselves and what we sold to gourmet restaurants. Another "happy circle": the folks we've trained up in our community gardens now grow and sell produce in their own front and back yards. A lot of the Keystone Food Hall folks had tables there, selling pierogis, breakfast burritos, fresh bread and pastries. Of course, we had our "Prosperity Club" table for people who wanted to find out more about what we're doing.

And how were we doing? The Prosperity Community Wellness Center was thriving under the enlightened direction of Dr. Kate, with an assist from Max Stone, our resident expert on treating drug addiction. And Raven was right: our social experiment created a magnet for artists, musicians and budding entrepreneurs. We'll be able to phase out our TimeBuck system in the next few months because we'll be generating so much revenue from new businesses. That's a big reason I was able to improve on my first promise, that everyone who wants a job can have one. Now they can find a job that pays real money, with real benefits.

As I walked home, I noticed how much this place had changed. Raven's joyous wall murals were everywhere, many of them commemorating our past. These included a celebration of the SteelTown Iron Men the year they won the Negro League World Series, a "heavenly hell" mural of the Forge blast furnaces during World War II (when women kept it going), and the greatest of all murals, a panoramic view of the first Prosperity Feast at the Community Kitchen.

Another change: there were more bikes than cars. Who needed a car when we had three (free) electric get-abouts? The streets were clean, and a thousand front yards were lush with fruit trees and garden vegetables of every kind. Best of all, people were sitting on their porches visiting with their neighbors.

I arrived home. Makayla was sitting on our front porch, ready to greet me. She has turned our home into an eco-paradise, with the help of Raven and Nick: solar panels, water-saving systems, an ultra low-energy fridge and lush gardens designed by Yandy. I now work about ten hours a week right here in these gardens. They grow enough produce for us to share with the whole neighborhood. Plus, we're making honey: our thriving beehive is surrounded by a riot of pollinators.

About Makayla: she's already licensed her Prosperity movie to a streaming service and sold her book to a publisher for a six-figure advance. She's a "Community Technology" contributor to Maggie Atwater's show on BlueNation. She hosts a 3-day a week "Community Power" podcast where she interviews all the heavy hitters in grassroots community transformation. The podcast gets two million downloads a week.

And all this started because we were able to get a measly three and half percent of the populace to join us: about three hundred people who believed in what we were doing, who were willing to change how the town thought of itself. They believed, and their faith has made all the difference.

Makayla and I aren't married: at least not yet. In fact, we're not even engaged. I was engaged to Tess for a year and a half, and I know that being engaged is an obstacle to getting married: when you're engaged it's too easy to find another excuse to push the thing off. Most days one of us wants to get married more than the other, and then we switch. We agree that if we both decide on the same day to get married, we'll get a license and then "self-unite." Turns out Pennsylvania is one of the few states that doesn't require a judge or magistrate to get married. The Quakers made it, so we just need a group of witnesses. We'll share our vows, then the witnesses will sign the marriage certificate. And of course we can always get the Rev to do a ceremony, or just be Witness #1.

So, what about the Rev? The First Church of Jesus Christ, Troublemaker is thriving. Every meeting is a celebration service, and every member of the church (including Nick, Raven, Makayla and myself) is required to perform ten hours of community service every week (easy to do in Prosperity). The church offers a wildly popular program of gospel concerts, jazz, and my fave, "1960s Soul'd Out Dance Celebrations." (Steve Dorsey's thriving New Prosperity Dance Hall has become the epicenter of the Great Polka Revival, with polka dances on Friday and Saturday nights and Sunday afternoons.)

I'm retired as Mayor: I'm now the Prattleboro Representative to the Prosperity Community Council, which is one more public office than Goodwin Tuttle holds. (He finished fifth in the Iowa Caucuses). I still work in the community gardens and the Wellness Center. I meet once or twice a week with the Trustees of the Prosperity Community Foundation. And I'm the Project Director of the Prosperity, Pennsylvania History Museum and Cultural Heritage Center, a (proposed) fifty-million-dollar tourist magnet that is going to tell our story to the world. It's pretty much the place that Makayla and I dreamed up that day. We are going to raise the fifty million from foundations and filthy-rich libertarian private donors. Yes, we are. Hell, we made one crazy dream come true, why not this one? In fact, doing fundraisers at Prosperity Clubs around the country (531 and counting) lets me share our story with thousands of people. I'll take five million donations of ten dollars, fifty thousand contributions of a thousand dollars, and even a single contribution of the whole fifty million from an enlightened

Libertarian billionaire willing to build one less moon rocket (and our place won't explode on opening day.)

Yandy once told me that if this thing took off, our biggest problem was going to be success. The Cubans were wildly successful in feeding people and growing a community. Then entropy set in: the regime started encouraging tourism. American dollars poured in, the national economy perked up, and people started drifting away from the gardens. And every one of those people tells Yandy that they miss the "Special Period." So, can we keep this going? Nothing lasts, except for one thing: the friendships we're making. "Happiness is love, full stop."

Plus coffee, of course.

THE END

THE UNDERBOOK

Life is a fundamentally cooperative enterprise that depends on diverse communities of living beings that self-organize to create and maintain the conditions essential to their individual and mutual existence. The living Earth that births and nurtures us is distinctive among all the planets we know because of its community of life. Our well-being depends, in turn, on that of the Earth. The implications of these truths run deep. They call us to transform how we structure and manage our relationships with one another and the Earth.

–David Korten

In this Underbook, I'll reveal my sources, provide recommendations for further reading and include some quotes that inspired me to write this book. This first quote is from David Korten, author of "Change the Story, Change the Future" and a tenacious optimist for the communitarian future described in this book. Here's how Korten describes the possible future we can create together:

We have yet to figure out how to get there and how it will all work, but these are some essential components of the vision now emerging:

- *Conflicts will be resolved peacefully. War will be confined to history books.*
- *Power will be shared within and among bioregionally self-reliant local communities, and most decisions will be made locally through radically democratic processes. Government and business will be accountable to the people they serve. Everyone will share in the ownership of and responsibility to care for the physical and intellectual assets on which their means of living depend.*
- *Each community will care for and seek to live within the means of its local ecosystems. Most material needs will be met with local circular supply chains, and we will vacation locally with minimal need*

for long-distance transport. Farms will be small-scale. Farming methods will feature regenerative soil care. And diets will be mostly vegetarian.

• Tools, appliances, and devices will be designed for easy repair and recycling.

• Cities will be designed to reconnect people and nature while meeting needs for personal transport with walking, cycling, and public transit.

NOTES

CHAPTER ONE

I drank coffee for thirty years. I had to switch to decaf when caffeine sent me to the emergency room with atrial fibrillation. I still dream of that pure, invigorating high I used to get.

CHAPTER TWO

Pulver Forge is a mash-up of several Pennsylvania steel towns. A great book that helped me here is "Homestead: The Glory and Tragedy of an American Steel Town" by William Serrin. Another is "Playing Through the Whistle: Steel, Football and an American Town," by S.L. Price. This is about Aliquippa, Pennsylvania.

CHAPTER THREE

This is the big idea of the book: "Changing What's Underneath." I first began pondering this back in the 1980s when I encountered the ideas of Werner Erhard. Erhard said that most of the time we react to the content of life: what's happening to us. And we react from our (mostly) unconscious ideas about the world, often learned in childhood. Erhard strove to change things by making the context conscious, then working to change it. Here's a quote:

A context is literally created by creating it. You just need to recognize that you have the power of context, and then you simply need to be willing to be responsible for creating it yourself, without reason, without the props of evidence – to simply say 'this shall be. I have the power of my word in my own universe. I have the power to determine the context of my own life. I give meaning to my life. The meaning doesn't come from outside…

Once you create a context, that context then generates a process in which the content — the forces and circumstances — re-order and align themselves with the context. For example, if you choose to shift the context of your life from 'I don't matter' to 'I make a difference,' the circumstances in your life, while they may not have changed, take on an entirely new meaning. This new meaning, then, begins to change the circumstances themselves. Soon the situations in your life begin to reflect that you do make a difference."

This is a liberating thought. If you want to know why something isn't working, look at the ideas that support it. The context of this failed rust-belt town is, as Mike Davenport says, *"People feel hopeless and powerless. It's, 'We're poor, helpless losers. Life's unfair. We give up.'"* The very name "Prosperity, Pennsylvania" is an intentional assertion of a new context for the town.

Most people think content dictates context, but it's the other way around. One of the best books on the power of context is Victor Frankl's masterpiece, "Man's Search for Meaning." Frankl said:

"We who lived in concentration camps can remember the men who walked through the huts comforting others, giving away their last piece of bread. They may have been few in number, but they offer sufficient proof that everything can be taken from a man but one thing: the last of the human freedoms — to choose one's attitude in any given set of circumstances, to choose one's own way."

The difference between those compassionate, generous souls who gave away their last piece of bread and the others in the camps is context: how they chose to hold their experience. The ability to choose one's attitude in any given set of circumstances is to create your personal context consciously.

The reason Abraham Lincoln is considered one of our greatest presidents is because of his mastery in creating a compassionate, humane context for a country torn apart by Civil War. Even as the country was being rent asunder, he spoke these words at his first Inaugural:

We are not enemies, but friends. We must not be enemies. Though passion may have strained, it must not break our bonds of affection. The mystic chords of memory, stretching from every battlefield, and patriot grave, to every living heart and hearthstone, all over this broad land, will yet swell the chorus of the Union, when again touched, as surely they will be, by the better angels of our nature.

Even when there was no logical reason to think the Union would survive, Lincoln led the nation from an empowering context that the Southern states were still part of the Union, and the Confederacy was a temporary rebellion perpetrated by a small group of landowning zealots. Every great leader shares this mastery of context with Lincoln. This group includes coaches, business leaders and teachers.

The ability to create and enlist others in a benevolent context is a super power. This whole story is about that super power.

CHAPTER FOUR

The character of Betty Chapel is inspired by two people:

The first is "Chef Molly" DeMers, the inspiring, paradigm-breaking Executive Chef of the Climate Collective and the first

female executive chef to open a major professional sports arena, the Climate Pledge Arena in Seattle. A good interview is here:
https://climatepledgearena.com/2021/06/11/cooking-with-pride/

A quote:

Stay genuine to the purpose and the goal because changing the world never happens by being small. You will be questioned on why you are doing something, but someday they will ask how you did it. If you can work through the uncomfortable phases of self-doubt or negative representations of other people's views, then what I found was pure beauty on the other side of fear.

The second is Chef Jose Andres, the celebrity chef and star of the National Geographic documentary "We Feed People." Chef Andres uses his money, fame, time and energy to fight hunger in disaster areas around the world through his organization, World Central Kitchen.

We are all citizens of the world. What's good for you, must be good for all. If you are lost, share a plate of food with a stranger…you will find out who you are.

CHAPTER FIVE

The Curse of Pulver Forge is based on something that happened in Homestead, Pennsylvania on July 6, 1892. The workers of Andrew Carnegie's Homestead Steel Mill knew Carnegie was making millions a year from their labor. They went on strike to prevent their wages from being cut. Carnegie, vacationing in Scotland, ordered his operations manager Henry Clay Frick to break the union in any way he could. Frick fired all 3800 workers and brought in 300 Pinkerton agents to occupy the plant. Thousands of workers and their families stormed the plant. In the ensuing battle, three Pinkertons and seven workers were killed.

The workers took control of the mill, but Frick prevailed: he got Pennsylvania Governor Robert Emory Pattison to send 8500 state National Guard soldiers to re-take the plant. By July 15, the plant was back operating with replacement workers laboring for the lower wage. Hundreds of Union leaders and workers were arrested and thrown in jail, crippling any attempt to organize the union members to stop the strikebreakers. Almost all these charges were later dropped.

The Union gave up in November. Some workers reapplied for jobs at the mill, agreeing to 12-hour work days and the lesser wage.

For an excellent history of America's labor struggles, try "There Is Power in A Union: The Epic Story of Labor in America" by Phillip Dray.

CHAPTER EIGHT

The story that Yandy Lopez tells of Cuba in the early 1990s is true. It is called the "Special Period" in Cuban history. The best account of this story is a documentary film, available on YouTube, called "The Power of Community: How Cuba Survived Peak Oil."
https://www.youtube.com/watch?v=aeM5emtaVC0&t=12s

This is a foundational story for this tale. Everything in the book—especially the power of cooperation, context and community—comes from what really happened in Cuba back then. It's astonishing what people can accomplish when they have to.

CHAPTER EIGHTEEN

A Charrette is a real creative process in which a group of stakeholders come together for a short-term, intensive work session. The difference between brainstorming and charretting is that a charrette must produce a result. Everyone in the room "agrees to agree" at the end of the session.

When Walt Disney was creating Disneyland, he became frustrated with the endless meetings he had with all his designers. He'd agree to give so much of the park to his ride designers, only to produce outrage in his landscape architects. To bring these meetings to an end, Disney had everyone get in the room for a two-day Charrette, with the stipulation that all the stakeholders had to abide by what was decided in the room. This model of Charretting has become common in the world of location-based entertainment.

Where did I get the number 3.5 percent as the core group needed to overthrow oppressive governments? Here's Rebecca Solnit in Harper's Magazine:

Political scientist Erica Chenoweth set out to determine whether nonviolence was as effective for regime change as violence. She found, to her surprise, that nonviolent strategies worked better. Organizers were enthralled by her conclusion that only around 3.5 percent of a population was needed to successfully resist or even topple a regime. In other words, to create change, you don't need everyone to agree with you, you just need some people to agree so passionately that they will donate, campaign, march, risk arrest or injury.

CHAPTER TWENTY

The character of Nick Barlow, Libertarian skeptic, is based on a hero of mine: Karl Hess. Hess was a conservative speechwriter for Barry Goldwater who became disillusioned with the right and became what he himself called a "left-wing libertarian" which means, by his definition, anarchist. He said:

Anarchists spring from a single seed, no matter the flowering of their ideas. The seed is liberty. And that is all it is. It is not a socialist seed. It is not a capitalist seed. It is not a mystical seed. It not a determinist seed. It is simply a statement: we can be free. After that, it's all choice and chance.

Hess decided to stop paying the tax on his income when that money went to finance the Vietnam War, and so the Internal Revenue Service seized his income. Rather than give in, Hess taught himself to be a welder and bartered for everything he needed as he wrote books. He organized for change in his community in ways portrayed in this story. My favorite book of his is "Community Technology." Here Hess lays out a vision for communities that take back power for themselves. He writes:

There is no reason in nature, in organization, or in science and technology for human beings to lead secondhand lives, under second-party rules, in second-class communities. Instead, there is every reason if they choose to, that human beings can participate fully in all the decisions that affect their lives, be responsible for their lives, and with other human beings live in precisely the communities suited to their capabilities and cares rather than bound to someone else's advantage or blueprint.

Hess tells his life story in "Dear America." He lays out his philosophy in the aforementioned "Community Technology" and "Neighborhood Power" (co-written with David Morris).

A final quote from Hess:

The most revolutionary thing you can do is get to know your neighbors.

CHAPTER TWENTY-THREE

The Cody Fortune chapters are (obviously) based on the disinfotainment brigade at Fox News. One of the most influential books in creating "Prosperity, Pennsylvania" is "Tribe" by Sebastian Junger. In the book, Junger says.

Human beings need three basic things in order to be content: they need to feel competent at what they do; they need to feel authentic in their lives; and they need to feel connected to others. These values are considered "intrinsic" to human happiness and far outweigh "extrinsic" values such as beauty, money and status.

This connection is what Pulver Forge had lost. My hero, Mike, understands connection from his time in the Army. His yearning to feel that again is what makes him commit to running for Mayor. Junger again:

The Army might screw you and your girlfriend might dump you and the enemy might kill you, but the shared commitment to safeguard one another's lives is unnegotiable and only deepens with time. The willingness to die for another person is a form of love that even religions fail to inspire, and the experience of it changes a person profoundly.

Junger addresses the toxic nature of corrosive narratives (like those of Cody Fortune). At the center of these narratives is the one attitude guaranteed to destroy a tribe: contempt, which is the core message of provocative, divisive media channels. Junger:

Unlike criticism, contempt is particularly toxic because it assumes a moral superiority in the speaker. Contempt is often directed at people who have been excluded from a group or declared unworthy of its benefits. Contempt is often used by governments to provide rhetorical cover for torture or abuse. Contempt is one of four behaviors that, statistically, can predict divorce in married couples. People who speak with contempt for one another will probably not remain united for long.

CHAPTER TWENTY-SIX – THE THIRTEEN (or is it fourteen?) PERSUMPTUOUS PREMISES OF PROSPERITY

This list is from a lifetime devoted to observing (and practicing) what works and what doesn't. What works is optimism, direct action, recruiting allies, finding a worthy mission, and having as much fun as possible doing as much good as possible. As Teddy Roosevelt once said, "Do what you can, with what you've got, from where you are."

CHAPTER TWENTY-SEVEN

Yandy's new job—farming the front lawns of homeowners and giving them a percentage of the produce in return for using their land—came from a great book called "The Urban Farmer" by Curtis Stone. Stone's book is "your complete guide to minimizing risk and maximizing profit by using intensive production and making a good living growing high-yield, high-value crops right in your own backyard (or someone else's").

Everything Yandy does has been done by Stone and other urban gardeners around the world.

The "Jarhead Sodbusters" are an expression of an expanding nationwide movement to heal traumatized war veterans by connecting them to the land, to generative tasks that include farming and beekeeping, and to their fellow veterans. A quick Google search will produce organizations like Farmer-Veteran Coalition, Warrior Farms, Armed to Farm, F.A.R.M. (Farmers Assisting Returning Military) and Victory Farmers.

A final note here: during the "Special Period" in Cuba, hundreds of specialists from Australia were invited to the island to help out. The Australians taught the Cubans principles of permaculture, a sustainable agricultural system that produced more produce with no pesticides and poisons. Hundreds of permaculture clubs are thriving everywhere in America. Many of these clubs would travel to Prosperity to help, to "train the trainers," and to make certain this experiment worked.

CHAPTER THIRTY

Converting school buses to electric power is already happening. Companies like Unique Electric Solutions are offering retrofitted electric propulsion solutions for delivery trucks, school buses, shuttle buses, and refrigerated trucks. The Logan Bus Company, largest contractor for the New York City Department of Education, is deploying diesel buses converted to Type C electric school buses in New York City.

CHAPTER THIRTY-THREE

The first question Mike Davenport is asked is, "What if I don't want to grow lettuce, or do any of this? Why should I?"

Mike says he's under no obligation to do anything. Later in the Q&A he refers to what's happening as "semi-self-organized anarchism." This is a wholly volunteer effort: no coercion, no compulsion, nobody forced to do anything. Everyone acts from their own enlightened self-interest.

Is this realistic? Once again, I rely on history. This is just what happened in Cuba during the "Special Period." An influential book on the likelihood of an experiment like this succeeding is "Humankind, A Hopeful History" by Rutger Bregman.

Bregman asks a provocative question: *"If there is one belief that has united the left and the right, psychologists and philosophers, ancient thinkers and modern ones, it is the tacit assumption that humans are bad...but what if this isn't true?"* Bregman takes us through 200,000 years of human history to prove that believing in human generosity and collaboration *"isn't merely optimistic — it's realistic. Moreover, it has huge implications for how society functions...if we believe in the reality of humanity's kindness and altruism, it will forge the foundation for achieving true change in society."*

In the epilogue of his book, Bregman says, *"In truth, it's the cynic who's out of touch. In truth...people are inclined to be good to one another. So be realistic. Be courageous. Be true to your nature and offer your trust. Do good in broad daylight, and don't be ashamed of your generosity. You may be dismissed as gullible and naïve at first. But remember, what's naïve today may be common sense tomorrow."*

I'm not writing science fiction. What happens in this book is not based on how I want human beings to act. It's based 200,000 years of how we naturally act toward one another when we're not hypnotized by media-generated narratives of fear and scarcity.

CHAPTER THIRTY-SEVEN

Luke Bramlett's Near-Death Experience is based on a number of NDE's. The most prominent of these is that of Howard Storm, described in his book "My Descent Into Death." Storm was a tenured professor of art who suffered a catastrophic attack of peritonitis. He then had an astonishing experience where he was rescued by Jesus and brought to heaven for a comprehensive life review and a conversation with angelic beings. Storm's life was transformed: he gave up his professorship, went to divinity school and became a minister for a tiny fraction of his previous salary. I've read and re-read this book: it's a go-to source of inspiration and solace for me. I believe every word of it.

CHAPTER FORTY-ONE

I spent ten years writing and segment-producing for so-called "reality TV" shows. I worked for Blade Kingston. I know Blade Kingston. I worked on the single worst reality TV show every produced for cable, "Secrets of Superstar Fitness." The show was so bad that the network, Discovery Health, actually went out of business shortly after our 13 weeks ended. (It became Oprah TV) It's impossible to reach the bottom of the cynicism of these people. They are in the train wreck business. They will do anything to make the deal, and then they'll do anything to get eyeballs, even if it means crossing up clients.

CHAPTER FORTY-FOUR

Floyd "Jelly Roll" Jenkins is based on Gus Greenlee. Greenlee is most famous as the owner of the legendary Pittsburgh Crawfords Negro League baseball team, with Satchel Paige, Josh

Gibson and Cool Papa Bell. A previous book of mine, "Sugarball," chronicled the exploits of these players when they ventured to the Dominican Republic in 1937 and ended up playing for their lives (true story).

Greenlee owned the Crawford Grille in Pittsburgh, where he brought in the greatest Black big bands (Ellington, Basie, Jimmie Lunceford, Cab Calloway). He owned prize fighters and staged fights. Like Jenkins, he got his start as a bootlegger and then became Pittsburgh's premiere numbers kingpin. Like so many of these men during the Depression, Greenlee is a fascinating mix of predator and benefactor. With his numbers racket, he happily took money from impoverished people, offering them the pipe dream that they could hit it big. He also took better care of the people in his neighborhood, dispensing charity and giving out Thanksgiving turkeys.

CHAPTER FIFTY-FOUR

"Wellness on Wheels" provides a mobile medical clinic after the July 4th riot. Again, would this happen? Here I refer to Rebecca Solnit's revelatory "A Paradise Built in Hell: The Extraordinary Communities That Arise in Disaster." She shows that the worst kinds of disasters—earthquakes, hurricanes, bombings—are consistently met with altruism, resourcefulness, kindness and generosity.

The common media narratives after these events rave about violence, looting and criminal anarchy. The truth is that they inevitably produce countless acts of charity, beneficence and compassion—like this one.

CHAPTER FIFTY-EIGHT

I've worked for many years in the themed entertainment/location-based entertainment business. Kennywood is a marvel. It's one of the very few traditional amusement parks from the early 20th century that made the transition to a competitive theme park in the 21st century. Kennywood is devoted to serving families, as expressed in this chapter, my tribute to the park.

CHAPTER SIXTY

Brandolini's Law is an internet adage formulated by an Italian programmer named Albert Brandolini in January 2013. It is known as the "Bullshit Asymmetry Principle": *The amount of energy needed to refute bullshit is an order of magnitude bigger than that needed to produce it.*

If you need me to provide examples of this after the 2016 election and three years of COVID misinformation, you haven't been paying attention.

CHAPTER SIXTY-ONE

I did a lot of research on doctors who have refused to give in to the ever-worsening Medical-Industrial Complex and stay true to their mission of healing people. The most affecting story is that of "Dr. Jim"—James Joseph O'Connell—as told by Tracy Kidder in the book "Rough Sleepers." Read it and be inspired.

Many of the characters in "Prosperity, Pennsylvania" are trying to answer the questions "Who am I?" and "What's worth doing?" The answers are often surprising, because they require shunting off the answers embedded in the master narratives of the American culture: "I'm here to make money and become famous." The real answers involve finding "right livelihood" which flows from Kahil Gibran's observation, "Work is love made visible." We're here to make a difference. We do this by serving others, because we love them, and that love makes us happy. This is what Kate has found, and also Mike, Makayla, Chef Betty, Nick, Raven and Reverend Luke.

The aforementioned David Korten says, "*Science is now confirming what we feel in our heart and daily experience. People who organize their lives around money and consumption to the exclusion of living relationships are prone to depression, anxiety, and low self-esteem compensated for by obscene displays of extravagance. We experience the fullness of life through the caring relationships of close friends and healthy caring families and communities and the positive rush we experience when helping a neighbor, volunteering, and giving. A connection with nature is essential to our health and happiness. We thrive in jobs that allow us to express creativity, exercise initiative, and be of service to others.*"

In a column in the Atlantic, happiness expert Arthur C. Brooks said, "*You only need two pieces of navigational equipment on that mission (to find the right job): the love in your heart and the will to be excellent. If you have those, you will find the answer to the question 'Who am I?' You will find satisfaction. And you will make the world a better place.*"

CHAPTER SIXTY-THREE

Should Prosperity, Pennsylvania tear down the statue of Enoch Cornelius Pulver? It's certainly true that Pulver—like Vanderbilt, Rockefeller and Andrew Carnegie—built fortunes by corrupting the rules of free-market capitalism and by subjecting workers to barbaric conditions that shortened (and sometimes ended) their lives.

On the other hand…what's best for Mike's project? The genius cultural blogger Seth Godin recently wrote this: *"More hope. More health. More security. More innovation. More breakthroughs. More connection. More creation. More joy. The more we ask for change at the top, the more we work to change our systems, the more likely we are to get it."*

Mike Davenport understands, like Godin, that the project can only move forward when the people doing the hard work feel connected to one another by a positive sense that they are doing something significant that will benefit everyone. Anything that divides the town has to be avoided. What makes this hard is that hate is energizing, and vilifying "the other" provides a delicious spike of self-righteous adrenaline. (If you don't believe me, watch any ten minutes of a cable pundit gabfest.)

Raven says it best. "Our job here is finding converts, not fingering heretics."

CHAPTER SIXTY-THREE

Headline, CNN, November 3, 2021: "Why Classic Cars are the Next Big Thing in Electric Vehicles."

Also, Forbes, December 25, 2022: "Forget About Teslas: Converting Vintage Muscle Cars Into Electric Vehicles Is Now A Thing"

Also, check out companies like "Make Mine Electric," and "Vintage Voltage." It's a thing, and it's growing.

CHAPTER SIXTY-EIGHT

The idea of turning the Pulver Forge Steel Mill into a tourist attraction is a natural. There's already an organization in the Pittsburgh area called "Rivers of Steel" that makes this offer: "Visit, learn, and experience all five of the Rivers of Steel attractions that showcase the artistry and innovation of southwestern Pennsylvania's rich heritage."

These attractions include a tour of a place very close to what Pulver Forge might have been: the Carrie Blast Furnaces, a legendary part of the United States Steel Homestead Steel Works that towers 92 feet over the Monongahela River. "Rivers of Steel" offers group tours, events and workshops. And this: "In recent years, Carrie has become an in-demand location for weddings and celebrations due to historic charm and authenticity."

CHAPTER SEVENTY-ONE

Here there's a discussion about what to do with Rockhurst Castle, the mansion of the Pulver Family. A lot of ideas are tossed around, but they all center around one idea: promoting Prosperity, Pennsylvania as a magnet for people interested in learning about the history and future of the town, especially how it transformed itself.

There's every reason to think this will work, because cities tell stories:

LOS ANGELES is the place to go to become a movie and/or television star.

ORLANDO is the place to go to have a memorable family vacation.

LAS VEGAS is the place to go to acquire instant wealth, because YOU and YOU ALONE are smart and lucky enough to beat the odds.

NEW YORK tells two stories: Make your fortune on WALL STREET and make your name as an actor on BROADWAY.

Perhaps the best analog to Prosperity, Pennsylvania is ASHLAND, OREGON, home of the Oregon Shakespeare Festival. Although struggling now, Ashland is a town of 14,000 people (just a bit larger than Prosperity) that, for decades, attracted 400,000 people a year to enjoy what critics called "a Disneyland of great theater."

CHAPTER SEVENTY-TWO

The moment when Makayla ponders why the group is giving all its power to Governor Tuttle will be familiar to anyone who has worked for a world-changing social movement or studied them. This is also something everyone knows who has turned their life around. First, a contextual thought from the great writer Salman Rushdie:

Those who do not have power over the story that dominates their lives – the power to retell it, rethink it, deconstruct it, joke about it, and change it as times change – truly are powerless, because they cannot think new thoughts.

The alternative comes from a writer and organizational psychologist named Dr. Ben Hardy. He said…

When you take responsibility for what is happening in your life, you're no longer the victim of circumstances. You no longer have to be a reactive object being acted upon by your environment. Instead, you can proactively act as an agent who impacts and changes your circumstances.

Like Makayla, we forget that we have power. This whole experiment in Prosperity, Pennsylvania is about seizing the power we, the people, have to create positive change in our lives. The Civil Rights leaders in the 1950s created an astonishing change in America by refusing to live by oppressive laws and social conventions thrust upon them by an oppressive, racist society. Going back to what Werner Erhard said above, the leaders created a context of freedom and responsibility. "I am free. My responsibility is to make a difference. I will live by these truths and teach them to others to liberate them from their illusion of oppression." That movement began with people taking back their power. Business blogger Seth Godin crystallizes the opportunity:

Whatever system we are living in or with, it would be nice if it were responsible for what happens next. On the other hand, knowing that we can connect, publish, inspire, lead, build, describe, invent, encourage and (especially) teach, means that there's no one better than us and no time like right now. And if it helps, go find, organize and connect with others who feel as committed as you do. Of course, it's frightening. But it's important and it's our turn.

"Laughter is the sound of freedom." So said the great Sheldon Kopp, author of "If You Meet the Buddha in the Road, Kill Him!"

CHAPTER SEVENTY-FOUR

I gave a lot of thought to this plot twist. The idea of secession still carries the stench of the Confederacy in the Civil War, where it was used to legitimize and perpetuate slavery. This is a book of ideas, and the biggest idea is the power of a group of people to shift the context of their own destiny from powerless to powerful. Going back and reading the words of the Declaration of Independence was galvanizing.

That, to secure these rights, governments are instituted among men, deriving their just powers from the consent of the governed. That, whenever any form of government becomes destructive of these ends, it is the right of the people to alter or to abolish it, and to institute new government, laying its foundation on such principles, and organizing its powers in such form, as to them shall seem most likely to affect their safety and happiness.

Thomas Jefferson was America's tragic genius. His words in the Declaration created the context for everything good about America:

We hold these truths to be self-evident, that all men are created equal, that they are endowed by their Creator with certain unalienable rights, that among these are life, liberty, and the pursuit of happiness.

Jefferson had the courage and imagination to create a new nation by pulling these words from the heavens. He failed to live up to them as a keeper of enslaved persons at Monticello. Mike Davenport just seizes the audacity of thirty-three-year-old Thomas Jefferson.

CHAPTER SEVENTY-FIVE

For two years (1991-92), I was the Entertainment Reporter for Channel 13 in Los Angeles. I have personal experience here. Television is all about visuals. (No shocking video, no George Floyd outrage.) When a film studio wanted to hype its latest summer tentpole blockbuster, their publicists handed me a 45-minute Electronic Press Kit with dynamite kinetic footage. All I had to do was figure out was how to edit myself into the piece and take credit for it. Makayla is being a smart producer here. Her savvy results in….

CHAPTER SEVENTY-SIX

…the piece on "Need to Know," the 60 Minutes-type network news magazine. The media loves a "both-sides" narrative, and Makayla serves it up with a jumbo soft drink and a bag of chips. She knows what every good television news producer knows: that people are so eager to get on network television to burnish their personal "brands" that they'll advocate just about anything, the more outrageous the better. She "feeds the beast" for the benefit of her cause.

EPILOGUE — TWO YEARS LATER

What's harder than creating a civic revolution? Keeping it going after the initial breakthrough. The "Special Period" in Cuba, where people took back their power to feed themselves and create the empowered communities they wanted, started to fade at the end of the decade, when Venezuela's Hugo Chavez sold Castro cheap oil and Vladimir Putin normalized relations, freeing up trade. Even so, thirty-plus years later, Cuba still has some community farms and gardens.

The best way to keep the revolution evolving is to achieve a critical mass of social and economic development. Any number of communities across American have made the shift from decimated urban wasteland to thriving village: Pittsburgh, Oakland, Indianapolis, Hartford, even Detroit. The formula rhymes with what happens in Prosperity: involve the community, engage people in constructive action, rehabilitate legacy buildings, revivify downtown (starting with cafes and restaurants), improve walkability, encourage young artists to live cheaply and share their talents, create green spaces that encourage picnics and social gatherings, and bring all these things together to create "buzz."

Chef Betty, Raven, Reverend Luke, Makayla and Mike are right to start this movement with food. Developing a program that turns aimless young people into cooks and chefs produces new, innovative (inexpensive) cafes and restaurants, which attract young trendsetters who are soon hanging engaging artwork on the walls of those cafes. Next comes galleries, boutiques, and clubs.

This a good outcome…but then comes the next challenge: "Brooklynization." Places become popular. Rents increase. The "creative class" — artists, designers and believers who created the first, vital wave of change— start getting priced out of neighborhoods by developers. This is why Raven's Community Development group is buying up all this distressed property: so that when it becomes valuable, the townspeople themselves have a say in what happens and who will benefit. (Do they want an Apple Store instead of a community art gallery? A Starbucks instead of a HuggaMug? They decide.)

I hope you enjoyed your visit to Prosperity, Pennsylvania. All along the way, I was guided by the words of Ursula K. LeGuin:

The storyteller is the truthteller…We will not know our own injustice if we cannot imagine justice. We will not be free if we do not imagine freedom. We cannot demand that anyone try to attain justice and freedom who has not had a chance to imagine them as attainable.

Never believe the dreams in this story are impossible. Everything here has happened somewhere. I just put these ideas and initiatives together in a new way. I just imagined them as attainable, because they are.

Finally, from one who knows:

Life can be much broader once you discover one simple fact: Everything around you that you call life was made up by people that were no smarter than you and you can change it, you can influence it, you can build your own things that other people can use.
Steve Jobs

ABOUT THE AUTHOR

R. Lee Procter is a writer and storyteller who works in the location-based entertainment industry. In 2018, the Themed Entertainment Association bestowed the title "Master of the Craft" on him for his work on more than a hundred projects, including The Abraham Lincoln Presidential Museum in Springfield, Illinois. His books with Black Rose Writing are: *Sugarball*, about Negro League Baseball, *Claude Monet Designs Yankee Stadium - A Love Story*, a funny and poignant romantic romp, and *Sanity Clause*, a droll update on Dickens' *A Christmas Carol*. With *Prosperity, Pennsylvania*, he's reaching for something more --a book that makes readers understand just how powerful they are to create the world they want. He lives in California and for fun collects classic movies, especially silent films.

OTHER TITLES BY R. LEE PROCTER

NOTE FROM R. LEE PROCTER

Word-of-mouth is crucial for any author to succeed. If you enjoyed *Prosperity, PA*, please leave a review online — anywhere you are able. Even if it's just a sentence or two. It would make all the difference and would be very much appreciated.

Thanks!
R. Lee Procter

p.s. By the way, the people of Prosperity have started a Substack to chronicle their adventures. You find that here:
https://prosperitypennsylvania.substack.com/

We hope you enjoyed reading this title from:

www.blackrosewriting.com

Subscribe to our mailing list – *The Rosevine* – and receive **FREE** books, daily deals, and stay current with news about upcoming releases and our hottest authors.
Scan the QR code below to sign up.

Already a subscriber? Please accept a sincere thank you for being a fan of Black Rose Writing authors.

View other Black Rose Writing titles at www.blackrosewriting.com/books and use promo code **PRINT** to receive a **20% discount** when purchasing.